'Once I picked it up **I could not put it down**'

Annette Cobb, Librarian

'**The best part about** *Spare Me The Truth* **is the characters**'

Worth A Read

'**Read it!**'

Meg Gardiner

'Nothing short of **brilliant**'

Michael Jecks

'A **top notch** thriller writer'

Simon Kernick

'**Genuinely unputdownable**. Hard to do anything else when you have one of CJ's books on the go!'

Andy Kirk, London cab driver for fifteen years

D0718354

CJ Carver is a half-English, half-Kiwi author living just outside Bath. CJ lived in Australia for ten years before taking up long-distance rallies, including London to Saigon, London to Cape Town and 14,000 miles on the Inca Trail. CJ's books have been published in the UK and the USA and have been translated into several languages. CJ's first novel, *Blood Junction*, won the CWA Debut Dagger Award and was voted as one of the best mystery books of the year by *Publisher's Weekly*.

www.cjcarver.com / @C_J_Carver

By the same author

The Forrester and Davies series
Spare Me the Truth

The India Kane series
Blood Junction
Black Tide

The Jay McCaulay series
Gone Without Trace
Back With Vengeance
The Honest Assassin

Other novels
Dead Heat
Beneath the Snow

TELL
ME
A
LIE

CJ CARVER

ZAFFRE

First published in Great Britain in 2017 by

Zaffre Publishing
80-81 Wimpole St, London W1G 9RE
www.zaffrebooks.co.uk

Copyright © CJ Carver, 2017

All rights reserved.
No part of this publication may be reproduced,
stored or transmitted in any form by any means,
electronic, mechanical, photocopying or otherwise, without the
prior written permission of the publisher.

The right of CJ Carver to be identified as Author of this
work has been asserted in accordance with
the Copyright, Designs and Patents Act, 1988

This is a work of fiction. Names, places, events and
incidents are either the products of the author's
imagination or used fictitiously. Any resemblance to
actual persons, living or dead, or actual
events is purely coincidental.

A CIP catalogue record for this book is available from the British Library.

ISBN: 978-1-785-76035-8
Trade paperback ISBN: 978-1-785-76291-8

Also available as an ebook

1 3 5 7 9 10 8 6 4 2

Typeset by IDSUK (Data Connection) Ltd
Printed and bound by Clays Ltd, St Ives Plc

Zaffre Publishing is an imprint of Bonnier Zaffre,
a Bonnier Publishing company
www.bonnierzaffre.co.uk
www.bonnierpublishing.co.uk

For Mark and Charlotte, with love

PROLOGUE

PROLOGUE

Thursday 22 January, Murmansk

Edik Yesikov listened to the tape with increasing disbelief. He forgot all about his guests milling in the gun room, the snow wolf hunt he'd organised, the fact they only had four hours or so to bag their trophies before the sun set. If what he'd heard was true, it was fantastic news.

'It's been verified?' he asked.

The Director of the FSK, the Federal Counterintelligence Service of Russia, glanced at Edik's father, who nodded. As usual, the power in the room was held by the old man, who had flown with the Director straight to the hunting lodge from Moscow this morning. Lazar Yesikov hadn't wanted anyone overhearing what he had to say.

'The British journalist says she heard it from Polina Calder directly,' his father said. 'I see no reason to doubt her.'

Edik felt a moment's alarm. 'We haven't kept her here, have we? The British government will go insane.'

'Of course not.' The old man looked affronted. 'We put her on a plane this morning.'

Edik arched both eyebrows into a question.

'She'll be dealt with when she gets home,' the old man told him. 'An accident. She bicycles to work. London is a dangerous place for cyclists.'

'And Polina Calder?'

'The same. Except she doesn't use a bicycle. She walks into town. Another accident.'

Edik pulled a face. 'Are you sure we can get away with it?'

A film fell over his father's eyes. His expression emptied. Edik knew that look. It meant anyone who stood in his way would, quite simply, be eliminated.

'Leave any troublemakers to me,' said the old man quietly.

'What about Jenny Forrester?' Edik looked at the woman's photograph. Tall and slim with sheets of blond hair, she looked intelligent as well as athletic; perfect for their purpose. 'You're sure her husband won't cause us any trouble?'

'He remembers nothing of his dealings with us,' his father assured him. 'He had a breakdown five years ago, when his son was killed. His memory never recovered.'

'To our advantage.' Edik found himself nodding. The plan was looking better and better.

At that moment, someone tapped softly on the door and Ekaterina stepped inside. She was holding a silver tray upon which stood a bottle of Zyr vodka. Distilled five times, filtered nine times and taste-tested three times, it was Edik's favourite for its exceptionally smooth and slightly astringent flavour. He pretended to watch her pour three glasses but in reality he was watching the Director, who was staring at Ekaterina as if he couldn't believe his eyes. His lips had parted, his tongue appearing briefly as though salivating.

Edik felt his ego swell. He enjoyed watching men drool over his prize, all the more since he knew Ekaterina was unimpeachable, and that he owned her, heart, body and soul.

'To the future,' said the old man, and raised his glass.

'You really think it will work?' Edik asked.

'Oh, yes.' His father smiled, his face creasing into folds of dried parchment. He only smiled when he knew he would win. 'It will work.'

Edik raised his glass high. He felt a rush of euphoria.

'To Russia's new future.'

CHAPTER ONE

Saturday 31 January

'Russia?' Dan Forrester stared at Bernard. 'You want me to go to *Russia*?'

'It's not on the moon.' Bernard looked amused. 'A four-hour flight, that's all.'

Dan glanced out of the sitting-room window. The radio had said it was snowing further north, but here it was a beautiful day with clear blue skies stretching over Welsh moorland. Jenny was going to go berserk. Ever since he'd moved out before Christmas he'd tried to fit in with her arrangements but now Bernard was here, the walk she'd planned with him and Aimee across the valley would be scuppered.

'Does Philip know you're here?' Philip Denton was Dan's boss and the head of DCA & Co, a global political analyst specialist service that he set up seven years ago. He used to be Bernard's colleague in MI5. The two men held a mutual respect for one another, along with a fair quantity of friendly rivalry, with Bernard always complaining that he trained the best officers only to have Philip poach them.

'Yes. Although not exactly why.'

'I see,' said Dan neutrally. At least this explained why Bernard had driven across the country to see him. But he didn't like Philip being kept out of the picture.

Bernard propped his hands in front of his face. Gnarled and heavily veined, they had surprisingly sensitive fingertips, which Dan supposed would be an advantage when he indulged his hobby: tying flies for trout and salmon fishing. They were sitting opposite one another, Bernard on the leather armchair that Jenny had inherited from her uncle when he died last year, Dan on the sofa. Jenny hadn't believed Dan when he'd said he hadn't known Bernard was coming and she'd gone from being soft and welcoming to furious in two seconds flat.

'I thought today was for us,' she spat. 'Your family.'

'It is,' he protested. 'Bernard didn't ring or text me. He just turned up.'

Her lips had tightened into an angry white line, showing she didn't believe him. He couldn't blame her, not after what he'd learned about his past behaviour. He'd been self-centred and obsessive from the sound of it, concentrating on himself to the exclusion of all others. Nothing like the man he was today. At least that's what he hoped. But from the look on Jenny's face it seemed nothing had changed.

She'd called him last week, saying she had something to tell him, something personal that she couldn't discuss over the phone, but before she could, his old boss had appeared. Talk about atrocious timing – how Dan was going to coax Jenny out of her foul mood he couldn't think. He wondered if she was going to broach the subject of divorce. So far, neither of them had mentioned it and he still didn't know how he felt. He was, he supposed, treading water, waiting for quite what he wasn't sure, but at the moment divorce didn't feel right although he couldn't give a precise reason why.

Bernard dropped his hands into his lap. 'We've been approached by someone who calls themselves Lynx. Someone we know nothing about. They're offering us a big story in Russia, something huge that will apparently have global ramifications.'

Bernard cleared his throat and leaned forward.

'They will only talk to you.'

Dan blinked. 'Why?'

'Apparently you met Lynx in Moscow ten years ago. They trust you.'

Dan waited for Bernard to fill in the gap.

'MI6 seconded you. You were pursuing the truth behind Alexander Litvinenko's death.'

Dan wanted to say he'd never been to Moscow, never been involved in the Litvinenko case, but he had to trust Bernard on this. A lot of his memory had been ruined, great chunks of his recall obliterated by what everyone now referred to as his 'breakdown' five years ago when his three-year-old son Luke had been killed in a hit-and-run. Strange how he couldn't remember Moscow or Lynx but could tell you every detail of the den he'd created at the bottom of the garden as a boy. Memories of his job at MI5 had been lost forever but there were faces from his school days and university that he knew as surely as if he'd created them himself.

'Lynx has been a dead agent all this time,' Bernard continued. 'They say you recruited them. It's only now that they feel they have something to say. To you.'

Dan's mind slipped over the code name *Lynx*. A wild cat with distinctive tufts of black hair on the tips of its ears. Large padded paws for walking on snow. A solitary cat. A cat that lived in the northernmost reaches of Russia, in Siberia. A cat that could grow to be the size of a Labrador. He knew all this, but couldn't remember Moscow. A kernel of frustration began to grow and he quickly caught it before it could balloon out of control, and let it go. As Dr Winter, his psychiatrist, had taught him, there was little point in getting angry over it. His memory was what it was and what had been lost would, apparently, never return. He had to learn not to let it get to him.

'How do you know Lynx is genuine?' Dan asked.

'We don't.'

A dog barked outside, a single deep *woof*. Dan took no notice, recognising that the tone wasn't an alarm but playful, as though the animal wanted a ball to be thrown.

Bernard glanced through the window, then back. 'They had the right fax number. The right code.'

Dan mulled things over. 'Could it be a trap of some sort?'

'I suppose so, but what sort of trap when you have no memory of them or the work you did?'

'Perhaps they don't know about my breakdown.'

'Perhaps,' Bernard agreed mildly.

Dan rubbed the space between his brows. 'You should send someone else. I'm not exactly current in trade craft.'

'Of course,' Bernard agreed, 'but Lynx refuses to meet anyone else. I offered them Savannah and Ellis' – two of Bernard's best and most trusted officers – 'but no go.'

'Does Lynx know I'm no longer with the Firm?'

'We have no idea. But they appear to be expecting us to persuade you to meet them.' Bernard's expression intensified a fraction. 'There's something else. They said their information involves you personally, but when we pressed for more details they clammed up. We're inclined to think they're using the personal angle to tempt you to meet them, but obviously we can't be certain.'

Dan's misgivings rose. He agreed with Bernard that the personal angle smacked of coercion, but what if Lynx was telling the truth? Uneasy, he looked at his old boss and said, 'What else?' He needed more information: why the Director General of MI5 had come all the way out here on a Saturday due to a 'dead' agent who might exist, but might not, and whose 'huge' issue might exist, but might not.

Bernard's mouth narrowed for a moment. 'Lynx told us that two FSB agents were coming to England on a top secret mission. Unfortunately, by the time we were alerted they'd already entered the country and vanished. We have absolutely no idea what they're doing in the UK.'

Dan's skin prickled. So, Russian state security were involved. 'When did they arrive?'

'The day before yesterday.'

Thursday the twenty-ninth of January.

'They're on tourist visas,' Bernard added. 'A couple, Ivan and Yelena Barbolin.'

'Are they actually married?' Dan asked.

'Doubtful.' Bernard watched him attentively. 'Lynx said they were sent by Edik Yesikov. He's an old friend of Putin's. Colonel-General of the FSB as well as Director General of Shelomov Gaz.'

Powerful as well as rich, Dan thought. A formidable combination.

'You've probably heard Edik Yesikov is being groomed to become Putin's successor,' Bernard added.

Dan nodded. He'd read about it in the newspapers recently. 'Any ideas what they might be up to?'

'Not yet.' Bernard pressed his hands together. 'But one thing we're sure of is that the Kremlin is becoming increasingly concerned that a revolution is around the corner. Annexing Crimea kept the lid on it for a while, then taking arms to Syria, but the people are getting more and more fed up with living under such a totalitarian regime.'

Bernard glanced at the window again, then back. 'The Russian economy is in its worst crisis of Putin's reign. It's only thanks to his control of the media that the people haven't rebelled yet. But what will happen when they learn the truth?'

Dan could see where this was going. Bernard wanted to know whether Putin's spies had anything to do with the President's need to keep Russia fuelled with patriotism, which could well turn to more annexations and war.

'I don't want any nasty surprises,' Bernard said. 'Which is why I've booked you on a flight to Moscow this afternoon.' He reached into his jacket and brought out a British passport, passed it across. Dan picked it up to see it had his photograph beside the name Michael Wilson. There were three separate tourist visas for Russia, each for thirty days; one in 2006, one in 2007 and one current. Bernard then passed over a mobile phone along with some wallet litter; membership cards and receipts in Wilson's name.

'With everything that's going on over there,' Dan said cautiously, 'won't I attract undue attention?'

'Sanctions may be in place but British businessmen are still moving in and out of the country. Not very many, certainly, but you shouldn't stand out.'

Dan checked the mobile phone and saw it had a list of contacts and a history of texts and emails.

'Your cover address is in London,' Bernard told him. 'Someone will vouch for you if enquiries are made. We've allocated you a retired officer in Ealing, Bob Stevens, who will cover the majority of issues but if things get sticky, he can bring in backup.'

Next came a driving licence and two credit cards. 'Try not to spend too much,' Bernard told him. 'And please bring back as many receipts as you can. Our accounts department will be eternally grateful.'

Dan turned the cards over in his hands. 'I don't speak Russian.'

Bernard sent him a sideways look and for a moment Dan thought he might demur but all he said was, 'Nor do most visitors.'

Something inside Dan quickened. Had he ever spoken Russian? His French wasn't bad, and nor was his Spanish, but what about other languages? Had they been consigned to the dustbin of his derelict memory?

Bernard didn't seem to sense Dan's sudden tension. He said, 'Lynx says they'll be in the lobby bar of the Radisson Royal Hotel at ten o'clock tonight. They will approach you with the words, "Have you visited St Clement's Church?" You will respond saying, "Not yet, but I have heard it is very beautiful."'

Dan stared.

'And before you go, I'd like to agree on some basic code words. Since you're meeting Lynx we thought *Mountain Lion* appropriate for yourself. If all is well, say it's meant to be *sunny later*. If you're injured or ill, it looks as though it's going to *cloud over soon*.'

As Bernard ran through more code words, a tingle started at the top of Dan's head and spread through his body. Every object in the room took on a harder, brighter edge. His hearing was amplified. He felt a rush of energy, close to euphoria and knew this was why he'd been addicted to his old job.

He closed his eyes and took a breath.

'Jenny's going to kill me,' he murmured.

CHAPTER TWO

'You didn't think to ask me first?' Jenny's eyes crackled with blue fire. 'We were supposed to spend the day together. Walk with Aimee and picnic at Pentwyn. She hasn't seen you for *ten days*, Dan. She's been so excited and you just throw it all away because Bernard asks you to.'

'I would never give up time with Aimee willingly. You know me better than that. It's a matter of—'

'And don't you dare say the words *national security*,' she spat.

He held up both hands. 'Sorry.'

'Christ.' She put a shaking hand to her forehead. 'It's just like the old days. You putting your job first. Vanishing God knows where for God knows how long. Leaving your family behind to sit around wondering when you'll return, and in what kind of state. I thought all that was behind us.'

'It is,' he said. 'I don't work for MI5 any more.'

'But when Bernard clicks his fingers you jump.'

'He's the Director General, Jenny.' He tried to keep his tone level. 'Not some middle manager. He wouldn't ask unless it was absolutely necessary.'

They'd shut themselves in the utility room to prevent Aimee overhearing and now the dryer kicked in with a rumble. Jeans and socks, pants and shirts tumbled. It used to drive him crazy that she used the dryer on a sunny day, when the washing could be hung outside to save electricity, but now he wasn't living here, she could do as she liked.

'It's too cold outside,' she said defensively. She was looking at him, looking at the washing. 'It'll freeze solid on the line.'

'You're probably right.' He wasn't going to argue.

Long silence. He tried not to look at his watch, to gauge when he should leave for the airport. Time was tight, but he didn't want to leave Jenny on a sour note. Desperately, he tried to think of a way to salvage the situation.

'I'll come down next weekend,' he said. 'Stay Saturday night at the pub. Take you both out for Sunday lunch.'

'We're with Granny and Grandpa then.'

'I thought they were coming over tomorrow.'

'So?' Her gaze turned combative. 'Or aren't they allowed to see their granddaughter two weekends on the trot?'

'Of course they are.'

He ran a hand over his head, looking at his wife and wishing he could find the right words to cajole her into a better mood. What to say? He studied her silky sheets of blond hair that he loved gently tucking behind her ears. The lush mouth that he loved kissing. Her high breasts and narrow waist. She was as beautiful as when they'd first met and although he still loved her with an aching passion that sometimes shook him to his core, he'd felt his only choice was to move out to give them both some space. Jenny had lied to him about how he'd lost his memory, and even though he could understand her reasons, he had yet to forgive her.

'What were you going to tell me?' he asked. 'That you couldn't say over the phone?'

Her chin lifted. 'It doesn't matter.'

'Come on, Jenny. You said it was important.'

She gave him a cold look. 'It can wait.'

Realising she wouldn't tell him if his clothes were on fire in her current mood, he let it drop.

'I didn't mean this to happen.' He spread his hands.

The cold look remained. 'I'll leave it to you to explain to Aimee why you're leaving when you've only just arrived.'

Jenny opened the door. She was about to step into the kitchen when she fell back with a little shriek.

Instantly he was in front of her, shielding her with his body. 'What is it?'

'The . . . your . . .' She took a breath and pointed.

The Rottweiler was flopped on the kitchen floor. She was looking at them, ears pricked, her amber eyes unblinking.

'Dog,' said Jenny. She was holding her hand against her heart. 'I forgot it was here.'

'Poppy's a she,' Dan said.

At the sound of her name the dog scrambled up and ambled over, her stumpy tail ticking from side to side in a happy wag. He'd rescued her from the RSPCA last month, where she was about to be put down. Few people wanted to adopt large breeds, let alone one that people perceived to be dangerous, and Dan hadn't been able to turn his back on her. Now he stroked Poppy's broad head and she leaned against him, emitting a throaty purr.

Dan looked at Jenny. Then down at the dog. He said, 'While I'm away, I was wondering . . .'

'No, Dan.' Jenny pushed past him. 'I am not having that thing stay here.'

'But Aimee loves her.'

'And that makes it OK? I don't think so.'

He gave Poppy another scratch before glancing at his watch. He had just five minutes left to annoy the other woman in his life.

Aimee was sprawled on her bed with a computer on her lap. She was wearing jeans and a bobbly sweater and her face was scrunched into an expression that Dan knew meant she was worried.

'Sweet pea,' Dan said, 'we've hit a problem.'

She pointed at her laptop screen. 'Daddy, it says it could happen in *weeks*.'

The screen said, in big black letters, HOW MANY DAYS APART EQUALS A LEGAL SEPARATION? Below, in smaller type, *Divorce in weeks from £37.*

'Aimee . . .' His voice was warning. She knew very well she wasn't allowed to go online unsupervised.

'It's not live, Daddy,' she said. 'It's what Tara sent me. She copied and pasted it.'

Aimee's best friend. Supposedly.

Dan sat on the bed and pulled her into a hug. 'We're not getting divorced. If we were, we'd tell you straight away. Remember what we said?'

Aimee stared at him, eyes wide. She'd stuck her thumb in her mouth, a sure indication she was feeling insecure.

'Mummy and Daddy weren't happy living together and we decided that it was best to live apart for a while.' He repeated what he and Jenny had been saying since he'd moved out. 'We both still love you very much and we'll always be your Mummy and Daddy.'

She unplugged her thumb. 'Why can't you come home?'

'We're trying to work out our problems.' He sidestepped the question, not wanting to give her false hope. 'Any decisions we make will have an effect on you so we'll always talk to you about what's going to happen. We won't do anything without discussing it with you first.'

He'd made a pact with Jenny to try not to say and do things that might make Aimee feel scared or confused. The best way they'd found was to always give her advance warning or an explanation of anything that was going to happen. When Aimee was properly prepared, she seemed to cope better with what was to come and without losing confidence and trust in them. So far, it seemed to be working OK. No thanks to her so-called buddy Tara.

'Anything else worrying you?'

She looked up at him. She'd just turned seven and had the fine bones and fair silken hair of her mother. She'd inherited Jenny's eyes as well, the same piercing blue that made his heart turn over every time.

'So what's the problem?' she said.

'There's been a change of plan.'

She stiffened and pushed herself away. 'You can't stay?'

'I'm sorry, sweetheart. Really sorry. But you know that man who turned up this morning?'

Reluctantly, she nodded.

'I used to work for him. He wants me to do something for him. You know I wouldn't normally put work first, but it's really, really important. I'll make it up to you, I promise.'

'Can't I come with you?'

She obviously assumed he was going to London and he didn't correct her.

'Maybe next time. We can go to Sea Life and meet some turtles. Oh, and they also have Gentoo penguins. Or so I've been told.'

'It's open again?' said Aimee, brightening. Sea Life had been closed over Christmas for refurbishment.

'Yup.'

'Can Mummy come too?'

'If she'd like to.'

Aimee slid off the bed and raced outside. 'Mummy!' she yelled. 'Daddy's going to take us to Sea Life! They've got penguins and fish but they've also got turtles, I *love* turtles . . .' She pounded down the stairs, streams of chatter following.

In the kitchen, Aimee kept up her running conversation with Poppy, who stood looking at her, head cocked and expression expectant, her tail steadily wagging from side to side. 'You can go snorkelling with sharks if you want,' Aimee babbled. 'But you can't snorkel because you're a dog. You'll have to swim, but then you might not like sharks . . .'

Relieved he'd deflected Aimee's disappointment, Dan looked across at Jenny. 'I'd better go,' he said.

A shadow slid across her eyes, but she nodded. 'I'll get Poppy's water bowl.'

'Can't Poppy stay here?' Aimee said. She looked between Dan and Jenny beseechingly. 'I'll walk her, I promise. And feed her. Pleeeeeeease!' She put her arms around the dog's neck and buried her face in fur. Poppy's eyes half shut as she heaved a contented sigh.

Jenny looked at Dan who shrugged his shoulders. It was Jenny's call but he didn't want to say so out loud. She would just love it if she was blamed for kicking the dog out.

'Oh, all right,' Jenny suddenly relented. 'The dog can stay.'

Dan blinked. Even Aimee looked amazed. She pulled back and stared at her mother. 'I thought you didn't like Poppy.'

'She's just a bit big, that's all.' Jenny looked defensive.

'Mummy, you're *brilliant*.' Aimee scampered over to Jenny and hugged her. 'Thank you! And Poppy says thank you too! Don't you, Poppy?'

Outside, Dan unloaded the dog's blanket from the rear of the car. 'I haven't got her bed or any food with me.'

'I can get something in Chepstow later.'

He looked at Jenny. 'Thanks,' he said.

As he held her eyes he saw her soften, the anger leaching out of her and making her lips relax and part a little. He saw she'd put on some sort of subtle lipstick – when had she done that? – and belatedly realised she was wearing her best jeans and a delicate cashmere top that only came out on tidier occasions.

'I'm sorry I went ballistic.' She gave a rueful smile.

'It's OK.' He smiled cautiously back.

'I wanted today to be perfect,' she admitted. 'To remind you of the good times. And show how good it will be when you come back.'

He knew he should reiterate the words *we still have to work out where we go next* but he didn't want to change her mood, which for some reason had lifted.

She stood before him, tall and proud and beautiful. 'I love you.' Her words resonated with the truth.

He wanted to say *I love you too* but it was too soon. He saw the hurt in her eyes when he didn't speak.

Dan said goodbye to Aimee who was dressing a contented-looking Poppy in Jenny's wool scarf, and gave her a quick run-down on Poppy's basic needs. Neither the dog nor his daughter seemed particularly perturbed when he left, which was a relief. He couldn't have borne a teary departure.

Jenny stood by his car as he climbed inside, started it up. He glanced at the clock on the dashboard. Even without having to find somewhere for the dog to stay he'd still have to put his foot down to make the flight comfortably. Winding down the window, he said, 'I'll be back in a couple of days.'

She was biting her lip, looking undecided.

'Everything OK?' he asked.

She looked away then back. Gave a nod.

Putting the car into gear he began driving down the track, his mind already racing ahead and planning what he needed to buy at the airport, from a pair of gloves and hat – Moscow would be below freezing at this time of year – to toothbrush and spare socks and underclothes. He was about to change into second gear when he heard Jenny's shout.

'Dan! Wait!'

She was running after him.

He rammed his foot on the brake, the tyres squirting gravel as he stopped.

'What is it?' He was already halfway out of the car when she ran up to him. Her face was flushed.

'What I wanted to tell you . . . Well, it's just that . . .'

She took a breath. 'You remember the last time we made love?'

Dear God. Not now. He struggled to change mental gears.

'It was after supper at Candy's,' he said. 'In November.'

She smiled at him, a smile of old that reminded him of when they first met. The smile that made his heart soar.

'Well, the thing is,' she said, eyes dancing, 'I'm pregnant.'

His mouth opened and closed. No sound came out.

'I thought . . .' She looked away, suddenly uncertain. 'Maybe Lucy could be godmother.'

'Lucy?' he managed. His mind was reeling.

'Your police constable friend.'

Dan drove to the airport his mind split in two, one half already striding across the airy foyer at Terminal 5, the other on PC Lucy Davies. Just weeks ago, Lucy had stopped him from making a monumental mistake, for which he was indebted.

As he joined the M25 from the M4, sweeping smoothly south, he decided Lucy would make a great godmother.

CHAPTER THREE

PC Lucy Davies was in the New Collections section of Marks and Spencer. Thanks to Stockton being one of the UK's most deprived areas the collection had to be the smallest on the planet, but despite this drawback it didn't stop poor old M & S being a magnet for every shoplifter in the district.

'Are you going to buy that, or just stuff it up your jumper?' Lucy's tone was conversational but Sharon leaped a mile. Lucy tried not to smile. She loved surprising potential offenders. Almost as much as she loved nicking them.

'Just browsing, if you have to know.' Sharon's lip curled. She retained her grip on the lace crop top.

Lucy eyed the soft red material edged with beads. Then she looked at Sharon, the woman's gaunt face, her lank and greasy hair, the shabby clothes a size too large and reeking of stale sweat and cigarettes. Lucy sighed. Sharon would no more wear the garment than fly to the moon.

'For dress-down Friday at the office?' Lucy said.

Sharon stared at her. Lucy looked calmly back, her body language open and unthreatening, but inside she was ready. Sharon was known for her volatile temper and Lucy had no intention of getting a black eye.

To her surprise, Sharon stepped forward and lifted the top to Lucy's face, cocking her head thoughtfully to one side. 'It really suits you, you know. You've got lovely skin. And the colour brings out your eyes. It really does. Makes them zing.'

'Zing or not, shoplifting is against the law,' Lucy responded.

Sharon sighed, let her hand drop. 'It's pretty,' she said wistfully.

Lucy wondered if Sharon had ever worn anything that wasn't second- or third-hand. She came from a family of six and had five children herself, three with different fathers. She had no job, had never had a holiday, and struggled to pay the heating bills.

'Very pretty,' Lucy agreed, feeling an uncharacteristic surge of gloom. Would someone like Sharon ever get out of the vicious cycle of poverty? As a kid, Sharon had been a runaway, and now her kids were also runaways and Lucy guessed Sharon's grandchildren would be doomed to repeat the same miserable behaviour patterns ad infinitum.

'Tango, tango, one-seven, all units . . .'

Her radio crackled the words. The divisional control room. Not wanting Sharon earwigging, Lucy moved away.

'. . . attend a shooting at Barwick House near Kirlevington.'

Lucy's pulse rose, her breathing went tight. Excitement and apprehension. She never felt more alive than when on a blue light.

CHAPTER FOUR

In the distance, Jessie Calder heard the distant wail of a police siren. The wind had to be coming from the north-west because normally they couldn't hear anything but the sounds of the countryside out here. Just the chirp of a robin, a sheep's bleat.

She raised her face to the weak winter sun. The smell of wet leaves, the creak of leather, the soft squelch of Templar's hooves. This was what it was all about. No school. Just getting up when she wanted, riding where she wanted and coming home when she wanted. She was looking forward to sinking into the armchair by the Aga with a mug of hot apple juice and a slice of chocolate butter cake that she and Mum had made yesterday.

Suddenly, the distinctive *boom!* of a shotgun echoed through the air. She felt the horse's muscles bunch beneath her, his head jerking up, ears pricked forward like twin arrows. His feet started to dance, clattering on the tarmac.

'Hey, easy boy.'

She soothed him gently and at the same time she heard another *boom!* She'd thought Dad had gone to a meeting this morning, but obviously he'd changed his mind. What was he up to? Shooting rats, probably. He was paranoid about rats. They peed constantly, ate the tack, ate anything. The feed might be in sealed bins but they still weed on the hay they fed to the horses. He'd bought a Jack Russell puppy last year in the hope it would keep the rats down but Lulu was more interested in foraging for titbits in the kitchen than doing anything useful in the stable yard. He might as well have bought a feather duster for all the use she'd been.

Boom!

Definitely rats, she decided.

You couldn't see the stables from here, they were around the back of the manor house, adorned with winter flowering jasmine and flower tubs. Her mother loved gardening almost as much as she loved painting but the estate grounds were too much for one person to look after and Dad employed a full-time gardener as well as a part-time horticulturist.

I like gardens very much, he'd said, *but I'd rather spend my weekends doing something I enjoy.*

Like shooting, Jessie thought, be it pheasants, partridge, or in this case, rats.

Crack!

The second after the rifle shot – a distinctly different sound from the gruff roar of the shotgun – a dog started screaming. All the hairs stood upright on her body. Templar tautened, throwing up his head, suddenly fearful.

Another shot and the screaming stopped.

Oh my God, she thought. What's happened? Who got hurt?

Crack, crack!

Panic began to rise. Had Dad missed a rat and hit Buzz, their Labrador, by accident? Why was he using the rifle? Sensing her alarm, Templar bunched into a sidling trot and she quickly gathered the reins and kicked him forward.

Silence fell. All she could hear was Templar's hooves clattering, the metal click of his bit, the sound of her own breathing. Mouth dry, Jessie pushed the horse on.

She didn't ride straight into the yard. She'd been brought up around guns and knew to exercise caution when people were shooting. At the side of the house she hurried Templar to one of the apple trees. Slipping from the saddle she hitched his reins over a branch. She was grateful that he stood quietly and gave him a swift pat. Her legs felt wobbly but she forced herself to run for the stable yard.

She paused before stepping into view, not wanting to be mistaken for a rat and shot.

'Dad?' she called out. 'It's me. Where are you?'

Nothing.

'Dad?'

She peered around the corner of the barn. She saw the flagstone paving, the hanging baskets, the fresh green and white paintwork, the horsebox parked at the far end alongside the Land Rover, Mum's Golf, what appeared to be two dogs sleeping.

Then she saw the blood.

Great pools of it spreading from beneath Lulu's supine form.

Jessie sprinted to the Jack Russell, a scream lodged in her throat. *No, no no no no no!* She skidded to her knees and reached out a hand, wary in case Lulu was wounded – she didn't want to get bitten – but in the next second she realised there was no need to be cautious. Half of Lulu's head had been blown away.

A high-pitched ringing started in her ears.

She looked over at Buzz. His muzzle was frothy with spittle and blood. His eyes were open but he wasn't seeing anything. He'd been shot in the stomach, but not with a shotgun. The rifle. It must have been Buzz who'd screamed.

'Dad?'

Jessie looked around wildly.

'DAD!' she screamed.

Jessie's mind dissolved into ribbons of sheer-white hysteria. Where was Mum? And what about Felix, Sofia and little Tasha? Galvanised, she leaped to her feet and bolted for the house. Pelted through the Italian sunken garden that separated the house from the stable yard, to the back door.

She gave a muffled yelp when she saw another form lying unmoving half-in, half-out of the doorway. Head lolling, blood clotting. Apricot, their elderly marmalade cat.

Jessie moaned. Stumbled to a stop.

She was trembling from head to toe.

Nothing made any sense. Who would shoot the dogs and poor old Apricot?

No. *No.*

Bewildered, frightened, Jessie stepped to the back door. Peered through the boot room and into the kitchen. The room looked unreal, the proportions odd and suddenly too large, the wall lights eerily over-bright as she took in the figure slumped face down on the rug in front of the massive open fireplace.

Her mother.

Her legs were spreadeagled, one arm flung wide, her hand clutching her mobile phone. Her other arm clutched a bundle of clothing partly beneath her, maybe some washing, but then Jessie's heart clenched and she saw it was little Tasha.

Stabs of panic pierced her. And through her fear Jessie knew they were, like the animals, dead.

Then she heard footsteps on slate. Strong and steady. Coming from the scullery.

A man's voice. 'Jessie?'

'Dad?' Relief made her feel dizzy.

'Where are you?'

The timbre of his voice was odd, raspy, as though he had a cold.

'K-kitchen.'

There was a movement at the scullery door but when Jessie dragged her gaze there it wasn't to see her father. The man might be wearing her father's clothes – moleskin trousers scuffed at the bottom, check shirt cuffs pushed above his elbows, same heavy tweed jacket – but it wasn't Dad. His expression was blank. His eyes were dead. Like a fish's.

He held the rifle in his hands. It was pointed at her waist.

'I'm sorry,' he said.

She saw the muscles in his hands flex and she knew he was going to shoot her. Like he'd shot Buzz and Lulu, Apricot, Mum and Tasha.

Unthinking, acting on nothing but instinct, Jessie spun around and ran.

CHAPTER FIVE

'Faster!' urged Lucy.

'I'm trying!' protested Howard.

They'd peeled off the A66 and on to the Yarm Road to find the traffic had thickened. Cars and vans hauled themselves to the side of the road at the sound of the siren, all except some twit in a Toyota Yaris who slowed to a crawl, dithering.

'Get out of the way you dozy . . .' Howard braked heavily, trying to second-guess the flustered driver. 'Pull over, you idiot. To the *left*, not into the middle of the fucking street . . .'

One of Stockton's oldest PCs at fifty-one, Howard was normally steady and even-tempered. He only swore under duress.

'Christ on a bike . . .'

Finally the Yaris stopped and waved them past.

'Cheers, mate.' He swung round the car, his voice sarcastic. 'It's not like we're in a fucking hurry or anything.'

They sped down Yarm High Street. Lucy kept quiet, not wanting to distract him. Too many things going on: traffic lights, crossings, delivery vans, pedestrians, kids, dogs.

Out of Yarm, screeching left on to Green Lane then immediately right, plunging on to a muddy country lane she'd never seen before. It made her realise she rarely set foot outside the centre of Stockton. This was a different world with hedgerows and rivers, sodden fields and stretches of woodland. What was it with a shooting out here? Had some country toff gone nuts? Or was it a couple of farmers having an argument? Her mind spun red and yellow. What about gang warfare? A hit of some sort? Control had said a girl had called emergency. Perhaps a teenager had gone off the deep end.

They were barely half a mile away when they met a massive green tractor taking up most of the road. No room for their vehicle to pass. The tractor was towing a huge piece of kit in matching green – Lucy had no idea what it was – and the driver waved frantically, indicating it would be faster if they reversed to let him past.

'For fuck's sake . . .'

Howard slammed the car into reverse but despite their best efforts, it still took them a good minute to manoeuvre past.

Lucy resisted the urge to scream with frustration.

A lot could happen in a minute.

CHAPTER SIX

Jessie sprinted through the back door and swung immediately right, legs pumping, driving for the corner of the house.

Crack!

A chip of stone struck her cheek but she didn't feel it sting or realise she was bleeding. She had to get away. She had to hide.

A childhood memory surfaced and she switched direction, running between the camellias and bamboo and diving through the garden door to come out on the west side of the drive. Ten paces and she was burrowing into an old childhood hidey-hole deep in an ancient rhododendron bush, leaves and branches wet and pouring rainwater as she moved them aside. She'd hidden there with Felix on countless occasions when they were little. The path they'd made through the boughs all those years had gone and she had to force her way through, crouching low and clawing her way deeper. The taste of earth was in her mouth, fresh wet air in her lungs. Finally she paused, huddling low, foliage brushing her cheeks and hands.

She tried to quieten her ragged gasps. I must keep absolutely still, she told herself. For as long as it takes. Until the police arrive and tell me it's safe to come out.

Through the leaves she could just make out the ghostly white of the fence edging the drive, but little else. Templar was just around the corner but she couldn't risk running for him. She'd be too exposed.

She started to tremble. Tears began to rise.

Do not cry, she commanded herself. You might make a sound that will give you away.

The faint rumble of an engine reached her.

She stiffened, listening, unsure where it was coming from. The stables? The front drive?

And then she heard a small sound behind her. Unable to see what it was, she began to shuffle away from the sound, terror like a rope around her neck and making it difficult to breathe. Had she left tracks on the grass? Footprints?

The sound came again.

She swallowed a scream and willed herself to keep still. She blocked out everything – the sound of a blackbird chattering, rooks cawing – and concentrated on what was behind her. Then she heard the tiniest of clicks. A minute metallic click she knew all too well. The sound of a safety catch being released.

It was right behind her.

Jessie bolted through the foliage. Head down, arms and legs driving for the other side, waiting for the bullet in her thighs, her back, her spine, and the next instant she was bursting into clear air, her legs pumping, propelling her across the drive for the orchard. *Crack!*

The sound of the rifle firing. It sounded so close!

She increased her pace, amazed she hadn't been hit, pelting for Templar, grabbing his reins from the branch and flipping them over his head, swinging him away from the yard and the rear drive. The five-bar gate was shut and although Templar was a fair jumper, if they botched it or he refused, they'd be trapped.

The horse was jerking his head, snorting and rolling his eyes at her urgency but he didn't back away – *good boy* – and he let her half leap, half scramble into the saddle. The instant she was astride she dug her boots into his ribs.

'Go, boy, GO!' she yelled.

She was ready for him to jibe, kick up a fuss as he usually did when she asked for a fast start, but it was as though he'd been waiting for this command all his life. His ears flashed forward. His shoulders rose and his great hindquarters bunched beneath her. He took off like a rocket.

He charged down the drive with Jessie lying low over his neck, willing him to go faster with every inch of her body. She glanced over her shoulder, her eyes focused on nothing but the rifle, the barrel pointed right at her.

Jessie reined Templar violently left. He responded immediately. She then reined him violently to the right.

Crack!

She heard the rooks exploding from the trees ahead, cawing frenziedly – *he hasn't hit me, he hasn't hit me* – and she hunkered even lower. Trees flashed past. Her senses were filled with nothing but the sound of Templar's metal shoes pounding against tarmac, the slap and creak of leather, threads of mane stinging her eyes. Templar's hot breathing.

Crack!

The sound of a bullet whizzed past her, like the snap of a bull-whip. *They had to get off the drive.*

Aiming the horse for the oak tree looming just ahead she pressured the reins, letting him know she wanted him to slow so they could swing down the bridle path. But Templar was enjoying his flat-out gallop and didn't want to stop.

Jessie leaned back and with all her strength, hauled the horse sideways, signalling to him to veer right. She was terrified they were going to overshoot the turning.

Please don't fire again, she prayed.

At the last second, Templar got the message. He dropped his head, put his rump down and spun for the bridle path, and although the huge body beneath her was angling for the path in the biggest slalom a horse had ever attempted, as his hooves met the grass they began to slip. He was suddenly off-balance and uncoordinated and she thought, *No! Please don't fall!*

It was as though he'd heard her. His rear hooves dug into the earth, powering him forward, but as he regained his balance the rifle fired, *crack!*, and Jessie felt something punch her in her chest. She didn't know what it was, she was urging Templar onward, and then another *crack!* and Templar gave a grunt as though he'd been winded and then the huge body beneath her began to buckle.

The horse crashed to the ground with horrifying force. Jessie was flung sideways as he flailed wildly, trying to right himself, and she could feel his hooves lashing madly as she urged him to get up, *please boy*, and he was twisting, desperately kicking his hind legs when there was another *crack!* and everything turned white. Blinding white, as though she'd been dropped on to an ice-covered mountain in bright sunshine.

She said something, she didn't know what, whether it was Templar's name or if she formed the single word, *Daddy.*

CHAPTER SEVEN

Siren still blaring, praying there weren't any more tractors in the vicinity or a herd of cows around the next corner, they flashed past a sign for Green Hall Farm.

'Steady,' she warned Howard. 'It's the next left.'

And sure enough there it was – a huge wrought-iron ranch-style gate with the name *Barwick House* sculpted across the top. Lucy's gaze went to the entry-phone pad to one side – would there be anyone to answer it? – but as Howard splashed the car forward the gate automatically swung open.

He switched off the siren. Lucy pressed button six on her radio. Code six. *Arrived at scene.*

An immaculate drive with manicured edges curved through water-logged grazing paddocks. According to the satnav the drive was half a mile long. The backdrop of moorland – they were a stone's throw from North York Moors National Park – was fringed by woods of oak and beech, monochrome grey and brown in the dripping countryside.

They were a third of the way down the drive when she spotted something large and dark humped on the ground. For a moment she thought it was one of those huge plastic-coated straw bales but as they neared she saw it was a horse. A girl lay next to it, motionless.

The car was still moving when Lucy erupted outside. Tore across. She skidded to the girl's side. The girl looked at her and she looked back.

'She's alive!' she yelled at Howard. 'Get the ambulance to hurry!'

The girl's puffa jacket was soaked in blood. Quickly Lucy unpopped the buttons. Pushed aside the girl's sweater. Dear God, it was a mess.

'What's your name?' she asked but the girl didn't answer. 'I'm Lucy. I'm going to find where you're hurt and try and help you, OK?'

Desperately she tried to find where the blood was coming from. She had to stop the bleeding or the girl would die. She could hear Howard talking to the ambulance. In the distance, more sirens but they were too far away, at least another minute. *Faster*, she urged them.

Lucy found the wound, pulsing, gushing blood, and put the heel of her hand over it. Pressed down.

The girl gave a shuddering cough.

'The ambulance is coming,' Lucy told her. 'They'll be here before you know it. They're really fast. They'll patch you up in no time.'

Jessie gave a groan, a sound of agony so deep Lucy started to sweat.

She forced herself to concentrate on stemming the flow of blood, which had, she realised to her horror, thickened and turned the colour of tar. Where was the fucking *ambulance*?

Jessie gave a soft hiccup, then her breathing began to labour. Blood bubbled through her nostrils.

'Daddy.' It was a gasp more than a word. 'Please ...'

'Hang in there ...'

The slender body gave a shudder. The girl's eyes were on Lucy's. They were deeply frightened.

'Don't give up, OK?' Lucy urged. 'The ambulance is seconds away ...'

The shaking increased. Lucy held her breath, willing the girl to keep breathing, stay alive ...

The girl's body tensed and gave a long, final shudder, then fell limp.

Lucy's mind howled. *NO!*

She started cardiopulmonary resuscitation. Thirty chest compressions then two breaths. She didn't stop until a paramedic caught her hands and drew them aside. While he bent over the girl, another began checking her vital signs. Lucy scrambled out of the way. Tried to steady herself. Get her brain working. She was trembling top to toe. *Prioritise!* she yelled at herself.

She looked away from the girl. It helped. Her mind kick-started. *Go ahead and secure the area. Help others who may be wounded. Stop anyone else from getting shot.*

Back in the car. Hands sticky with blood. Heart thumping. Howard driving, talking to Control, giving them a running commentary. He'd already warned them about the girl but the medics would still try and resuscitate her.

'We're approaching the house from the north,' Howard kept up his commentary. 'The doors and windows to the house are closed. I can't see anyone. I'm driving past the house and through a set of columns. Arriving in a stable yard.'

He'd made a sensible decision, Lucy decided, not to get out of the car straight away in case the shooter was still around. Her eyes went to two dogs lying on the ground, obviously dead. Oh, shit. Her mouth tasted sour. She prayed this wasn't what she thought it was.

'There's a horsebox,' Howard continued, 'a Land Rover, a Jaguar XF and a VW Golf.' He rattled off the vehicles' registration numbers, a precaution in case someone did a runner in one of them.

He stopped the car. Cautiously they climbed out. Lucy looked around, every sense attuned to detecting movement. The rise and fall of a chest. The blink of an eye. Fingers squeezing a trigger. She didn't want to die today.

'TFU are on their way,' Howard hissed. Tactical Firearms Unit.

'How long?'

'Three minutes.'

It didn't sound long but they couldn't wait. Their priority was to preserve life. They had to find the shooter. Arrest them if they could.

They headed for the rear of the house. Lucy's dread increased when she saw a dead cat lolling half-in, half-out of a doorway.

They put their radios to silent. Stepped into a boot room. Ancient flagstone floor. A chest freezer on the left. Loads of muddy boots and wellies, waxed jackets. They crept down a corridor, peered into a kitchen. Her eyes went straight to the figure lying face down on the floor.

The woman's legs were splayed apart, one arm flung wide, the other clutching a bundle of clothing partly beneath her, maybe some washing, but then Lucy's heart clenched. It was a child.

They both sped over. Although the bodies were still warm, both were dead. Her stomach twisted violently when she saw the glistening blue of an entrail showing through the mess of the woman's sweater. She guessed a shotgun had been used and she swallowed drily, trying to quash the wave of nausea that followed. Legs unsteady, she rose when Howard did. He raised his eyebrows at her. *You OK?* She nodded.

Back in the corridor. Rooms to the right and left. Ahead was a spacious hall with silk-lined walls and deep red Turkish-style rugs.

Howard gestured left, asked the question with his eyes. She gave another nod. He was beginning to move away when Lucy's heart jumped. She thought she'd heard something.

'Ssst,' she hissed. He stopped.

Nothing.

She pointed upstairs. Howard came and stood with her, listening.

Zero.

Be careful, he mouthed at her.

While he headed back to check the rooms leading from the kitchen, she moved quietly into the hall. Took the first door on the left and into a library. Thick tartan carpet, open fireplace, walls of books. As soon as she saw the room was empty, she moved into what appeared be an artist's studio with York stone floors, an easel, lots of paint pots, canvasses, jars and brushes. Also empty.

The next was a family room. Big squashy sofas, widescreen TV, oversized portraits of several children on the walls, books and toys scattered, a playpen. As she scanned the area she caught the smell of something off. Cautiously she moved forward. With each step the smell got worse. Faeces, urine, fear. Her stomach became oily as she took step after step, searching the room.

She found him behind the second sofa.

A boy. A teenager, maybe thirteen or fourteen. He lay at an angle, his shoulders twisted. One arm lay stretched out, reaching towards Lucy. He'd had his throat cut. Blood saturated his chest. His eyes were open, staring past her, his expression surprised. With a shaking hand, she quickly checked for his pulse. His skin was still warm, but no pulse. Not even a flutter.

Lucy exhaled. Sweat greased her skin. Her heart was pounding so hard she wondered she didn't feel faint. She crept to the door. Where was the killer? Still here? Or had they gone?

She slipped back into the hall and to her horror saw a man at the far end, tiptoeing for the kitchen. Six feet or so, broad-shouldered, mid-fifties, dark curly hair. He was carrying a shotgun and even from where she stood she could see the blood that stained his clothes. He was covered in it. He was stalking Howard.

No thought. No hesitation.

'POLICE!' she yelled. 'FREEZE!'

The man swung the gun around. His eyes were wild, his mouth caked in spittle.

Lucy dived back into the family room.

No gun went off. She hadn't been shot. Sweat was pouring off her and she could hear panting. It took her a second to realise it was coming from her own mouth.

'Police!' she yelled again. 'Put your weapon down!'

'How do I know you're police?' The man's voice was raspy and racked with tremors. 'I can't see you.'

She wasn't going to stick her head around the corner and get it blown off. 'Put the weapon down and I will show myself.'

'How do I know you won't shoot me?'

'My name is Lucy Davies. I am a police officer. Put your weapon down.'

Silence.

'Sir.' Howard's voice. Soothing and mild, like soft caramel. 'If you would look at me, you will see I'm wearing a uniform.'

Silence, during which she prayed the man was looking at Howard and not about to shoot him.

'Now I will show you my warrant card.'

Cautiously Lucy slid to the doorway and peered round. As she'd hoped, the man was gazing at Howard who was holding up his card but she wasn't sure the man was seeing it. Good news: he'd lowered the gun. But she didn't like the fact he was still holding the damn thing.

'Police.' The man's voice shook. 'I rang you ages ago. *Where have you been?*'

'Sir. Give me the gun.'

Howard held out his hand.

Something on Howard's face made the man crumple. 'Oh, God.' He made a guttural sound, almost a groan. To Lucy's immense relief, he handed the gun over.

As soon as Howard ejected two shells Lucy tore down the corridor. 'Sir, you have the right to remain silent. You do not have to say anything, but it may harm your defence . . .'

As she neared, she brought out her handcuffs. She wasn't going to take any risks with this guy. She wanted him cuffed and in the back of the car with the doors locked. To her horror, he took one look at her closing in, glanced at Howard, and in that moment, Lucy knew that she had done exactly the wrong thing.

CHAPTER EIGHT

Before Lucy could call a warning to Howard, form the words *stop him!* the man ran into the boot room, slammed the door and bolted it.

Fuck! She couldn't have timed it better if she'd tried. She was hanging up her uniform in two weeks to start as a detective and she was going to look *so stupid* . . .

Spinning on her heels she tore for the front door, flung it open. Erupted on to the porch and pounded round the side of the house, past a rhododendron and an apple orchard. Pounded into the stable yard. Empty. Wildly she looked around. He couldn't have got far. He was larger than her, more bulky. She was small and quick, whippet-like. If she knew where he'd gone she'd catch him up in no time.

Two police cars rocketed into the yard but she didn't pause to tell them what was going on. She had no time to waste. *She had to find him.* She broke into a run for the stable yard. Glanced inside the first stable.

Hell, she thought.

A little grey pony lay dead on the straw.

The next stable was empty but the next, a big loose box, held another dead horse.

She jogged past a horsebox. Joined Howard briefly to check out a smoking oil drum where a pile of bloody clothing was blazing. What looked like the remains of a tweed jacket, sturdy trousers, leather shoes. The smell of an accelerant hit her, petrol maybe. The man had obviously tried to burn his clothes earlier to cover forensic evidence, but he hadn't bargained on them turning up so soon.

A police officer was running towards them with a hose already spilling water. They left him to it. While Howard ran to a five-bar gate, she tracked the drive around the house, coursing the ground like an agitated hunting dog. She came almost full circle before she saw footprints leading from the massive rhododendron bush. Two sets. One smaller than the other. Both led to the drive. From there, she followed the prints until she saw the smaller ones leading into the orchard.

An ambulance drove into the stable yard. More police cars arrived. In the distance she heard the distinctive clatter of a helicopter approaching. Saw a bunch of cops begin to move out. The hunt was on. She had to find the man before someone else did. The last thing she wanted was to start her new job looking like a total prat.

The footprints didn't go far. They led to a mess of ground churned up by a horse. The hoof prints headed up the drive. Lucy scanned further to find a set of larger footprints – they looked the same size as the ones from the rhododendron – heading deeper into the orchard. She followed them. The air was changing rapidly, the temperature dropping. On the news this morning, the weather girl had predicted light showers, but Lucy was wondering if they were in for something more serious, like a snow storm.

She worked her way through the orchard and over a fence acting as a boundary from a stretch of woodland. A police helicopter passed overhead, the whirring sound vibrating against her breastbone and in her ears. She continued cautiously, carefully scanning the ground as she walked, occasionally ducking beneath a branch, stepping over muddy, leaf-filled puddles. The wood was dense with low-lying limbs and shrubs, and from time to time she lost sight of the man's tracks and had to pause and scan around before she found them again.

She came to a slope and began to climb. The woods grew darker. Sleet began to fall. Pulling up her collar, she plodded on.

She tried to keep her bearings but it was difficult and after a while she wondered if she'd find her way back. She glanced over her shoulder, unnerved at the thought. She wasn't from the country. She was city born and bred and found the dark stillness oppressive, almost threatening.

Stop being a baby, she told herself. You're twenty-six years old. There are no goblins here.

Slowly, carefully, she followed the tracks until suddenly, the woods parted and she came to a lane. She looked up and down. No traffic, no parked cars. Just the sound of rooks cawing. She scouted the area searching for more footprints but found nothing. Had the man left a car here? If he hadn't, then as far as she was concerned he might as well have vanished into thin air.

Shit, shit, *shit*.

She'd bloody well lost him. Howard had done a top job in dis-arming the man and in her eagerness to cuff him, she'd stuffed up. A rookie could have done better.

Despondent, she turned and began retracing her tracks. Her trousers were soaked and smeared with moss and green fungus and mud. Her hands were freezing and her mind had fallen as grey as her surroundings. She felt like doing nothing but going home, turning up the heating and drowning her sorrows with a bottle of anything. Vodka, wine, she didn't care as long as it took the edge off her failure.

She wondered where the man had gone. Assuming he was the father, she would have expected him to commit suicide after killing his family, but perhaps they'd disturbed him before he could finish the job. What a *waste*. She couldn't comprehend what had driven him to kill his wife and kids, the animals. What had the horses and dogs done to deserve such brutal treatment? And that poor bloody cat . . .

She'd been walking for a good twenty minutes before she real-ised she was lost. She'd been walking in her own tracks but at some point had started following an animal trail without think-ing for who knew how long. For fucksakes, not only was she a crap police officer but her orientation skills were less than zero. Standing next to an ivy-coated tree, she looked around, listening intently, hoping for some kind of clue to her whereabouts.

Overhead, the canopy of branches parted to show nothing but a dimming sky. Please God it wasn't *that* late. She checked her watch to see she'd been out here for well over an hour. Crap.

It was going to be dark soon. Pulling out her phone she saw Mac had texted her.

The first message said: *Are you OK?*

The second: *I need to know.*

Third: *I'm on my way.*

That was the trouble with having had a relationship with a fellow cop. Not that it had been a relationship as such being an orgy of wall-to-wall, beach-to-beach full-on, fantastic sex, but DI Faris MacDonald didn't see it like that. What was going to happen when he became her full-time boss in two weeks, God only knew.

She sent him a message back: *Don't come. I'm OK.*

Then she texted Howard. Her fingers were shaking with cold and she had to retype most of the message before it became comprehensible.

After she'd tucked her phone away, she spotted a patch of leaves that were darker than the others, as though they'd been disturbed. She crouched down, wondering if an animal had been here and then she looked ahead, and saw something out of place. A piece of wood hammered into a tree trunk.

Carefully she stepped forward. Pushed past some branches. A structure appeared. She looked up to see a tree house. Her heart gave a bump. Sitting in the tree house was the man. He was partly protected from the elements by a roof but his legs were dangling outside and were soaked. He didn't seem to notice. He was staring blankly into the distance.

'Hello,' she said.

He didn't respond.

His skin was white and waxy-looking, his eyes dark hollows. Pain was etched into every pore.

'I'm PC Lucy Davies,' she added. 'What's your name?'

Nothing.

'You must be feeling cold. I certainly am. We've been out here for over an hour by now. Time to go and get a hot cuppa, don't you think?'

He didn't move a muscle. Didn't blink. Just stared his dead-eyed stare God alone knew where.

She knew she ought to radio Control to tell them she'd found him, but since she couldn't bear the humiliation of having to admit she didn't know where she was, she thought she'd wing it for the moment. She looked at the wooden ladder propped against the tree. Looked up at him. 'Mind if I come up? I hope it's not too high as I'm not great with heights.'

Still he didn't move. Didn't give any indication he knew she was there.

The rungs were slippery but firm enough. When she reached the top she had to crouch in order to enter. The house had three walls and was open on one side, which was where the man sat. It was small and empty of anything but a floor covered in rotting leaves and a dead mouse in one corner.

'I'm coming over to join you,' she told him. 'I could do with a rest. It's not often I go for a walk in the country. I'm more used to pavements, to be honest. My boots are soaking.'

Lucy shuffled over to join him, her senses alert in case he did something unpredictable, like attack her. But she didn't think that would happen. He appeared catatonic.

She settled next to him, careful not to touch or startle him in any way. She kept up her one-sided conversation, her voice modulated and calm, non-threatening, as she took in the view. Trees, trees, and more trees. Some were brown, others black but as the temperature continued to drop, everything started to freeze. Like her feet. She couldn't think when she'd last felt so cold.

Then it started to snow. Soft fat flakes the size of pennies. Great.

She stuck her hands under her armpits. Swung her legs back and forth, trying to keep the blood flow going. At this rate, she was going to get hypothermia. And what about him? He was wearing nothing but a suit. Albeit a blood and mud spattered suit. Black leather shoes that were covered in mud. He must have changed into the suit after he'd set fire to his clothes. It was his bad luck the police had arrived before they'd turned to ashes. At least she was wearing a thermal vest and a thick pair of woollen socks. She'd learned to dress warmly since she'd been transferred up here.

She felt her phone vibrate as messages began coming in, no doubt from Howard and Jacko, her sarge, and everyone in between. She didn't move to answer them. She didn't want to spook the man.

'You know we can't stay here all night,' she said. Her teeth were chattering, her whole body racked with shivers. 'We'll freeze.'

No reaction.

'Neither of us are dressed for this,' she added. 'I don't know about you, but I don't want to get sick. I have people who depend on me.'

She was picturing Howard as she spoke and didn't think she'd said anything profound, but for some reason he turned his head and looked at her. His gaze wasn't distant any longer, it was focused on her, one hundred per cent.

He said quite clearly, 'I'm sorry.'

And then his face crumpled. His grief showed in his eyes, from deep within his core, and wrenched Lucy so hard she felt her own emotions rise in response but she couldn't show any reaction, she was a police officer. The man turned his face skywards, his face still creased with pain.

She fell quiet, wanting to give him some emotional space but the snow had thickened and was now falling rapidly, settling on every surface and painting the woods white. Time to get a move on before they froze solid.

She said, 'I'm Lucy. What's your name?'

He didn't answer for a moment. But then he said, 'Adrian.'

'Well, Adrian. It's getting dark. And if you hadn't noticed, it's snowing pretty hard too. It's time to go.'

'Polina loves the snow.' His voice was rough and hoarse.

'Polina?'

He didn't respond.

'Adrian, who is Polina?' Lucy asked, wanting to get him talking.

'My wife.'

Long pause.

'She ...' The word trembled. He cleared his throat. 'She w-wants to take the kids to Russia next Christmas.'

'Why Russia?' Lucy said.

'She's Russian.'

Was the dead woman with the child in her arms his wife? If so, why had he used the present tense? Shock? Or was it simply denial of what he'd done?

'It gets down to minus fifty out there,' he added distantly. 'Snow up to your armpits. This is nothing.'

'Feels cold enough to me,' she said.

He turned his face to Lucy. His eyes were rimmed with red in a face the colour of stale putty. He looked exhausted, about to collapse. 'I didn't kill them.'

She'd heard enough guilty people protest their innocence to know not to say anything in response.

'I loved them. Why would I harm them?'

That's for the shrinks to find out.

He looked back at the woods. Snow coated his knees but he didn't seem to notice. 'Why didn't they kill me?' he mumbled. 'I don't understand. What harm did Polina do anyone? Tasha?' As he spoke the names, his face collapsed once again. 'Felix,' he whispered. 'Jessie.'

Lucy was thinking about shuffling backwards for the ladder and encouraging him down, when he suddenly said, 'Dear God. What about Zama?' He grabbed Lucy's arm and gripped it tight.

His sudden animation made her nervous. She glanced down. It wasn't far if she had to jump, maybe fifteen feet or so and on to what looked like a nice deep litter of leaves, but if she landed on a stump or rock or a sharp-broken branch, she could do horrible damage – lacerate an artery or break a bone.

His grip was like iron. She could practically feel the bruises forming. 'Adrian, you're hurting me.'

He dropped her arm as though scalded, expression dismayed. 'I'm sorry. I didn't realise.'

'We can find out about Zama if we go back to the house. Are they a relative?'

He hesitated. Something cautious rose in his eyes. For the first time, she saw he was thinking.

'He's, er . . .' Calder licked his lips. Glanced away. Thought some more. 'Earlier,' he said. 'In the house. You were going to arrest me.'

I still am, she thought, but instead said, 'I'm looking forward to getting into some dry clothes and having a hot drink. My feet are like ice blocks.'

'You have to believe me,' he said. 'I'm innocent.'

Yeah, right. You and every other person I've ever nicked.

'If I'm arrested,' he added, 'who will look for the killer?'

He looked at her solemnly, waiting for her response.

When she didn't say anything, he glanced down at the ground then back. Shuffled his backside forward a fraction. Nearer the edge.

Shit, *shit*, she thought. He's about to jump. Do another runner.

'Adrian, if you don't come with me now,' she said, 'it's going to make things really difficult for you. Not just because you're soaking wet in sub-zero temperatures, but because every police officer will take your absence as a sign of guilt.'

He peered down as though judging how far it was to the ground.

Please, don't jump. I want to go home, not chase you around the fucking forest all night.

'They've got tracker dogs and infra-red cameras,' she told him. 'You won't stand a chance.'

She felt as though he was waiting for something to help him decide whether to stay with her. She wished she had the magic words he wanted to hear but since she couldn't mind-read, she settled for the prosaic.

'You'll get hypothermia if you stay out here any longer. That won't help you find anyone, will it?'

He looked at her for a long time. She looked back, trying to emulate a benign and gentle persona rather than an enthusiastic copper who was dying to slap him behind bars.

'Will you help me find who killed my family?' he asked.

She didn't have anything to lose. Let him believe what he wanted. Anything to bring him in.

She nodded. 'Yes.'

'OK,' he said. 'Let's go.'

As they trudged through the snow, she heard him say very gently, 'Yes, my love. It's not as cold as it is in Russia.'

CHAPTER NINE

Saturday 31 January

Dan disembarked at Sheremetyevo Airport trying to shake off his state of dazed confusion. He had to start concentrating on the job at hand but Jenny's voice trailed like a continual banner in his mind, her joyous smile imprinted on his retina.

I'm pregnant.

They'd been talking about having another baby but that had been months ago and before they'd separated. He hadn't realised she'd come off the pill. He remembered their making love when they'd returned from Candy's that night. Nothing earth shattering or remarkable or spectacular, they'd simply undressed and climbed into bed and turned to each other, moving seamlessly, touching one another where they knew they liked being touched as they'd done a hundred times before. Afterwards they had curled together, their legs entangled, her arm around his ribs, her head pillowed on his chest, and he'd fallen asleep with her scent on his skin.

And then things had skewed and he'd moved out. But now . . . he drew in a deep breath. They were going to have a baby. And according to the text she'd sent just as he boarded the aircraft, it was going to be a boy.

He wondered how she felt about having another son. Luke had been their firstborn and Aimee just a baby when Luke had died, as Jenny believed, in a hit-and-run just off Brick Lane. He'd been three years old. Dan processed the fact that if he hadn't rushed off on this mission, he could have asked her, but then he recalled the joy sparking in her eyes when she'd told him the news, and he knew things would be OK, and that she'd love their second son unreservedly.

With his satchel slung over his shoulder – bought in haste at the airport – he took a moving walkway to Terminal E and caught the Aeroexpress train to Belorusskiy Vokzal. From there, he used the metro, busy even on a Saturday with families and the elderly absorbed in their e-book readers. He couldn't remember being in Moscow but had little trouble understanding the system, buying a multi-ride card and travelling without any trouble, aware of things that he'd only know if he'd been here before, recognising the *perekhod* signs that linked underground passages between interchange stations and knowing that when two or more lines met, the intersecting stations could have different names. Strange how the memory worked. Dr Winter continually encouraged him to trust his subconscious and let it be his guide. Sometimes it surprised him. Like when, on an inexplicable impulse last month, he'd entered an exclusive-looking men's shop in Mayfair to be warmly greeted by one of the tailors saying, 'Mr Forrester, so good to see you again.' He'd held an account there for five years and although he couldn't remember it, an instinct had driven him to grasp the polished brass door handle and step inside.

Now, he rode the escalator to the surface at Kievskaya, icy air sweeping to greet him and cutting the skin on his cheeks like cats' claws. Tightening his scarf he settled his hat as low as he could – his ears were already burning with cold – and strode out. Traffic roared past, slushing through ice and snow. Pedestrians walked hunched in calf-length woollen coats and fur, their eyes watering, hastening to get to their destinations and out of the cold. Ahead, the imposing Gothic facade of the Radisson Royal reared against the dark sky, dominating the area with its pale and stately Stalinist architecture.

By the time he reached the hotel his nose had gone numb at the tip and his fingers were tingling. He stripped off his gloves as he entered the foyer, a massive expanse of marble floors and gleaming white pillars. He checked the time. Nine forty-five p.m.

A security guard looked him over. Dan walked past him as though he didn't exist. *Always look as though you belong. As though you know where you're going.*

The bar was busy, nearly every sofa and armchair occupied. The sound of voices and laugher, glasses chinking, background music. Men and women, visitors and business types, all unwinding on a Saturday night. Dan shucked off his coat and settled on a stool at the bar and ordered a tonic water and ice. Something that looked as though it contained vodka. Surreptitiously he studied his neighbours. A man, running to fat, was gesticulating expansively to another man who appeared bored. Two women chatting and drinking champagne. One blonde and elfin, the other dark and slender, all fierce angles and fire. Both women were stunning. Could such beauties be professionals? he wondered. If so, he doubted they'd be taken seriously by their male colleagues. The issue of gender equality and overt sexism in Russian society was a continual concern to ordinary Russians but how he knew this, Dan wasn't sure.

He studied the women carefully. Not professionals, he decided. They used their sexuality too openly. However, it was hard to tell whether they were daughters or girlfriends of high-echelon officials or a pair of high-class prostitutes. They could even be university students looking to pick up a sugar daddy to help fund their studies but he wouldn't bet on it. Again, he checked his watch.

Nine fifty-five.

A man entered the bar, alone. Young, cheeks dark with stubble, he wore jeans and loafers and an air of casual wealth. Was he Lynx? Dan let his gaze drift past to an elderly lady with red-painted nails who was peering at one of the orchids that adorned an occasional table as though checking for greenfly. Another young man arrived to greet the first. Dan watched them approach the bar and start to flirt with the two women.

He wondered what Jenny would make of the hotel's opulence, the potted palms, thick carpets, grand staircases and chandeliers. Aimee would love it. She'd be pop-eyed with excitement but what about his wife? He didn't think he'd taken her anywhere so overtly sumptuous. They usually stayed in top-end B & Bs or, for special occasions like their wedding anniversary, a boutique or country house hotel. She'd enjoy it here, he decided, but more out of curiosity than real pleasure.

His heart squeezed at the next thought.

What would they call their baby boy?

What would their second son be like? Luke had had bright blond hair like Jenny and a wild streak that came from Dan, but which Dan had learned to repress. Jenny told him he used to love watching Luke play in the garden with the sheer abandonment of irrepressible youth.

His gaze was drawn to the dark-haired beauty at the bar. She wasn't his type, but there was something in her expression and manner that he found so absorbing, he found it hard not to stare. It had to be the sheer beauty of her. It was almost hypnotic.

Ten o'clock.

Something caught his attention at the far end of the room. Two men in suits. Hard and unsmiling. They scanned the bar as though looking for someone, then left.

The minutes ticked past. Ten past ten. Ten twenty. Ten forty. Dan ordered a light bar snack. Would Lynx turn up? Had they been scared off or delayed? No way to tell, so he ate his snack and ordered another tonic and ice, outwardly relaxed, internally vigilant.

Eleven o'clock came and went. Dan made the decision to wait for Lynx until the bar closed even though something told him that if Lynx wasn't here by now, they wouldn't appear. It was looking as though it would be a wasted trip, which wouldn't please Bernard.

Out of the corner of his eye he saw the two women preparing to leave, picking up their handbags, slipping off their stools. They were laughing, their lips stretched over pearly white teeth, but their eyes weren't amused. The men tried to stop them going. One of them gripped the dark-haired beauty's arm and she tried to brush it away but his grip tightened and she grimaced in pain.

Dan's gut tightened. He resisted the urge to intervene. The last thing he needed was a bar fight.

She snapped something at the man but he ignored her. She flashed Dan a look. It was almost as though she expected him to rise and defend her. Then she shrugged as though to say *it's not my fault* and when she next spoke to the man restraining her, she nodded at Dan. The men turned to stare at him. He stared back.

What had she said?

She released her arm from the man's grip. Both women sashayed their way over to him. The petite blonde kissed his cheek, trailing a delicate scent of vanilla and anise, and then left without a word. The dark woman stood so close her hip touched his. She delicately placed a hand on his shoulder and bent her head to his. She smelled of dark amber, nutmeg and ginger lily. Spicy and exotic. She murmured in English, 'Put your arm around my waist.'

Her voice was low and smoky, accented in Russian.

He complied.

The men continued to stare.

He didn't drop his gaze from theirs.

'Pull me closer,' she said.

The material of her dress was slippery and cool, her body pliant and smooth. She moved her hand to the nape of his neck. Caressed his hair.

She dipped her head to his once more. Her lips were so close to his ear he felt the tiny hairs tremble when she spoke. Goosebumps rushed up his arm and across his chest.

'I told them you were my pimp.'

One of the men sent Dan a disgusted look. The other gave him a final glare. Finally, they both turned away and began scanning the room for further prey.

The woman slipped on to the stool next to him. Laid a proprietorial hand on his thigh. Long, slender fingers. Magenta nail polish. A silver ring in the shape of a skull. Nothing on her wedding ring finger. She said, 'Buy me a drink.'

'Champagne?' he asked.

'Cristal,' she said.

He called over the barman. Thought of Bernard's accounts department. *Try not to spend too much.* At over fifty quid a glass someone's eyebrows would rise when they checked his expenses.

'Yes, sir?'

'A bottle of Cristal, please.'

'Certainly, sir.'

Dan watched it being poured. Touched his champagne glass to hers.

'You are waiting for someone,' she said. Her sultry, almond-shaped eyes held his, appraising.

'Not really.'

'Is she pretty?'

'I'm married,' he said.

'You don't wear a ring.'

He'd taken it off at the airport, a simple precaution to protect his family rather than signal that he was single.

'Are you here on business or pleasure?' she asked.

'A little of both.'

Her hand remained on his thigh, as light as a butterfly. 'Have you visited St Clement's Church?'

Without pausing he responded, saying, 'Not yet, but I have heard it is very beautiful.'

'Perhaps we could visit it together. It is renowned for its baroque interior, along with a set of gilded eighteenth-century railings.'

'Perhaps,' he agreed. His tone was dispassionate but inside his mind was racing. He'd recruited this woman? This was Lynx? How old had she been when they'd met ten years ago? He could remember nothing about her. Not her smoky eyes or stunning body or tumbles of silken hair.

'Tomorrow morning,' she said decisively. 'Ten o'clock. If you're late I will wait for you like a cat waits at the window for its human to return.'

It was a veiled reference to her code name and he gave a nod of acknowledgement.

In one fluid movement she rose and slipped from her stool.

He watched her cross the room. Every eye followed her, men and women alike, riveted by her sinuous, exquisite beauty. Dan supposed he was affected as much as the next person but his defences were raised against a honey trap. He wished he could remember her. She would have to have had a speciality for him to have recruited her and – apart from her obvious sexuality – he wondered what it was. He hoped he'd find out tomorrow.

He drank another glass of champagne while he checked the Internet on his phone. St Clement's Church wasn't far so he decided to spend the night at the Radisson. Hopefully he'd get the information Bernard wanted by tomorrow lunchtime and be on the next flight back to Heathrow. He paid the bar bill with Michael Wilson's credit card and headed back to reception who allocated him a classic room. Small with no view, but comfortable enough.

He showered and climbed into bed. He fell asleep wondering if they'd have their baby boy christened in church, and whether Lucy would come.

CHAPTER TEN

Sunday 1 February

It was hot and stuffy in the interview room, making Lucy feel irritable and edgy. Which wouldn't normally bother her, except for the malevolent belch of smoke crouching at the corners of her mind. It was there when she'd awoken earlier – talk about bad timing. She wanted to be on form, sparkling and alert, not struggling with her 'moods', as her mother called them. She'd only taken five days sick leave over the span of her police career because of them, but luckily nobody knew the real reason why. Everyone believed she suffered from migraines, which was the perfect cover and as close to what she suffered as to make it plausible.

There was no colour in her mind, just grey. Apparently she had a type of grapheme-colour synaesthesia where her mind lit up with colours when stimulated emotionally in some way or her brain was making – or trying to make – a neurological connection of some sort. It wasn't anything to worry about, her friend and GP had told her recently.

Hating the dreary grey, she hoped if she kept busy and didn't drop her guard, the colours would come back. She must remember to eat regularly and keep her fluid levels topped up, that always helped. The last thing she wanted was to be pole-axed and forced to take time off.

Adrian Calder sat opposite, with his brief. Eyes bloodshot and rimmed with red, Calder appeared exhausted. His skin was as grey and dry as cement dust and he looked as though he'd been incarcerated for weeks rather than fifteen hours. The clock was ticking – they had nine hours left before either charging him, or releasing him.

'If you're innocent,' said Mac, 'why did you run away?'

Calder looked at Lucy. He had deep grooves on either side of his nose, running down to his mouth, that she hadn't noticed before. Canyons of grief and fatigue.

She was waiting for him to say *no comment* but he surprised her by saying, 'I panicked, OK? She scared me.'

Calder's brief – a stocky man called Justin Tripp, who had a wind-beaten, ruddy face, reminding Lucy more of a farmer than a lawyer – turned to Mac and said, 'I need a word with my client.'

'Leave it,' Calder said.

'Adrian,' Tripp began to protest, 'I really –'

'Leave. It.'

Silence.

'Lucy scared you?' Mac raised an eyebrow. 'She's barely five four.'

'It was her whole attitude,' Calder said. 'She was going to arrest me, and from the way she was waving her handcuffs around . . . well.' He raised his hands as if to say, *what do you expect?*

'I can understand how you felt,' Mac said wryly, 'she scares me too sometimes.'

Although she knew Mac was being empathetic with the suspect, she sent him a filthy look. *What is this? Bash Constable Davies Day?* Despite her irritation she couldn't help noticing he was looking particularly good this morning, brown curly hair slightly messy, mismatched grey eyes clear and bright. When he glanced at her, her stomach did its usual flip. Hurriedly she looked away. Turned her concentration firmly back to the interview.

'Why were you burning your clothes?' she asked Calder.

'We went over this last night,' Justin Tripp quickly interjected.

'But not with me,' said Lucy. After she'd handed Calder over to the custody sergeant in the station, she'd been endlessly debriefed, then released to hammer out her report. Although she'd protested – she'd wanted to be the first to question Calder – Jacko had sent her home. Which had been a good move in retrospect as the instant she'd turned her key in the lock of her front door exhaustion had overcome her. She'd awoken on the sofa six hours later from a dream about Jessie, where the girl had been alive and begging for help, and although the clock said five a.m. Lucy hadn't bothered trying to get back to sleep. She'd put on her uniform and gone to the station.

'Look, I didn't . . .' As Calder began to speak his solicitor held up a warning hand as he turned to Tripp and said fiercely, 'I've nothing to hide. *Nothing.*'

'But you know what I said about –'

'I want to *help* the police,' Calder went on in the same fierce tone. 'I want them to find who killed my family. This policewoman said she'd help me and she can't do that if you want to bloody hog-tie me all the time!'

Silence.

'I didn't burn any clothes.' Calder looked at Mac, but Mac didn't say anything. Just folded his hands on his lap and maintained a neutral expression. Mac was her DI and the SIO – Senior Investigating Officer – but until she was transferred to CID he wasn't yet her boss. She was still answerable to her sarge, Jacko, and it was only thanks to Jacko that she'd been allowed to stay on the case. *To get some CID experience before you start officially*, he'd said, but in reality he'd done it because she'd have made his life hell if she hadn't been allowed to see the Calder case to completion.

Calder said, 'I was wearing my suit . . .' – he took a shuddering breath – 'which was covered in blood because I tried to see if I could save Tasha. And Felix . .'

Lucy had never seen a more devastated lawyer. If Justin Tripp could have put his hands on his head and wept, he would have done. She could almost feel sorry for him, but not today, not with a murderer trying to confess, or wriggle free. It was hard to tell quite what Calder thought he was doing.

'The shotgun I was carrying was loaded because I didn't know –'

'Adrian, I need a word' Justin Tripp made a last ditch attempt at controlling his client but Calder kept going.

'– whether the killer was still around. And I didn't want them to kill me!' He shuddered again. 'I did not kill my family. You have to believe me.' He looked desperately at Lucy. 'I wouldn't do such a thing. *I couldn't.*'

Lucy thought back to the familicide she'd attended in London two years ago, where a father had stabbed his three children before jumping into the Thames and drowning. She already knew that in over two-thirds of all cases of murdered children the parent was the principal suspect and Lucy had no reason to believe this case was any different. The only thing that really bugged her was the fact Adrian hadn't killed himself. Yet.

'Who's Zama?' she asked.

Adrian Calder's expression didn't change one iota. 'Who?' he said.

His brief, however, wasn't as composed. Justin Tripp reacted as though he'd heard his phone ring – the involuntary response of surprise.

Lucy said, 'When we were in the tree house, you said *what about Zama?* Why were you worried about him? Is he a relative of yours?'

Calder shook his head. 'You must be mistaken. I don't know anyone called Zama.'

He was lying. Why?

Long silence while she considered him. Then Mac spoke. 'I'd like you to tell Lucy about your business.'

Adrian Calder nodded. 'I run a chain of fast-casual restaurants called Melted.'

Lucy knew Melted. They were all over London and when she'd been at the Met she'd used them at least twice a week. Her favourite melt had been La Dolce Vita, slices of fontina with salami Napoletano and rocket, on garlic bread. Seriously delicious.

'Over a hundred restaurants,' said Mac, checking his notes.

'A hundred and eleven,' Adrian Calder said.

'Any debts?'

Calder leaned back and rested his hands in his lap, holding Mac's gaze openly, seemingly relaxed, but the little hairs on the back of Lucy's neck rose. Calder's shoulders had crunched slightly, almost infinitesimally, just like her father's used to when he felt defensive.

'I have one bank loan. And a mortgage on the house.'

Justin Tripp revived fleetingly to say, 'Is this really necessary?'

Calder rounded on his lawyer. 'Shut up and let them do their job.'

Tripp sank back with a sigh, hands held high, expression long-suffering as if to say: *I did my best.*

Mac took Calder through his finances, what he owed at what percentage, how he offset his mortgage, how his business loan with the bank worked, and although Calder's body language appeared unperturbed, the tension in his shoulders remained.

'You've sold some restaurants,' said Mac. 'Fifty-two, am I right?'

'As franchises,' Calder agreed and as Mac changed the subject, Calder's shoulders dropped. The movement was tiny, caused by a release of stress, and she doubted Mac would have seen it, but to her it was like watching her father all over again, denying he'd been down the pub, denying he'd been unfaithful, denying he was leaving them, denying he was emigrating to Australia with a yoga teacher called Tina who lived just down the road . . . Dad would look Lucy and her mother straight in the eye as he spoke, but his shoulders gave every lie away.

Lucy let Mac and Calder talk about the restaurants for a while before she tested Calder's tell. By leaning forward, she let Mac know she had a question. He gave her a nod. She brought out her pocket book and pretended to check something. 'I just wanted to go over what you said about debts.'

The instant she said the word *debts*, he leaned back and affected a casual, confident air, but his shoulders crunched. And when she released him from the subject, handing the interview back to Mac, the same delicate dropping movement occurred.

Gotcha, she thought triumphantly. They'd have to check his debt situation really closely now. Make sure every decimal point was accounted for and then check again, and again.

'Why is your company being investigated?' Lucy asked.

'It's not,' Calder said. He didn't seem perturbed by the question. No shoulder crunching. 'It's just that HMRC didn't like the fact my income reduced so radically, so quickly. There's nothing illegal going on.'

Lucy looked at him.

Calder spread his hands. 'The franchise restaurants have been losing money. They used poor advertising and poor quality control. Then there was a health and hygiene scare in Manchester last year. It put customers off.'

Put them off? Lucy stared. It had nearly killed them if the newspapers were to be believed. Over a hundred people had been hospitalised. When the health inspectors went in, they found salmonella in the chicken products and listeria in the cheese. Lucy hadn't eaten in a Melted since then and she wasn't the only one. Even Howard, a confirmed Melted addict, hadn't been back.

'All outlets started making a loss,' Calder added. 'Hence the reduced income. I declared less income which meant I paid less tax, hence the investigation.'

'Your income disappeared to nothing practically overnight,' Mac remarked placidly. 'A financial correspondent in one of the newspapers at the weekend said you could be facing bankruptcy if things don't turn around fast.'

Calder looked away. 'It's just a glitch.'

It was the first time he'd looked ashamed, unable to meet their eyes, and Lucy felt a welcome wave of anger. Anger was good. Anger kept the mood demon at bay. Had Calder been unable to bear his family facing poverty, the shame of it, the fall of societal ideals? Was that why he'd murdered them?

Daddy.

She heard Jessie's desperate whisper in her mind. The girl had just turned fourteen. Her life had barely started. What a horrific waste. And all thanks to the arrogance of Calder's actions. The sheer unadulterated conceit of the man thinking his wife and kids wouldn't be able to cope with a drop in living standard. But it wasn't about them. It was about *him*. *His* shame. *His* failure. *His* inability to stand in front of them and their friends and admit he'd fucked up. *His* stupid macho ego.

She looked at Adrian Calder but inside her head she was trying to staunch Jessie's gunshot wound, seeing the fear in the girl's eyes, seeing his wife sprawled dead on the kitchen floor, her lifeless baby daughter in her arms.

'What did your wife think about the state of your business?' she asked. Her tone was brittle, making Mac glance across, but she ignored him.

Calder blinked. 'What do you mean?'

'Did you discuss the fact you wouldn't be able to pay for your children's private education?' Both Felix and Jessie had gone to Ampleforth, one of the finest co-educational boarding schools in the country. The annual fees for one kid came to more than she earned in a year.

'Of course.' He looked baffled, as if to say *who wouldn't?*

'And?' Lucy prompted.

'She agreed we'd have to talk with the school heads. See how to transfer them to state school with minimum disruption. Polina was upset, understandably, but she didn't panic. She's made of sterner stuff than that. She knows what's important and it's not private schools. They're a luxury.'

'A luxury?' Lucy repeated, hoping to dig a bit deeper into his wife's psychology and expose him for what he was. A family annihilator who couldn't cope with having no money. Because without the money, he couldn't keep up appearances. He'd killed his wife and kids because he couldn't face them knowing he was a failure.

'Her mother, Irene, is Russian,' Calder said. 'She was brought up during Stalin's time. The purges.'

Lucy remembered what he'd said in the tree house. That his wife loved snow and had wanted to take the kids to Russia. 'Go on.'

'Godawful time, from the sound of it. People who spoke out against the regime were executed. They died in their millions.' He rubbed a hand over his forehead. 'Irene's father was quite powerful in the party apparently, but even so her in-laws were sent to death camps. Although she was born in England and has never been to Russia, Polina's marked by her mother's experiences, her stories. If we weren't starving in some hovel in sub-zero temperatures, then we were OK. That's what she believed. She's a strong woman, like her mother.'

'Did she believe there was a way out of your financial problems?'

'Er . . .' For a moment, Calder looked nonplussed. 'I don't think so. I mean, she agreed we had to start pulling our horns in. Downsizing. Economising.'

'So, no more horses and ponies to play with.'

Her tone had been more acidic than she'd planned and Mac turned his head and frowned at her. Tripp leaned across to Calder, about to say something, but Calder spun round like an angry snake, hissing, 'Let me be, for fuck's sake. They have to *know*.'

Shaking his head, the lawyer sank back into his chair.

'Polina understood what was going on,' Calder said. 'We hadn't discussed the details of how to downsize, but we'd already agreed we wouldn't get rid of the children's horses. Not Squirrel, anyway. All the children adored that pony. That would have been awful.'

Lucy stared at him. She made sure she held his gaze as she spoke.

'By "Squirrel" I assume you mean the little grey pony in the stable? The little grey pony who'd been shot in the side of his face, shattering his jaw? The pony who was left to bleed to death in the most appalling agony?'

What little colour Adrian Calder had drained out of his face.

Lucy leaned forward. 'Why did you kill the animals?'

'I didn't!' He looked horrified. 'I could no more harm them than harm my children!'

'Did you think nobody could care for them as well as you did? Was that the reason you gave yourself? That they'd be happier dead rather than being alive and looked after by someone else?'

'No!' His voice rose. 'I didn't kill them! I swear it!'

Mac made dampening motions with his hands. Intellectually she knew she should remain unemotional and not give the defence any ammunition they could use against the police later, but she couldn't bear him sitting there protesting his innocence when she'd touched the bodies of his wife and daughter, and young Felix, still warm.

'You had wealth,' she continued. 'You had possessions, went on foreign holidays, African safaris, skiing in Europe. Thanks to your restaurants going down the pan you couldn't give your family any of these things any more. You killed them as an act of mercy in your eyes. To prevent them having experiences of any hardship and—'

'NO!' This time Adrian Calder leaped to his feet. His face had turned red with fury. 'You are bloody well WRONG! I AM INNOCENT!'

She snapped her mouth shut as Calder's lawyer jackknifed to his feet, both hands raised. 'Time out,' he snapped.

Lucy didn't bother with any niceties. She simply pushed back her chair, got to her feet and walked out. The demon was now well and truly gone from her mind. No dark cloud, no fog. But at what cost?

Behind her, she heard Mac's angry footsteps in the corridor behind her. He yelled: 'My office, NOW, Lucy!'

CHAPTER ELEVEN

Lucy dragged her feet all the way to Mac's office. Nobody likes being told off and even though she knew she had to get it over with she still dawdled, chatting to people she met in the corridor along with a couple of undercover cops who'd just returned from a stake-out.

Finally, she was outside his door. He's just a cop, she told herself. He's not even your boss yet. Focus on that, and not the spectacular sex you've had with him, and you'll be fine. You just have to go in there, let him tear a strip off you, and leave. Simple.

Lifting her chin, she rapped on the door.

'Come in!'

She stepped inside to see Mac turned away from her, frowning at his computer screen. Strong jawline, broad shoulders, hands with square fingertips that were big and strong but could feel as gentle as velvet. God, what she'd do to feel them on her skin again, but it wasn't to be. Yes, he was delicious, and yes, the sex was fantastic, but the last thing she wanted at this stage of her career was to be undermined by having a relationship with her boss. She'd already been transferred once, booted out of the Met to land in poverty-stricken Stockton, and she had no intention of being transferred again. If she dated Mac and it went tits up, well, it wouldn't be him – rising star Detective Inspector – who'd be shovelled off to Land's End or John O'Groats and forgotten about. It would be her, a lowly constable, who was expendable.

At least that's what she told herself, but the truth went far deeper: she couldn't risk falling for him. She was terrified that if she allowed him to see her as she really was, showed him the truth of her, that he'd run a mile. Just look at Nate, her last boyfriend. Nate had pronounced her crazy and got his GP to put her on mood-suppressing drugs. It had been like living in the bottom of a milk bottle and the minute she'd ended the relationship and headed up here, she'd chucked the pills in the bin.

If Mac saw how crazy she got sometimes, he'd dump her without a second's thought and she'd have to see him every day, work alongside him while her heart was breaking. Much easier not to start a relationship. It was the only way she could protect herself.

Mac swivelled his chair round, rose to his feet. Folded his arms and propped a hip against his desk.

'Your temper,' he said.

'Sorry,' she said. She kept her eyes glued firmly on the wall past his left shoulder, her body straight, as though she was on parade. 'But he was acting so innocently, being so goddamned *helpful*, I couldn't bear it any more.'

'You're going to have to learn to bear it, OK? You've got to appear non-judgemental and not fly off the handle. It could be incredibly destructive in an investigation. You're bloody lucky Calder's brief isn't making a complaint.'

Bully for him, Lucy thought, feeling sulky, but she knew Mac was right. She'd behaved in a totally unprofessional manner and although she kept her head raised and didn't let her gaze waver, inside she was squirming at her behaviour.

He looked at her a long time. She tried not to fidget.

Finally, he let out a sigh, ran a hand over his face. 'I suggest I get you on an interview skills course. The sooner the better.'

'Great,' she said. She looked at him warily, wondering why he wasn't chewing her out.

'Fancy a drink later?' he asked.

'What, tonight?' She blinked. No way would he have time for anything but the case.

'Is that a yes?'

He'd laid a trap and she'd nearly fallen for it.

'No,' she said. Before he could ask why or press any further, she told him about Calder's tell, which seemed to distract him nicely.

'I didn't see anything.' He looked sceptical.

'It's minuscule. But believe me, it's there.' She didn't tell him about her father. She didn't want to get personal.

'I'll look out for it,' he said. 'Meantime, I guess we'd better go over his accounts again.'

'Any luck on the footprints I followed through the woods?' she asked.

'We're pretty sure they weren't Calder's. He's size eleven, and these were around nine. They can't tell us much more apart from the fact they were made by a pair of boots.'

Calder had been wearing leather shoes.

'Were they made the same day?' she said.

'Difficult to say.'

She tried not to cringe at the possibility she'd followed an old set of prints that belonged to a trespasser, someone walking their dog, the gardener. God, she'd been a shambles yesterday. Thank heavens she'd brought Calder in or she'd be a laughing stock.

'Can I go now?' she asked.

'Any clue as to what you might be doing next?' he asked. He was being ironic because he knew she liked working odd angles on a case, alone. And because she appreciated the long leash he gave her – something her old boss refused to do – she paused to answer.

'I'm going to interview Polina's mother to see if he's telling porkies,' she told him. 'Assuming she's not in Moscow or anything.'

'Scarborough.'

Nice one, she thought. She quite fancied a trip to the seaside.

CHAPTER TWELVE

Mac watched Lucy go, wishing he could call her back, wishing he could get over his idiotic obsession with her.

But how to do that when he saw her practically every day?

It had been OK when she'd been working out of the beat office. They could go for days without seeing one another. But now she was going to be a detective, how the hell was he going to get her out of his mind?

They'd first met on a team-building exercise in Wales, for new recruits. He remembered meeting her in the car park and trying not to stare. He couldn't keep his eyes off her and, at the time, it seemed she felt the same way as they'd spent most of the week bunking off before they'd made passionate love beneath the hot September sun. It had been thrilling and intense, and when she'd vanished towards the end of the week – her mother had fallen ill, apparently – he hadn't thought too much of it until she ghosted him: abruptly stopped taking his calls and answering his texts.

He asked a friend at the Met about her and everything became clear when he learned she had a boyfriend – Nathan Beamish – who she lived with. Which was a shame, because Mac thought they'd had something really good together, but if she was taken, well, she was taken.

And then he'd been transferred to Stockton Police, and there she'd been, as gorgeous as ever and, more importantly, single. At least that's what he'd thought, but now he wasn't so sure.

Was she seeing someone?

Without realising it, he entered the major incident room with a huge scowl on his face. Twenty computer screens were crammed on the single long table in the middle of the room. Twenty screens for twenty cops. Dozens of things needed doing, involving media liaison, SOCO, pathologists, coroners, witnesses, relatives and the world and his dog, and Mac had to ensure he was at the hub of all this information, being kept abreast of everything, checking that nobody was getting pissed off with anyone else and that the team was working closely together and as much in harmony as a bunch of angels playing the harp because a detective inspector wasn't just a cop. He was a manager.

He poured himself a coffee and took it to the whiteboard. Studied the chart. One adult and four kids, all dead.

Polina, the mother. Jessie, Felix, Sofia and little two-year-old Tasha.

One horse, three ponies, two dogs and an elderly marmalade cat, all shot to death as well.

Mac had worked several murder cases, but this was his first family annihilation. What had Calder been thinking of when he'd loaded his weapons? Had he already worked out who to kill first? Which child to kill last?

He turned his wrist and checked his watch. The psych was interviewing Calder at the moment. He'd be interested to see what she had to say, but if she even started to intimate that it was all Mummy's fault that Little Adrian murdered his family, then Mac would leave the room. He didn't buy the idea that you could blame your childhood for your adult actions. He had issues from his own childhood and he hadn't turned into a smackhead or a murderer. Mac had spent some time seeing a counsellor, to make sure something from his subconscious wouldn't trip him up, and then he'd got on with his life, because he was a mature man who could make his own decisions and they didn't include killing people just because his childhood sucked.

Yeah, he was mature all right. As crazy as a hormonal teenager held enthralled by his first infatuation.

What to do about Lucy?

He thought of her bright brown eyes, always so expressive. Her temper, always volatile. He thought of the way she held herself, confidently, always alert and active, her body small and lithe and quick. He thought of the way she felt in his arms, the little whimper she made when she came, and at that moment Mac realised the only way he'd stop obsessing over her was if she went out with him. He had to persuade her, somehow, and if it worked, great, and if not, fine. They were both adults, right? And once they were going out, he'd be able to relax.

CHAPTER THIRTEEN

Polina Calder's mother lived in a red-brick house on the eastern extremity of Scarborough, slap bang in the middle of the headland that separated North and South Bay. Partial views to the south showed the harbour and the steely North Sea. To the north stood a perpendicular rock face topped with castle ruins.

Lucy didn't bother looking for anywhere to park. The streets were narrow, single track, and she didn't want to waste time driving around the town waiting for someone to vacate their space. Instead she parked on a double yellow line outside the house and next to a panel van, hoping she'd be able to keep an eye out for parking wardens. She already had three parking tickets outstanding and didn't want another.

She climbed out into a stiff northerly breeze that rang with the sound of seagulls, boat engines and the distant clank of halyards. The air smelled of the sea and from somewhere came the faint aroma of hot oil. Chips, she thought, salivating. She'd have fish and chips for lunch.

Irene Cavendish greeted her at the front door, a formidable woman, tall and handsome, her cable sweater tight across her wide shoulders. She was in her eighties and although her hands were curled into claws from arthritis, she appeared pretty fit for her age. No walking frames or wall rails that Lucy could see. The only indication her life had been devastated by the murder of her daughter and grandchildren was her eyes. Red-veined and puffy and full of anguish.

Lucy offered her condolences. Irene nodded. Then she announced, 'You will have tea.' Her tone was thick and gravelly with tears but brooked no refusal.

Lucy allowed herself to be shown into a room filled with dark, heavy furniture graced with copious quantities of lace doilies. Through the double window she saw a wind-blasted balcony with a view of the harbour. Her car was just visible. No parking wardens that she could see.

'Sit,' Irene said.

Lucy sat. The tea came from a copper samovar and when Lucy asked for some sugar, she was offered a spoonful of raspberry jam.

'You like it?' Irene watched Lucy closely as she sipped.

'Yes,' Lucy said, surprised. The brew was thick and strong and the jam worked well. 'Thank you.'

'So. You have questions.'

'That's correct,' said Lucy, 'I spoke with –'

'I also have questions.' Irene rode straight over Lucy. 'Why is my son-in-law in a cell? Why am I not allowed to see him? He is innocent. He did not kill Polina.' Irene was fierce. 'Or his children. He loves his family! Absolutely!'

'Adrian will remain at the station until we have finished our inquiries,' Lucy said impassively.

'Yes, yes.' Irene was impatient. 'But you will find the person who did this, yes? Then he can come home and I will look after him. If you have an easy life, then you can't be good. Adrian is a very good, very hard worker. His family are all very calm and he is wonderful with his lovely children. He is a good father and husband. He has done nothing wrong.' For a moment her face collapsed and Lucy thought she was going to cry, but she quickly squared her shoulders. Fixed Lucy with a steely brown gaze.

Lucy gazed back, feeling nothing but admiration for the woman's strength.

'What are the police doing?' Irene demanded. 'To find the person who killed my beautiful Polina and her babies?'

Wanting to divert Irene away from the police investigation, Lucy said, 'Tell me about Adrian's business.'

'Ah, his restaurants! They are fantastic!' She flung up her hands in a gesture of approbation. 'He has dozens all over the country. He is a big success. Look at how he lives. How he cares for his family.'

The way she spoke made Lucy think Adrian's mother-in-law might not be up to speed with the company's catastrophic downfall since Melted's Manchester health scare. Wanting to keep to the subject of Adrian's company, she said, 'Tell me how he got started. How he became such a success.'

Irene detailed a classic tale of a man starting with one shop, and building on its success exponentially. He'd taken loans along the way but never missed a repayment. He was a model employer who cared for his workers, paying them more than the minimum wage and treating them with respect. From Irene's account her son-in-law was an exemplary businessman, a mathematical genius and consummate entrepreneur.

'Tell me about his debts,' Lucy said.

Irene looked baffled. 'He has a loan from the bank. For his house and business. I have told you this, yes?'

'I'm talking about a different loan.'

'Different?' She appeared genuinely perplexed. Lucy decided to go out on a limb and shake the tree a bit.

'Not from the bank, but someone else.'

Irene shook her head. 'I know nothing about this.'

'Did any of his friends loan him money?'

Again the shake of her head. 'I don't know this.'

'Did Polina ever say anything about another loan?'

'Never.'

Lucy asked about loan sharks and unlicensed lenders before asking whether Polina had ever had any debts – none – but every question produced the same responses: No, or don't know.

Surreptitiously Lucy glanced outside. Several seagulls stood on the sea wall. A man walked a West Highland terrier. Still no traffic wardens.

'Did Adrian or Polina mention the business was in trouble?' Lucy asked.

Irene sat without moving a millimetre. Not a blink. She could have been a Russian matryoshka doll for all the expression on her face.

'He franchised nearly half of his restaurants,' Lucy said. 'He told us about the health scares. The bad publicity. Even he admits his business is in serious trouble.'

Irene flicked a glance to the window as she thought but then her nostrils flared and she gave a nod. 'Adrian, he tells Polina his difficulties. He was worried she'd be upset, be angry with him. But she is a strong woman. She loves her husband very much.'

'Did she know they were probably going to lose everything? The house, the horses?'

The lines on Irene's face deepened. 'Yes, she knows this. She cried a little bit. But she is made of steel, like me. Adrian says they have to move children's school: she says OK. He says they might be poor: she says OK.'

'She sounds very understanding,' Lucy said. 'Not every wife would be so accommodating.'

Irene pulled back as though she'd smelled something bad. 'Understanding?' Her voice was scathing. 'She is a wife who loves her husband. Loves her family. What do you think she would do? Run away? You silly girl, you know nothing!'

She rose to her feet and walked across the room to a side table. Opened a drawer and brought out two black-and-white photographs. Gave one to Lucy. Lucy stared.

It showed a pile of corpses. Fifty, maybe sixty, all carelessly heaped on top of one another in the snow.

'This was life for us,' Irene said. 'Fear. Lies. Terror. Death camps.' She jerked her chin scornfully at Lucy. 'You are a child in such things. Polina is twenty times the woman of you. She knows the value of her life.'

Lucy let the woman's derision wash over her. 'Who are they?' she asked. She was still looking at the photograph.

'They are all part of me.' Her voice broke. 'And I am . . .'

When Lucy looked up, she seemed to pull herself together. 'It was a terrible time. People saw enemies in every room. People betrayed neighbours. Children betrayed parents. But when you chop wood, the chips fly.'

Irene passed over the second photograph. Lucy's breath caught. Five children lined up and staring into the camera. No expression. It was hard to tell their sex because they were so thin. Bones and rags. Distended stomachs, their heads appearing huge, their skulls fleshless.

'Kazimir made this,' Irene said. 'He made famine. Made the army raid villages. His men stole the harvest and all the food. Many people died in the street, in their home. Women ate their own children.'

Jesus Christ. Lucy tried not to look appalled.

'Who is Kazimir?' Lucy asked.

'Kazimir,' Irene repeated. Her gaze grew distant. 'He is a general in the army. Much decorated. He and Joseph Stalin were like this.' She twisted her index fingers together. 'Kazimir implemented Stalin's purges.'

She walked to Lucy and took back the photographs. 'You know nothing of suffering.'

Lucy didn't argue.

'But Polina . . .' Irene chewed her lower lip. 'She knows she has much luck. Of course she has an understanding of her husband's problems. She stands with him. She knows what's important. She can see the situation in its correct place. She has . . . How do you say it?' She looked expectantly at Lucy.

'Perspective?' she guessed.

'Yes,' Irene said, nodding. 'Polina has perspective. She knows the value of life. She knows her family will not starve in this country. She will not be sent to a camp to die because her husband has a bad business. She would not run away. She loves her family. Absolutely.'

Irene's eyes remained on Lucy. 'You understand?'

'Yes,' said Lucy. 'I understand.'

She recalled Adrian Calder's anger and fear, the way his eyes burned with grief, the way he refused to say *no comment* to every question. He hadn't acted like a guilty man, and now it appeared he'd told his wife about his problems. He may have been losing his ability to keep up his family's lifestyle, but he didn't seem to see the problem as insurmountable. Things were not as clear-cut as she'd first thought.

Lucy said, 'Who's Zama?'

There was the tiniest movement – a flicker, no more – in Irene's dark brown eyes. *She's heard the name before*, thought Lucy, *she knows who they are*.

'Who?' Irene frowned, ostensibly perfectly puzzled.

'Adrian was worried about him.'

Irene's mouth downturned as she shrugged in a seemingly genuine *who cares?* attitude. She said, 'When can Adrian come home? Be with his family?'

'Is Zama a relative?' Lucy pressed.

'I don't know any Zama.' Irene looked irritated. 'Now, please. Tell me what you are doing for Adrian . . .'

Although Lucy would have loved to have pushed the subject of Zama further she decided it would be prudent to do it another time; she didn't want to be reported for traumatising a newly bereaved relative. Lucy told Irene she'd keep in touch and at the same time she glanced outside to see a traffic warden approaching her car. She jackknifed upright. 'Excuse me,' she said, and practically galloped outside.

CHAPTER FOURTEEN

Using every ounce of self-control she possessed, Irene watched the young policewoman run down the stairs and along the pavement. She felt like falling to her knees and wailing, rending her hair with grief but she refused to collapse, show how distraught she was. She was stronger than that, a woman made from steel.

She watched PC Davies approach the traffic warden. Even through her wrenching grief she felt a surge of contempt for the police officer, that she thought it more important not to get a ticket than to spend time with the victim of a catastrophe. She might as well be back in Siberia for all the help the policewoman had offered. Not a word about when Adrian might come home. Nothing about what they were doing to catch the killer of her beloved daughter, her darling grandchildren.

She felt a cold breeze on her neck, laced with the smell of snow.

Your babies will never live.

Unbidden, her father's voice snaked through her head.

They'll sicken and die.

She tried to push him away, but as she stood there in the cold wintry air his voice increased in volume.

I want to save you from having to bury them. Can't you see? I'm doing it to protect you.

He stood in her mind as clear as day. Broad and as powerful as an ox, his KGB uniform perfectly pressed, his jackboots highly polished. He was glaring at her through eyes the colour of wet peat.

No, Papa, she said. You're wrong. He's strong. You just can't see it. Give him a chance. Please.

Irina, he is a weakling. Her father spread his hands as though appealing to her would change her mind. *He is pathetic. Even the dogs laugh at him. He will sire nothing but weaklings.*

Dmitry was anything but a weakling. He had strength of character her father could only dream about. Instead of bullying, he helped others. Instead of using intimidation and oppression he used encouragement and respect. He was slender and beautiful and as resilient as a flute reed. He smelled of warm bread and clean hair. It was the smell of freedom, the promise of a life without violence.

She couldn't live without him.

She raised her chin, refusing to quail. I love him. I want to marry him.

Her father laughed, a genuine belly laugh that had her skin springing with sweat. The last time he'd laughed like that he'd been dragging her mother around the dining room by her hair, pulling out great chunks of it. The next day, when she'd tried to help Mama comb her hair over the raw bald spots, they still showed through, the size of soup spoons and weeping blood.

I forbid you to see him.

She held herself very still. I'm seventeen. I can see who I like. *Not unless I say so.* His eyes hardened.

Stomach churning, she looked at the four men who stood with her father. Three were low-level soldiers whose names she didn't know. Military haircuts and lean, hard faces. They were fighters and killers, brutal henchmen who would gut a child if her father commanded them.

The fourth man spoke.

Your father's right. Dmitry isn't right for you. He's as wet as a piece of piss.

Yesikov stood seven inches taller than Papa, and where her father was sturdy with a good layer of fat, Yesikov's frame was tall and angular. Twenty-six years old with sleek blond hair and piercing blue eyes, wide shoulders, a strong jawline, he had women fluttering after him in droves. But his good looks were deceptive. He had no charm, no kindness in his soul, just layers of cunning and depths of cruelty that terrified her. She'd been eleven when he'd shown her the scar across his kidneys where he'd been knifed. When he told her he'd trussed his attacker from the ceiling in return, slicing out his kidneys with a filleting knife and forcing him to eat them while he died – she'd had to run from the room to vomit. Yesikov had laughed, thinking her a great joke. He was a heartless butcher, a brutal creature, and her father's favourite pet.

Her father spoke quietly. *I've heard Dmitry is* bélaya kost.

White bone. Blue blood. An aristocrat.

You heard wrong, she lied. Her fear rose. Dmitry was indeed related to the royal family, but you wouldn't know it. He had no airs or graces, didn't expect to eat off silverware or demand wine with every meal.

Stop lying, her father snapped. *How can he not be a tsarist shit with Prince Vladimir and Princess Sofia Kasofsky as parents? I've seen the photographs of their palace, dripping with jewels and droves of servants. Tsarist scum, the lot of them, sucking the life out of good, honest hard-working people.*

Stop it, Papa! she cried. You know things aren't like that any more! They're just like us! Dmitry's father works for Gosplan and his mother cleans the local government offices. They work as hard as the next man!

I bet he's an agitator for the old elite. His gaze turned crafty.

Of course not! Her voice reverberated with the truth. Dmitry was a schoolteacher and had no intention of campaigning for a cause that he knew would bring his parents and his school's children into danger.

Are you sure?

I'm sure. Desperately she looked between the men. Who had been spying on her? Who had told her father?

I'm disappointed in you. Her father lit a cigarette, throwing the match on to the floor. One of his henchmen scurried to pick it up. *Of all the men, you choose an autocrat. It's unbelievable. What have I done to deserve this? One son's an alcoholic, the other runs away to the West. My eldest daughter threatens to defect. I can't allow them into the house any more! Ach.* He made a sound of disgust. *My children are a plague on me.*

Long silence during which her father looked at Yesikov, then at her.

Why don't you marry Lazar here? He's one of us. He's intelligent. He's strong, a real man. He's perfect.

If you like pigs. She spoke without thinking.

Her father burst out laughing. *Lazar, what do you make of that?*

Lazar Yesikov held her gaze for long seconds. *I think she doesn't know me well enough.*

His eyes were hooded and there was an emptiness there, a blank glassy look she'd seen too many times. It was the look he gave before he hurt people.

Perhaps you should both get to know one another better. Her father gave a low chuckle.

Yesikov blinked, and the look vanished.

The silence held until her father turned and walked for the door.

She hadn't run straight to Dmitry and his parents to warn them, because she knew she'd be followed. She'd been forced to wait until an opportunity presented itself where she could slip away unseen. In the meantime, she pretended to be absorbed in preparing the house for yet another party, this one for Joseph Stalin's birthday. Everything had to be perfect, and although she presented a calm exterior, untroubled and carefree, her little brother sensed something was up. Timur was seven years younger than her and the age gap meant she found him mostly an annoyance, playing tricks and hiding things, and now he became almost unbearable, springing from behind doors shouting, '*Salka!*' Surprise! and scaring her every time.

She knew he was only trying to gain her attention but she found his constant demands to play exhausting. Until the day came when she said goodbye.

'I'm sorry,' she said, 'for being such a mean sister.'

'You've been horrible lately,' he said, lower lip stuck out. 'I don't know what's wrong with you.'

She pulled him to her and hugged him tight. For once, he didn't struggle but hugged her back. She rested her face against his hair – thick and dark like his father's – and breathed in his scent.

'If you ever want to surprise me again,' she told him, 'you mustn't hesitate. Because although I shout at you sometimes, deep down I love it when you surprise me. I've just been distracted recently. A bit stressed over the party. I love you, Timur. Don't forget it.'

She'd left her father's house without a backward glance. She didn't know where she was going, what the future might have in store for her. All she knew was that she was going to run away with Dmitry. It didn't matter where. They just had to get away and start a new life, where nobody knew them or their pasts.

Now Irene Cavendish breathed in cold air that tasted of snow. She was glad her father was dead. But instead of suffering a deadly fate for his cruelty and violence he'd been pensioned off with an apartment in Moscow and a *dacha* in the countryside, dying of heart disease in 1965. Some people thought of him as a hero for helping Stalin bring industrialisation to Russia – cities and streets were named after him – but Irene would spit on his grave if she could.

The young police officer was still talking to the traffic warden. Could she trust Lucy Davies with her family's secrets? Would the police officer keep them safe? She gave an inward shudder. Intellectually she knew the British police were far less corruptible than their Russian counterparts but she would rather lie down and let wolves devour her than share a word with them. She'd have to face things on her own. It wouldn't be the first time.

CHAPTER FIFTEEN

'Oh, come on,' Lucy said. 'I'll be two minutes. I'm not in anyone's way and –'

'Don't tell me.' The warden put a finger against his mouth in a parody of thought. 'You expect special dispensation because you're a police officer.'

'No way!' she objected but it was true. She'd hoped he'd give her at least ten minutes before slapping a ticket on her windscreen.

'I'm glad to hear it.' He stood back with his arms crossed, foot tapping and making it obvious he wanted her to climb into her car and drive away while he waited. *Officious little bastard*, she thought furiously. She only needed five minutes to wind up the interview with Irene Cavendish and now she had to spend God knew how long searching for a sodding parking space before she could return.

Without another word she jumped into her car and drove up the hill, turned left. Miles of nothing but narrow cobbled lanes lined with double yellows and pretty houses in cream and white. No room to park a bicycle let alone a car. She had to double-back to Castlegate Street and finally, right at the top of the hill, opposite a church, she found a grass parking area for fifty-plus vehicles, empty aside from a lone Fiesta. PRIVATE. She ignored the sign. She was only going to be a second – all she wanted to do was give Irene her business card – besides which the place was hardly going to fill up in the ten minutes she'd be gone. Lucy jogged back down the hill.

As she approached Irene's house, she saw a couple standing on the front porch. They were talking to Irene. Although it appeared to be a friendly conversation – neighbours or relatives dropping by to offer condolences perhaps – Lucy could tell something was wrong. Where the couple were standing, relaxed and apparently at peace with the world, Irene was so tightly strung that Lucy reckoned if she plucked her with a finger she would twang. She increased her pace and at the same time, Irene looked across at her. Her face went suddenly slack with relief.

The couple turned to follow Irene's gaze. A good-looking pair in their thirties, the man with a broad face and cleft chin, the woman small and chic with large hazel eyes. He wore a dark tailored woollen coat over trousers and shoes, the woman a rich camel jacket with a fur collar and a pair of sexy high-heeled oxfords with a glossy finish. Their eyes travelled slowly over her uniform with studied indifference.

Lucy trotted up the steps. Without saying anything the couple moved from the porch and made to walk past her, heading for the street.

'Excuse me,' Lucy said. She put up a hand, expecting them to stop. But they didn't. They brushed past her and kept walking.

She turned and walked after them. 'I'd like a word, please.'

The couple ignored her.

'I'm investigating a serious case regarding Mrs Cavendish's family.'

No response.

Lucy walked faster in an effort to get past them but each time she tried they walked faster too. It was like some kind of farce and if she wasn't so wary of them she might have expressed her annoyance. When they beeped open their car – parked in the same space she'd used, sadly the Officious Little Bastard was nowhere to be seen to help delay them – she stood in front of the vehicle and crossed her arms in order to make herself look larger and more official.

'Did you know Polina Calder?' she asked. 'Irene Cavendish's daughter?' She was looking for a response. She got nothing.

The man opened the passenger door and shut it once the woman was inside. As he walked to the driver's side, Lucy said, 'Did you know Polina was murdered?'

Still nothing.

'From your behaviour, I'm thinking you have something to hide. And when I find out who you are I will come after you and next time, you will have no choice but to answer my questions.'

Without even a glance in her direction the man climbed into the car, started the engine, put the car into gear and drove around her.

She watched them go, frustration biting. No time to run up the hill and get her car and follow them. They'd be long gone by the time she returned. Pulling out her pen, she made a note of their number plate in her pocket book.

She returned to Irene but this time she wasn't invited inside.

'Who were they?' Lucy said.

For a moment, Lucy thought the woman wasn't going to answer but then she said, 'They say they are friends of Polina's. I've never see them before.'

'What are their names?'

'They didn't say.'

If they were Polina's friends, Lucy thought, *surely they would have introduced themselves? Stopped to talk to a police officer? And why had Irene been so tense?*

'They came to say sorry she is dead.' Irene's tone was flat. She had regained her composure and held Lucy's gaze as though daring her to accuse her of lying.

'Do they live locally?' Lucy asked.

'I know nothing of these people.' Her contemptuous tone had returned. 'Nothing.'

They'd looked pretty sophisticated and gave Lucy the impression they could be as at home rubbing shoulders with the millionaire farmers of Yorkshire as city traders in London. Aside from the car, which was a plain no-nonsense Ford Mondeo. From their clothes she would have expected at least a Mercedes or BMW.

'You were relieved to see me,' Lucy remarked.

Irene's gaze turned cold. 'You have more questions? Or are you going now?'

A stiff cold breeze lifted Lucy's hair from the nape of her neck but she didn't move, didn't shiver. She looked straight at the older woman. 'Irene.' Her tone was sombre. 'Do you want us to find who killed your daughter and your grandchildren?'

A flare of astonishment. 'Of course.'

'Then *help* us. This means you tell us who Zama is, and who those people were.'

The woman's expression closed as hard and fast as Adrian Calder's had in the interview room when she'd asked him about Zama.

'Look.' Lucy tried to be reasonable. 'If you withhold what could be vital information, the killers may never be caught, and whose fault will it be?' She let a silence fall but Irene looked unmoved. Lucy sighed. Brought out her business card. 'If you want to speak to me, here's my mobile number. Call any time.'

Irene pocketed it and, without another word, took a step back and closed the door in Lucy's face.

As she walked back up the hill, icy wind biting her neck and wrists, Lucy rang Mac and filled him in.

'I'll run the number plate,' he told her. 'Look, when we've solved this case, I think we should go out and celebrate. Shall we pencil in next Saturday?'

She couldn't help but admire his optimism. 'You really think we'll have it wrapped by then?'

'I don't see why not.' He sounded remarkably cheerful. 'Let's have dinner. I've found a great little pub near Rosedale. They do a great roast pheasant, lots of roast potatoes and gravy.'

'Are you talking about those beautiful birds I see on the moors, with long tails and pretty little ear tufts?'

'Is that a yes?' he said.

'No.'

Phone back in her pocket, she strode for her car, arriving just in time to catch the Officious Little Bastard putting a ticket under her wiper.

'It's private,' he told her smugly. 'And open to the public only when the Pay and Display signs are –'

She didn't waste time listening to him but snatched the ticket free, jumped into the car and took off, twin spots of fury burning on her cheeks. Another thirty quid wasted. She had to start parking legally or she'd never be able to pay her rent.

Lucy drove back to the station. Being Sunday, traffic was almost non-existent and the journey time practically halved. Bliss. As she walked into reception, she saw a man talking to the desk sergeant. Early thirties, sun-bleached hair, a couple of days' stubble, silver earring in one ear, brown leather necklace, a couple of ethnic bracelets on his right wrist. A rucksack hung from one shoulder. She walked past. She assumed he was an undercover cop but paused when he said, 'I'm here to meet Justin Tripp. Adrian Calder's lawyer. He said he'd be here around three.'

Lucy turned around.

'You can wait for him over there.' The duty sergeant gestured at the row of plastic chairs sitting below a variety of posters exhorting how to defeat alcohol and domestic violence.

'No problem,' said the man.

Lucy watched him take a seat. His demeanour was calm. The rucksack lay neatly beside his feet. She was surprised when he didn't immediately bring out a phone and begin checking his messages but sat quietly without moving. He looked as though he might be meditating.

'Do I know you?' he said.

His eyes clicked to her. Murky green. Strangely luminous.

'I'm sorry?' She was momentarily wrong-footed.

'You've been staring. I thought it might be that we've met somewhere before.' His gaze was open and affable. 'I'm an ex-cop, so it's possible.'

'You don't look like one,' she remarked.

'What do I look like?'

'A surfer.'

'Good observation.'

She held his eyes. Strong jawline, lean body. He was bad-boy good-looking. Not someone she'd forget in a hurry.

She stepped closer, expecting him to rise to meet her, but again he surprised her by remaining seated, lifting his face to maintain eye contact. 'Tell me, do you know Adrian Calder?' she asked.

'I've seen him on the news.'

The door banged to one side, letting in an icy blast but neither of them looked round.

'Who are you?' Lucy asked.

'Nicholas Blain. Why, who are you?'

Her name was stitched on her epaulettes but she didn't mention it. 'I'm one of the investigating officers on the Calder case.'

Interest sparked. 'I see.' But he still didn't rise.

'Are you sure you don't know Mr Calder?'

'As I said, I've seen him on the news.'

He'd sidestepped her question and she was going to ask him why he'd come to the police station to see Justin Tripp – it seemed an odd place to meet a lawyer, especially at the weekend – but the door gave another bang and a voice said, 'Lucy.'

It was Mac. He was staring at Nicholas Blain.

Blain looked at Lucy, then at Mac. He smiled. Mac didn't.

Mac headed out of reception. Lucy joined him.

Halfway down the corridor she said, 'Do you know that guy?'

'Nope.'

'Are you sure?'

'Yup.'

'He's an ex-cop,' she said. 'Or at least that's what he told me.'

Mac didn't say anything. She looked across at him. He looked back but there was something odd in his expression that made her press further.

'You worked together?'

He turned away with a shrug. 'I didn't like the look of him, that's all.'

Her jaw dropped. Dear God, she thought. He's jealous. How the hell was that going to work when he became her boss?

From the beat office, she called the desk sergeant and asked him to ring her when Justin Tripp arrived. Ten minutes later she got the call and she jogged back to reception to find Nicholas Blain and the lawyer standing closely together, absorbed, talking quietly, intent on the screen of an iPad. As she approached the light shifted making the image on the screen perfectly clear to her.

A man's face, close up. Slightly blurred as though he'd been on the move and unaware of being photographed. Clean cut, strong jaw, short brown hair, serious expression. A fair-haired woman was just behind him and her features were out of focus and unclear.

Lucy's eyes widened and at the same time Nicholas Blain swept the iPad away from Tripp and slid it into his satchel.

'Yes?' Blain asked.

His expression had turned cold, speculative, but it wasn't this that stopped her from asking about the man in the photograph. It was because of *who* the man was that stopped her.

She said, 'I wanted to ask Justin something.'

'Go ahead.' Blain's words were casual but the cold look remained. 'Don't mind me.'

'Privately,' she said, allowing an edge into her voice.

He shrugged and stepped aside, allowing the lawyer to walk a few paces away. Turning her back to Blain she stood close to the lawyer. Lowered her voice. 'You know Zama.'

'I'm afraid I don't.'

'OK. Know *of* him. Please, don't split hairs.'

His expression didn't change. 'I can't say. Client privilege, I'm afraid.'

'But if he's in danger, as Calder seemed to believe, shouldn't you be concerned?'

His lips tightened. 'I have nothing further to say.'

He returned to Nicholas Blain. Murmured a few words. They walked outside together. Lucy followed to see them head across the station forecourt and cross the street to a silver Mercedes. They shook hands. Tripp beeped open the Mercedes and slid inside. Lucy watched him cruise up the street, turn the corner and disappear.

Blain walked in the same direction Tripp had travelled. Lucy dawdled, curious to see what car he drove, but he didn't stop. He kept walking. She looked at her car then at his rapidly diminishing figure. He walked deceptively fast. She couldn't follow him on foot. She'd stick out like a walking traffic light being in uniform. Lucy hopped into her car. Bridge Street West was incredibly long and his figure soon became a dot in the distance. She'd lose him if she wasn't careful. Lucy started the car and followed him. To her relief he didn't turn around, didn't look behind him, but turned the corner into Boundary Road. She eased after him, driving unhurriedly under the old iron bridge but she couldn't see him. She pressed the accelerator. Came to a muddled junction of three roads, a car park and a discount exhaust shop on the opposite corner. Still no Blain.

She drove slowly, turning her head from side to side. *Where had he gone?*

She extended her search but couldn't find him. It was as though the second she'd lost sight of him, he'd evaporated.

Lucy turned the car around, her mind on the man she'd seen on the iPad. The last time she'd seen him had been outside a junkyard that had been crawling with police and Security Service personnel. Both of them had been exhausted. Both had blood on their clothes.

What was Calder's lawyer doing with a photograph of ex-MI5 officer Dan Forrester?

CHAPTER SIXTEEN

Sunday 1 February

After he'd dressed, Dan checked his phone and saw that Lucy Davies had called. Her message was brief. *Ring me. It's important.*

When he'd last seen Lucy she'd been sitting slumped and exhausted on a London pavement, bruised and bloody. He remembered offering to introduce her to Bernard, get her a job with MI5, and she'd laughed, genuinely amused.

Now, he rang Lucy back, but the line was busy. He didn't leave a message.

After a leisurely breakfast buffet, Dan headed to the metro, glad he wasn't pressed for time and could take a circuitous route to Tretyakovskaya. He paused occasionally to check if anyone was following, doubling back on himself and popping in and out of kiosks. He thought he saw the same woman a couple of times and when she stepped on to the same train as him he waited until she was forced further down the carriage – ostensibly trapped – and at the next station when the doors were about to close, he stepped off and caught another train.

He then ran a further two hours of counter-surveillance, making him question why he was being so careful. After all, who could know where he and Lynx intended to meet? Maybe his tension came from a primeval instinct that recognised he was on an assignment. Dr Winter said he retained a myriad of memories that weren't necessarily memories but subliminal associations of what was around him; sounds, colours, body language, actions, incidents. His instinct told him to make sure he approached the rendezvous with Lynx alone.

He walked past the church, a massive five-domed two-storey building that stood behind a row of trees devoid of leaves, but couldn't see her. He returned, looking up and down the road as traffic roared and splashed through slush alongside. Finally, he walked into the church.

He found her standing just inside the main entrance. She was gazing at the ceiling, her perfect features serene. She wore a full-length fur coat the colour of syrup and a matching fur hat. He'd thought he was immune from her beauty but when she turned and looked at him with those wide almond eyes, his breath caught.

'So,' he said quietly, determined not to let her see he was affected, 'why do you want to see me?'

'Shhh.' She pointed at the people scattered throughout the church. Three contemplating, two couples on their knees, praying. A cleaner dusting a pew. 'Let's go outside,' she whispered.

He followed her on to the broad pedestrian pavement. They walked past a bank, then a pedestrian crossing. Few people were about. It was too cold.

He said, 'What's your name?'

She turned her head to look at him. A tiny frown marred her perfect brow. 'I'm sorry?'

'Your name.'

She stopped and faced him. Held his gaze. He couldn't tell what she was thinking. He couldn't read her at all.

'My name is Ekaterina.'

It meant nothing to him. He said, 'How do we know one another?'

'You're saying you don't know who I am?'

Something in her tone made a prickle of unease sweep over his skin.

'That's right,' he said. He didn't apologise or explain. He wanted to try and get her to show her hand. Friend or foe? He couldn't work her out.

'I see.' Her tone was non-committal, giving nothing away.

Dan was aware of a bus trundling past, a woman standing at the pedestrian crossing, a car overtaking another on the one-way street.

'What's your surname?' he asked.

When she didn't answer, he stepped a little closer, forcing her to raise her chin to meet his gaze but she wasn't easily intimidated and didn't back away. 'Tell me,' he demanded.

She held his eyes, composed and enigmatic, heartbreakingly beautiful in the icy air of the street.

Finally, she took a step back and put her head on one side, studying him.

'I heard something about you losing your memory,' she said. 'But I didn't know it was true.'

'How did you hear?' he asked.

She didn't answer but continued to study him.

'So this is like the first time we've met,' she said.

He didn't want to make it easy for her and didn't reply. Instead, he said, 'I need to know your surname.'

'This isn't about me.' She was curt.

A gust of wind nipped his cheeks, making his eyes water and the hairs in his nostrils freeze.

'OK,' he said. 'So what is it about?'

'You can't remember *anything*?' This time her scepticism broke through.

'Of course I can.' He couldn't help feeling irritated. He hated it when someone remembered him but he couldn't remember them back. 'How do you think I got dressed this morning?'

She made a dismissive gesture to show that wasn't what she meant.

'You can't have forgotten the City Space Bar,' she said.

He just looked at her.

'Or Dominika's Club, surely.'

He tried not to grit his teeth, but it was an effort.

'What about sexy little Milena?' Her gaze turned sly. 'Don't tell me you can't remember her either?'

Silence.

She put a hand over her mouth. 'Oh, my God,' she said. Her eyes widened. 'It's true.' For a horrendous moment he thought she was going to laugh. He wasn't sure what he'd do if she did.

'What happened?' she asked.

For the first time, her guard lowered fractionally. He couldn't help it. He responded to whatever it was in her expression, and felt his chest tighten with an emotion he couldn't identify. Whatever it was, it left him feeling off-balance and vulnerable.

'Was it an accident?' she pressed. 'A trauma? I've heard of such things from our soldiers, but never –'

'Why am I here?' he cut over her. He didn't want to give her any information that wasn't absolutely necessary.

Something shifted in the atmosphere between them. She narrowed her eyes. Looked away, then back. She was thinking, he realised. Thinking fast.

'OK,' she said. She seemed to have come to a decision. 'We are here to talk about Edik Yesikov. President Putin's successor. His plans for Russia's future.'

She reached into her coat pocket and brought out a photograph, showed it to him. He didn't touch it. Simply studied the picture of a man with dirty blond hair dressed in hunting attire. He was kneeling on the ground, smiling broadly, holding open the jaws of a dead bear. Blood smeared his hands and wrists.

'How do you know him?' Dan asked.

She didn't answer. Pocketing the photograph, she turned and began to walk along the street. He walked beside her, close enough so their coats brushed.

'This will be the only time we see each other,' she went on in the same businesslike tone.

'How can I trust you?'

This made her pause. 'You have to have faith.'

'Are you with any of the authorities?' he asked. 'FSB, GRU?'

'I am not with any intelligence agency.'

'Then, what?' He was puzzled.

'Edik Yesikov,' she said determinedly. 'He secretly sent two agents to your country last week.'

'How do you know this?'

'Trust me. They arrived in London on Thursday the twenty-ninth of January.'

'Why?'

'Edik is an FSB officer,' Ekaterina went on. 'Also Director General of Shelomov Gaz. He's powerful and rich, but he's nothing special. Putin would prefer an inspirational leader down the line, a man who unites his people and commands respect around the world. He's looking for a man the people will love. Who they'll write poetry about and fight wars for.'

'And stop the next revolution.'

'Correct.'

Ekaterina slowed her pace with his to make way for a couple passing them.

'You've heard of Kazimir?' she asked.

As she spoke, a fissure opened in his mind and a picture of a broad-shouldered man in KGB uniform appeared. 'He was a KGB general,' Dan added. 'Stalin's most trusted aide.'

She turned, her expression filled with consternation. 'You remember Kazimir?'

'Not exactly.'

She stared at him, her gaze so piercing it was like having a laser drill through his skull. He could almost hear the words: *How can you remember Kazimir but not me?*

'It happens occasionally,' he admitted. 'Something breaks through.'

She continued to stare at him.

'But it's not often,' he added, suddenly feeling awkward. Defensive. 'Maybe a couple of times a year.'

Did her stare intensify? He wasn't sure, because she suddenly whipped around and began walking again. She didn't say anything for a while, just walked. They passed a small park with a frozen waterfall, the trees covered in a dusting of snow turned grey by pollution. Past a bus stop. Another bank. Another pedestrian crossing.

'The people remember Kazimir clearly,' Ekaterina told him. Her voice was steady and calm. 'They're scared of him, but deep down they revere his great strength, his wisdom. Kazimir means "keeper or destroyer of peace" and if he was still alive, they'd probably walk through fire to follow him.'

She halted at a zebra crossing but the traffic didn't stop and she made no move to cross the road.

She said, 'The two FSB agents in your country are called Ivan and Yelena Barbolin. Their mission is to find a British journalist. Jane Sykes.'

'Why?'

'Jane Sykes was told a secret by a friend in the UK. She came to Moscow to verify it. She was overheard by the FSB, talking about it.'

'What secret?' he repeated.

'Where to find Zama Kasofsky.'

Dan frowned. 'I don't understand. Who's Kasofsky?'

She turned to stand in front of him, expression sombre. 'This is where it gets personal.'

'OK,' he said.

'Because your wife –'

'My *wife*?' He reacted as though he'd been slapped. 'What has she got to do with –'

'Just listen.' She cut across him, her tone earnest. 'She is an accountant, am I correct?'

'Well, yes.' He was bewildered. 'But only small-time. She looks after local farmers and beekeepers.'

'She used to work in London, yes?'

'Yes, but –'

'For McInley and Krevingden?'

His stomach dropped. 'What has Jenny got to do with this?'

She nodded as though he'd confirmed something she hadn't been sure of. 'I'm sorry. I had to be certain. But it's not her so much as –'

Suddenly her hand was flung sideways and she staggered backwards. The look on her face was one of shock.

In the same instant he heard a shot, a distinct *crack!* that cut through the sound of traffic.

He didn't have time to move before her body doubled over as though she'd been punched in the abdomen and she toppled to the ground. Instinctively Dan dived to her side.

He should have run. He should have got away, sprinted down the street. But he couldn't leave her. He pulled open her coat to see blood seeping from her breast and through her dress. She was moaning, turning towards him.

'Daniel,' she said. 'Run.'

His mind was scrambled. He felt sick with helplessness. 'I can't.'

'You must.'

'No.'

Her eyes went past him. She opened her mouth but nothing came out. He followed her gaze to see an Audi approaching, pulling over. His stomach hollowed as he saw the driver's door beginning to open. They were coming to finish the job.

CHAPTER SEVENTEEN

Lucy checked her phone again to see that Dan had rung, but hadn't left a message. She left another voicemail message as well as a text, but he didn't respond. There was little she could do but wait until tomorrow – Monday – when if she still hadn't made contact, she could ring his office.

'Calder's twenty-four hours are up at five this afternoon.' Mac's voice broke into her thoughts. Everyone in the MIR groaned. 'At which point we need to charge or release him. Judge Dalton – that's Judge Dredd to you and me – has already expressed concern about the lack of gunshot residue on him and his clothing, so let's pull our fingers out and find evidence that irrefutably ties him in. I don't want a defence lawyer making mincemeat of us.'

Mac was drowning, clutching at straws, but determined to find something to nail Calder. Even Lucy, who knew how fast things could change, didn't feel optimistic. They'd brought the entire team to work over the weekend, an expensive process with overtime costs and meal allowances, and blowing Mac's budget to kingdom come. Uniforms were talking to everyone who knew the Calders, checking out the kids' friends, everyone who lived within a five-mile radius. When Lucy heard uniforms were trying to trace a couple who had visited the family two weeks before the Calders' murder, long-lost relatives apparently visiting from South Africa, Lucy immediately thought of the good-looking young couple who'd stood on Irene's doorstep, scaring her.

She asked Calder about the couple who'd visited his family.

'Robin and Finch Stanton,' he told her. 'They're Irene's nephew and niece from Cape Town. We haven't met them before. Didn't know they existed until they turned up.'

'What do they look like?'

'Er . . .' Calder tried to think. 'Short. Wiry. Not much like Irene in all honesty. Dark hair. Finch wore hers in a ponytail. Robin's got a moustache. They're both pretty brown. All that South African sun . . .' He struggled to say any more.

'Well dressed?'

'Not particularly. Jeans and fleeces. Trainers.'

With their suntans and casual dress, they didn't sound like the smart couple who'd stood on Irene's doorstep and this was confirmed when the smart couple's vehicle number plate check came through, matching a hire car from Heathrow. Hertz. Loaned to Ivan and Yelena Barbolin, from Russia.

Lucy rang Irene Cavendish and asked if she knew the Barbolins.

'No.'

'Did Polina ever mention them?'

'No.'

Lucy made a note in the file and moved on. The team continued sweating the small stuff, checking every convicted burglar in the Cleveland area, as well as plenty they hadn't been able to convict. Calder's bank accounts were scrutinised but appeared clean. There appeared to be no insurance on his wife's or children's lives. So far they'd had nothing but useless tip calls.

The newspapers were full of what had been dubbed the Barwick House murders, broadcasting Calder's failing business, how he would have had to sell his multi-million pound home to keep afloat, pull his kids out of private school and spend his holidays at Scarborough instead of the Seychelles. The consensus was the same as Lucy's conclusion had been: that he couldn't bear his family to suffer a loss in lifestyle and status. The press printed photograph after photograph of Polina and her children. They were an attractive family and made good subjects for the front pages.

She was doggedly going over the Calders' financial records for what felt like the thousandth time, looking for something, *anything* to give them a clue where to go next, when one of the team, a skinny DS called Barney, said, 'What do you mean, another one?'

His tone of voice, genuinely surprised, made everyone look across.

'Yeah, yeah. We'll check it out.' He hung up and looked at Mac.

'Boss, that was a friend of mine at the Met. He's just heard of another family annihilation, it's on the news. It's near Bristol . . .'

He trailed off as Mac led the charge to the TV in his office.

A red banner at the bottom of the TV screen read *Breaking news*. A woman journalist stood on the street in the pouring rain, in front of a pretty stone cottage bristling with police officers.

'A suicidal mother has killed her two daughters and her grandson, who was just four years old. It appears she poisoned them before poisoning herself. There was no note.'

Apparently Oxana Harris had been known to suffer from depression and although it was rare for a mother to kill her family, it wasn't unknown. Nobody said a word until the journalist started repeating herself, when Barney said, 'I can't see it's got anything to do with our case.'

'Nor me,' said another DS.

Mac obviously agreed because he announced briskly, 'Back to work!' and turfed everyone out. He was about to turn off the TV but Lucy said, 'Wait.'

She flipped channels until she found another reporter outside the same cottage – a man with a reddened nose hunched beneath an umbrella. He said nothing the female journalist hadn't but, sensing Mac's rising impatience, Lucy held up a hand.

'. . . a tragedy for the rest of the family after Oxana Harris's eldest son Lewis last week killed his two young children and himself by driving his car into a quarry and drowning. His wife survived, and is being comforted by Oxana's youngest son Ben, who turned twenty-one just before Christmas.'

She stared at the TV. 'That's weird,' she said.

'Yes.' Mac was also staring.

'Can you be genetically disposed to kill your family?' she asked.

'God knows,' said Mac.

'Or did something else trigger their behaviour? Did Lewis suffer from depression too? Were they all control freaks?' Her mind was glowing orange, racing ahead, skimming and leaping as it tried to find connections. 'Maybe there was sexual jealousy on the mother's part. A reverse Oedipus complex or whatever it's called.'

'Electra,' he supplied.

'Or someone was leaving the family, or threatening to break it apart, or emigrating –'

'Lucy.'

She halted.

He said, 'It's not our case.'

Lucy lassoed her mind and hauled it back. 'Sorry.'

He looked across at her. 'Fancy a drink later?' he asked.

She rolled her eyes to the ceiling.

'When will you stop asking me out?' she said.

'When you say yes.'

'No.'

She returned to the MIR, struggling to turn her mind from the Bristol suicides. She found it odd to have three family annihilations so close together and, making sure she couldn't be overheard, she picked up the phone and rang the Bristol police. The SIO who was working Oxana Harris's case wasn't available, but when Lucy said it might concern the Barwick House murders, she was put through to a DI who was cognisant of the events that had taken place. Yes, he said, once she'd introduced herself, of course he'd try to help.

'I want to know if Oxana Harris and her family are related to the Calder family in any way. If they know one another through friends, business or some such.'

'I'll have to check and get back to you.'

'That would be great.'

She asked if a forensic psychologist had been brought in, but apparently not.

'It's pretty cut and dried the mother and son did it,' the DI said, but his voice had changed slightly, making Lucy come alert.

'But . . .?' Lucy prompted.

'It's just odd.' He sighed. 'According to the survivors there were no signs. Makes you wonder if every seemingly happy family is seriously fucked up in some way.'

'Perhaps,' said Lucy wryly.

'Yeah.' He gave a half-chuckle. 'Mine's not exactly a hundred per cent.'

'I wonder if something in their genes made them do it?' Lucy pondered aloud.

There was a short pause.

'It's funny you say that,' he said, tone turning thoughtful, 'because the only survivors were Lewis's wife, and Oxana's youngest son, Ben. Ben is, apparently, adopted.'

'Interesting,' Lucy murmured.

'For a geneticist maybe,' he responded. 'Look, I've got to go. I'll get back to you, OK?'

Lucy hung up, her mind unable to stop chewing on the Oxana Harris case, and it wasn't until she began going through Polina Calder's finances that her attention finally shifted. It appeared that even during the halcyon days Calder's wife had never had a particularly extravagant lifestyle. Yes, she'd had regular manicures, the odd facial and spa day with a girlfriend, but nothing that could be termed excessive or wasteful. She appeared to be remarkably frugal considering her wealth, and when Lucy delved into her spending over the past quarter it appeared she'd recently stopped all beauty treatments aside from her six-weekly bikini, underarm and leg wax. This did nothing more than prove that Calder had told his wife about their financial difficulties and that Polina was prepared to – as he'd said – pull her horns in. Downsize. Economise.

Lucy pushed her chair back and rubbed her forehead. What if Calder hadn't killed his family? What if someone else had? Like a debt collector? Did Calder gamble? Had he fallen foul of a loan shark?

She went and fetched a coffee. Sipped it while she trawled through Calder's accounts to see that – surprise, surprise – everything appeared to add up. She'd just started studying the individual restaurants – choosing one in Leeds that she'd gone to a couple of times – when out of nowhere all her energy vanished, sucked out of her as though her soul had been vacuumed.

Go away, she told it.

Suddenly it was too bright. The lights felt as though they were piercing her eyes.

Leave me alone.

She couldn't move. She felt an urge to put her head on her arms and sleep forever.

She had to keep busy and *fight it*.

She forced herself back to the restaurant accounts, fighting her lethargy, wondering how Calder was paying his bills. Did he already have a bunch of creditors in place? He was at the tipping point of going under but few people seemed to realise it, not with all those supposedly successful sandwich bars to his name. How had he been paying the household bills? How was he paying his lawyer?

A grey wave washed through her brain. She pinched the bridge of her nose hard enough to make it hurt. Fought to keep the murk from devouring her. Sod it. Had she been wrong about Calder's tell? She pictured the rise and fall of his shoulders and knew she had to keep digging until she found what was bugging him. Fighting the grey in her mind, she rose and stepped into the corridor. Walked up and down, trying to keep the blood flowing and get her brain to colour once again and come up with something new.

Zilch.

Lucy headed to the beat office, hoping for some inspiration but when she got there it was empty aside from Howard, who was unwrapping a sandwich.

'Where is everyone?' she asked.

'Fight at the Reindeer.' He took a bite and pulled a face. 'God, this is crap. Bought it at the garage. Won't be doing that again.'

Out of nowhere, a crimson thread floated through her mind. She said, 'How do you fancy a Melted sandwich?'

When Lucy asked her sarge, he refused to let Howard join her on her Melted mission and she couldn't blame him. It wasn't as though she had a concrete lead to follow, but with the DCI's endorsement of her *superlative lateral thinking* on her last case along with the fact she'd be on Mac's team next week anyway, Jacko decided it would be politic to let her go.

Swiping a pool car she headed to the Melted restaurant in Leeds, situated at the entrance into the Merrion Centre. She parked opposite on Wade Lane – no yellow lines, just a parking restriction – hoping that since she was in a police car she might avoid getting moved on too soon. Unless the Officious Little Bastard had a cousin in town, of course.

She watched the restaurant for a few minutes. A couple sat in the window chatting, a young guy at a table behind them, working on his laptop. It was quiet, but then the shopping centre wasn't exactly heaving either; the cold weather was keeping everyone at home. She gave a shiver as the car began to cool. With its warm lighting, red and dark green Victorian lampshades and leather club chairs, Melted looked cosy and inviting but she thought she'd watch a little longer before she went inside. She turned on the radio. Listened to the news. The newsreader had just handed over to the sports presenter when her phone rang. She felt a rush of affection as she answered.

'Hi, Mum.'

'Can you talk?'

'Yup. I'm just sitting in the car staking out a sandwich bar.'

'Sounds exciting.'

'Hardly. It's freezing.' Lucy stretched. 'Everything OK your end?'

'Everything's fine. I just wanted to check in, make sure you're OK. That's all.'

Lucy had rung her mother the day of the Barwick House murders, just after she'd put her clothes – stiff with Jessie's dried blood – in the washing machine. It had been her mother who'd instructed her to run a hot bath and curl up on the sofa with her duvet and a mug of hot chocolate.

'Yeah.' Lucy exhaled as the vision of Jessie's frightened eyes returned. 'I'm OK. But thanks.'

'Proud of you,' she said.

Lucy's mind hummed a soft yellowy peach. Of all the appro-bation she'd received before Christmas, it had been her mother's that meant the most. After Dad abandoned them, Mum had struggled hard to bring Lucy up on her own, ploughing every-thing into supporting her every step of the way and when she finally saw her daughter graduate from police college, she'd cried. And she was even more proud now Lucy was joining CID. Lucy'd better not mess things up; it would kill her mum.

'Any chance you can come home for Easter?'

'Doubtful,' Lucy said, and stretched again. 'Being single with no kids means I get last dibs.'

'That seems unfair.'

'Not really,' said Lucy, thinking of Howard and his wife, their three children on an Easter egg hunt. 'Besides, I like having time off out of school holidays. It's cheaper and a hundred per cent quieter.'

After they'd hung up, Lucy checked the area for traffic war-dens before climbing out of the car and walking across the road. The instant she opened the door she was enveloped in a cloud of freshly ground coffee, melted cheese and toasting bread but her saliva glands did nothing. She could have been breathing fresh air for all the effect it had. Not for the first time she found it dis-concerting how badly her mood affected her appetite. *She must*

make sure she ate something. Even if it was only a few mouthfuls,
it would help.

She considered the health scare briefly, but it had been ages
ago, and salmonella hadn't been found in any of Calder's restaurants but franchised stores. So she should be safe.

A girl with dyed black hair, black T-shirt and a nose ring
came over. Her name badge read *Tammy*.

'The Flamenco, please,' Lucy asked. Flame-grilled chicken,
crispy onions, chorizo, smoked paprika and chilli tomato sauce,
roast red peppers and creamy cheese. 'To take away.'

While Tammy made her melt, Lucy looked around. 'It's pretty
quiet,' she remarked.

'It's always quiet,' Tammy said.

'What about before Christmas?' Lucy asked. It should have
been rammed with all those shoppers walking past.

'Busier, but we weren't exactly rushed off our feet.'

'How come?'

The girl opened her mouth to say something but thought better of it, and shrugged.

Lucy settled in the car to eat her sandwich but could only
manage a couple of bites. *I must eat.* She ate another two bites
but it was like trying to eat a flannel for all the appetite she had,
and the demon fog was thickening, tempting her to go home
and lock the doors, curl into bed and sleep. The problem was,
if she gave in to it, she might not move for days. The last time
she'd succumbed had been in London when she'd been with
Nate. What a mess. If it hadn't been for Nate covering for her,
she might well have been found out. Now she was on her own,

she couldn't afford to let go. She had to fight it every step of the way until it passed.

You won't win, she told it.

She drove to another Melted, this time in York. Once again, the restaurant had a great location and interior decor, with an art deco snug and roomy service area. Just five customers. This time, Lucy bought a sea-salted chocolate bar.

'How come it's so quiet in here?' She nodded at the café opposite which, although it didn't look half as nice, was heaving.

The barista looked away, obviously uncomfortable.

'Surely it's not that health scare,' Lucy said. 'It was over a year ago.'

'People have long memories,' the barista replied.

Wasn't that the truth? Until today, Lucy hadn't eaten at a Melted since the scare, proving she was just as cautious as the next person. Still fighting the demon, she headed to Newcastle and two more Melted restaurants. Both in top locations, both quiet. On another day she would have given up by now – it was getting late – but she wanted to take advantage of the light traffic. More importantly though, she had to keep working to fight the murk in her mind, knowing the instant she stopped she'd be felled. At the last restaurant she asked to see the manager, a young Chinese man with quick brown eyes and a ready smile: Lee Adamson.

'Yes, the scare affected us really badly,' Lee agreed. 'Overnight we went from over two hundred customers a day to under thirty.'

'And now?'

'They're coming back, but slowly. Adrian's convinced if we sit tight things will return to normal but it's taking longer than we thought.'

'So what were your weekly takings back then?' she asked. 'And what are they now?'

He fetched them both a coffee before settling them at a rustic teak table in the window. Booted up his laptop. There, he showed her the weekly records. Everything added up.

Her eyes went to the door as a man entered the restaurant. Big woollen coat. Blue-striped beanie. Large features. He had a tatty nylon messenger bag across his chest.

'Excuse me,' Lee said. 'I won't be a minute.'

She watched Lee approach the man, whose fingers went to the plastic clips at the front of his bag but stopped when his eyes clicked to Lucy. She was wearing civilian clothes – trousers and boots, red sweater beneath a jacket – but this guy pegged her within a nanosecond. She put on her most bland, disinterested expression, but she could practically see the thought form in his mind, surrounded by blue flashing lights and fireworks.

POLICE.

The man's hands fell from his bag. He turned on his heel and without looking left or right, walked outside.

Lee stood there looking baffled. Then he returned to Lucy.

'Who was that?' she asked.

'A friend of Adrian's. I don't know his name.'

A shimmer of silver edged the grey cloud.

'What was he doing here?'

'He comes in once in a while and drops something off for the boss.'

A tingle started at the top of her head. She said, 'Do you know what?'

'Usually it's a present for one of his kids. A book or something that he wants to keep secret.'

Yeah, right.

She quickly ascertained that the man made a delivery to Adrian roughly once a month. There was no pattern to the delivery that he knew. No particular day. Lee would text Adrian to tell him when it arrived and Adrian would come by and collect it, usually the same day. The biggest package Lee had taken delivery of was the size of a case of wine, but a quarter of the weight, and the smallest an A4 padded envelope. The deliveries had been going on for the past year.

'I haven't done anything wrong, have I?' Lee looked at her anxiously.

Since she couldn't be sure, she decided not to offer any opinion. 'Has the man ever left a package when you're not here?'

'He's pushed an envelope through the letterbox once or twice. But usually he hands it to me or one of the staff.'

'If he comes in again,' she said, 'please ring me immediately.'

She gave him her card, which showed her office number as well as her mobile. Thanked him for the coffee. And left.

She didn't go far.

She was pretty sure the man would return.

And when he did, she'd be there.

CHAPTER EIGHTEEN

Sunday 1 February

Dan saw the Audi was still moving. Several people were watching but nobody came to help. He wished he had a gun. He wanted to be proactive, not a fixed target for whatever assassin had been sent. He put one arm beneath Ekaterina's shoulders, the other beneath her knees. With a surge of strength he rose to his feet, holding her in his arms. He was about to head back to the church, the only shelter he could think of, when a woman shouted.

'Daniel!'

He glanced round to see a woman standing beside the Audi. She was waving frantically.

'Get in!'

It was Ekaterina's elfin friend from last night. Her stunning companion who'd been at the bar. She ran to open the rear door. Nobody appeared to be inside.

'Quick!' she shouted. She leaped back into the driver's seat, edging the car closer to him, shouting for him to *hurry!*

He charged for the Audi. Another shot rang out. He hadn't been hit. What about Ekaterina? No time to think. He scrambled on to the back seat, still clutching Ekaterina, and slammed the door behind him. Her friend immediately took off with the rear fishtailing in the slush before settling on to the road.

A clank of metal told him a bullet had hit the car. Then the driver's window shattered, spraying glass, but although the woman gave a small scream, she was gutsy and didn't pause. She drove hard to the end of the street and spun right, gunned down the next street. Dan looked through the rear window but couldn't see anyone following. Had a sniper been in place? Hidden somewhere unobtrusive and static? Was that why they weren't being chased?

'Who are you?' he asked.

'Call me Maria.'

'Maria, where are we going?'

'A friend's place. Katya told me that if anything went wrong, we should go there.'

Dan settled Ekaterina better on his lap. He was soaked in sweat and his coat and hands were covered in blood. He hadn't realised he'd taken off his gloves. He had no idea where he'd put them. He put his hand over her wound and pressed hard, trying to slow the blood flow. Then he saw another wound, lower down. She'd been shot twice. His heart clenched. 'She needs a hospital.'

'We cannot. They will find her.'

'Who is "they"?'

'Katya told me no matter what happens we must not go to a hospital or to any authority. No police, nobody official or they will find out.'

He repeated his question. 'Who is "they"?'

She said, 'The FSB.' Her voice was scared.

Russia's domestic intelligence agency. Which had fingers in every security pie from the police to border control and counter-espionage. Dan let the information settle in his mind. He said, 'Does this friend of Ekaterina's know a doctor?'

Maria didn't answer.

'Who shot her?' Dan asked.

'I don't know.' Her voice shook. He looked at her in the rear-view mirror. Her mouth was trembling, her enormous eyes wide with fear.

'You're doing great,' he said. 'You saved our lives.'

'She said it might be dangerous. I didn't really believe her. I thought she was exaggerating.'

'What were you doing there?'

'I drove us to the church. Katya, she asked me to look out for her. She was worried that she was being watched. I thought she was being paranoid. I didn't realise . . .' She paused as she ran a red light. Sounded the horn as a pedestrian began to cross the road.

'Who's watching her?'

'All she said was that she needed my help. I went with her last night, as a cover. So she could meet you discreetly.'

'She told those men I was her pimp.'

Maria met his eyes in the mirror. 'We are not prostitutes.' She said it very flat.

The Audi crossed the Moskva River. They appeared to be heading west. It started to snow.

'How is she?' Maria asked.

Ekaterina's face was paper-white. Her breathing was shallow, her pulse weakening. 'How long until we reach your friend?'

'Ten minutes.'

'Don't give up,' he told Ekaterina fiercely. 'Keep fighting, OK? We'll get you to a doctor. They'll fix you up.'

He felt Maria looking at him in the mirror. He met her gaze. 'Please,' he said. 'Tell me everything she told you about me.'

'She was nervous at seeing you. She wasn't sure how you'd react.'

'What else did she say?'

'That to meet you was the most important thing in her life.'

'Why?'

'She didn't say.'

Raising his gaze he saw the streets were less busy and that Maria had increased her speed, the Audi rocketing along. Finally she slowed and turned right, and at the end of the next street, pulled up outside a block of apartments. Without saying anything, she got outside, jogged to the front door and pressed an intercom button. Spoke briefly.

Thirty seconds later, no more, a lanky man in his forties came out and hurried to the car. Thick dark hair going grey at the temples, dark eyes, sallow skin. He wore a green patterned sweater over a pair of grey trousers. When he saw Ekaterina, his face went tight with shock.

'Katen'ka,' he whispered. He rounded on Maria, who spoke urgently. The man looked dismayed, then horrified. He snapped something at Maria, who said to Dan, 'We must get Katya inside.'

Between them they carried Ekaterina into the building and up two sets of stairs. Into an apartment that smelled of stew and cigarettes. Into a double bedroom. Piles of clothes everywhere, CDs and books. They placed her gently on the bed. The man and Maria spoke swiftly in Russian. When the man referred to Ekaterina he used the diminutive Katen'ka. Where Maria used Katya, appropriate for friends and work colleagues, Katen'ka was only used by close family members. Or lovers.

'How do you know Ekaterina?' Dan asked the man.

'I'm her brother.'

His name was Fyodor. He was a playwright, divorced with two children – who apparently lived with their mother – but he didn't say any more. Maria stayed with Ekaterina while Fyodor went to a phone on the wall and made a call.

'Who are you ringing?' asked Dan.

'A doctor.'

The doctor arrived fifteen minutes later. Small and thin, with angry red spots around his nose, he looked about eighteen, but he was confident and gave the impression that he knew what he was doing. When he had finished, the doctor moved into the kitchen where he and Fyodor spoke. Their voices rose. Fyodor seemed to be pleading with the doctor who responded with angry gestures.

'What's going on?' Dan asked.

The doctor shrugged, picked up his bag and made to leave.

'Katen'ka needs blood,' Fyodor said. His fists were clenched. 'He wants a thousand dollars. I don't have this.'

'What do you have?'

'I only have roubles. Four thousand.'

Approximately a hundred and thirty dollars.

Dan brought out four hundred dollars from his own wallet and combined the amounts. 'That brings it to over five hundred dollars.'

Dan went and stood next to the doctor. Showed him the money. 'This is enough, yes?'

The doctor licked his lips.

Dan looked down at the man, waiting.

The doctor swallowed. Took the money.

'*Da.*' Yes.

He scurried outside.

Dan tried to think what to do next. He'd come to Moscow to meet Lynx, who had been shot before she'd managed to impart much information. He recalled her questions about Jenny, her nod of satisfaction as she said, *I'm sorry. I had to make sure. But it's not her so much as –*

As what? How was his *wife* involved?

He brought out his phone and although he was tempted to ring Jenny, he didn't want to risk it. He might not have been shot but Ekaterina had, twice. Was Jenny in imminent danger? He felt an urgency descend upon him. He had to get home. Make sure she and Aimee were safe.

Dan looked around for Maria but couldn't see her.

'She left,' Fyodor said.

Dan moved to the window to see Maria's brave red Audi was no longer there. She must have slipped away when they'd moved into the kitchen with the doctor. 'What's her real name?'

'I've never seen her before,' said Fyodor with a shake of his head.

'How do I contact her?'

Fyodor shrugged. 'She is a stranger to me. You will have to wait for Ekaterina to wake up.'

CHAPTER NINETEEN

Milena Zhukov brushed the glass from the driver's seat of her car and drove straight to the Audi dealership. She was grateful it took over an hour to get there. An hour for her to stop shaking. An hour to get her head around what had happened. Which was for Katya to get shot while meeting the Englishman.

She'd thought the church visit a romantic tryst until she'd seen who Katya was with. She'd thought Katya's references to danger were allusions to Edik's temper should he find out she was being unfaithful. And with a Westerner! He hated Western capitalists. He'd like to see them lined up and shot, tossed into a pit and their bodies burned. Little wonder Katya had wanted to keep her meeting with Dan Forrester secret.

She could remember when they'd first met him, at an embassy party over ten years ago. He was a good-looking man with humour on his lips and promise in his eyes, but what caught their attention was the aura of danger that surrounded him. Instantly attracted, they'd both made a play for him. Subtly of course, so Edik wouldn't hear of it, but the Englishman hadn't been interested. He'd flirted, to be sure, obviously flattered at their attention, but neither of them had scored.

At least that's what Milena had thought, but now she wasn't so sure. What was Dan Forrester doing here now? Was it coincidence he'd been at the Radisson, or had Katya organised it? Perhaps he'd been the one to make contact. Perhaps he and Katya *had* had an affair – or were even still involved – and Edik had found out and ordered Katya to be killed? He could be violent, jealous and brutal but he had a soft spot for them, which they occasionally exploited, but carefully, and never in excess. And what about Dan Forrester? If Edik had gone after Katya, wouldn't he have killed him as well? But instead Katya had taken two bullets and Dan none.

Nothing made any sense.

Fear roiled in her belly as she thought of Edik. She wished she'd kept her mouth shut when he'd asked what was up with Katya. She'd been unusually flighty and nervous over the past week or so and he was concerned.

She hasn't got herself into something she shouldn't? he'd asked.

Milena had said no, she didn't think so, but then Edik said, *I wanted to see her on Saturday night but she said she's busy. She's never been busy to me before.*

And, stupid woman that she was, Milena had told him that they were going on a girls' night out at the Radisson. She hadn't known Dan Forrester would be there. She'd thought Katya just wanted to kick up her heels and have a night out without their guardian. A night of freedom. Edik had seemed to understand, but now she remembered how paranoid he was, how he saw spies under every bed, eavesdroppers in each crevice of every wall. Had he spied on Katya, found out she was seeing the

Englishman today? With a lurch of terror she realised this was highly likely.

She gripped the steering wheel so hard her knuckles went white. Why had she told him where they were going? Why, why, *why*?

For the same reason that Katya hadn't told her to keep their night out a secret, she realised. It was always far better to be open with Edik so you didn't get caught in a lie. Early on he'd had them followed when they'd said they were going shopping, and again when they'd told him they were away for the weekend helping a friend move house. Those were the times when they'd known they were being spied on but now Milena guessed they'd been kept under surveillance more than they'd realised.

And what about her? What was Edik going to do now she'd helped Katya and Dan? She felt sick with fear. Started shaking again. Tears coursed down her cheeks. Why had she helped them? What in God's name had made her act the way she did? She wasn't any kind of heroine . . . When she'd heard the shots ring out, for a moment she'd almost fled, but then she'd seen Katya fall. She hated herself for it, but she'd hesitated. She'd nearly driven away, abandoning her childhood friend to bleed on the pavement. That was what their current life had done to them. Made them venal and selfish, only thinking of keeping their own skins safe. Dan Forrester hadn't run away. He'd sheltered Katya with his body. Then he'd picked up her friend and even though it was probably futile, had begun to run for the church. It was as though he'd demonstrated to Milena what she should be doing. Showing her what true courage was.

She wasn't brave. She was terrified.

What should she do? She pictured Edik, sitting in his high-backed leather chair with his feet resting on the skin of a grey wolf he'd shot five years ago at the Kingisepp camp. His dirty blond hair. His broad knuckles with starbursts of scars. His seemingly friendly smile that could turn as mean and hungry as an alligator's.

They'd met Edik when they'd been nineteen, fresh from Irkutsk and as naive as a pair of kittens. They'd just been signed up by a modelling agency and were celebrating at the Simachev Bar when Edik had walked in. They'd been dazzled by him, his power, the way everybody kowtowed, toadying to his every whim. He'd flattered them, spoiled them, showering them with praise and presents. They'd lapped it up, secretly thrilled to have found such a wealthy benefactor, someone powerful who would protect as well as indulge them. An old man of fifty at that, who was married to a woman the same age as him, but who was rarely seen. No kids. Not that they would have cared.

They immersed themselves in his life, pampered and pandered, always thankful that he didn't demand sexual marathons or any disgusting or unnatural acts, just basic rutting sex and the occasional performance between the two of them, which was no big deal. They weren't lesbians, but it didn't bother them, not when he paid for their apartment, their cars and clothes. He'd bought them, they knew that, and they'd never regretted it. Not until today.

What would Edik do?

Would he forgive her? She didn't want to have to abandon their beautiful apartment, turn her back on her luxurious and privileged lifestyle. She revelled in the parliamentary parties, the trips away, rubbing shoulders with influential people who spoke unguardedly in front of them, their discretion trusted and proven over the years. Milena began to cry. She couldn't bear it if she had to start again. She still did a bit of modelling but nothing like she used to, and although she knew she was still beautiful, there were younger and more beautiful girls out there now. How could she avert the disaster heading her way? What miracle should she start praying for?

She wiped her eyes as she pulled into the Audi garage, making a concerted effort to bring her emotions under control. She had to hide her distress or the sharks would start to circle. Using the vanity mirror, she reapplied her make-up before taking a deep breath and climbing out of her car. She demanded to see the service manager.

'A hunting accident,' she told him with an arrogant flick of her fingers. 'My boyfriend. He's a jerk.'

He surveyed the blown-out window and bullet hole in the rear wing without expression.

'It'll need valeting,' she added. 'His friend bled all over the back seat on the way to hospital.'

His face still held no expression. 'We'll need it for a few days.'

'I want a perfect job. He's paying.'

'Of course.'

She wasn't looking at him but she felt his eyes slip past her coat and latch on to her breasts, her waist. She gave him a small, practised smile, the one she used when she wanted a man to feel as though they shared a secret, that she thought he was special, to keep him on side. He flushed. *Good boy.* He'd make sure of a top job.

Milena let him order a taxi for her. She felt better now she was out of the blood-soaked car. The bitter air helped clear her head. A nugget of hope edged into her mind. What if it hadn't been Edik who'd arranged the shooting? What if it was someone else? She mulled this over for a while and eventually decided she'd go to Edik and confess everything. He'd know what to do, and if he *had* arranged the shooting, surely he'd reward her for trying to help Katya in all innocence, as well as being honest?

She decided to wear her primrose silk dress, his favourite, and the vintage white-gold earrings he'd bought her in the summer. But first she needed a bath, to wash off the stench of fear that clung to her.

The taxi dropped her off outside their apartment, and she was walking to the front door, keys in her hand and still planning what to say to Edik, when two strong arms wrapped around her from behind and lifted her off the ground. She took a breath to scream but another man suddenly appeared and before she could move, punched her straight in the face.

CHAPTER TWENTY

'Mummy?' Aimee whispered. 'Are you awake?'

Jenny heard her daughter through the fog of sleep. 'Not really,' she mumbled. She just needed another twenty minutes or so. That was all.

'Can I watch cartoons?'

Normally she didn't like Aimee watching junk TV, but after Dan letting them down yesterday she thought Aimee could do with a bit of a treat. 'Sure.'

She didn't hear Aimee leave but the TV blared downstairs briefly before the volume was hurriedly turned down. Jenny closed her eyes.

The next she knew, sunlight was flooding the room. She blinked a couple of times, surprised, before she took in the time. Ten o'clock! She hadn't slept in for as long as she could remember. Was it because she was pregnant? She didn't think she'd ever overslept when she was carrying Aimee but for some reason this baby took more energy out of her than Aimee had. She remembered Luke had had the same effect. Was it really going to be a boy? When she'd got the test results back she'd been told so, but she'd been sceptical. How could they be so definite so soon?

Aimee had, predictably, gone crazy when she'd told her she might be having a baby brother and for a moment she'd regretted saying anything. What if it was a girl?

'I'll call her Camel,' announced Aimee. 'She can be Neddy's best friend. But if it's a boy he can be Gobber.'

Great, Jenny had thought, half-amused, half-horrified at the thought of having a son named after Gobber the Belch, a six and a half foot tall hairy Viking out of the movie *How to Train Your Dragon*.

Tenderly Jenny placed a hand on her belly, which had just started to curve gently. 'Good morning little one,' she said. 'How did you sleep?'

She'd talked to Aimee before she'd been born, Luke too, and she found herself doing the same for this child. She'd read somewhere that unborn babies participate in the emotional state of their mothers, whether watching a disturbing movie or a comedy, and that within hours of birth, a baby already prefers its mother's voice to a stranger's, suggesting that it must have learned and remembered the voice from the womb.

She wished Dan was here to talk to the baby. Before Aimee was born he'd taken to resting his head on her belly and telling Aimee stories. When he'd learned that the foetus could listen, learn, and remember at some level, he'd spoken French to her, and Italian, reading from city guidebooks on Paris and Florence.

So she won't be scared of languages, he'd said. *Or travel.*

And when he'd told unborn Aimee a story about a dolphin, he said, *so she won't be afraid of the water.*

Jenny felt a mix of emotions rise. Sorrow, anger and love. Sorrow for Luke, who would never meet his younger sibling. Sorrow that Dan wasn't with them. Anger for the same. Where was he? Where had Bernard sent him? Was it Russia again? Or Turkey? Or just plain old England? She'd never know. Dan never told her about his missions. Never had, and never would. She remembered when she'd first found out that he was a spook. They'd been going out for over a year and she was head-over-heels in love with him. So much so, she hadn't given much thought to his habit of keeping arrangements flexible and occasionally changing things at the last minute. He'd told her he was head of marketing for a global pharmaceutical company with a demanding boss, who would sometimes call him out of hours, claiming his time.

When he'd confessed, she'd been astonished, then curious, and then she recalled all the times he'd changed arrangements: leaving her halfway through a weekend telling her he had to do an impromptu presentation at nine on Monday; being forced to collect an overseas colleague from Heathrow with virtually no notice; flying to a week-long conference in America with barely a days' warning. None of it had been true. She was stunned.

You've been lying *to me all this time?*

I didn't want to. Dan's face was pale. *I'm sorry but I had to.*

She was deeply shaken at his ability to deceive her.

I believed every word you told me.

I know. He was contrite, almost on his knees in penitence. *I'm sorry. Please forgive me. I didn't have the courage to do it any earlier. I didn't want to mess up what we had. Please, Jenny. What can I do to make it up to you?*

She'd demanded to know more. He told her everything he was allowed to tell. Then she demanded time out with him.

I can't think when you're around. I'll ring you when I've thought things over.

He had looked gratifyingly horrified. *Are you saying you don't want to marry me any more?*

I don't know.

She'd let him dangle. She couldn't live without him, she knew that as well as she knew how to reconcile a bank statement, but could she live with being a security service wife? As it turned out, she could, but it was far harder than she imagined and when he came home after being away for weeks on some undercover mission, unshaven, underweight and with a faraway, absent look she hated, she'd considered separating, but she couldn't. She could no more leave him than cut off her own hand. And just when she'd planned a weekend to reunite them, give Dan a chance to forgive her and move back home, Bernard had snapped his fingers and Dan had jumped, gone who knew where, and there was nothing she could do about it.

'Time to get up,' she told the baby. 'See what Aimee's up to.'

She pulled on her dressing gown – a soft snuggle shawl robe that her parents had bought her for Christmas – and went and put the kettle on. Tea in hand, she walked into the sitting room to find Aimee, still in her pyjamas, slouched on the floor with Dan's dog. Which she had completely forgotten about.

She thumped down her mug of tea. 'The dog's got to go out,' she said. 'It's late. Has she made a mess anywhere? I'd better get some newspaper and bleach . . .'

'Mum!' Aimee rolled over. 'I've already done it. She peed and pooed outside and then she came in and I gave her breakfast.'

Jenny blinked. 'She's been out?'

'Yes.' Aimee rolled over to continue watching TV. The dog looked amiably at Jenny but didn't move.

'She didn't run away?'

'Daddy told me to show Poppy her breakfast first, so she had something to come back inside for.'

Clever Daddy, thought Jenny. She sat on the sofa looking at the dog who watched her back unblinkingly. 'Good dog,' she said. At that, Poppy rose and ambled over, stuck her head on Jenny's lap. Carefully she stroked the broad forehead and then the ears. 'Gosh, her ears are soft.'

'They're like bunny's ears.'

Bunny's ears or not, they had to take her for a walk at some point. Luckily their garden was quite large, and although it was unfenced at the end – she and Dan liked having the unbroken view across the valley – the field didn't contain any livestock at the moment.

She was finishing her tea when Poppy went to stand in front of the French windows. Her body was alert, her ears pricked as though she was watching something outside. Maybe a rabbit? There were loads of them even in winter – she'd seen four grazing the edges of the drive yesterday morning. For no good reason she could see, the dog suddenly turned and raced out of the room.

'Maybe she needs to go out again,' said Jenny on a half-yawn. 'Or she wants to go rabbiting.'

'Show her a titbit first!' called Aimee.

Yes, Madam. Jenny found Poppy with her nose pressed against the front door. 'Just a minute,' she told the dog. In the fridge she found a piece of Cheddar. She tried to show it to Poppy but the dog wasn't interested.

As she opened the door the dog muscled her aside and set off at a run across the drive. Her head was low, her hackles up. She moved silently and with purpose. Puzzled, Jenny tried to see what she might be after. Please God it wasn't a sheep. Farmers had zero tolerance for sheep worriers and Dan wouldn't just kill her if she got his dog shot, he'd –

Her thoughts stalled. There was a man. He was running hell for leather through the trees at the edge of the drive. Poppy was running straight after him. The man jinked left, deeper into the woodland, and vanished from view. Hotly pursued by Poppy.

Her heart went into her mouth.

'Jesus Christ.'

What would happen if the dog caught the man? Rottweilers were guard dogs – would she bite him? Savage him? Would he be hospitalised? Would he sue? Ramming her bare feet into a pair of wellies, yanking on an old Barbour of Dan's over her dressing gown, she tore after them.

'Poppy!' she yelled.

Her breath poured steam in the icy air as she galloped down the drive, Barbour flapping around her dressing gown.

'Poppy!'

She heard a man's shout and then Poppy's bark. Deep furious *woofs!* that reverberated through the trees. Sick with apprehension, she raced towards the sound of the barks, her wellies slipping on the damp ground, cold muddy water splashing up her bare legs. *Please don't bite him.*

She found Poppy at the base of a tree. Just out of reach, standing on the low branch of an ancient oak and hugging the trunk was a man. Red-faced and panting. He said, 'Call him off.'

The dog glanced at Jenny then looked back at the man. She continued to bark until Jenny put her hand on her shoulder and said, 'Quiet.'

The sudden silence rang in her ears.

The man said, 'Put him on a lead.' His voice was unsteady.

She cringed. 'I don't have one. Well, not with me. I have one at the house but –'

'Take him to the house. Shut him in.'

She gripped Poppy's collar. The dog immediately came close to her side.

'He's obedient.' The man sounded surprised. 'Is he yours?'

Jenny looked at the man. He wore dark green trousers and a big camouflage jacket. A beanie covered his hair. Thirties, light brown stubble. A pair of binoculars hung from his neck. A birdwatcher, maybe? Odd time of year for it, but what did she know – she'd never gone birdwatching in her life. He didn't look particularly threatening, but she wasn't going to tell a stranger Poppy was only on loan. He had, after all, been on their property.

'It's a she,' she said. 'And yes, she's mine.'

'Can you keep hold of her while I come down?'

'Yes.'

She tightened her grip on the dog's collar but although Poppy watched him, she didn't move as the man scrambled to the ground and began dusting bits of bark and lichen from his clothes.

'How long have you had her?' He looked interested.

She didn't want to tell him. Instead, she said, 'Are you bird-watching?'

He glanced at the binoculars. 'Not really. I was going for a walk and my host – I'm staying with the Taylors in the village – insisted I take them.'

She knew the Taylors, a robust elderly couple who lived in the Old Rectory with their two spaniels, and felt herself relax.

'I'm so sorry she chased you.' Her body language turned apologetic. 'I thought she was after a rabbit.'

'No harm done, apart from to my pride.' He gave a wry smile. 'Was I trespassing?'

'Yes, I'm afraid so.'

'In that case, I deserved what I got.' He settled his binoculars straight on his chest. 'I wanted to walk to Pen-y-parc and thought this was a shortcut.'

'It is, but it's private property.'

'I'm sorry.' He looked genuinely apologetic. 'I won't do it again, promise. Would you mind holding your dog until I go?'

'Of course not. I'll take her straight to the house.'

Back inside she gave Poppy the piece of cheese whereupon her own stomach growled, reminding her how late it was. She was about to ask Aimee if she wanted cereal or eggs for breakfast when her parents rang. 'Darling,' said her mother. 'We're crossing the bridge now. Your father wanted to warn you.'

Crap, she thought. She'd completely forgotten they were coming over for coffee. Thank God for Dad or they would have been caught out.

'See you soon!' she told her mother brightly.

'Soon!' her mother replied in the same cheerful tone and hung up.

Jenny bolted to the living room. 'Aimee, get dressed. Granny and Grandpa will be here soon.'

'But I'm watching –'

'*Now*. And turn off the TV.'

Aimee knew when not to argue and followed Jenny upstairs in a flurry. It didn't take them long to shower and get ready, and by the time her parents arrived, they'd blow-dried their hair and straightened the house, looking as though they'd been up for hours. At least she hoped so. Her mother wouldn't approve of them lounging around in sleepwear for half the morning. She'd been brought up on a farm, rising before six a.m. no matter what the weather, and was baffled by anyone who rose any later. Something Jenny's academic father still had trouble with, being a bit of a slugabed himself.

Aimee helped put out the cakes she'd baked for the weekend. Carrot cake, Dan's favourite, and a batch of chocolate and nut brownies, also his favourite and maybe Poppy's too by the way the dog was salivating. Unbidden, an image of Dan rose. Dan in the shower, turned away from her, when he didn't know she was looking. His body tall and fine and strong, his thighs and backside well muscled, his calves well defined. He didn't know it, but he had a beautiful body. She loved every inch of it, even the scars on his ribs and knuckles, the twist of scar tissue on his stomach where a bullet had grazed him.

'Does the baby like chocolate, Mummy?' Aimee asked.

'You could always ask him.'

Aimee put her face against Jenny's stomach and yelled, 'I bet you DOOOO!'

'You don't have to shout!' Jenny laughed. 'His ears will be ringing for a week! Mine too!'

Aimee patted her belly and said, 'Sorry.' She was smiling.

Jenny was glad she'd involved Aimee in the pregnancy from the start, letting her accompany her on any doctor's visits to try and lessen the possible jealousy that would occur.

At that moment, the phone rang. Ronny Field, a local builder, wanting to know if she was in. He wanted to drop off his personal accounts.

'You're a day late,' she scolded. She must have told him a dozen times the cut-off date for him to pay his tax was the thirty-first of January.

'I know, love, but I forgot. The wife reminded me as we were getting on the plane.'

'What plane?'

'Canary Islands. Holiday.'

'It's all right for some,' she told him drily. 'It's going to snow later, you know.'

'Can you do it next week? Submit it for me?'

She grabbed her phone and brought up her diary, had a quick look. 'Yes. But how do I get hold of your paperwork?'

'Bobby Taylor said he could drop it all round. He's got keys to my place. Would you mind ringing him?'

'No problem.'

She called Bobby Taylor who said yes, he could drop Roland's paperwork round later that day. She said, 'I met your friend this morning. My dog gave him rather a fright.'

'What friend?'

'The one staying with you. He seemed rather nice.'

Pause.

'But we don't have anyone staying with us.'

'What?' She was confused. 'He told me you'd loaned him your binoculars to take on his walk.'

'I haven't loaned anyone my binoculars. Did he give a name?'

'No.'

'How odd.'

She described the man to no effect. When they'd hung up she went to the French windows and looked out. Poppy came and joined her. She rested her hand on the dog's shoulder, suddenly glad the Rottweiler was there. *Who was the man? Why had he lied?*

CHAPTER TWENTY-ONE

Milena must have lost consciousness because the next she knew she was lying on the ground. Blood ran across her face and down the back of her throat. Panic rose. She felt as though she was drowning. She scrabbled on to her side and coughed up some blood. She heard a feeble, pathetic whimpering and it took her a few seconds to realise she was making the sound.

She forced open her eyes. She could see snow. Blood on the snow. Her blood. She was panting hard and fast through her mouth. She couldn't breathe through her nose. Her sinuses were swollen and scorched with pain and felt as though they had been blow-torched.

'Welcome back, beautiful.'

Edik's voice. She saw his boots. Leather brogues, hand-made in London. She recognised the tiny scar in the leather shaped like a sickle.

She put her hands on the snow and tried to rise to her knees but he put a boot between her shoulders and shoved her down so hard she lost all the air in her lungs.

'Don't fucking move unless I say so.'

She lay there, fighting to breathe.

'Now,' he said. 'I have a question for you.'

She rolled her eyes to see she was lying at the end of an alley. Refuse sacks lined one wall, spilling frozen debris on to the ground. Above the rubbish, spread across the wall, was a piece of graffiti featuring a withered rose on a pile of corpses. She immediately recognised it. She was in the alley that ran between the rear of her apartment block and the park. She was barely three hundred yards from the back door.

'If you answer my question correctly,' he continued, 'you will be able to come home and resume your life as though nothing has happened. If you don't, or if you try to lie, you will find yourself in so much pain you will beg to die.'

'Please,' she choked. 'Please d-don't . . .'

'Where is Ekaterina?'

'Please,' she begged. Quietly, she began to cry.

'Wrong answer.' He turned aside. He said, 'Deal with her.' He walked away, his shoes crunching in the snow.

She inched her head round. Took in three more men. She barely looked at the two thugs because her eyes went straight to the old man. The man who held the power. He was tall but stooped, and leaned on a cane. Wrinkled skin draped over aquiline features. He would have been handsome in his youth.

She wanted to weep. She wanted to howl in anguish. She knew him. She knew what he was capable of. She was scared of Edik but his father frightened her even more. It was said he was best friends with Kazimir's ghost, and that they dined on their victims' souls every Sunday after church.

'Sir . . .' she choked. She didn't dare say his name. 'Please. Have mercy.'

His expression didn't change. It was as though she hadn't spoken. Her dread increased. She might tempt a younger man, persuade him with promises or her money – she had over fifty thousand roubles tucked away – but not this hooded old bird. Desperately she looked along the alley, but Edik had gone. Nobody was there. Nobody walking along the adjoining alley, nobody driving or bicycling or walking their dog.

'Please,' she begged again. 'Call Edik . . .'

The old man's eyes were rheumy but they turned as sharp as icicle points. He stepped forward. He looked down at her dispassionately.

'Edik can't help you now, you silly bitch,' he said. 'Nobody can.'

His voice was dry and rattled like broken twigs.

'If you think he'll protect you because he's been fucking you for the past decade, you're deluded. You're a woman. You're insignificant. You're of less value than a piece of dog shit. Can't you see? He's abandoned you. He won't help you. But if you help us, we might consider helping you. Answer me. Where is Ekaterina Datsik?'

She closed her eyes and thought about Katya. Their playing in the woods when they were children, the evening sun lighting the grass and birch trees gold. The swing suspended between two pines. Hedgehogs, foxes and garter snakes. Their walking to school together. Sharing homework, clothes, nail polish, lipstick. The first beauty contest they'd entered. Their shared hunger for Moscow, their unflagging thirst for something new and exciting, the newest events, the latest fashions, the hottest places to be seen.

'You'll let me go?' She tried not to sound pitiful but with her nose smashed flat against her face, her voice was feeble and weak.

'Of course. What do you think we are? Animals?'

She looked at his ancient, arrogant features, clean-shaven, his expensive coat and shoes.

She muffled, 'What will you do to her?'

'Nothing that you need to know about.'

Milena listened to the distant hum of traffic and tried to think past the pain. Work out what to do.

'Where is she?' he asked.

'Presnenskiy Val ulitsa,' she said. 'Block number eight. Apartment eleven.'

'You wouldn't be lying, would you?'

She started to shake her head but the pain was too much and she said, 'No.'

'So when we send a car there, we'll find Ekaterina Datsik.'

She remained silent.

'If we don't find her, I will get my friends to cut off one of your fingers. They will continue cutting until you give me the right address and we have found her.'

How could she survive this? Desperately she tried to make a plan.

'Do it,' he said.

The first thug bent over her and when she saw the pruning shears she gasped, 'OK, OK.'

She didn't see she had a choice. Gulping, weeping, trying to play for time, she said, 'I'm not sure of the exact address. I've never been there ...'

Before she could move the thug had gripped her hand. He placed the blades on either side of her thumb. She was sweating and whimpering. 'Please don't, please –'

'Tell me.'

'It's an apartment block on ulitsa Peredelkino. It's the third on the left if you come at it from Chobotovskaya alleya.' She gasped out an apartment number and floor. She closed her eyes. *May God forgive me.*

CHAPTER TWENTY-TWO

Dan managed to persuade Fyodor to ask a neighbour if he could use their phone. He had no idea whether Fyodor's apartment would be bugged or not, but thought it worth taking the precaution. Instinct told him not to use his mobile. He didn't want his call traced. Fyodor's neighbour, a small woman in a blue dress, led him inside, her sagging middle-aged face as long and melancholy as a bloodhound's. When Dan offered to pay her for the calls, she refused in a voice surprisingly deep for such a fragile-looking frame.

The phone was in the hallway, a narrow space filled with books. Books were crammed on shelves, others on the floor and piled on top of one another in messy towers. He saw the names of the greats, Dostoyevsky, Pushkin, Tolstoy. Also some modern literature. He recognised Lyudmila Ulitskaya's *The Kukotksy Case* and recalled it had won an award of some sort. How he knew this he didn't know. The knowledge was just *there*, like he knew how a glass of milk would taste.

He raised the receiver, listened to the buzz. Dialled 8. Waited for a second dialling tone then dialled his home number. It rang four times before it was answered.

'Hellooo?' a voice sang. It was Aimee.

'Hi munchkin.'

'Daddy!' Her ecstatic squeal almost split his eardrum. 'Where are you? Are you coming home? Granny and Grandpa are here, we've had chocolate brownies and some carrot cake but the brownies were the best because Mummy put white chocolate buttons on the top, we'll save some for you if you like, they were yummy and . . .'

As her prattle continued he felt relief trickle through every cell in his body. Aimee was OK. She was with her grandparents and everything was OK.

'Sweet pea,' he tried to interrupt. 'I need to speak to Mummy.'

'When will you be back?'

'Soon.'

'Like for the weekend?'

'I hope so.'

'Mummy!' she yelled. 'It's Daddy!'

He heard sounds of cloth brushing and soft thumps as she carried the cordless phone to her mother.

'Love you, munchkin.'

'Love you tooooo!'

Small pause. Then Jenny said, 'Dan.' With that one word he knew he'd made her happy. His heart squeezed and out of nowhere he felt a rush of emotion so powerful he could have dropped to his knees and wept. He loved his wife *so much*. Why had he moved out? The answer came in a rush, shocking him with the truth. *Because he was punishing her.*

He rested his head against the wall. Closed his eyes. He said, 'I'm sorry.'

'My love.' Her voice was gentle, cradling him, forgiving him.

'I'll make it right when I get back. I promise. But right now, I need you to do something for me.'

'Anything.'

'I need you to take extra-special care of yourself and Aimee until I get back.'

'Of course.' Her voice was warm.

'It's just that . . .' He took a breath. She wasn't going to like this but there was no way to avoid it. She had to know. 'Something's come up at work. That might involve you.'

'Like what?' Her voice sharpened.

'I'm not sure. But it could be dangerous.'

Silence.

'I want you to –' He swallowed his words as Fyodor burst into the hallway.

'The police!' His expression was wild. 'They come!'

'Hold on,' he said urgently to Jenny.

Fyodor dragged him out of the apartment to the stairwell window. A police car had turned into the street, along with an unmarked vehicle sporting government plates.

'Maria.' Fyodor spat out the word. 'She has told them where to come. Traitor.'

Dan spun round, wanting to race back to the phone but the old woman's door was shut and didn't open when he knocked. She didn't want to get involved any further, not now Fyodor was in a panic and the police were in the street.

Dan looked outside again to see the cars were cruising slowly, obviously unfamiliar with the place.

'We have to move her,' Dan said.

'Yes.'

They had to work fast. Inside the apartment Fyodor threw several items into a bag. Glanced at Dan. Moved to a cupboard and seized a pair of trousers and a khaki-coloured fleece, tossed them across. 'You must change.'

Belatedly Dan realised his clothes were blood-stained from holding Ekaterina. Swiftly he swapped garments. The trousers were tight, but he managed to haul them on, along with a baggy fleece. Fyodor grabbed a bunch of keys. 'My car,' he said. 'It is down the street. I will bring it to the rear of the building.'

Dan checked outside to see the cars had pulled up outside the apartment block. Two uniforms were climbing out of the first car. Two plain-clothes cops climbed out of the second.

He carried Ekaterina to the rear of the building. Stood outside on the step with her in his arms. He could hear the whine of the elevator, and music playing somewhere. Then Fyodor was there with a weather-beaten Lada Samara sedan. Nought to sixty in fourteen seconds or so, and that was in a straight line, on a dry road. Fyodor left the engine running as he went to open the rear door. Dan hurried with Ekaterina to the car, trying not to slip on the ice. He'd barely taken four steps when he heard a shout.

He didn't look round. He simply put Ekaterina in the back and said to Fyodor, 'I'll drive.'

Fyodor looked as though he might protest.

'In my last job,' Dan hastily told him, 'I used to instruct racing car drivers.'

Fyodor immediately scurried onto the back seat with his sister. Another shout.

'Hurry!' Fyodor told Dan.

Dan slid into the driver's seat. Slipped the car into second gear. Swift glance in the rear-view mirror to see one of the plain-clothes cops. He was running after them. He was on the phone.

Dan pressured the accelerator, careful not to make the tyres spin in the slush and lose traction. He changed into third. Then fourth. They made steady progress down the back street. The plain-clothes cop had stopped running and was gazing after them. He was still on the phone.

'Turn right here!' Fyodor told him. His voice was high with tension.

Dan turned the corner, picking up speed, feathering the steering wheel, unconsciously getting a feel for the car, its weight and behaviour. Light steering but reasonably accurate. Soft suspension, body roll through the corners but a fairly decent grip.

As soon as they were out of sight, Dan changed down a gear and rammed his foot on the accelerator. Drove flat out. He revved the engine high, keeping the speed up, hands light on the wheel, ready for anything. Streets and junctions flashed past.

'Take the next left!' Fyodor continued giving directions. 'Over the bridge!'

'No bridge,' he said. Bridges were exposed areas. They could be trapped.

'Straight ahead,' Fyodor quickly amended. 'Right at the cross-roads.'

As Dan drove, his concentration was focused on planning ahead, looking at where he wanted to go. You look at the corner of the building you're skidding around, you drive into the corner of the building. So he fixed his gaze at the next corner, not at the road he was driving along, his concentration fixed, every sense taken up with correcting and assessing what was ahead; traffic lights, pedestrians, trams.

He raced past a scattering of vehicles. He had to veer a little to pass a truck and the tyres broke traction. They began to skid straight into the path of an oncoming bus.

'*Chert!*' exclaimed Fyodor. Oh, shit!

Resisting his instinctive reaction to lift off the accelerator Dan instead increased the pressure, easing out on the steering wheel at the same time. The Lada's rear tyres pushed back on to the road just in time for Dan to nip round the front of the bus.

'*Spasibo, Gospodi*,' Fyodor breathed. Thank you, Lord. Dan saw him cross himself.

'Where are we going?' Dan asked.

'South. To Yasenevo.'

Dan was barrelling down a busy street full of shops when he heard the sirens. Quick glance in his rear-view mirror showed two cop cars at the end of the street. They had larger engines, better performance. They were catching up.

He rode tight behind a Lada Niva, inches from its rear bumper, waiting for a truck driving from the opposite direction to pass. The second it was in his peripheral vision Dan popped out and zipped past the Niva, tearing down the street, overtaking at every opportunity, aware of nothing but his grip on the steering wheel, the road, the laboured scream of the engine and the snapshots in the rear-view mirror of the police cars overtaking traffic behind him.

Dashing past a row of three cars, he hit some rubbish or debris, or simply a patch of ice, he had no way of knowing, but the car's rear end suddenly stepped out. The car flew sideways but his hands were already turning to correct the skid, preventing the vehicle snapping into a full spin. Then he was off again, flat out, his focus and determination on the traffic lights ahead.

'Fyodor.' He waited until the man looked at him in the rear-view mirror. 'Do you have anyone who can help you?'

Fyodor's face was pale. 'Yes.'

'If I drop you off, will they come and fetch you?'

'Yes.'

Dan flew down the next straight. When the slush parted he let the car race howling to the corner until he was nearly past it and then he lifted off the accelerator and shoved his foot hard on the brakes. The nose of the car dived under his heavy braking and he spun the steering wheel right, the rear swinging out, the whole body of the car rolling, shuddering and creaking as he pushed through the turn. As the car squealed past the apex of the bend he floored the gas and they flew out of the corner towards the next corner, and the next one after that.

The police cars appeared briefly in the rear-view mirror but quickly faded into the background.

'Fyodor. When I tell you, I want you to get out of the car with Ekaterina. I will drive on. Draw them away.'

Fyodor didn't protest.

'You can't stay in Moscow,' Dan told him.

'No.' The man's voice shook.

'I want you to ring a number. Tell them what happened. They will help you.' Dan gave him Bernard's direct line. 'Give them the code words *Lynx* and *Mountain Lion* and say they're in *Colorado* looking for a *fast river*.'

Fyodor stared at him.

'Repeat the number,' Dan said.

Fyodor stumbled once, but remembered it the second time.

'What are the animals?'

'Lynx and mountain lion.'

'Where are they?'

'In Colorado.'

Dan scrubbed down his speed for the traffic lights ahead, planning his right turn around an artic lorry and a bus.

'Looking for?'

'A fast river.'

'Now the number, Fyodor.'

He repeated it flawlessly.

Dan slipped past a lorry. The street ahead was filled with delivery vans, shoppers, market stalls, awnings, trays of vegetables, platters of meat. Lots of bustle, lots of cover. Plenty of places for them to hide.

'Here,' said Dan. 'Get ready.'

He waited for a gap in the cars parked by the kerb and slewed the car into a space. Fyodor already had the door open and his feet on the kerb by the time Dan stopped. It took five seconds, no more, for Fyodor to lift his sister outside and slam the door shut.

Dan didn't waste time seeing where they went. He pulled straight out and pushed through the market, hand on the horn and weaving round delivery trolleys and shoppers until suddenly the road was clear. He floored the accelerator with no clue where he was going. He just knew he would drive and keep driving as fast and hard as he could, lead them away from Fyodor and Ekaterina for as long as he could, at least until he ran out of petrol. Which could be now or in twenty minutes, he had no idea; the fuel gauge didn't work.

He wasn't going very fast, maybe fifty, down a narrow residential street, when he heard the distinctive clatter of rotor blades. Sweat sprang along his spine. A helicopter. He was surprised it had taken them this long to get one in the air. Now they could coordinate a road block. Shepherd him where they wanted before trapping him. Time to abandon the car and run on foot. He started looking for cover. A wooded park would do, or a warren of busy streets filled with shops and arcades.

He tore around the next corner into another street. Broad with snow-covered trees dotting the pavements.

His stomach hollowed.

Two police cars and a police bus blocked the far end.

He glanced in the rear-view mirror.

Clear.

He swiftly came off the gas, the car's weight coming forwards to provide grip at the front end. He took a big bite of the steering wheel and turned in a single fluid motion, simultaneously pressing the clutch and pulling on the handbrake.

The rear wheels locked, started to slide.

As the back of the car came round, he let the wheel slip through his hands. Controlled, smooth.

The car spun round.

The second he was facing the other way, he released the handbrake, knocked the gearstick into first and brought out the clutch with enough revs to spin the wheels slightly.

And rocketed back the way he'd come.

He was looking at the end of the street, planning to turn right, when two more police cars careened into view, straight in front of him. Two vans followed.

He was trapped.

He saw men in black flak jackets and helmets pour out of the vans: each carried an assault weapon. OMON: Special Purpose Mobile Unit.

Dan slammed on the brakes.

The car was still moving as he went for his phone.

He could have done this earlier but he'd hoped it wouldn't come to this, that he might get away . . .

His hands shook as he dialled.

The OMON team fanned out fast, their weapons trained on him.

He poured sweat, praying she'd answer. That she hadn't left her phone at home. That she would hear it ringing.

'Love,' she said. Her voice was warm, filled with happiness.

Four police dropped to their knees, their weapons steady on him. Another half-dozen began to approach, cheeks against their weapon stocks, ready to fire.

'Brimstone, Jenny.' He was gasping in haste. 'Brimstone.'

'What?'

'Brimstone!' He was almost screaming. 'Do you remember what we said about Brimstone?'

'Yes.' Her voice suddenly came alert.

'Do it!'

'Yes.'

'And my phone!'

'I'll do it now.'

He ripped out his micro SIM card. Grabbed the car key and belted the card against the dash, cracking it. He then put the SIM card into his mouth and with absolute determination, swallowed it.

The police continued to approach. They were shouting, gesticulating for him to get out of the car.

Dan put up his hands, showing he didn't have a weapon.

One of the cops came close to the car, gesturing violently with his gun.

Dan reached for the car door. He kept his other hand up and open for them all to see. He opened the door. Raised both hands once more. Kicked the door wide.

The second he began to swivel to exit the car they were on him. Shouting and screaming, they dragged him bodily out of the car and pushed him to the ground. Ice and gravel scraped his face.

He felt the cold steel of a weapon against his neck; another dug painfully into his kidneys. His legs were kicked apart, his hands forced behind his back. Handcuffs clamped around his wrists.

One of the men kicked him in the ribs, obviously letting off steam. Another joined him but backed off when a man barked an order. A dry, rasping voice that had the men standing to attention.

Dan struggled up to see an old man leaning on a cane. Aquiline features. Alert blue eyes. He came forward, studied Dan. In fluent English, he said, 'Where did you learn to drive like that?'

CHAPTER TWENTY-THREE

Jenny had to force herself to move. She felt as though she was having an out-of-body experience, numb and disconnected. Shocked.

Brimstone.

Dan had practically screamed the word.

Do you remember what we said about Brimstone?

How could she forget? After his breakdown Dan had lost great chunks of his memory, from what his favourite food used to be to where he used to work, and when he learned he'd been employed by the Security Service he demanded she tell him everything she could remember. She'd been brutally honest, saying how much she'd hated his job, and how the final straw had come when his cover had been blown one day and he'd rung her with their code word *Brimstone*.

Brimstone meant an emergency. That they were in the gravest danger. That things had turned catastrophic and in order to survive they had to implement a previously agreed plan.

Which was for Jenny to take Luke and go into hiding immediately. Without telling anyone where they were going. Not Dan's boss. Not even her parents.

She had to vanish without leaving a trail.

She had to hide for as long as it took, days or weeks. Until she heard the release code: cloverleaf.

Fortunately, she and Luke had only been out of the house for three hours when Dan rang with the release code, but it was the worst three hours of her life, not knowing what was going on, whether Dan was alive or dead. When she'd said this to Dan last year, however, he said he thought Brimstone and what it represented an excellent idea, and despite her trying to assert that life was over he'd insisted they keep Brimstone in play. *Just in case*, he'd said. He'd even gone so far as to get a credit card in a different name. Mr & Mrs Fisher. She had no idea how he'd done it and didn't ask – she decided she'd rather not know. He'd also put aside some cash for them to use, which occasionally they dipped into when they were short but which he quickly topped up. She called him paranoid; he said he was prudent.

She started to shake. She never thought she'd be back here again. With her family's life in danger.

What was going on?

No time to think.

She had to get out.

But first she had to wipe his phone. That was the priority. Quickly she grabbed her laptop. Logged into Dan's account. Two more taps on the screen and she found the icon she needed, *erase iPhone*.

Done.

She desperately wanted to see where he was, using the locating feature on his phone, but she would be wasting precious time. He could be in Brazil or Bristol and the situation would be the same. She had to pack for her and Aimee. She had to be organised in case they were gone a long time. She had to shut up the house properly but she mustn't get bogged down doing things that weren't vital. No pausing to clear the fridge or take out the rubbish.

Thank God her parents had left earlier. Small mercy. They'd never have understood the situation.

Pack and leave.

Preferably within five minutes. And while remaining completely calm.

'Aimee?' she called and, as she turned round, she almost collided with Poppy, who'd been at her side. She'd forgotten about the dog. Another thing to worry about. She couldn't leave the dog behind. Besides, Poppy had proved herself useful, chasing that man away.

Jenny glanced through the window but saw nobody hiding in the trees, nobody running down the drive. Just sheets of sleet and snow billowing over and around her car. She'd have to pack warm clothes. DVDs. A couple of games . . .

She strode into the living room. 'Aimee, that was Daddy on the phone.'

Her daughter looked up from her colouring book.

'We have an emergency,' Jenny said. She knelt down, looked at Aimee seriously. She'd learned over the years that if she talked to her daughter openly, matter-of-factly, she responded far better than if she tried to hide the truth. 'We have to leave home right now. Daddy couldn't tell us exactly what the emergency was, but that it's to do with his work, and that we might be in danger if we stay.'

Aimee's eyes went as wide as soup plates. 'What sort of danger?'

'I don't know.' Jenny was honest. 'But when I find out I'll tell you, I promise. But in the meantime, we have to leave now, OK?'

Aimee looked at her colouring book then back at Jenny. 'But I don't want to go anywhere.' Her voice rose into a whine. 'I want –'

'I'm going to pack some things for us.' Jenny spoke calmly, wanting to prevent Aimee from stepping on to a hysterical spiral. 'Would you pack for Poppy? She'll need her dog bed and bowl, biscuits and –'

'Her ball!' Aimee jumped up, immediately distracted. 'And she'll need some treats too!'

As she started to run to the hall Jenny called out, 'Don't go outside, please. Just put everything by the front door. I'll pack the car in a minute.'

'Okaaaay!'

As Jenny hared upstairs she could hear Aimee talking to the dog over metallic clanks of the dog bowl. She never thought she'd be glad of Dan's dog but right now she could have hugged the creature for preventing Aimee from having a meltdown. Diving into the spare room she grabbed two holdalls from the divan drawers. No time to fetch the suitcases, which were in the loft.

She flew across both bedrooms, grabbing underwear, socks, shirts, jeans and jumpers. Toiletries. Books, crayons, sparkly nail polish, Neddy the stuffed horse. Everything shoved haphazardly into the bags. A framed photograph of Dan was shoved on top.

'Ready!' yelled Aimee.

'Gosh, that was quick.' She lugged the bags downstairs to find dog and daughter standing by the dog's items, looking expectant. 'Do we have her lead?'

'Yes.' Aimee held it up proudly.

'I'll be one minute and then we'll pack up the car.'

Laptop, phone, chargers, DVDs, more books, waterproofs, wellies, handbag, car keys. Big leather wallet which held passports, marriage certificate, birth certificates, paper driving licences and a handful of Euros left over from a previous holiday.

Quick glance outside. Nobody there that she could see.

'Let's go.'

They ducked their heads as they ran to her hatchback. The wind was viciously cold, biting their skin and the sleet stung their eyes. Jenny flung their things in the rear. The dog would have to take the back seat.

'Buckle up,' she told Aimee.

'Can I sit with Poppy?'

'If there's room.' She wasn't going to argue and waste time.

Jenny was about to set the alarm when she remembered her phone. Taking it out of her handbag she ran with it to the house. Left it on the hall table. Even if it was switched off she couldn't use it; it could still be traced. Dan had said it was far better to leave it behind and buy a new one. What else? Frantically she ran a mental checklist, but stalled as soon as she got past the essentials: passports, cash, emergency credit card.

She switched the heating to fifteen degrees. Did a fast sweep to check the windows were locked, then she set the alarm and left the house.

As she headed down the drive she searched for the man in the trees but saw nobody. Was it because he wore camouflage clothing, or was he simply not there? No car followed her through the village. No vehicle behind her as she wound her way down the mountain. Her heartbeat began to settle, her sweat cool.

'Where are we going?' asked Aimee. She was scrunched into one corner with Poppy's massive head on her lap.

'Kent,' Jenny said. 'Lots of walks for Poppy there.'

'Kent?' Aimee looked blank.

'Well, we've never been there before, and Daddy and I thought it would be a bit of an adventure.'

She didn't like going somewhere she didn't know, but that was what they'd decided. For her to go to a safe house near Canterbury, owned by a fellow spook and friend of Dan's called Max Blake, who had agreed they could use it, pitch up without warning, any time of day or night. Plus Kent was close to major airports, ferries and the Eurotunnel. And London too, if they needed to get into the city for any reason.

'Did you hear that, Poppy? We're going to Kent for an adventure . . .'

While Aimee prattled on, Jenny's mind burned ahead. She could hardly remember anything about the safe house except that it had a public phone box nearby. Would Max Blake be there? She'd never met the man. What if she couldn't find his house? Panic rose and she forced it down.

Cross bridges when you come to them.

She would use her laptop to access phone numbers she needed. Like Aimee's school. Her parents and her clients. She'd use the story she and Dan had come up with back when he was still with MI5, that Dan's father had died overseas. Bill Forrester was alive and well in Weston-Super-Mare, but since the only people who were likely to check would be whoever they were running from, she wasn't concerned.

She gave a shiver. Checked her rear-view mirror to see nothing but a windswept country lane.

Where was Dan? Was he OK? What was happening?

She reran their earlier conversation. Heard his voice in her head as he said, *I'm sorry*. It had been filled with regret and sorrow and she knew he'd forgiven her. That when he came home, it would be *home*, with her and Aimee, and not to the flat he was staying at, in London. She wanted him to come home *so much*.

She felt tears rise and forced them down. She didn't want to scare Aimee.

Jenny drove across the country. As she joined the M25 the bad weather eased and the sun came out. They stopped briefly for fuel and to use the loos, buy some lunch and walk Poppy. She bought some food supplies from M & S with Mr & Mrs Fisher's credit card. She had no idea how it would get paid but there seemed no point in worrying about it. Pasta and sauce, pizza, bread and jam, some eggs, simple things because she had no idea of the cooking facilities ahead.

Back in the car Jenny accessed her laptop and retrieved the postcode for the safe house. Tapped it into her satnav. Continued driving east as the sun moved overhead. They passed Canterbury and she took the A28 towards Margate for a few miles before ducking right and into the countryside.

Five p.m. and it was nearly dark.

Aimee appeared to be asleep. The dog too.

You have reached your destination, her satnav suddenly announced.

Jenny looked up and down the lane to see nothing. No building, no lights.

She dropped her speed. Passed a farm before crossing a bridge over a river. She kept turning her head to the right and left, peering past trees and hedges, desperate to find the safe house. Please God it was here. She was exhausted.

And then there it was. A small brick cottage set back from the lane. A neat gravel drive to the front door. As she turned through the gate, her headlights lit a small wooden sign that read *Sparrow Cottage*. No car outside. No lights. It looked empty. Her spirits rose a little.

'Stay here,' she told Aimee. She wanted to check it was the right place. She walked to the front porch. Lifted the flowerpot to find a single Yale key.

Great security, she thought, *but who cares. We're here. We're safe.*

She brought in their bags. The cottage was cold, the air dead. Nobody had been here for a while. She switched on the lights, tracked down the boiler and turned on the heating before having a quick look round. Neutral walls, neutral furniture, no personal touches. Three bedrooms, one bathroom and a downstairs loo. A linen cupboard that looked as though it held everything they'd need. Her spirits lifted further when she saw the sitting room. Wooden beams, an overstuffed sofa and two big armchairs. TV, DVD player and stereo. An open fire already laid with logs and newspaper, a box of matches on the hearth.

She went and fetched Aimee and the dog. 'Why don't you choose a room,' she said to Aimee, knowing it would be guaranteed to keep her occupied for at least five minutes. Poppy scouted the garden before she came in and checked the cottage, working her way from room to room, busily inspecting every corner, every wastepaper bin, every inch of carpet.

Jenny filled up the dog's water bowl before feeding her. She opened the kitchen cupboards to find basic supplies: long-life milk, rice, beans, oil, tins of soup and tuna. Two jars of honey. The fridge held a bottle of vodka and another of tonic and – her eyebrows lifted – two bottles of rather good Chablis. The freezer was empty apart from a tray of ice and a packet each of frozen peas and broad beans.

She cooked some pasta for supper, and after reading Aimee a story and putting her to bed with Neddy and her nightlight – thank God she'd forgotten neither – she lit the fire and poured herself a large glass of wine. Poppy settled at her feet with a sigh.

The wine tasted delicious, especially having not had any since Boxing Day, when she'd missed her period and guessed she might be pregnant. *Sorry little one*, she told the baby. *But this is an emergency.* She took another sip and closed her eyes. Part of her couldn't believe this was happening, but the other part was saying, *Things could be worse. You and Aimee could be dead, kidnapped, held at gunpoint, the safe house could have been a dump, filled with vagrants, filthy, but it's actually pretty decent.* She tried to keep positive thoughts in her mind but she couldn't help the tears hovering.

How long would they have to stay here? Where was Dan? What was going on?

She switched on her laptop. Logged into Dan's iPhone account once more. Asked the software to *find my device.*

Nothing happened.

Heart in her mouth, she waited.

Finally the screen changed. She felt a rush of horror. The green pin wasn't in England. It was in Russia. Dan was somewhere in Moscow.

She wanted to ring Bernard and shout at him, scream abuse for coming back into their lives, sending Dan on a mission doing God alone knew what. But she couldn't. She wasn't supposed to ring anyone. Even the head of MI5. That was what Dan had asked, and that was what she'd promised.

Trembling, nauseous with anxiety she turned on the TV, desperate for some distraction. She was staring at the news, not taking in a word, when a car drove slowly past. She didn't hear it. Nor did she hear the light footsteps outside as a man checked her number plate. And made a phone call.

CHAPTER TWENTY-FOUR

Monday 2 February

The room Dan was brought into was painted battleship grey and furnished with two desks facing one another. A pair of battered filing cabinets that looked as though they'd been there since time began stood to one side. The walls held maps of Moscow and a portrait of the Prime Minister. Another of Putin. It reeked of cigarettes.

A man in police uniform sat behind one desk, smoking. He was overweight and his jacket was tight across his chest and arms. Late forties or so. Pale face, pudgy fingers. Grey hair, close cropped. He didn't say anything. Just looked at Dan.

Dan didn't say anything either. He went to the window and looked out to see an ice-packed car park, and beyond that, what looked like office buildings and a snow-covered church tower. He had no idea where he was. Or what they were going to do with him. He felt dirty and tired after a night in a cell, his muscles aching.

He heard someone enter the room behind him, and turned to see the old man enter the office, leaning on his walking stick. He wore a grey suit and shirt and smart black shoes. His eyes glittered as he surveyed Dan. He might have been old but somehow his intellectual energy made him seem much younger.

'Good morning,' he said to Dan in English, perfectly polite.

'Have you contacted the British Embassy yet?' Dan demanded, wanting to keep up his camouflage of innocent businessman abroad, even if it was shaky.

'No.'

'Why not?'

'Why does a British high performance instructor flee from our security services?'

'I wasn't fleeing. I just drive fast.'

The old man arched his eyebrows, threadbare wisps of grey. 'You certainly do that.'

'You can't keep me. I've done nothing wrong.'

'Aside from driving dangerously, endangering pedestrians as well as other drivers. It's a miracle you didn't kill someone.'

Dan gave a snort. 'I'm a professional, trained to the highest level to drive in complete safety . . .' He went on to give a mini lecture on his driving abilities, maintaining his cover and detailing his expertise in teaching police and ambulance drivers how to drive excessively fast in the safest way possible on public roads. It was the job he used to do before he started with DCA & Co.

'Yes,' the old man said. 'We checked with your colleague in London.'

Bob Stevens, Dan's allocated cover. He wondered if Bob had had to bring in backup yet, or if he was fending off the Russians

OK on his own. He'd spoken to Bob before he'd flown out, to cross a few t's and dot some i's and now he hoped it was enough.

'What's going on?' Dan continued playing the injured tourist. 'Why am I here?'

'Where is Ekaterina Datsik?'

'Who?' Dan looked blank.

The old man clicked a finger at the policeman who rose and passed Dan a handful of photographs. They showed the bar at the Radisson, Ekaterina and Maria talking to two young men, and then another handful of photographs of Ekaterina coming to sit with Dan.

'Oh,' he said. 'I didn't know her name. She picked me up.' He gave a wry smile. 'I'd heard Russian hookers were good-looking but not *how* good-looking.'

'She is not a prostitute.'

'Oh,' Dan said again. Once again, he kept his expression blank.

'Why did you meet her at St Clement's Church?'

'She suggested it.'

The old man stared at him.

'She's a beautiful woman,' Dan sighed. 'I would have met her in a crypt if she'd asked.'

'You are married, yes?'

Dan's mind streaked like lightning through the replies he might give. He wanted to protect Jenny but he didn't want to be caught in an outright lie. And now he knew Ekaterina had been under surveillance, no doubt followed to St Clement's Church, there was no reason for him to believe their conversation hadn't been listened to. But his legend was that he was single. His stomach hollowed. If he admitted he was married, he'd be flying into uncharted territory. *Please God, Jenny and Aimee were safely at Max's cottage.*

'She is an accountant,' stated the old man conversationally. 'Local farmers and beekeepers.'

Dan's skin turned cold.

The old man had used the exact words Dan had spoken to Ekaterina. Proving that he'd heard everything he and Ekaterina had said. The old man knew Dan was a spy of some sort and was letting him know that he knew.

Ekaterina: *Edik Yesikov secretly sent two agents to your country last week.*

Dan: *How do you know this?*

'Where do you live?' the old man asked, flicking through Dan's passport.

Dan gave him his cover address in Ealing.

More questions followed about Dan's job, where he went to school, university, his hobbies and interests, all of which he had to cobble together with his real life because his legend wasn't extensive. Dan couldn't understand what was going on. The old man hadn't asked for his real name or confronted him. What game was he playing? Then the old man turned to ask about Dan's family.

'No children,' Dan lied, perfectly calm. 'We've been trying, but no luck yet. Now, look. I don't know what all these questions are about. I know my driving got up your nose, but you can't detain me indefinitely.'

'Do you know Jane Sykes?'

Ekaterina had said Jane Sykes was a British journalist and Dan frowned, pretending to search his memory. 'I think Ekaterina mentioned her, but I can't be sure.'

'And Zama Kasofsky?'

Dan kept frowning. Having had his conversation with Ekaterina recorded, he knew he had to stick close to the truth. 'She said something about Edik Yesikov's interest in these people.'

The old man gave a nod as though to say *Yes, that's what she told you.*

'Your wife,' said the old man. 'She used to work for McInley and Krevingden?'

Dan stared at him, fear tingling along his veins. *Leave my wife out of this!*

'How long did she work for them?' the old man pressed.

Calmly, Dan said, 'I am not saying another word until you get me a lawyer.'

Long silence.

The old man gazed at Dan, wrinkled and hunched, frail with age, but his eyes were alive and active as a man in his twenties. 'What do you know about Russia?' he asked.

Dan waited a time, and finally said, 'As much as anyone who listens to the news.' He was cautious. The last thing he needed was to get into a political debate.

'What do you think will happen when Mr Putin dies?' The old man was watching him carefully.

'There's no risk of that, is there?' Dan said, startled by the question. 'He's very fit for his age. At least that's how the photographs depict him. Strong and healthy.'

'He's a strong man,' the old man agreed. 'That's why he is so popular with the people. Why they stood shoulder to shoulder with him when he brought Crimea and Sevastopol home again, to Russia.'

Dan wasn't surprised at the man's imperialistic attitude, but it made him wonder if the old man was truly patriotic or if, deep down, he was as cynical as some of his countrymen.

'When Mister Putin goes, we will need another strong man to take his place. A man who loves Russia in his heart, and who they can trust and depend upon to look after them.'

Dan stared. Was he talking about Edik Yesikov? He said, 'Do you have anyone in mind?'

The fierce blue eyes fastened on Dan's face. 'Perhaps,' he said.

The old man held Dan's eyes for a few seconds longer. Then he turned his head and spoke to the policeman briefly in Russian, who responded with, '*Da, ser.*'

The old man walked out of the office. Baffled, Dan watched him go. He couldn't work him out. Was he an ally or an enemy? Ekaterina had been shot, but he'd escaped without injury. Why? Had he met the old man when he was last in Russia? Was the old man a double agent of some sort? His mind flew over various scenarios but he quickly brought himself back on track because from the way the old man had treated him, like a stranger, he was fairly certain they hadn't met before.

Who was Zama Kasofsky? Ekaterina had told him that Edik Yesikov had sent two agents to Britain to find a British journalist, Jane Sykes, because she knew where to find Kasofsky. Was he a whistleblower? They wouldn't be the first Russian informant to flee to the UK. Dan ran a hand over his head. How was Jenny involved in all this? Was Zama Kasofsky one of her old clients? Were McInley and Krevingden, Jenny's old employers, involved somehow? He couldn't think how else she'd be entangled in whatever was going on.

The policeman's mobile rang. He spoke briefly. Then he looked at Dan and said, 'Come.'

He led Dan back to his cell.

CHAPTER TWENTY-FIVE

Lucy called Dan's office but he was apparently out for the day – back tomorrow – and all she could do, yet again, was leave a message. Where was Dan? What was he doing? She didn't want to ask Justin Tripp or Nicholas Blain why they had a photograph of him without speaking to Dan first. She didn't want to blow what might potentially be Dan's cover. He was an ex-spook and who knew what he might be up to.

She'd barely hung up the phone when Mac announced that Adrian Calder had been officially charged with murdering his wife and children. Even though he was considered a serious flight risk as well as potentially suicidal, he'd received bail. His lawyer had obviously done an exemplary job.

'Hell.' Lucy was surprised. 'I thought we'd keep him banged up for ages yet.'

'I know,' Mac agreed. 'But the good news is that our legals say that with nobody else in the frame, we could well get a conviction.'

'What if he didn't do it?' Calder's helpfulness still niggled at her, along with his honesty with his wife about their facing potential bankruptcy. But instead of winding Mac up, her comment simply made him look weary.

'He did it, Lucy.'

She decided not to mention the other family annihilation, the Oxana Harris case near Bristol because that really would irritate him. Plus she hadn't heard back from the Bristol DI so she'd be talking out of her backside. She made a hurried mental note to chase the DI. It would be a feather in her cap if she found a connection to Adrian Calder and would encourage Mac to keep her on a loose leash rather than a stranglehold when she began full-time in CID.

She'd told Mac about the mystery man at Melted and his packages and the fact that although she'd waited until closing time, he never returned. Mac hadn't agreed with her idea of assigning a surveillance team to watch the restaurant, saying it didn't *offer good value for money* especially since they didn't know whether the man would reappear. When they'd questioned Calder about the deliveries, he'd simply shrugged.

'Gifts,' he said. 'That's all. Things I order on the Internet and don't want Polina or the kids to see. Things like a new Sonos speaker for Felix's birthday. And, um . . .' He thought for a bit. 'A gardening book for Polina. A new iPhone for Jessie.'

Each time he mentioned his wife or his children's names, his breath caught and the pain rose in his eyes.

'I even got half a dozen bottles of Polina's favourite Sauternes delivered there once,' he added.

Lucy might have believed him if his shoulders hadn't done their little crunching trick. *He was lying*. It was at that moment her mind emptied out everything but the need to know what was in those packages. Her heart thumped and a sudden energy swept through her, lighting up her mind with shimmering rainbow colours. The grey was banished, replaced by her single-minded mission; she must catch Mystery Man, she must solve the case. She was suddenly on a high, focused on nothing else.

'I'll stake out the restaurant if you like,' she offered Mac. 'I'll find him.'

Mac shook his head. 'I can't justify it.'

Now Calder had been charged, everyone had reverted to working shifts. Lucy's current shift finished at eleven a.m. and then she was supposed to be having her two days' allotted time off, and if she continued to work past eleven she would officially be on overtime. Overtime, however, was limited by Mac's budget, which had apparently fallen to below zero.

'He has a package to deliver *right now*.' She could shake Mac for not seeing how important it was. 'He couldn't deliver it yesterday with me there. Lee hasn't rung, so he hasn't been back yet. He will be there soon, I know it. Any second now. *Now.*'

Mac stared at her. 'Are you OK?'

'Fine, fine. I'm great. Fantastic.' Everything was amplified. Phones ringing, radios crackling, the smell of instant coffee. Excitement filled her. 'I need this, Mac. Can I go? I'll do it in my own time. No problem.'

He stared some more. 'Your own time?'

'Yes, yes.' She was already striding for the door.

'You're not tired?'

'God, no. Could keep going forever.'

'Keep me posted!' His yell followed her down the corridor.

Lucy ducked home to dress down. Frayed jeans, fur-lined suede booties to keep her feet warm, sheepskin-lined leather jacket. She tied her hair back with a crimson scarf and rammed on a bobble hat. Grabbed spare clothes, undies, deodorant, toothpaste, laptop, chargers, a book of crossword puzzles, another of sudoku. Ear buds so she could listen to music on her phone. En route, she stopped at a service station and filled up her car. Bought bottles of water and a variety of snacks from sandwiches to bags of Maltesers – her favourite – and nuts. High-energy food.

She felt nice and inconspicuous in her own car. The repair shop near her mum's – that the family had used for decades, being distant cousins – had done their level best to iron out the dirty great dings she'd collected on her last escapade (and where she'd first met Dan) but there was no way she'd get decent money for the Corsa when she sold it. A two-year-old could tell it had been trashed at some point.

As soon as she arrived in Newcastle she checked with Lee to make sure no package had been delivered.

'When he turns up,' she told him, 'text me immediately. I'll be just around the corner.'

She walked along Nun Street, assessing where to wait. Parking was limited, but at least the street was outside the vehicle restriction zone, even if by a whisker. At night she'd be OK but during the day it was going to be another matter; she'd have to stick her car in a car park. Her luck changed when she discovered the McDonald's on the corner was open twenty-four hours a day, seven days a week. Not only could she park her car there but it would be dry and warm, and she had an unimpeded view across the street of the Melted restaurant. *Yes!* She punched the air in her mind. She'd found the perfect spot.

Settled on a stool at the window, she drank tea, had a burger. Walked up and down Nun Street. Browsed the jewellery store, the Oxfam shop. Returned to McDonald's. Drank more tea. Played with her phone. Listened to some music. *He will come, he's on his way, I will catch him.* She was absolutely focused, absolutely convinced.

Night fell. She didn't talk to anyone except to order more tea and a sweet chilli crispy chicken wrap that left her feeling strangely bloated and heavy. Hadn't someone tried to live off McDonald's once? She seemed to recall the man who'd tried it ended up with a knackered liver and malnutrition. She looked him up on the Net, her fingers racing over the keys, her thoughts on fire.

Suddenly she came to, as if she'd fallen asleep, to see that it was morning. She hardly knew how she'd got through the night. After a walk, bracing and wet, she returned and ordered a cappuccino and a sausage and egg McMuffin.

Another walk. More tea. She had endless energy. She kept trying Dan Forrester with no luck. Occasionally she rang Mac. He kept asking how she was.

Fine, I'm fine. Fabulous.

She was glad he wasn't witnessing her hyperactive mood. On a stake-out it worked to her advantage, being able to survive without sleep, and all she could do was hope and pray it wouldn't be followed by a mind-numbing crash.

Tuesday came and went. Wednesday morning, six thirty a.m. and another McMuffin breakfast. The staff didn't seem to make much of her practically living in their restaurant, probably because she kept to herself and didn't smell or cause problems. She washed and brushed up in the toilets, taking as little time as possible in case she missed something vital.

She was swallowing the last of her cappuccino when she took in a man approaching from Grainger Street. A man dressed in a heavy coat and nubuck boots. Early thirties, sun-bleached hair, strong jawline. Bad-boy good-looking.

All the hairs on her body stood upright.

Nicholas Blain.

The man who'd shown Adrian Calder's lawyer a photograph of Dan Forrester on his iPad.

She slid off her stool at the window and out of sight. What was he doing here? It couldn't be a coincidence, surely. Carefully she inched her head round the corner of the window to see him walking steadily down Nun Street. She wanted to follow him but sod's law being what it was Mystery Man would probably arrive the second her back was turned. A lorry turned into Nun Street, blocking her view of Blain. To her frustration, it pulled into the parking bay opposite, filling her view with advertising. FISH 'N' CHICK. COMMERCIAL QUALITY FOODS.

Her brain sizzled orange and crimson. She wanted to scream. She couldn't see Blain and she couldn't see Melted any more.

Throwing on her coat and scarf, she pulled her bobble hat low over her head. Grabbed her rucksack and hastened outside.

Casually she skirted the lorry's rear, ostensibly heading for Grainger Street. Carefully slid her eyes left.

Her heart gave a single, giant leap.

Mystery Man was stuffing an envelope into Melted's letterbox.

He didn't turn round. Didn't look at her.

Keeping her footsteps steady, she walked around the corner. Waited a few seconds before walking casually back to see Mystery Man climbing the access ladder into the lorry's cab. Lucy returned hastily to McDonald's. Wrote down the lorry's details, from the company's logo – a white cockerel's head inside the circle of a blue, happily smiling fish – to its number plate.

Yes!

She watched the lorry drive up Nun Street and, with some difficulty, turn the tight corner at the end.

Six thirty-eight.

She was itching to get her hands on the envelope. Longing to see what was inside.

Six forty. Only another twenty minutes until Melted officially opened its doors.

Six forty-five, Lee appeared to open the restaurant, get things started. He'd barely put his key in the door when she was at his side.

'Hey,' Lee said as a greeting.

'Hey.'

He stepped inside and picked up the envelope. Adrian Calder's name was printed on the front in black felt pen. Nothing else.

She put out her hand. He passed it over.

'Can I get you a coffee?' he said on a half-yawn. 'On the house.'

'Another time. Thanks.'

Carefully, she opened the envelope, peeked inside. Somehow she wasn't surprised when she saw the stacks of cash, all in twenties and fifties. Around three thousand pounds in total, she guessed. All used notes.

Had Nicholas Blain come to collect the money for Adrian Calder? Was this how Calder was paying his lawyer? If so, who was providing the cash?

'Has anyone else ever collected packages on behalf of Adrian Calder?' she asked Lee.

His eyes slid away as he shook his head. 'No. It's always Adrian.'

She described Blain to him in case he was familiar, and although he shook his head again, something was off and she wasn't sure if she believed him. Was he protecting Calder? Protecting Blain? She knew of employees who were so loyal they'd lie and steal for their bosses. Was Lee one of them?

She trotted to her car. Had a quick flit through Google before ringing Mac, but it switched to his voicemail. She didn't bother leaving a message.

She'd just climbed into her Corsa when Mac texted her.

Missed your call. Where are you?

On my way back.

All OK?

All OK.

What time are you due in?

She nibbled her lip. She'd planned to stop off at the station to log in the cash, but she didn't want to stop. She wanted to head straight south, to Thetford.

Tomorrow, she told him. She didn't want him waiting to pounce on her, let alone delay her or scupper her plans. She was on a roll, she didn't want to be diverted.

OK, he texted. *See you then.*

An hour later, Lucy quickly logged in the cash before going home and having a long, soapy shower. Heaven. Dressed in a fitted red sweater, blue jeans and thick-soled boots, she shrugged on her sheepskin-lined leather jacket and mussed her hair. Looking as though she'd just stepped out of the cab of an eighteen-wheeler, she walked on to the street to find Mac parked on the other side of the road, climbing out of his car.

CHAPTER TWENTY-SIX

For a moment, Mac thought Lucy was going to make a run for it, bolt down the street, but she obviously thought better of it and she paused, watching him. What was she up to?

He strode across the street to stand before her. Tried not to think how good she looked. Then he took in her tote bag.

'Going somewhere?'

'Gosh,' she said, widening her eyes. 'How did you guess that? You must be a detective.'

'Seriously, Lucy.' He fixed her with a hard glare. 'I know you're still on your allotted time off, but since you're not actually taking time off and are working the Calder case I need to know what you're up to. It's not that I don't trust you, I just want to make sure you're on the radar and keeping safe, OK? And I can't do that if I don't know where you are.'

Lucy was looking past his shoulder and wouldn't meet his gaze.

'Also,' he went on, 'I don't appreciate your telling the DCS that you're due in tomorrow only to have him tell me that you're actually downstairs logging in some cash from your stake-out. In future, when I ask you what you're doing, I want you to tell me, not fob me off.'

'Take a chill pill, would you?' Lucy gave him a look of contempt. 'You're not my mother.'

'No,' he snapped. 'Thank God. But I will be your boss in ten days' time and –'

'Eleven,' she said.

'What?'

'I start on Monday the sixteenth. It's Wednesday the fourth today, so that makes it eleven days. Unless you're counting today, of course, which would make it twelve. Meantime, Jacko's my boss, and I start my shift tomorrow at seven a.m. and finish at four. What I get up to today is my business.'

'It's not if you're fucking *working*, Lucy. You're running around like some sort of demented Lois Lane –'

'Isn't she a journalist? I'm not a journalist.'

He felt like tearing his hair. 'You know what I mean.'

She raised her eyebrows. 'Do I?'

God give me strength . . . 'Are you going to be like this when we're working together?' He could hear the frustration in his voice but he couldn't seem to help it. She drove him nuts.

'Like what, sir?' She gave him a pretty smile and lifted her tote, indicating she was ready to leave.

Insufferable, he thought, but instead he said, 'Insubordinate.'

Her eyes flashed.

'You want me to kowtow?' she snapped. 'Salute you at every turn? Sure, I can do that.' She executed a smart salute, worthy of a drill sergeant.

'No,' he ground out. 'I just want to know *where you are going.* I do not want to hear you've gone missing, been kidnapped or shot at, without knowing roughly which hornet's nest you've prodded.'

'OK, OK.' She held up a hand. Dropped her head. He saw her take a breath. Noted her reluctance to speak. What on earth was she going to say?

'I'm heading to Thetford, OK?' she told him. 'I want to check out Fish 'n' Chick. Talk to the driver of the truck that delivered Adrian's envelope full of cash.'

She shifted from foot to foot, suddenly anxious, and with a flash of perspicacity he realised she was waiting for him to protest, to stop her going, maybe even give someone else the task.

'I see,' he said.

Another silence. Mac looked at Lucy and she gazed at her boots.

If he stopped her going, he thought, she'd resent him and probably make his life hell. If he let her go and she trod all over Norfolk constabulary, stirring up God knows what muck and mess, they'd give him hell. Not a great choice, and here she was scowling at her feet like a furious child waiting to be grounded, and it was all thanks to him.

He let out a breath he hadn't realised he'd been holding. 'That sounds like a good plan,' he said, carefully neutral. 'You're taking your car?'

Her head shot up. She stared at him in surprise. 'You'll let me go?'

'Keep a record of your mileage,' he told her. 'Log your fuel receipts along with any other expenses. And keep me informed. Because unless you do, I won't give you half as much leeway next time, OK?'

She was still staring at him as though she couldn't quite believe her ears. 'Let's use this as a tester,' he told her. 'If you can manage to report regularly to me, and not go on any wild goose chases without letting me know, then maybe we can forge a good working relationship and build a good rapport to our mutual benefit. OK?'

God, now he sounded like an HR manager.

'OK,' she said. She raised her tote bag, took a couple of steps down the street. Her body language had shifted subtly, come alert. She reminded him of a hunting dog on the scent, wanting to get away before its owner grabbed it and stuck it back in the kennel.

He stepped aside, hands open, letting her know she could go.

She looked at him, deep brown eyes holding his.

'Thanks,' she said. And she smiled. A megawatt smile that lit her face as brightly as the sun emerging from behind a thunder-cloud.

Impossible for Mac not to smile back.

He continued to smile like some kind of halfwit for the rest of the day.

CHAPTER TWENTY-SEVEN

Two p.m. and Lucy was deep in the Norfolk countryside. Lots of flat land, open spaces and big skies. Not much traffic. She pushed her little Corsa harder, ignoring the rattle that accompanied her increased speed. The car was overdue its 60,000-mile service, that was all. Once she got the filters changed, oil, fuel, air, whatever, gave it a bit of TLC, it would be fine. She hoped. She'd bought it from one of her mother's friends for just under five thousand pounds three years ago and so far hadn't had any trouble, but the more it rattled, the more she became convinced it might be terminal. She should get it to a garage as soon as possible.

Not long later, she drove past a chicken farm. Rows upon rows of low-slung barns with huge silver feed hoppers at each end. The grass in between was neatly trimmed, the whole place immaculate. Three miles later she came to a factory and processing plant. Industrial buildings, an office block, a forecourt with two trucks busy loading up, car parking for a couple of hundred people.

Just past the factory stood a pair of wrought-iron gates, beyond which was a lake and beyond that a mansion with huge mullioned windows, turrets and towers. Great Huntingdon Hall. Where, if Wikipedia was correct, the owner of FISH 'N' CHICK resided. Obviously sales of fish and chicken were doing well if they could afford to pay the heating bills.

She returned to the factory. Parked in a slot marked VISITORS. Headed for reception. Lots of posters on the walls showing happy chickens knee deep in straw (did chickens have knees? she wondered), on grass, in the sunshine. Apparently the company provided raw and cooked portions of poultry and fish to hotels, restaurants and airline caterers throughout the UK. Lucy ran her eye down a long register of satisfied customers and was disillusioned to see her favourite gastro pub listed, which meant the delicious chicken and leek pie she always ordered wasn't home-made after all but mass-produced in a factory in Norfolk.

Lucy showed her warrant card to the receptionist and asked to see whoever was in charge of the company's transport, drivers and deliveries. Three minutes later the transport manager scurried inside; a compact woman called Nina with tight curly hair and a worried expression. She looked confused when she saw Lucy. 'I was told someone was here from the police?'

Obviously Nina hadn't considered that she might be meeting a detective in plain clothes. Lucy showed her warrant card.

'Oh,' said Nina. 'How can I help?'

'I want to know who was driving one of your trucks earlier today.' Lucy recited Mystery Man's number plate.

'That's Boris's truck.' The worry increased. 'What's happened? He hasn't called in or anything. Has there been an accident?'

'No accident,' Lucy assured her. 'Is Boris around? I'd like to speak to him.'

'He's not due back until later today. But I'll check. Please, follow me. Everything's in the office.'

The office was a Portakabin set to one side of the forecourt and opposite the loading bay. Two desks, two computers. Time sheets and rosters covered the walls.

'He hasn't done anything wrong, has he?' The worry was almost palpable.

'If you could tell me when he's due back?'

'Of course. Sorry.' Nina went to a chart on the wall and ran her finger down a column. 'Five o'clock. Give or take an hour. It totally depends on the traffic out of Nottingham.'

'What's Boris's surname?'

'Gol . . . something. I can never get it right. Hang on a sec . . .' Nina went to her computer and clicked her mouse a few times, scanned the screen.

'Golubkin.' She spelled it out.

Lucy frowned. 'Where's he from?'

'Russia. Moscow, I think.'

Vivid green and blue ran like rivers through Lucy's brain, connecting, linking and breaking apart again.

'Would you like me to call him?' Nina asked. 'Let him know you're here?'

'No. I'll wait until he arrives. If you could tell me how long he's worked here? What checks you undertook before employing him? Where he lives, when he came to the UK . . .'

Nina did her best but Lucy could tell she was terrified of stuffing up in some way, either dobbing Boris in or creating something the police might take the wrong way. A typical response from someone trying to protect someone they liked, and one that Lucy was used to, but it was interesting to see Nina thought that Boris was an OK bloke and not a total shyster. Which put a keen twist on the situation because she'd assumed Boris was dodgy through and through and here he was, presenting as an upstanding truck driver with a great sense of humour, a lovely wife, three great kids and a Labrador called Orlaf.

All rather confusing, if she was to be honest.

Along with Nicholas Blain. She kept picturing his relaxed and assured walk, his murky green eyes. He was involved in all this too. How? She recalled his spark of interest when she'd said she was on Calder's investigative team. The way he hadn't answered her question when she asked if he knew Adrian Calder. The fact he had a photograph of Dan Forrester. And then there was the way he'd vanished on her. Like a professional. Like someone who did it all the time. Perhaps he was a spook, like Dan used to be?

She got the sense she was slipping below the surface of something frighteningly complex, with tendrils that stretched further than she could imagine. Out of nowhere she heard Adrian Calder's voice. *Polina loves the snow. She wants to take the kids to Russia next Christmas.*

Russia, she thought. The case is all about Russia.

'Excuse me? Hello?'

Lucy came to as she heard Nina speaking. 'Yes?'

'Can I get you a coffee or anything while you wait?'

'Coffee would be great.'

While she sat waiting for Boris Golubkin she trawled the Internet on her phone, checking out the company, its directors and policies. Then she leaned back and half-closed her eyes, putting everything she knew together. Irene Cavendish, mother to Polina, grandmother to Jessie, Felix, Sofia and little two year-old Tasha. The photographs Irene had shown her of piles of corpses, all carelessly heaped on top of one another in the snow.

This was life for us. Fear. Lies. Terror. Death camps. Polina is twenty times the woman of you. She knows the value of her life.

Then there was the elusive Zama, who had made Justin Tripp flinch.

And what about the couple who had frightened Irene so much? The well-dressed couple on her doorstep? Ivan and Yelena Barbolin?

They say they are friends of Polina's. I've never see them before.

Lucy continued to think, her head kicked back against the wall, staring at the lists of rosters as she listened to Nina instructing, coordinating, getting trucks into Gatwick and out of Heathrow, to chains of pubs and hotels in time for wedding parties and conferences.

When Boris arrived it was dark. Nina pointed out his lorry, parked at the far end of the forecourt. 'He has an early pick-up tomorrow,' she said.

'Will he come in here?'

'He has to sign in. Yes.'

Lucy stayed where she was, head back, legs stretched out, seemingly half asleep.

When Boris opened the door he was already starting to talk to Nina, his big round face relaxed and warm but the second he saw Lucy, his whole body tensed. He snapped his mouth shut.

'Hi, Boris,' she said.

For a moment, from the way his eyes flickered past her to the window, then to the side, she thought he might flee, but he didn't move. He stood with one foot inside the Portakabin, the other on the step outside, his hand on the door handle. Half-in. Half-out. Frozen.

'I just wanted to tell you that your delivery went OK.' Lucy stretched and yawned. 'The one received by the Manager of Newcastle's Melted at six thirty this morning.'

Nina looked between them, tense and uncertain. Loyal to her employee but also wanting to do The Right Thing.

The seconds ticked past.

Boris licked his lips.

'What was in the envelope, Boris?' Lucy asked.

As soon as she said the word *envelope* he reached into his jacket and pulled out a phone. Dialled.

'I'm not sure if I want you to do that,' Lucy jackknifed to her feet but he didn't pause. He started to speak into the phone. In Russian. Rapidly. His tone was urgent.

'Hey,' she said. 'Hang up, Boris.'

He spoke faster, his eyes fixed on her as she approached.

Then he stopped speaking. Hung up.

To her surprise, he offered her his phone.

She took it and checked the last number dialled, a landline. The name listed was *Aleksandr Stanton.*

'You rang the owner of the company?'

He sent Nina an imploring look. Nina sent a panicky one back. The atmosphere was tense and uncertain. Boris remained half-in and half-out of the Portakabin and when the desk phone rang, they both jumped. Nina answered it.

'Oh,' she breathed. Her body seemed to collapse in on itself. 'OK. Yes, yes.' Her eyes flicked to Lucy then back. 'Yes. OK.'

Nina looked at Boris, then Lucy. She said, 'Mr Stanton's on his way.'

From the way Boris and Nina slumped in relief, the fact Mr Stanton was coming was a Good Thing.

'How long until he gets here?'

'Oh.' Nina looked surprised she should ask. 'A couple of minutes. That's all.'

'Great.'

They stood resembling some strange tableau until the desk phone rang again, someone complaining about a late delivery. The atmosphere relaxed a fraction as Nina became absorbed. Boris eased his position so that he stood outside the Portakabin. Lucy stayed still, watching both of them.

The sound of a powerful engine came from the forecourt. Boris turned his head expectantly.

The engine was switched off.

Quiet.

The slamming of a car door. Rapid footsteps.

Aleksandr Stanton strode into view, a tall and lean figure clad in a beautifully cut dark suit with a bright white shirt and red silk tie with a diamond stud. Shiny shoes. Manicured hands. Not a hair out of place. Late fifties, Lucy guessed, or a very fit sixties. He looked as though he worked out, or went running a lot. He had that sinewy, hungry look of a marathon runner. He came to Boris and stopped. Looked at Lucy then at Nina and back to Boris. He stood there almost quivering, assessing the situation like a bird of prey before it struck.

'What's going on?' he said. His English was cut-glass. Public school.

Lucy introduced herself. 'I want to ask Boris about a delivery he made in Newcastle this morning.'

'What delivery?'

'He dropped off an envelope to a Melted restaurant in Newcastle. It was addressed to Adrian Calder. I'm one of the investigating officers –'

'You're trying to find who killed Polina and the children?' He cut over her.

She blinked. 'We're trying to find answers, yes.'

He held up a hand and said something to Boris in Russian, who immediately ducked his head and scuttled away.

'Hey!' Lucy stepped forward. 'I want to talk to –'

'It's me you need to speak to,' Stanton spun round to face her. 'Boris only does as I tell him. Is the Corsa yours?'

'Yes.'

'Follow me.'

Without waiting for her response, he strode to his vehicle, a hulking great SUV of some sort. He didn't wait for her to climb into her car, just took off. She had to scramble to follow him. The journey took less than three minutes, most of that spent waiting for the pair of electronic wrought-iron gates to open to Great Huntingdon Hall. Inside the house, he rang a bell on a rope. A young woman appeared in a black-and-white uniform.

'Yes, sir?'

'Is the fire lit in the study?'

'Yes, sir.'

'Tell Vanessa we'll take tea in there.'

'Certainly, sir.'

'And bring a cover for the guest chair.'

'Yes, sir.'

And three bags full, sir, Lucy echoed as she followed him along a corridor lined with oil paintings of shooting scenes. He paused to straighten an already straight picture before leading her into a wood-panelled room with gold-leaf bound books in glass-fronted cases and a carved mahogany fireplace. As they crossed the room, Lucy saw the young woman was covering a gilt armchair with what could only be termed a dust sheet.

'Please.' He indicated the same chair.

Lucy knew she looked scruffy, but she didn't think she was *dirty*. 'We can always talk somewhere else,' she offered. *Like the pig pen.*

He ignored her, taking the chair opposite, one without a dust cover, and stretched out his legs.

Lucy sat where she'd been told and made a show of getting out her pocket book and a pen.

'Ah,' he said when the door opened. 'Tea.'

Lucy expected Vanessa to be matronly, maybe in her forties, but instead a lissome brunette twenty-something brought in a three-tier china cake stand covered with tiny sandwiches, bite-sized sausage rolls and home-made cakes. A big pot of tea followed.

'Please, help yourself,' he told Lucy.

'No, thank you.' She was coolly polite. She clicked her pen, indicating she was ready to start.

He didn't make anything of her refusal. He poured himself tea and helped himself to several sandwiches, devouring them in single bites, totally unselfconscious that he was eating alone.

She said, 'Tell me about Boris's delivery this morning.'

A pair of sharp blue eyes surveyed her over a fragile-looking teacup.

Lucy said, 'Boris dropped off an envelope containing –'

'Three thousand pounds exactly.' He put the cup down in its saucer with a little click. 'Yes, I know. I sent it. Adrian needs a bit of a helping hand until he gets back on his feet.'

'This isn't the first time,' Lucy stated.

'I've been helping him out since his business got into difficulties. There was a health scare at one of his franchise stores the November before last.'

'So we understand.'

Stanton shrugged. 'What's a gift between friends?'

'A gift?' she queried, remembering Calder's shoulder crunching.

Something calculating slid across the back of his eyes. 'One day he will repay me. Until then, I can afford to be generous.' He tilted his chin to indicate the sumptuous room with its gilt furniture and antique rugs.

'What interest rate do you charge?' Lucy asked.

'That's our business.'

'Not any more,' she said. 'I'm here on a murder investigation and that means I can demand pretty much any information I require.'

'No interest,' he said.

Liar, she thought. 'How many times have you sent him money?'

'Enough to help him.' He leaned forward, suddenly intent. 'Do you know who killed Polina and the children?'

'You don't think Adrian did?'

'Of course not!' He looked affronted that she should ask. 'What a ridiculous suggestion.'

She let a pause develop.

'How do you know Adrian?' she asked.

He arched his eyebrows at her. He obviously thought she should already know this. When she didn't respond, he said, 'We're related.'

Ah, she thought. Now we're talking.

'In what way?' she asked.

'Polina is my . . . *was* my . . .' He paused and tilted his head, his expression going distant. For a moment she thought he'd heard something but she couldn't think what. All she could hear was the crackling of the fire and the fat ticking of a grandfather clock.

'Your . . .?' she prompted.

He rose and walked to the wall and pressed a bell. Came back and sat down.

'Cousin,' he said.

'So you know Irene?' Lucy said. 'Polina's mother?'

'Of course.'

An emotion flashed across his face, so fast it took her a moment to recognise what it was.

'You don't like her,' she stated.

He shrugged. 'We can't choose who we're related to.'

Wasn't that the truth. Lucy couldn't stand some of her relatives and when Christmas came, she avoided them like the plague. She shifted on her chair. 'Why the secrecy over loaning Adrian money? Why use Boris?'

'Adrian didn't want anyone to know . . .' He paused as Vanessa came in, a question on her face. 'Take it away,' he told her with a flick of the hand.

Vanessa cleared away fast and without expression. When she'd left, Stanton added, 'He wanted to retain some dignity.'

'And Her Majesty's Revenue and Customs?'

Once again, the calculating look returned. 'It is Adrian's responsibility to declare it, not mine. We were doing nothing illegal.'

Unless he was involved in some criminal activity and money laundering through Calder's restaurants, but there was no evidence of that. The takings were small, matching a small customer base. She was inclined to think Stanton was telling the truth but it still needled her. She ran through a bunch of questions ascertaining that Stanton had been married for forty years and had no children.

'My fault, I'm afraid.' He was surprisingly candid. 'Low sperm count.'

Lucy maintained what she hoped was an impassive expression and remained silent. Luckily he didn't appear to expect a response and went on to tell her his ancestors were Russian. 'We're from Irkutsk originally,' he told her. 'One of the largest cities in Siberia. One of the coldest too. I like it when the easterly wind blows here because it reminds me of my roots.'

It was a wistful remark, and reminded her of what Calder had said about his wife loving the snow. *It gets down to minus fifty out there. Snow up to your armpits.*

'We come from a big family,' Stanton continued when she pressed him about his origins. 'But we were persecuted so badly many of us fled. My father included.'

His gaze turned distant. 'He died when I was a baby. My mother remarried but died fourteen years later. Septicaemia of the heart.' He went on to tell her that he'd been lucky, he'd got on extremely well with his stepfather, who'd bought an ailing chicken farm in Suffolk and rebuilt it, expanding and developing the business into a national success before he in turn died, leaving it to him. It was he, Aleksandr, who had added the fish side of things.

Something about Stanton had become almost too relaxed during his little speech, pricking Lucy's curiosity. His face had lost its mobility and was unnaturally impassive, as though he didn't want to give anything away. She said, 'You lived with your father after your mother died?'

'My stepfather. Yes.'

'Do you have any siblings?'

'No. There's just me.' Stanton's face was unreadable.

Something wasn't quite right here, but she put it down to an inherent wariness of the authorities, making him careful of giving anything away that he didn't deem necessary.

Irene's voice trailed through her mind.

So-called enemies of the Soviet people were not tolerated. People saw enemies in every room. People betrayed neighbours. Children betrayed parents.

Hereditary caution aside, she still didn't like the amount of death in the family. Both his parents – albeit years ago – and now the Calders.

'How did your real father die?' she asked.

He studied her for a moment before saying, 'He was killed in a car accident. A pile-up on the M1.'

'I'm sorry,' Lucy said.

Stanton gave a nod to acknowledge her commiseration. Then he steepled his fingers, tapped their ends together. 'So. You were asking about my business . . .'

He droned on about food products and marketing while Lucy tried to think if there was another angle she could find that might help further the investigation.

'I import from all over the world,' Stanton was saying. 'Salmon from Alaska, blackfin sea bass from the Pacific, tuna from the Cape . . .'

Her mind gave a little shimmer and abruptly she recalled the South African couple who they had yet to trace. The couple who'd visited the Calder family two weeks before their murder, long-lost relatives apparently, visiting from South Africa.

'Do you know Robin and Finch Stanton?' she asked.

Stanton maintained his easy bonhomie but his body posture came alert. 'Who?' he said.

'Irene Cavendish's nephew and niece, from Cape Town.'

'I've never heard of them.' He sounded disinterested but the alert attitude hadn't left.

'If you're Polina's cousin, then that would make them . . .'

'More cousins.' He made a dismissive gesture. Rose to his feet. 'I don't just have relatives in England but in Australia too.'

'What about Zama?'

'Who?' This time when he said the word he appeared genuinely baffled.

'Adrian mentioned him the day his family was killed. He was worried about him.'

He frowned for a moment before shaking his head. 'I don't know of any Zama. How strange. I can't think who he might be referring to. Now, if you'll excuse me, it's getting late and I still have lots to do.'

Lucy followed him out, pausing at the antique table in the hallway, laden with silver photograph frames showing pictures of Aleksandr Stanton on his wedding day, his bride a stunning red head. Another showed them at what appeared to be an opening meet, foxhounds milling. Aleksandr in immaculate country attire looking up at his wife astride an elegant grey mare. She was looking down at her husband, and their shared smile was intimate and filled with love.

Aleksandr saw her looking and she glanced away feeling slightly embarrassed, as though she'd intruded.

'You hunt?' she said, more to deflect her discomfiture than out of any genuine interest.

'I don't know one end of a horse from the other,' he admitted. 'But Elizabeth's mad for them.'

He briskly escorted Lucy to her car. She had barely picked first gear before he'd returned inside the house and shut the front door. She was so absorbed with replaying the meeting, the extravagance of the surroundings, Aleksandr Stanton's peculiarities – was he OCD? – that she hardly noticed the car that passed her on the drive. She was aware of a pair of headlights, a dark sedan. Nothing else. And when she was questioned later she could have kicked herself for being so taken up with replaying the calculating look in Stanton's eyes as he spoke about Adrian Calder.

One day he will repay me.

CHAPTER TWENTY-EIGHT

Thursday 5 February

Dan sat on the floor, his back propped again the bunk, hands on his knees. On his right another detainee sat next to him, talking to a man perched on the end of the bunk. Three more men were on the bunk with him. Another fifteen sat or kneeled or stood. Twenty of them stuffed into one holding cell. No windows and no heating. Nearly all of them smoked and the air was foul with stale smoke and nicotine. There was a hole in the floor to be used as a toilet, where sewage bubbled up. There was no sink, no taps and no fresh water. Rats squeaked at night.

He couldn't think how long he was going to remain here. Couldn't think what the plan was. There had to be a plan, right? The authorities couldn't simply leave him here, could they? *Oh, yes they could*. Lawlessness had reached epidemic proportions in Russia, where lawyers could be jailed for testifying against corrupt police officers, judges and criminals. Take Sergei Magnitsky. He'd tried to expose a £140 million theft from his country by the authorities only to be put in an isolation cell, handcuffed, and beaten with rubber batons by eight riot guards until he was dead.

It had been documented and was in the public domain, world-wide, but the Russian authorities hadn't cared. They'd holidayed in St-Tropez and shopped at Harrods. They got away with what they liked.

Which didn't bode well for Dan. He was off the grid. If he died in this cell, his body would be disposed of and nobody would know. Dan wondered if Fyodor had managed to contact Bernard, and whether he'd remembered the code words. *Colorado* meant he and Lynx were compromised, *fast river* that their lives were in danger. Bernard would have pressed the panic buttons but if he didn't have any on-ground intel, what could he do? Since Dan's meeting with the old man, he'd been locked in this stinking cell for three days, during which he'd been ignored. He'd tried to engage the guards but they'd obviously been told not to interact with him as each time he spoke or tried to gain their attention they turned away.

Which meant they'd been briefed about how to behave towards him. *Ignore the foreigner.* For how long? And what about Jenny? Had she made it to Kent, to Max's? Was she taking Brimstone seriously? He tried not to worry – it was pointless and merely made him feel nauseous – but he couldn't stop the image of her and Aimee hand in hand and fleeing from an OMON team.

His mind continued its relentless circuit of speculation, wondering about Jenny and McInley & Krevinden, whether they'd been unwittingly involved in some scam or other; whether Fyodor and Ekaterina had got away; whether Fyodor's friend had been able to help them; whether Ekaterina had had a blood transfusion; whether she was alive or not.

Every time he thought of Ekaterina, pictured her wide almond eyes looking into his own – *Daniel, run* – he couldn't stop the emotions that followed, all of them contradictory, all confusing. Suspicion and desire. Anxiety and hunger. Guilt. Fear. Yearning. He couldn't deny his attraction to her. What man could? He'd seen the way everyone's eyes had followed her sinuous walk through the Radisson. Even though she'd scarcely been with him for three minutes at the bar, barely tasting her champagne, he'd felt possessive of her. Protective too, but deep mistrust warred with his enjoyment of her.

Had she been a honey trap and betrayed him in the past? Or had it been him who'd abandoned or betrayed her in some way? Bernard had said she was a dead agent, that Dan had recruited her.

How do you know Lynx is genuine? he'd asked Bernard.

We don't.

He flinched inwardly when one of the inmates grabbed the bars and began to yell. A guard finally appeared. The inmate spoke rapidly and the guard went away. Half an hour later the locks clattered and the door opened, and the guards pushed another six detainees into the cell, forcing everyone sitting on the floor to stand. They all started to smoke and Dan felt his lungs seize up. He could barely breathe.

An hour or so later a shout came from the corridor. Another clatter.

The man next to Dan nudged him with an elbow. Jerked his chin towards the bars. Dan couldn't see anything past the press of bodies.

Another shout.

Several detainees turned their heads and looked at Dan. A man yelled something. It sounded like an order.

The man next to Dan grabbed him and pushed him forward, muttering. Hands urged him onwards and there was more muttering as detainees made way for him. When he reached the front, the guard opened the gate and hauled him outside. Led him down the corridor and past two more holding cells, all rammed with detainees. Over a hundred people awaiting court appearances or transfer to jail.

Dan was taken to a shower room. Given a block of soap and a towel. His clothes – taken off him three days ago – were placed in a pile by the door, his watch on top. He stripped out of the thin prison suit, dropped it on the floor. Turned on the water. Freezing cold. No point in waiting. He already knew it wasn't going to get warm. Holding his breath, he ducked beneath the spray. He couldn't help his involuntary grunt. He stepped aside, soaped himself down, lathered his hair. By the time he'd rinsed, his fingers and feet were numb. He towelled himself vigorously, trying to get warm. Got dressed. Raked his fingers through his hair. Without a razor there was little he could do about his beard, but at least he was clean. He walked outside to be taken up the stairs. Through reception and outside.

It was snowing.

Not a light dusting, but a full-blown blizzard. He could hardly see his hand in front of his face.

'Come.' A guard led him to a government four-wheel-drive vehicle idling on the kerb. He opened the rear door and gestured

Dan inside. Nobody there. Dan climbed in. Waves of heat enveloped him. Blissful warmth. His skin started to tingle.

The car pulled away. He said, 'Where are we going?'

The driver didn't respond. He pressed on.

Dan looked outside to see factories and warehouses, depots, trucks. Lots of snow. He looked around the car. He wasn't locked in. He wasn't under guard. He could jump out any time. Or take control of the vehicle. He waited a while, wanting to see if he recognised anything, and then they were on a dual carriageway and he saw a road sign with an aircraft on it. Then another. They cruised for half an hour or so before taking an exit signed with an aircraft. Dan's heartbeat increased. He sat back, hoping and praying, and when the driver eventually pulled up outside the departures doors of Domodedovo Airport, he exhaled.

The driver popped the glovebox and withdrew an envelope, passed it to Dan.

'*Do svidaniya*,' he said. Goodbye.

Dan flipped open the envelope to see his passport, wallet and mobile phone. An Aeroflot ticket to London, Heathrow. One way. He didn't hang around any longer.

'*Spasiba*,' he responded. Thank you.

He made the flight with ten minutes to spare. An aisle seat over the wing. Safest place to be. He fell asleep seventy seconds after the Airbus 320's wheels had lifted into the air and awoke on touchdown at Heathrow. Five minutes past eight in the evening.

Inside the terminal, Dan headed for a public phone and rang Bernard. He wanted to go straight to Jenny, but didn't dare.

'I'm back,' he said.

'Good to know,' said Bernard cheerfully. There was the faint sound of voices in the background, some music. Not the TV, Dan thought, perhaps a drinks do of some sort. 'Come to the office. Eight tomorrow.'

'Eight,' Dan acknowledged, and hung up.

He caught the Heathrow Express into town. At Paddington he threw away his phone – he didn't trust the Russians not to have infected it in some way – and bought a new one. He then bought a postcard of the Queen and a first class stamp. Sitting on one of the chairs in front of the departures board, he wrote his postcard, filling in the address from memory. A wave of exhaustion washed over him but he forced himself to his feet and back on to the Underground, posting the card on the way. When he got to the flat it was empty. Max had left a note, saying he'd gone to Corsica on an impromptu holiday, which was code for being called away on a mission. He was still with the Firm and was one of the few people who'd remained in touch with Dan after Luke was killed. Max had apparently been a good friend when Dan worked for MI5, and it was he who had recently helped him fill in various blanks over his ruined memory. Max had also reminded Dan of Brimstone and reiterated that if he ever needed to use his cottage, he was free to do so. And it had been Max, too, who'd offered him his London flat when Dan moved out from home.

Dan pulled a pack of Italian meatballs and pasta from the freezer and microwaved it. Wolfed it down. He desperately wanted to go to the cottage, see Jenny and Aimee, check they were OK, but he wouldn't risk it. Not until he knew it was safe.

He didn't think he'd sleep, his mind was churning so fast, but he lost consciousness almost the second his head hit the pillow, awakening to the sound of a recycling lorry outside the building just after dawn. He was at Thames House North at seven thirty. Bernard arrived five minutes later. Looked Dan up and down.

'I suppose I've seen you looking worse.'

Bernard's office overlooked Vauxhall Bridge, which was shiny with rain and already filled with commuting traffic. He closed the door behind them. Said, 'I received a phone call from someone called Fyodor two days ago.'

Dan had dropped Fyodor and Ekaterina at the market on Sunday. It was now Friday, and he wondered what had taken Fyodor so long to make the call.

'The code words were genuine,' Bernard said.

'Yes. I gave them to him.'

'Tell me what happened.'

Dan didn't leave anything out and when he finished, his old boss looked past him, expression distant. 'As soon as we got the call from Fyodor, we pressed the diplomatic emergency button. We were told you were in jail, arrested for reckless endangerment, and we were all set to create a diplomatic stink but you were released in the next breath, lots of guff about local police making a mistake, that sort of thing.'

'What about the OMON team?'

'It means someone's pulling some major strings over there. Someone right at the top.'

'Why did they hold me for so long?'

Bernard studied him. 'Perhaps they wanted you out of the way.'

Dan hadn't thought of that and gave a shiver inside, praying that Jenny was safely tucked up away in Max's safe house.

'Fyodor,' Dan said. 'Did he say anything about Ekaterina?'

Bernard picked up a pen, turned it between his fingers. 'He asked me to tell you that his sister was in recovery.'

The relief Dan felt was inappropriate for an acquaintance of such a short time and he looked away, suddenly embarrassed. Not that Bernard would think any less of him, though. Agents and assets could forge a bond closer than lovers in some cases, especially when the asset was in a dangerous position and the agent running them responsible for their life.

'Did he say anything else?' Dan asked, hoping to find out about his history with Ekaterina. Old friend or old enemy?

Bernard put down the pen. Regarded Dan speculatively. 'If you're hoping I can fill in any blanks, I'm afraid I can't help. You were off the grid back then and Fyodor wasn't giving much away.'

Dan was surprised to realise how disappointed he was.

'I'd like you to look at some photographs Six have sent over.' Bernard's voice turned brisk. 'Try and identify everyone.'

Dan nodded.

Bernard buzzed someone, saying, 'He's ready.' A brisk young woman from MI6, navy suit – *Hi, I'm Emily* – came and escorted him to another office. Offered him coffee, then sat him in front of a laptop. Put an obviously pre-selected program into operation. As a succession of portraits crossed the screen, Dan leaned back, making himself as comfortable as possible. *This could take a while.* Emily took up position on the other side of the desk, tapped away on her computer keyboard.

Dan let his mind wander as the faces paraded. Some in colour, some in black and white. Some were head shots while others included groups of people dining or at parties, others at official functions. He recognised the Russian Prime Minister but not the man he was talking to. When Magnitsky's photograph came up his intuition pinged until his conscious mind kicked in, reminding him he'd never met the man but simply recognised him from the newspapers. He settled back again. Barely five photographs on, his heart gave a bump.

There!

He pounced on the mouse to stop the slide show.

Ekaterina and Maria at a party. Maria holding a glass of what looked like champagne and laughing at whoever was taking the photograph. Ekaterina was smiling too, her hand on a man's arm. Her touch looked light, and he recalled the feeling of her slender fingers on his thigh, as warm and soft as vapour. Both women wore stunningly provocative full-length dresses, and although he knew nothing about haute couture he'd bet his last penny they'd cost a fortune.

'Who do you recognise?' Emily asked. She was standing at his shoulder. He pointed at the man, recognising him from the photograph Ekaterina had shown him. 'Edik Yesikov,' he said. Then he pointed at the two women. 'Who are they?'

'Ekaterina Datsik and Milena Zhukov. He picked them up at a bar when they first arrived in Moscow and made them his pets.'

For a moment Dan was transported into the back of the Audi and he was looking into Maria's eyes – Milena's eyes – in the rear-view mirror. *We are not prostitutes.*

'He has other women but those two have stood the test of time. He trusts them. They go where he goes. He likes showing them off.'

'Apparently I recruited Ekaterina,' he said. 'A while ago.'

Emily appraised him, respect in her eyes. 'Good choice.'

He couldn't help his next thought. *But exactly who had recruited who?*

Emily returned to her desk. Dan clicked the mouse and restarted the parade. An hour passed. Then another. He broke for a coffee. Came back. It was almost midday when his intuition kicked in again but he couldn't see why. He'd been looking at a collection of photographs taken at a ball. Carefully he scrutinised each one, checking each face, no matter where they were in the picture.

And then he found him.

The old man.

He was behind a circle of bejewelled women and men in dinner jackets and was turning away from the photographer as though he didn't want to be seen. He was younger there, in his forties maybe, but Dan knew it was the same man. He had the same upright posture, the same cut-glass angles on his face. Refined and arrogant.

Emily came to stand at Dan's shoulder again.

He pointed at the old man.

She squinted at the screen. Returned to her computer. Tapped away for a while. Turned her screen so he could see the photographs scrolling, but there was no clear head shot of the man. All were of other people, with him always in the background, never centre stage.

'His name is Lazar Yesikov. Edik Yesikov's father, apparently. Ex-KGB. He's been around for years, one of the old guard, but we've never pinged him before.' Her gaze was bright on Dan. 'Not another of yours, I suppose?'

He shook his head before quickly telling her about his being questioned by Lazar.

'Shame. He seems to know everyone.' She clicked through more pictures. Yesikov hovering behind Dmitry Medvedev. standing next to Patriarch Alexander Kalinin, the head of the Church, and President Putin. Yesikov standing over a dead wolf with his son at his side.

'We'll work on him,' Emily said. 'Get a proper backstory together.'

Dan returned to Bernard's office. Told him about Milena and Ekaterina, otherwise known as Lynx.

'You say you don't remember her,' Bernard looked at him carefully. 'Even though you recruited her.'

'Correct.'

'And she said that meeting you this time was the most important thing of her life,' Bernard reiterated, 'and that Jenny is somehow involved.'

Dan licked his lips. 'Yes.'

Bernard swivelled his chair to look over the Thames. 'Ekaterina knew about the FSB agents entering the United Kingdom. That they want to find Zama Kasofsky.'

Long silence.

'Why?' Bernard swivelled back. 'Who is this Zama Kasofsky? Why are they –'

He stopped speaking when one of the phones on his desk rang. He picked it up. He didn't say anything, just listened. Finally, he said, 'I don't like it.' Then, he lifted his eyes to Dan. 'I don't like it at all.'

Bernard hung up. He said, 'Bad news I'm afraid.'

Dan felt his stomach hollow. Desperately he tried not to think of Jenny and Aimee.

'Jane Sykes,' Bernard said. 'She was killed the day after she returned to England. Cycling accident.'

Dan stared at Bernard, nerves humming.

'We have to find Ekaterina Datsik.' Bernard's eyes focused on Dan, intense. 'We need answers, *now*.'

CHAPTER TWENTY-NINE

When Ekatarina awoke it was the intense light she first became aware of. It seemed to pierce her eyelids and drill into her brain. She moved her head to the side and lay there, feeling the mattress against her spine, the dense pillow beneath her head. She tried to suppress the whimper as pain pulsed from her stomach and chest into every corner of her soul.

She knew where she was. She didn't need to open her eyes. Hospitals always smelled and sounded more or less the same. A mixture of antiseptic, stale urine and anxiety. Fyodor had brought her here. She'd wanted to dissuade him but she was so close to death she could no longer speak. He was sobbing as he left her in the emergency room, torn between letting her die in his arms and giving her a chance of survival in hospital, but with an uncertain fate.

She swallowed carefully. Her mouth was dry and tasted sour. How long had she been here? She had no idea of knowing. It could be days, or weeks. Everything was a blur of pain and terror. The last clear thing she remembered was Dan Forrester holding her in the back of Milena's car.

Don't give up.

His voice had been fierce, as though he remembered her, but he hadn't, not really. Not like her. When she'd seen him at the Radisson she'd had trouble containing her hate. And when he'd put his arm around her waist, although her body had melted, seamlessly fitting against his, it had taken a huge effort not to slap him.

She was amazed he hadn't seen her loathing, hadn't felt it burning like a river of lava, destroying everything in its path. He'd been insouciant, almost blasé when she'd approached him, but when she'd walked away she'd felt his eyes follow her like they used to. Her body had responded in kind, her hips swinging a little more, her waist tautening. She'd forgotten how he used to affect her, how mercilessly attractive she'd found him. Broad shoulders, muscular waist, eyes grey and deep as the ocean, framed by charcoal lashes.

Milena had purred when she'd first seen him. Ekaterina hadn't stood in her way, but Dan hadn't been interested. He'd only had eyes for her, which had made her life easy since Edik had told her to befriend the Englishman. Poor Milena, she knew nothing about her and Dan, their twisted and bitter history. Dan had spoken Russian then, but he didn't any more. Strange to think he didn't remember her. She wasn't sure how she felt about this. She'd been angry for so long, nurturing her hate, that it was difficult to see past it, but life had a strange way of closing the past. She never thought she'd have anything to do with Dan Forrester again until she overheard Edik talking about Dan's wife.

She'd been tempted to ignore what she'd learned, but the ramifications went further than Dan and Jenny, further than the FSB and MI6's machinations. She couldn't turn her back. She loved her country too much to do that. And now she'd been caught out and Dan was gone who knew where, she had to find another way of reaching his wife. She had to stop this train of conspiracies from reaching its hideous destination.

Cautiously, eyelash by eyelash, she unglued her eyes. Saw a linoleum floor. A glossy blue wall. She swivelled her eyes to the far end of the room to a small table where an old man sat. Aquiline features exuding a sharp intensity. He was looking straight at her. 'Good,' he rasped. 'You're awake.'

The wave of fear drowned out her pain. She couldn't help it – she released a trickle of urine.

Leaning on his cane, he rose to his feet. Clicked his fingers. Five men appeared. Big men. Goons.

He said, 'Bring it in.'

One man vanished. The other four stood quietly. Lazar Yesikov looked at Ekaterina.

'I expect you think I'm here to kill you.'

A whimper fluttered in her throat but with a herculean effort she quashed it. She didn't want him to see her terror. She'd heard it only irritated him, made him more brutal.

'I considered it,' he told her. 'But you're more useful to me alive.'

The man he'd sent outside returned. In one hand he held a heavy iron bucket. In the other, a metal rod.

Yesikov came and stood over her. He said, 'I want you to be a warning to others.'

Dread drenched her. She clenched her teeth to stop him hearing them chatter.

Another click of the fingers. Four goons moved swiftly, pinning her to the bed. One man wound her hair around his fist then twisted her face to one side, pressing her head down into the pillow so hard she thought her skull might crack. She could feel tears trickling down her cheeks but she made no sound.

The fourth man came over with the bucket. Took off the lid. Immediately she felt a waft of scalding heat. Smelled the thick scent of blazing coals. The man raised his metal rod and she saw it had a design on the end, glowing white-red hot. It was a brand.

The whimper ballooned in her throat. Tears poured.

'Suka,' the old man said. 'That is now your name.'

Suka was the prison word for *traitor*. It was also the word for *bitch*.

He looked at the brander. 'Do it.'

The man brought the brand straight towards her. She was overcome with horror.

Not my face!

She tried to struggle, to fight, but she was already weak and barely moved against her captors' grip.

The man thrust the brand against her cheek, then tilted it to sear the corner of her mouth, then moved up to her eyelid.

The pain was so huge, so shocking she couldn't even take a breath to scream.

The last thing she remembered was feeling the brand push against her eyeball, melting it with a hissing, popping sound that would stay with her until the day she died.

CHAPTER THIRTY

Dan stared out of the window and along the Embankment, barely seeing the people scurrying beneath their umbrellas, heads and shoulders hunched against the driving sleet. He was listening to Lucy on the phone with increasing bafflement, trying to find his way through the maze of information she'd imparted.

'Let's get this straight,' he said. 'You're saying that this Nicholas Blain has a photo of me. And the man he showed it to is the lawyer for Adrian Calder, who apparently killed his family, and whose wife is the daughter of Irene Cavendish. Irene is of Russian extraction.'

'Yes.'

He hadn't told Lucy about his Russian visit, or that Jenny was in hiding. He never liked sharing information without good reason, even with the police, and unless he thought it might help Lucy open another avenue of investigation – or vice versa – he decided to keep his trip quiet for the moment.

'Ask the lawyer about Blain,' Dan said, 'and why he has a picture of me. As much information as you can get, please.'

'No problem.'

She was brisk and efficient and he pictured her vividly, her narrow, intelligent face, her vivid brown eyes. Although she'd laughed at his offer of working for the Security Service before Christmas, he thought she'd make an exemplary officer. She was tough, smart and resourceful, but most importantly, her thinking was original.

After they hung up, Dan tried to see how, if at all, any of Lucy's investigation fitted with Ekaterina and the old man in Moscow. And what about the two FSB agents? Ivan and Yelena Barbolin? Had they found Zama Kasofsky yet?

He checked his watch to see it was past five p.m. He'd spent all day at Thames House North, looking at more photographs, talking to the Russian desk, reading up on Edik Yesikov, trying to piece information together, and he didn't think he'd learn anything further. It was time for some fieldwork.

He took the Tube to King's Cross. Exiting the station, he pulled up his collar against a bitingly cold wind and walked to Kings Place and the offices of *The Guardian*. Dan pushed open the glass door, welcoming the flood of heat that enveloped him. He shrugged off his coat and folded it over his arm. Told a receptionist he was meeting the editor, and absorbed the sleek and chic surroundings, the rumble of traffic, the unobtrusive down lighting, acres of space.

He was ushered up a stainless steel and glass staircase and into an office with a glass table and two designer-style squishy chairs in vibrant yellow and blue. The editor-in-chief, John James, was a lean, spare figure with dark skin and intensely dark eyes. When they shook hands, his grip was strong and dry.

'I was sorry to hear about Jane Sykes's death,' Dan said.

'We're still getting our heads around it,' James admitted. 'Most of us cycle to work. It's made us jittery.'

'I can imagine.'

Small pause.

'So,' said James. His look was appraising. 'You want to talk about Jane's recent trip to Moscow.'

'Yes. Why she went, who she saw, that sort of thing.'

'I couldn't tell you anything in detail. She has . . . I mean *had* an apartment there, you see. She used to split her time between that and her parents' place in Chiswick.'

James gave a rough outline of what Jane had hoped to achieve, listing a handful of contacts. Dan recorded them. He didn't recognise any names.

'Did she mention someone called Zama Kasofsky?'

At that, caution rose in the man's eyes. He said, 'Ah. So you know about that.'

Dan blinked. 'You know Kasofsky?'

'I know *of* him.'

'And you know where to find him.' It was a statement, not a question.

James scratched his neck with a finger. 'Not really.'

Irritated by the man's reticence, Dan said, 'Please, this is important.'

'Look.' James swallowed audibly. 'Your lot told me not to talk about this Kasofsky. Not to anyone. You gave me the gypsy's warning.' He glanced around the office, giving a nervous laugh. 'You scared the crap out of me, to be honest.'

All of Dan's hairs rose on the back of his neck.

'Our lot?' he said.

He looked at Dan as though he'd asked something stupid. 'SIS. Same as you, right?'

'What were their names?'

James blinked. 'It was a couple. Ivan and Yelena Barbolin. They were undercover but they gave me a number to ring to authenticate their credentials. I checked, believe me. I even rang your office. I wasn't going to let them take Jane's stuff without ensuring they were legit.'

Ekaterina's voice: *Edik Yesikov secretly sent two FSB agents to your country last week. Ivan and Yelena Barbolin. Their mission to find a British journalist. Jane Sykes.*

'They spoke English?' Dan asked.

'Of course they spoke English,' James said with a touch of impatience. 'They *were* English.'

The Barbolins were good, Dan thought, to have hoodwinked James so successfully. He'd tell James he'd been scammed so he could avoid the same thing happening in the future, but not yet. He didn't want to distract the man.

'Tell me about Zama Kasofsky,' Dan said.

'Why?' James said nastily. 'Don't you guys talk to each other?'

Dan just looked at him. The man looked away, his Adam's apple bobbing.

'Tell. Me,' Dan repeated stonily.

'OK, OK.' The editor flung his hand up. 'I don't know much, to be honest. Just that Jane was friends with someone who told her a secret – and before you can ask, no, I don't know what it was. However, Jane said that if it was true, it was one of the best stories she'd ever get. Pulitzer Prize-winning. She was thinking of writing a book about it too – as it involved politics as well as being an incredible human interest story.'

'Who's the friend?' Dan asked.

The man took a deep breath, exhaled. Looked straight into Dan's eyes. 'Have you been watching the news lately?'

'Of course.'

'You saw that man who killed his wife and kids up near Stockton?'

Dan felt as though a dozen cockroaches had scurried along his spine. Adrian Calder. The man Lucy had arrested. 'What about him?'

James said, 'I'll give you the same information I gave your colleagues, OK? I told them to go and talk to Polina Calder. It was Polina who told Jane this secret.'

'When did the Barbolins see you?' Dan asked.

'Thursday the twenty-ninth of January. In the evening.'

Dan's ears began to ring. Jane Sykes had been killed first thing on Friday morning, and Polina Calder and her children murdered the following day. Had the FSB killed Jane Sykes and Adrian Calder's family? If so,*why*?

CHAPTER THIRTY-ONE

Saturday 7 February, 10.00 a.m.

Jenny poured cereal and milk into a bowl for Aimee before making some toast for herself and spreading it with peanut butter, something she usually only ate on holiday. They weren't on holiday, but the situation made her feel as though they deserved treats. They'd been here for *six whole days*. She could hardly believe it. She had to keep reminding herself of the urgency in Dan's voice when he'd yelled *Brimstone!* down the phone. That they were in the gravest danger she hadn't doubted, but the fear factor had fallen to almost zero in such benign surroundings.

In daylight the cottage was chocolate-box pretty with roses and wisteria – all neatly pruned back for winter – climbing its walls. There was a bubbling stream at the bottom of the garden with a pretty hand-hewn bridge leading to the field opposite, an apple orchard and a garden shed that contained a lawnmower along with some outdoor furniture. It felt more like a holiday cottage than a safe house and she kept expecting Dan's friend to walk in any moment now it was the weekend, and demand she leave.

She kept checking the location feature on Dan's iPhone in the faint hope something would appear, but nothing did. His phone was obviously defunct. That he'd been in peril had been evident and she tried her best not to dwell on scenarios of doom. He'd been in danger before and had come home. He'd do the same again. At least that was how she managed to get through each day and night. By having faith in his ability to survive.

She dropped a piece of crust on to the floor where Poppy lapped it up. The dog had been a godsend as far as Aimee was concerned, giving her a positive structure to the day, feeding, walking and grooming the animal. Poppy had taken to sleeping on the landing outside their bedrooms, and Jenny hadn't demurred. Having over a hundred pounds of muscular bodyguard armed with teeth and claws just yards away was immensely comforting.

She'd emailed her parents as well as Aimee's school, explaining about Dan's father's fictional illness, but how long could she keep up this particular lie? For as long as it was needed, she supposed, to keep them safe. But today, in the bright winter sunshine, it felt ridiculous. She had such a longing to go home she could scream. They would go to the coast today, she decided. Whitstable or Herne Bay. Nobody would know them there. Their little expeditions to a supermarket on the outskirts of Canterbury yesterday and Wednesday hadn't been enough. They were both getting cooped up and irritable and –

Jenny's heart just about leaped from her chest when Poppy suddenly erupted into a series of barks and bolted outside.

'Stay here,' she told Aimee. 'I'll go and see who it is.'

Poppy was by the front door, barking with such force her front feet were jerking off the ground. Adrenaline hammering, Jenny peered outside to see a small red van drive down the road. The postman. Relief flooded her, making her knees go weak.

'Poppy . . .' She touched the dog on the shoulder and Poppy fell quiet and moved aside. Jenny picked up the mail. A bill for Max Blake, the cottage's owner, a flyer for a retirement village and a postcard of the Queen.

When she turned the postcard over she started to tremble. It was Dan's writing; clear, bold and precise.

My darling,
I'm sorry I can't be with you. Wait for me. I will come soon.
All my love to my precious girls, x

Jenny dropped to her knees and burst into tears.

Dan was OK. And he was in London, if the postmark was to be believed. Please God he hadn't given it to someone else to post. Surely the fact sent it meant he was OK? She felt Poppy's head nudge her and she turned and buried her head in the dog's shoulder and sobbed. Stress, anxiety and relief washing through her all at once.

'Mummy?'

Aimee stood there, looking scared.

'It's OK.' Jenny leaned back, giving a wobbly smile as she wiped her eyes. 'I'm just having a cry because Daddy sent us a postcard. I miss him so much. Here . . .' She showed Aimee the card saying, 'I wonder if he went to see the Queen?'

'I'd like to see the Queen,' said Aimee solemnly. 'I'd wear my best dress, the one with the lace collar, and I'd wear my red shoes and put a red ribbon on Neddy as I couldn't go without *him* . . .'

After they'd washed up the breakfast dishes Jenny packed everyone into the car. Her first priority was to mail a postcard to Dan in London, and once that was done, they walked the dog along a pebbly beach. She wished she could have told Dan the number of the pay-as-you-go phone she'd bought, written it on to his postcard, but as he'd said all that time ago, what if someone was checking his mail? If they had her phone number they could find her. She couldn't email him either. If the wrong people were looking, they'd find them. He'd insisted they do things the old school way, the *safest* way, even if it seemed to take decades to communicate.

After their walk they looked around some quirky shops where she helped Aimee buy a stuffed penguin for the baby.

'Neddy and I will look after it for him,' Aimee said proudly. 'Until he's born.' Whether she'd actually give it to the baby or not remained to be seen, but even so, Jenny was immeasurably touched that her daughter had even thought of the baby. Mind you, Aimee hadn't been exactly reticent about the matter, telling everyone from the postman to her head teacher that she was going to have a baby brother soon, and that it was going to cry a lot but that was OK because Mummy said so.

They bought some sandwiches and a KitKat and ate them on the seafront. By the time they returned to the car they were windblown and tired and Jenny was thinking of little other than what they might have for supper, when Dan might come for them – maybe after the weekend? – when Poppy suddenly switched her head round and gave a low snarl.

Pulse rocketing, thinking someone might be about to attack them, Jenny spun on her heel.

She only caught a glimpse of him. He was at the far end of the car park, vanishing behind a camper van but her nerves fizzed.

He hadn't been wearing a beanie, and nor did he have a pair of binoculars hanging from his neck, but something about him made her think of the man who Poppy had chased at the house, and who had lied about staying with the Taylors in the village.

Jenny hustled Aimee and Poppy into the car and locked all the doors. She brought out her phone. Dialled.

'Police,' she said when it was answered. 'A man has been following me and my daughter. I'm scared.'

When the police car turned into the car park, Jenny drove to meet it. The police checked behind the camper van but the man wasn't there.

She thanked the police effusively and when they offered to escort her home, she accepted. Nobody followed them. Relief mingled with embarrassment. She was obviously getting paranoid.

Back inside the cottage, Jenny let Aimee feed Poppy. She felt a little pulse of affection for the creature. It was nice to have someone on their side, even if it was just a dog.

CHAPTER THIRTY-TWO

Lucy met Dan in a coffee shop in Yarm, a pretty boutique-lined town just outside Stockton and where she reckoned they wouldn't be spotted by anyone who knew them. He had called her last night, saying he thought he'd discovered a Russian connection to her murder investigation, but that he didn't want to give his information officially, was that OK? Sure, she said. Who was she to refuse a gift horse galloping up the M1?

She'd chosen a café on the high street and when Dan arrived he immediately moved them to the back, close to the rear exit and where they'd be harder to spot from the street. He was taller than she remembered, broader, but just as self-contained.

'Have you heard of a journalist called Jane Sykes?' he asked. 'She's a friend of Polina Calder's.'

He didn't beat around the bush or bother with any niceties. Simply jumped straight in. She liked him for that. She knew where she stood.

'No, I haven't,' she said.

'Can you ask Adrian Calder about her? Ask him what secrets Jane held with his wife?'

'Sure.' She waited for him to give a reason for his request but he gave a minute shake of his head. A waitress was heading their way. Gingham apron, cheerful smile. Lucy ordered a cappuccino, Dan an Americano and a bacon sandwich with lots of butter, no sauce. He obviously wasn't concerned about his arteries.

'Why do you think Adrian Calder is innocent of killing his family?' he asked. 'The media seem convinced he's guilty. Nobody else is in the frame.'

'Lots of reasons,' she responded. 'But mainly because he told his wife he was facing bankruptcy. Aside from spousal revenge, family annihilations usually occur when the husband loses his ability to keep up the lifestyle. They don't tell anyone they're in trouble, usually because they're making money illegally. One morning they wake up to the fact that they're broke, and that when they go to jail they'll never be able to make that kind of money again. They suddenly realise they're stuffed, with no way out of the situation, and they can't face it.'

'But not Adrian Calder.'

'No. Not only does he appear to be squeaky clean, but he was totally open with Polina about his financial problems.'

Dan mulled for a moment before saying, 'If he's innocent, then who killed his family? And why?'

That's what I want to find out, Lucy thought. She went on to fill him in on everything else, finishing with the Russian couple on Irene's doorstep. 'They rented a Hertz car. Ivan and Yelena Barbolin.'

Dan stared at Lucy. 'They visited Irene Cavendish?'

'She said they were friends of Polina's but she didn't know their names. For some reason, they scared her. But she wouldn't say why.'

Dan went on staring into Lucy's eyes. She'd surprised him, she realised. Shocked him, even.

He cleared his throat. 'Number plate?'

She checked her pocketbook, read it aloud. He didn't write it down. His memory was obviously better than hers.

Their coffee arrived. Dan looked at his bacon buttie and for a moment Lucy thought he wasn't going to eat it, but then he tucked in and devoured it quickly, clearly hungry.

'Who are Ivan and Yelena Barbolin?' she asked.

He gave her a single shake of the head. Obviously out of bounds. Dammit. She'd hoped Dan might have brought a new lead for her to follow, but so far she'd got zilch. Perhaps meeting with an ex-spook was always like this; a one-way street filled with traffic driving against you.

He seemed to sense her disappointment. 'All I can say,' he told her quietly, 'is that I'm doing this investigation at the behest of my old firm.'

She felt a little frisson across her skin. MI5.

'How sure are you that Calder's finances are clean?' Dan asked.

'Pretty sure,' Lucy answered. 'Why?'

'The Russians are famous for coming to the UK to launder money.'

'I haven't found anything,' she admitted. 'Nor have our analysts.'

His look turned distant and she guessed he was thinking *but it doesn't mean it's not there.*

'Any luck with Nicholas Blain?' he asked.

She shook her head. 'He says he's an ex-cop, but the only Nicholas Blain who's been employed by the police was killed when his vehicle crashed during a police pursuit in 2001. I've tried to ask Calder's lawyer about him, but Tripp hasn't answered my calls. If he doesn't get back to me by the end of the day, I'll nip round and see him. I've got his home address.'

'I'll be interested to hear what he says.' Dan's expression narrowed. 'Because I suspect Blain isn't who he says he is.'

Reaching into his rucksack he brought out a padded envelope, passed it across. Lucy flipped open the flap, and saw a black box half the size of a cigarette packet. 'A tracker device?' she said disbelievingly.

He said, 'I've programmed your mobile number into it. Mine too. We'll be able to see where the device is on Google maps, in real time.'

It was her turn to stare.

'If you see Blain's car, would you mind attaching it?' he asked.

You must be fucking kidding.

'Please,' he added.

She looked at the device again.

'It's magnetic,' he told her. 'It'll take you less than three seconds to duck down and slap it on the underside of his car.'

'I don't think I can do that,' she said.

He just looked at her.

She felt a tap of dismay beneath her diaphragm. 'I could get into awful trouble, and my boss . . .'

'Doesn't have to know,' he said. 'This is between you and me.' He leaned forward, expression intense. 'I need Blain, Lucy. Please, will you help me? The people I'm working with?'

'I don't even know if he drives a car,' she said, reluctance crawling through her. 'He was on foot when I saw him.'

'In that case . . .' He had another rummage in his satchel, came out with a small clear plastic bag and passed it across. 'Stick this in his pocket.'

Lucy held the bag up to see a small black plastic object inside, the shape and size of a peanut. Another tracking device apparently, with global GPS and the capability to report to Lucy and Dan where it was in the world at any time. While part of her was excited about being involved with MI5, the other was screaming caution. This wasn't official. Should she be discovered planting a tracking device on Joe Public, i.e. Nicholas Blain, she could be in deep shit.

'You're serious,' she said in a strangled tone.

'One hundred per cent.' He finished the last of his coffee, put his cup back in its saucer with a little click.

'OK.' She took a deep breath. Put both devices in her handbag. 'But the chances of my seeing him –'

'You'll find a way,' Dan said smoothly.

Yeah, sure.

A silence fell. Lucy fiddled with her teaspoon trying to think what else she needed to cover and not obsess over the tracking devices and their implications. Summarising the case to herself swiftly, she realised all of a sudden that she hadn't mentioned

Zama but before she could open her mouth to tell Dan, her phone vibrated. A quick look told her it was Mac. 'Sorry,' she told Dan. 'It's my boss. I won't be a moment.'

She turned aside to answer it. 'Mac, I'm with a –'

'Aleksandr Stanton is dead.'

It took a second for his words to sink in.

'*What?*'

She felt more than saw Dan stiffen.

'He was found this morning with a broken neck. He went riding first thing. The horse came back riderless, which is when they started searching for him. He was found near a tiger trap. It's a sort of jump, I'm told.'

Lucy's ears started to ring. 'But he didn't ride.'

'Why do you say that?'

'Because he told me he didn't know one end of a horse from the other. It's his wife who's mad about horses.'

Brief silence.

'I want you down there *now*,' Mac said. 'Liaise with the local force. Find out what's going on.'

He hung up.

Lucy turned back to Dan who was watching her expect-antly. 'Polina's cousin, Aleksandr Stanton, is dead,' she told him. 'Horse-riding accident. Except he didn't ride.'

Dan's unblinking eyes didn't change expression.

'I've got to go,' Lucy said. She grabbed her handbag, her keys. 'My boss wants me down there.' Her mind was already racing ahead, wondering whether she should go home and grab an overnight bag, if there would be a pool car available and if not, whether Mac would loan her his or if she'd have to drive her own crappy car, which she still hadn't had serviced.

She paused when Dan raised a hand.

'One thing you should know before you go.' He breathed deeply. 'Ivan and Yelena Barbolin. The couple who you saw talking to Irene Cavendish. They're FSB agents.'

Dan watched Lucy jog along the street and climb into an ageing Corsa with a shabby repair job on its side and rear panels. It took a couple of turns of the ignition before it started. Ever vigilant, he memorised the number plate before heading for his own vehicle, a black BMW coupé that struggled to accommodate Poppy on its rear seats, though luckily the dog never seemed to mind. He hoped Jenny had got his postcard by now and sent one in return, which, owing to the weekend, he wouldn't get until Monday. It should contain coded instructions where to meet, on which day and when, and if one of them couldn't make the assignation, the other would make sure they were there every three hours from the time Jenny stated, for the next three days.

When this was over, he'd take Jenny to Rome. Just the two of them, as it had been when they'd first met, and before his memory became ruined. Where they'd walked through ivy-draped palazzos and along streets smelling of herbs and roasting garlic overlaid with clouds of pungent coffee. Where they'd made love every afternoon. Jenny wearing nothing but his shirt at breakfast on their tiny balcony. Jenny, eating ripe peaches, juice running down her chin. Jenny, whose arctic beauty turned heads – but it was her smile, filled with a joy that poured from her like sunshine, that Dan had fallen in love with.

For no reason he could think of, a vision of Ekaterina seared his mind. He'd never seen her smile. He'd bet she looked even more devastating. He couldn't help wondering where she was now. If she was OK. If she'd survived the shooting, or not. An odd feeling of regret mingled with longing came over him as he guessed that he might never know.

Dan headed out of Yarm and picked up the coast road south, to Scarborough. He didn't listen to the radio. He concentrated on driving fast, overtaking slower traffic with precision, his senses heightened, aware of farm entrances where a tractor or an animal might suddenly appear, ready for the unexpected, reading the road ahead and matching his speed to the conditions. It didn't take long before he came to the outer limits of Scarborough and he dropped his speed, let down his window a little. He'd been brought up in Devon, near the beach, and he loved the briny smell of the sea.

As he approached Irene Cavendish's street, a car vacated its parking space just ahead. With Lucy's voice ringing in his ears – *Officious Little Bastard* – Dan quickly took it.

He climbed out of the car into a brisk wind. Patches of ice clung stubbornly to the foundations of walls and telegraph poles. To the south the North Sea rolled slowly, the colour of pewter. He pulled up his collar. Walked to the Russian woman's door. Knocked. Stepped back so that he could be seen clearly from an upstairs window, if need be.

He sensed someone looking at him. He kept his face bland, his body language unthreatening. If what Lucy said was true – that the woman had survived Stalin's purges – she'd have a suspicious and guarded nature and wouldn't take to strangers lightly.

He knocked again. Called, 'Mrs Cavendish. My name is Dan Forrester. Ivan Barbolin suggested we meet.' He had no idea if Irene Cavendish knew Barbolin, but he needed to show that he had information for her and hopefully encourage her to open her door.

A car drove past behind him. He turned his head a little to watch it disappear round the corner, and at the same time he heard someone move inside the house. Slowly, he turned back to face the front door. Left his hands open and by his sides and waited some more.

Finally the door opened.

'*Jissus*, I'm sorry mate.' A sun-browned man with a thatch of dark hair stood in the doorway looking harassed. He held a small drill and had a piece of sawdust clinging to the corner of his moustache. 'I heard you knocking but I was right in the middle of some DIY, kind of beyond the point of no return if you know what I mean.'

From his accent and deep tan, Dan took the man to be South African. One of the visiting cousins Lucy had told him about, he guessed.

'Robin Stanton?' Dan said.

The man blinked, looking momentarily disconcerted. 'You know me?'

Dan stepped forward, hand outstretched, and introduced himself. The man's grip was damp from exerting himself, perhaps, and strong.

'Nice to meet you, Dan,' Robin said. 'But I've got to ask. How the hell do you know my name?'

'I've just come from a meeting with the police.' Dan was enigmatic, hoping the man would assume he was with the authorities. 'I heard you visited Adrian and Polina Calder two weeks before they were killed.'

'Ach.' He made a disgusted sound at the back of his throat. Shook his head. 'That poor bloody family. We had no idea Adrian was so screwed up. And to kill the animals as well.' More head shakes. 'I mean, man. That was sick.'

'There are some who think he might not have done it,' Dan said mildly.

Robin Stanton looked astonished. 'You're kidding me. I thought he was bang to rights. Honest to God, I thought he did them because he couldn't keep up the living standard. And hell, what a standard. It was seriously fantastic. If I was him I'd kill myself rather than give it all up.'

A distant clatter of plates came from inside the house. It sounded like someone unloading a dishwasher.

Robin turned and yelled, 'Hey, sis. Someone's here who says Adrian didn't do it.'

No response but the crockery clattering stopped.

When Robin turned back, Dan asked politely, 'Is Irene in? I'd like to see her.'

'Sorry. She's gone to see a relative in the Lake District. We're visiting from Cape Town and she said we could use her place while she was gone. Do you want her phone number?'

'Yes, please.'

Robin had barely taken a step back when a woman appeared beside him. Same wiry build, same dark hair but tied in a ponytail. Like her brother, she wore jeans and a work shirt.

'You think Adrian didn't do it?' she said. Her gaze was vivid and aware.

Dan said, 'I believe I said there are some who think he might not have done it.'

'That is so English!' Amusement rose. 'I still can't get used to you guys, so non-committal. Look, you want to come in for a coffee? Tell us who these people are? God knows, we don't want Adrian to be guilty. He's such a nice guy. I'm Finch, by the way . . .'

Dan didn't particularly want to go inside the house, but something in the way Robin looked at his sister – with an odd kind of rebuke – made Dan accept. If they were hiding something, he'd like to know what it was.

Finch continued to talk as she led the way to the kitchen, where she finished unloading the dishwasher before making them all coffee. 'Until we came here, we'd never met any of our relatives,' she told Dan. 'Dad warned us we might not like some of them but mostly, they've been really nice.' A flash of emotion crossed her face, momentarily startling Dan. It looked like regret. 'I wish we all lived closer together,' she added quietly.

'Except for Gregory,' Robin remarked in a dry tone. He stood with his back to the cooker, his hands cupped around his mug.

His sister pulled a face. 'If I never saw him again it would be too soon. Revolting man.'

'What makes you say that?' Dan was genuinely curious.

'He's a Holocaust denier.' Finch raised her chin. 'Anti-Semitic and racist. I've never met such a bigoted arsehole before. Personally, I'd like to see him exterminated from planet Earth.'

Dan blinked.

Robin ran a hand over his head, looking uncomfortable. '*Ja*, he's not a nice bloke, that one. He says the Holocaust was just some Jewish hoax to gain sympathy. He also believes that Stalin and his cronies were heroes for their ethnic killing campaigns. He says Stalin was one of the greatest leaders who ever existed, blah, blah, blah.'

'I see,' Dan remarked.

His tone was neutral, but it seemed to act like a tub of ignited rocket fuel, because Finch spun on her heel to face him. Her eyes crackled with fury.

'Stalin was nothing but a murdering bastard. Seven million Ukrainians were starved to death thanks to him. You've heard of the Butcher of Ukraine? General Kazimir?'

Dan didn't nod, didn't move a muscle.

'He was Stalin's henchman. He was responsible for millions of innocent people starving to death.' Her body was trembling with outrage. 'And Gregory fucking Stanton thinks the sun shines out of his arse!'

Robin touched Finch's arm. 'Hey, steady sis.' She pulled away. Her gaze was concentrated on Dan.

'He's just been elected to represent UKIP in Sunderland,' she told Dan. 'What do you think of that?'

Dan blinked. He hadn't realised she was talking about the self-confessed neo-Stalinist UK Independence Party candidate. Gregory Stanton had created a storm in the press recently by announcing he wanted to stop all non-white immigration into the UK.

She added tightly, 'Imagine what fun you'll have when he starts shit-stirring in the corridors of power.'

Robin held up a hand. 'Hopefully that won't happen.' His tone was conciliatory. 'Everyone will see through him.'

Finch glared at her brother. 'I wouldn't be so sure.'

Small silence.

Dan picked up his mug and took a sip of coffee. Instant, weak and bitter. He swallowed. Put down his mug.

'Thanks for the coffee,' said Dan. 'If you wouldn't mind giving me Irene's mobile number?'

'Sure.' Robin walked out of the room to return with a slip of paper, which he passed to Dan.

Finch exhaled. She put a hand over her eyes. 'God, sorry, man. I didn't mean to rant like that but that Gregory . . . he really got to me. I can't believe I'm related to him. Fascist bastard.'

Although she'd apologised for her outburst, Finch didn't look him in the eye again.

CHAPTER THIRTY-THREE

From her bedroom window, Irene watched Dan Forrester disappear around the corner. He was a nice-looking man. Very self-contained. She'd seen the way he'd stood on the doorstep, not too close, but not too far away either. Respectful and polite. She would have liked to have met him, spoken to him about the people who believed her son-in-law hadn't killed his wife and children, but now was not the time. She was glad her nephew and niece had been here to cover for her.

She walked back downstairs.

'Thank you,' she said.

'Not a problem,' Robin said.

Why Timur and Michaela had called their children after birds, Irene couldn't think. Robin and Finch. To her it was ridiculous and showed a nonsensical side to her brother she didn't particularly care for, but that was Timur for you – intense and intelligent but occasionally extremely silly. He'd left Russia fourteen years after Irina, aged twenty-four. He hadn't gone straight to South Africa, but had come to England first to visit her. They'd had a spectacular row, but despite the fallout, which even now could make her weep if she dwelled on it for too long, Timur wasn't a bad man.

She battled a wave of exhaustion. Robin and Finch had been out last night, to dinner and a film in York and hadn't returned until after midnight. She'd woken when they let themselves in and for a moment she'd thought it was Polina coming in late and that her daughter was a teenager and in that split second she'd been cross because her daughter would be tired for school the next day and then she remembered Polina was dead. Her beautiful grandchildren, dead.

She couldn't get to sleep again, her mind raw red and screaming with grief. She'd visited Adrian yesterday and she'd been shocked. He'd lost a lot of weight and his skin was grey and sagged like an elderly elephant's hide. His movements were listless, his voice dull. She prayed he would pull through this. That they both would. But he was in a worse state than she was. He was being accused of his family's murder whereas she, Irina, was free of any charges. But what was freedom when such a thing happened? She couldn't say if she'd stayed in Russia that things would have been better, because she knew it wasn't true.

She went into the kitchen, started washing up the coffee mugs. Finch joined her.

'Are you OK?' the girl asked gently.

Irene smiled and Finch smiled back. They had been a godsend, her nephew and niece. She hadn't realised how much she missed having people in the house and the energy they brought; their noise and chatter was a balm against her pain. She had people to shop and to cook for, to wash and iron for, and although they'd protested, she found keeping busy eased her sorrow far more than drifting aimlessly and weeping all day. She'd learned that years ago, when she'd fallen in love with Dmitry.

'Robin's nearly finished the utility room window,' said Finch. 'Shall we have lunch when he's done? I saw you bought a quiche . . .'

But Irene wasn't listening. She had forgotten at that moment about the cold light coming through the kitchen window, the china mugs, the soapy water in the bowl. She had forgotten that she was in Scarborough, a tourist town with sandy beaches, cafés and arcades, on the coast of North Yorkshire. Her mind had turned to Dmitry. How he and his family suffered at the hands of General Kazimir, Stalin's henchman.

She remembered how Dmitry had come home from teaching at school one day to find a large sign hanging outside his apartment block. On it were the names of his parents, two of their cousins and his own name. Next to his parents' names was written 'former prince and princess, currently not working,' suggesting they were spongers living off the labour of others. Next to Dmitry's name was 'son of a former prince, currently not working.'

All of them were then fired from their jobs. Nobody wanted a 'former' person working for them in case they were accused of sheltering enemies of the state. They struggled to find other work. Dmitry's family sold all their personal belongings to raise money for food but it soon ran out. Bread was rationed but as outcasts, they weren't entitled to ration cards. Dmitry tried to raise rabbits, but the animals died. They began living on a soup of water and potatoes.

Against her father's wishes, Irina brought them food and supplies, and tried to find them jobs. But late one night, several soldiers arrived at their apartment with an arrest warrant for

Dmitry. He was put in an NKVD 'black raven' and driven away to eventaully be incarcarated in a gulag.

Irina raced home to beg her father to help. Dmitry, she choked. Tears streamed down her cheeks.

Her father lifted an eyebrow.

Please, can you help Dmitry? she begged. I love him. I want to marry him.

He suddenly jerked to his feet. He was trembling head to toe. *Love?* he hissed. He strode to Irina and drew back his hand and slapped her, first one cheek and then the other very hard. *There's a war going on and you're busy doing nothing but fuck tsarist shits! You're nothing but a slut!*

Her head snapped from one side to the other. She thought her neck might break. For a moment, she thought he was going to kill her.

Get out of my sight! You disgust me!

She stumbled outside. Lazar Yesikov lounged there, smiling. He'd heard every word. They stood for a moment, looking at one another. They both knew that once someone quarrelled with her father it was over between them. They might as well be dead. And with Yesikov there to drip toxins into her father's ears, Irina knew she'd lost her father's love.

Yesikov raised a hand, as though to touch her hair, her face, and she felt a surge of panic and forced herself past him, running for her rooms. Trembling and frightened, she stood in her bedroom, unsure what to do next. She had an urge to flee but she knew she couldn't be impetuous. She had to be careful, as cunning as a fox, and form a plan. One that would work for her and Dmitry. She went to the window and looked out at the acres of snow and ice covering the city. The security forces guarding the house.

She put on her heavy winter coat and walked outside. When she came to the gate, a soldier barred her way. He was apologetic, almost cringing. *I'm sorry. I have orders not to let you pass.*

But I want to go shopping. I need a new dress. Some shoes.

Sorry.

It was as she'd guessed. She was now a prisoner.

Don't worry, she said. I understand. He was, she knew, just doing his job. She returned to the house. She had to think long-term. Lull them into a sense of security. Let them think she had given up. She hardened her resolve and for the next weeks plotted and laid her plans. Finally, her elder sister came to visit. While she was talking with Papa, Irina crept into the boot of her car, praying nobody would realise she was missing. When the car started and drove to the gates, the fear of being discovered made her feel sick, but nobody opened the boot. Nobody discovered her.

Her sister wept when Irina told her what had happened. *What has happened to Papa?* she lamented. *We had such a happy time when Mama was alive. Playing on the farm, those beautiful gardens, the woods to hide in, all those wild berries to pick.*

He's changed, said Irina.

Yes. Some days I think he is quite insane. And Yesikov! He is deplorable. Her sister was angry enough to use her contacts and the power of their father's name to get Dmitry released from the gulag. Angry enough to smuggle them out of Russia and into

India, where Irina and Dmitry went to the British Embassy and formally petitioned for political asylum, changing their names to escape their past. They were married in London three weeks later and when they made love, she wept.

She'd thought they'd live together into a ripe old age, growing vegetables and picking apples in their orchard, but her father's reach stretched further than she'd imagined. After she'd given birth to their child, Dmitry was killed. A single bullet to the head when he was driving to a business appointment. An assassination. The police thought it was a case of mistaken identity but Irene knew differently. Her father had got his revenge.

That's when she changed her name again and moved out of London to start anew for the second time. It seemed to have worked because her father never bothered her again.

Irene returned to the present with a jolt when the telephone rang. Finch raised her eyebrows at her. Irene nodded. She didn't want to talk to anyone at the moment. She suddenly felt incredibly tired and wanted nothing more than to sleep.

She began to move for the stairs, for her bedroom. She heard Finch talking behind her. A small beep indicated she'd put the phone back in its cradle. Silence followed.

'Irene?' Finch's voice sounded odd.

She turned and saw that Finch was looking at her, with a peculiar expression on her face.

'It's about cousin Aleksandr. I'm afraid I've some really bad news.'

CHAPTER THIRTY-FOUR

With Lucy heading south to investigate Aleksandr Stanton's death, Dan had agreed with her that he would call on Justin Tripp. Like Lucy, Dan had tried ringing the lawyer to no effect. Frustrated, aware he could be wasting valuable time searching for answers to release Jenny from the safe house – he still had to talk to Jenny's old workplace in London – he drove to the lawyer's home, a converted mill nestled at the bottom of a deep valley in the North Yorkshire moors.

He found Tripp kneeling in a barn with his left hand clutching the wool of a ewe's back, the other inside her uterus.

'Your wife said I would find you here,' Dan said.

'Hang on, would you?' The lawyer's facial muscles were scrunched in concentration. 'It's got elbow lock. I've had to push the lamb slightly back to extend the legs . . . Hang on girl . . . We're nearly there . . .'

Dan watched silently as Tripp helped the ewe give birth to what appeared to be a healthy male lamb. While the ewe made *hunka-hunka* noises over her new charge, Tripp swiftly gave her an injection of long-acting antibiotic.

'Always do that after an assisted birth,' he told Dan cheerfully. 'Now, let me wash my hands, and then you can tell me what you're doing here.'

Dan followed the man into a stone-walled room with a tin sink where he lathered his hands and arms, cleaning them of mucus and blood before drying them on a faded green towel hanging on a hook. Then he took off his apron and said, 'Right. Fire away.'

'I want to know who Nicholas Blain is. And why he's got a photograph of me.'

Tripp stared at Dan. He said, 'Who are you? And who is Nicholas Blain?'

Dan felt completely wrong-footed. He didn't think the man was a good actor. He simply hadn't a clue.

Dan said, 'Nicholas Blain met you at Middlesbrough Police Station last Saturday. Constable Lucy Davies saw him show you a photograph of me on an iPad.'

The man's eyes flickered to Dan and away several times, indicating he was thinking, assimilating information. Finally, recognition dawned. He'd put the photograph together with the man standing before him.

Dan said, 'I take it Blain isn't his real name. What is it?'

Tripp shook his head. 'Sorry. I can't say anything more.'

Dan stepped close to him. Tripp wasn't very tall, maybe five six or seven, but he held his ground.

'Perhaps if you could tell me how you found me?' Tripp asked. 'My private address isn't publicly listed.'

'Sergeant Lucy Davies gave it to me.'

'Why don't I ring her,' Tripp suggested. 'And she can explain why you're here.'

Dan took a step back and folded his arms. 'My name is Dan Forrester.'

'Yes,' he said. He didn't appear frightened or unnerved in any way but looked at Dan, openly curious. 'Look, I'd really like to help you, but I still can't say anything.' He sounded sincerely apologetic. 'Client confidentiality is all very well, but sometimes it can be a real double-edged sword.'

'What do you mean?' Dan wanted to ask if he knew of Jenny, but he dreaded saying her name. He wanted to protect her, not draw attention to her.

'Sorry . . .' Tripp shook his head.

'How do I find Blain?'

Tripp frowned as he thought further. 'I suggest you go and talk to Adrian Calder.'

Dan was opening his mouth to ask another question but Tripp forestalled him. 'I'll give you his phone number, OK? That's as much as I can do. He's currently on bail but whether he'll talk to you or not is another matter.'

'You can't tell me where he is?'

'Good God, no. I might as well chuck in my job if I did that.'

Dan started punching Calder's number into his phone. 'Do you know a Jane Sykes? *Guardian* journalist? Apparently she was a friend of Polina Calder's.'

The lawyer shook his head. 'Sorry.'

As Dan walked for his car, Tripp called after him, 'Good luck.'

Adrian Calder's phone was on voicemail so Dan put one of Bernard's trusty bloodhounds on his trail to find out where he was. He hadn't gone home, apparently, no doubt because the second he did the media would camp on his doorstep. Calder would have to keep the police informed of his whereabouts, so it shouldn't take long, and not for the first time Dan wished he still worked for the Firm. It would have saved a lot of time if he could have gone to the police station, shown them his ID card and got the information first-hand.

He wasn't sure whether to stay in the area or not, but found the financial questions concerning Jenny, Calder and Russia were chiming so loudly in his mind that he couldn't help but be drawn back to London. The fact that Aleksandr Stanton had just died couldn't be a coincidence. Dan wanted to follow the money trail of Melted Restaurants and Aleksandr Stanton's envelopes of cash to Calder. Was Stanton possibly using the restaurants to launder Russian money somehow? And could Jenny have been unwittingly involved in Russian affairs when she worked for McInley and Krevingden?

His worry over Jenny was a continuous gnawing in his belly and every time he thought of her, Aimee and the baby, his breathing caught and he'd find himself momentarily unable to function. So he kept his family in a compartment in his mind that he only opened occasionally and when he knew it didn't matter if he was distracted.

As he drove down the dual carriageway of the A19, he kept Calder's number on re-dial, but it wasn't until four hours later when he was driving through the outskirts of London that finally Calder picked up the phone.

'Hello?' His voice was hesitant and quavery. He didn't sound like the strong-looking man shown in the newspapers. He sounded a hundred years old.

'Adrian Calder?'

'Yes. Who is it?'

'My name is Dan Forrester.'

Long silence. Then Calder said, 'I think we'd better meet. Don't you?'

CHAPTER THIRTY-FIVE

Lucy arrived at Great Huntingdon Hall as the sky was beginning to darken into evening and far later than she'd wanted, thanks to having to wait an extra hour for a pool car. Her Corsa was now making awful rattling noises and she knew she couldn't trust it to do anything more than run her to the supermarket and back until she got it fixed.

A huddle of paparazzi stood by the front gate, their vehicles parked along the road, half-on, half-off the verge. Lucy wound down her window to the PC on duty and heard the whirr and click-clicking as her photograph was taken. If they managed to find out who she was – which was pretty doubtful since she was in mufti – it would give them a pretty headache trying to work out what a Middlesbrough cop was doing down here. Good luck to them. She showed her ID and the PC radioed for the gate to open. More click-clicks as she wound up her window and drove through.

Parking at the end of a row of vehicles, which included a couple of patrol cars and a forensics van, Lucy climbed out of her car and stretched. A cold wind whipped her hair across her face and she quickly grabbed a scrunchy and tied it back. She stretched again, trying to clear her mind after the four-and-a-half-hour journey.

She'd spent the entire time with her head buzzing, fighting to work out why the Federal Security Service of the Russian Federation was involved with Adrian Calder. Dan said he was concerned the FSB had killed Polina and her children, but why hadn't they killed Adrian? He'd been armed with a shotgun, had he scared them off? She'd have to talk to Adrian Calder again and ask him about it.

She introduced herself to the investigating team, who'd been expecting her thanks to Mac preparing her way, and when she said, 'He didn't ride,' they said, 'Yeah, we know.'

'So how did he die?'

'Broken neck.'

She looked at the SIO who pulled a face. 'We're keeping an open mind, OK?'

Lucy walked to a field behind the stables where Aleksandr Stanton had been found beside a jump made out of rails. Not being part of the forensic team she couldn't get too close, but she could still see Aleksandr's body. He looked diminished, small and elderly and nothing like the tall and energetic man she'd met.

'Cervical dislocation.' She overheard the pathologist talking to the SIO and moved closer to eavesdrop. Apparently Aleksandr had lain here for a while as his body was stone cold. 'Could have been here for six hours or twelve, hard to say.' He went on to say that the man's neck had been snapped either forwards or backwards, and not broken from the side as far as he could tell. As he moved away to take some more photos, Lucy puttered back to the house. Headed for the stables. She looked at the horse that had supposedly thrown its rider. It had been untacked and stood quietly in its stall, half asleep and not apparently bothered by the bustle of a police investigation.

'What did you see?' she asked the horse softly. 'What happened?'

'Do you normally talk to animals?' A haughty woman's voice sounded behind her.

Lucy turned to see an elderly woman in trousers and muddy leather boots. An enveloping fleece the colour of pondweed hung to her thighs.

'Only when I wish they could talk back,' said Lucy. She put out her hand. 'I'm Lucy Davies. I'm with the police.'

'I'm Margaret. Elizabeth's mother.'

'I'm sorry about Aleksandr.'

'Yes.' Margaret's face crumpled briefly. 'Elizabeth's devastated. But still, she wanted me to make sure Clarence was OK.'

At Lucy's blank look, Margaret said, 'The horse.' She went to the stable door and opened it, stepped inside. 'Hey boy,' Margaret murmured. The horse swung its head and nuzzled her palm. Lucy watched the woman move her hands over the horse's body, from behind its ears down its neck to its shoulders.

'Aleksandr told me he didn't know one end of a horse from the other,' said Lucy.

Margaret shot her a look. 'You met him?'

'On Wednesday.'

Margaret frowned. Before she could think any further, let alone jump to any conclusions about her visit, Lucy added, 'I talked with him about Adrian Calder.'

'Oh.' The woman faltered, put a hand to her forehead. 'Poor Adrian, accused like that. I believe he killed his family about as much as I believe he could fly to the moon. I hope you're close to finding who did it.'

'We're working extremely hard.' Lucy was careful to be neutral.

'I'm glad to hear it.' Margaret moved her hands expertly over the horse's legs, raising each foot and inspecting the hooves.

'If Adrian didn't kill his family, who do you think did?' asked Lucy.

'Some crazy person on drugs, no doubt. It's at times like these that I wish we still had the death penalty. There . . .' She patted the horse briskly on the neck. 'No harm done to you, my fellow. Elizabeth will be relieved. She bred him, you know. She adores her horses. They're like children to her.' The woman came out of the stable and slammed the door shut with more force than Lucy thought necessary. 'I don't want to speak ill of the dead, but if he'd let my daughter have children she'd find them a comfort right now. But all she's got is her horses. I like horses very well, but they're not the same as *children*.'

Her voice was fierce and filled with bitterness.

'I'm sorry,' said Lucy. She looked into the angular face of Elizabeth's mother; the old skin stretched over the bones of her head like cream parchment that had been foxed by damp. Anger radiated from every pore. At not having grandchildren? Or was it something more?

'Did they ever consider adopting?' Lucy probed.

Margaret reared back in astonishment. 'Why on earth would Aleks adopt when he could perfectly well have children of his own?'

Lucy stared. 'I thought he had a low sperm count.'

The woman gave a snort. 'Is that what he told you?'

'Er, yes.'

'The lying bastard.'

Margaret started to stomp towards the house. Lucy followed her into a light, chill drizzle. What was it with this family? When she'd seen Aleksandr he'd been strangely cautious on the subject, and now his mother-in-law was here full of resentment. Normal family tribulations? Or did it go deeper?

'Why didn't he want children?' Lucy asked. 'I mean, most men would like a child to leave all this to . . .' She swept her hand to indicate the mansion and hundreds of acres of grounds.

'He wasn't *most men*, as you call him,' Margaret snapped. 'He was highly unusual. Highly intelligent, highly successful. It wasn't that he disliked children per se. He just didn't want them himself. He was quite adamant about it. Elizabeth did fall pregnant once, you know. She thought he'd come round. He loved her so much, and she him, but . . .' Margaret's lips thinned. 'He demanded she get rid of it. Can you imagine it? Your husband doing such a thing?'

They stepped around a line of tubs filled with evergreen shrubs.

'And did she?'

'Yes. He took her to the clinic himself.' Margaret turned her head to look at Lucy. 'They nearly divorced, though. They were separated for ages afterwards.'

'But they got back together.'

'Eventually.'

'Perhaps he had a congenital disease he didn't want passed on to his children,' Lucy said, wondering if OCD was hereditary.

'Rubbish,' Margaret said roundly. 'None of his relatives have anything like that. They're all as healthy as horses. He was a selfish prick, that's all. And now he's dead.' She looked darkly at Lucy. 'Elizabeth is too old to have children now. She's fifty-eight.'

Lucy recalled a male friend of hers who'd never wanted kids but refused to tell his fiancé before he got married, thinking they'd be fine as they were. It was only way down the line when his wife started making baby noises that he confessed. They'd split up soon afterwards. His ex-wife remarried and had a child almost immediately. Her friend was still single. He hadn't wanted kids because of the financial burden, and because he wanted the freedom of life without them. Had Aleksandr felt the same? That he would feel trapped if he had kids?

Margaret paused on the doorstep, shaking her head. 'I'm sorry,' she said. 'You must think I am frightfully odd talking to you like this. I think it's the shock of his death that's made me bang on so. Elizabeth's my only child, you see. I miss not having grandchildren terribly, and now Aleks has gone . . . well, I can see how very lonely my daughter's going to be. Damn the man for being so selfish . . .'

'Please, don't worry about it,' Lucy said, and something must have resonated in her voice – she'd known people share far stranger things after a loved one died – because Margaret looked at her and said gently, 'You are kind.'

Since Margaret seemed to have accepted her company with equanimity, Lucy stuck by her, hoping for some more family titbits. They walked through the echoing spaces of a rear hall and scullery, a capacious kitchen, and eventually they were crossing the main hall into a drawing room. A very different room from the one where Aleksandr had talked to Lucy, this one was decorated in pale greens and pinks and was far more feminine. His and Hers rooms, obviously. At the far end a tall door led to a conservatory. Lucy's eyes went to the woman who was in there. She looked as though she was weeping.

'Elizabeth,' Margaret said.

She went to her daughter, but she didn't embrace her. Just stood close. Margaret might not be visibly distressed, but Lucy knew people responded differently in shocking situations and didn't think anything less of Margaret for keeping her ramrod-straight posture and her emotions under lock and key.

Lucy was so absorbed in the tableau of the two women she nearly had a heart attack when a man spoke right next to her.

'Well, well, well.' His voice was soft and deep, like molasses. 'If it isn't Constable Davies.'

She turned to find herself looking straight into a pair of murky green eyes. Strong jawline, lean body. Bad-boy good-looking.

Nicholas Blain.

CHAPTER THIRTY-SIX

'What are *you* doing here?' Lucy asked. Her voice sounded unnaturally high and she hurriedly cleared her throat, trying to retain her composure.

His eyes were cool on hers.

'I'm a friend of the family.'

'What kind of friend?'

'A friend-friend.' He put his head on one side and surveyed her. 'Why? What are *you* doing here? This isn't your jurisdiction, surely?'

It was none of his business but she didn't want to alienate him. She said, 'My boss sent me.'

'DI Faris MacDonald.'

She nodded.

'Found anything for him?'

Lucy held his eyes as she said, 'Just you.'

'Me?' His tone was filled with mock innocence.

'Oh, yes.' She gazed back steadily at the man who, the last time she'd seen him, had been walking down the street outside Adrian Calder's Melted restaurant in Newcastle. 'Can I ask you something?'

'I can't guarantee I'll answer it,' he said. 'But I'll try.'

'Why do you have a photograph of Dan Forrester on your iPad?'

Blain widened his eyes. There was nothing involuntary about his expression of surprise, she realised. He wanted her to understand that he appreciated her knowledge.

'Why do you think?' he parried.

Since she hadn't a clue, she was forced to make a guess. 'Because of Adrian Calder.'

'In other words, you don't know.' Amusement rose.

'Why were you showing the photograph of Dan Forrester to Justin Tripp last Saturday?'

'Sorry.' He looked regretful. 'I'm not at liberty to say.'

'Are you perhaps at liberty to tell me who Zama is?'

'Who?' His expression appeared genuinely mystified.

He didn't appear to be acting, and Lucy wondered why Adrian Calder and Justin Tripp knew the name, but Nicholas Blain didn't.

'Nobody important,' she lied.

He gave her a narrowed look. 'Like I believe you.'

Momentarily she regretted giving him the name but if she didn't ask, she'd never get any answers.

'I don't suppose you fancy coming for a drink sometime?' he said.

'What, so you can pump me for information?' she snorted. 'I don't think so.'

'Are you usually so suspicious?'

'Only with men who give me a false ID.'

'Ah,' he said. 'I can see how you might find that off-putting.'

CJ CARVER | 277

'What's your real name?'

He put his head on one side as he surveyed her. 'I'll tell you if you join me for a drink.'

'Sorry.' She was stiff. 'I'm not open to that sort of bargaining.'

'What a shame. I thought you were more adventurous than that.' He shook his head with a faintly sorrowful look before walking away. Lucy looked at the mother and daughter, then back at Blain, dithering over who to stick with, but with Dan's tracking devices burning a hole in her handbag, she decided she'd better go after Blain. Find his car and slap a tracker on it before he buggered off.

Outside, the drizzle had turned to rain. She saw Blain talk to one of the uniformed policemen and when he moved out of sight, she went to the cop and said, 'You don't know which is Blain's car, do you?'

'Who?'

'That man, there.' She pointed him out.

'Sorry.'

Lucy trailed after Blain until, to her relief, he beeped open a sedan and opened the boot. She watched him grab a waterproof jacket and pair of wellies from the boot, put them on. When he began to head for the east side of the house, she realised he was probably going to see Aleksandr's body. Great, he'd be gone for at least twenty minutes.

Lucy sped to his car, a boring old grey Vauxhall. She'd expected him to drive something more exciting, like a sports car or performance coupé, but the vehicle could have been pulled from any police pool around the country. Perhaps that's where it

TELL ME A LIE | 278

had come from? She hurriedly made a note of the number plate. Then she ducked down and, pretending to fiddle with her shoe, stuck the device behind the left front wheel.

Easy.

Feeling pleased with herself, Lucy returned to the house where she rang Mac, and then texted Dan to tell him: *Tracker attached as requested.* She spoke with a couple of cops from the investigating team but learned nothing further. She was wondering if it was time to leave when she saw Blain return. At his side walked Elizabeth. Her tears were under control and she was talking to him earnestly. Margaret watched unhappily from the porch.

Blain appeared to be protesting but Elizabeth wasn't having it. Finally, he flung up his hands. Made a call. After he hung up, he nodded at the two women but he didn't look pleased. Finally Blain unlocked his car and climbed inside. Lucy watched Elizabeth watching him drive away. Her expression was strange. It held grief and anguish but there was something else there as well. Lucy didn't know what it was. Hope? Yearning?

Was Blain having an affair with Elizabeth? It would be a bit weird if he was – there had to be twenty years between them – but Lucy had learned over the years never to be surprised by human nature. Was he really a friend of the family? She was pretty sure he was delivering money between Aleksandr and Adrian Calder, so he had to be a trusted acquaintance. Or was he an employee of some sort? Maybe a relative?

She walked over to Elizabeth. 'Hi,' she said. The woman might have been nearly sixty and stricken with grief but she was still incredibly beautiful. Her hair was threaded with silver but still held its auburn colour and her skin was unlined, nearly flawless. She was tall and as slender and elegant as a racehorse and made Lucy feel like a Shetland pony in comparison.

'You're with the police,' Elizabeth said politely.

'Yes. I'm terribly sorry about Aleksandr.'

The woman's mouth spasmed but she held it together enough to say, 'Thank you.'

Lucy looked down the drive where Blain's Vauxhall was cruising between arches of mature beech trees. 'May I ask what your relationship is to Nicholas Blain?'

'Oh, he's a friend of Adrian's. He's helping the family out.'

'I see,' Lucy said. 'How do they know each other?'

Elizabeth put a hand to her forehead, suddenly looking frail. 'I'm sorry, but I really don't feel very well . . .'

Margaret swooped to her daughter's side and Elizabeth let her put an arm around her waist and help her back inside the house, but their body language was stiff and awkward and although Lucy felt briefly sad for Margaret, she had no doubt she'd borne her own part in their seemingly uneasy relationship.

She would, she decided, return another time and talk to Elizabeth. She wanted to iron out the family ructions. Find out exactly what had gone on. They were niggling in her mind as bubbles of mauve and white.

Her phone rang while she was walking to her car. A number she didn't recognise.

'Hello?'

'Hi. It's DI Penman here. Sorry it's taken me so long to get back to you.'

It took her a moment to place who he was but then she remembered the other family annihilation near Bristol and her wanting to see if Oxana Harris was associated to Adrian Calder in any way. She said, 'Any luck?'

'Sorry, no. But I thought I'd give you a call in case you've found anything your end.'

'Zilch,' said Lucy. 'I can't see there's any connection between our cases, except . . .'

'What?' His voice sharpened.

'Well, Adrian Calder has Russian links. And isn't Oxana a Russian name?'

'She's from Ukraine, not Russia.'

'Even so . . .' Lucy couldn't say why, but she was reluctant to drop the idea that the two cases might be related.

'Look, I've got to go.' The DI suddenly sounded harried. 'But I'll keep an open mind, OK?' Which on balance was all she could ask for.

In her car, Lucy checked the satnav on her phone and saw that it would take her a couple of hours to get to London. Jacko, with Mac's approval, had agreed that since it was the weekend – Sunday tomorrow – she could go and visit her mum, as long as she was back in Stockton first thing on Monday. Before she started her journey, Lucy checked to see if the tracking device was working and felt a little thrill when she saw that Blain's car – a little red dot on her Google map – was heading south-west along the A11. She frowned. For some reason she'd expected him to head north. Where was he going? She felt a smug smile emerge when she realised she'd soon find out, thanks to Dan's gizmo.

Lucy was beetling around the M25, already looking forward to a curry and a pint with her mum at their local, when Dan called. His voice was tense.

'Where are you?' he asked.

'Er . . .'

'Are you still in Norfolk?'

'No. I left a while back. I'm actually going to see my mum –'

'*Where are you?*'

Shit. She'd better sharpen up. She was talking to the man whose investigation was at the behest of MI5.

'I've just turned on to the M25 from the M11 and am heading west, for –'

'Turn around. I want you heading south, after Blain. He's just passing Purfleet.'

'But that's in the opposite –'

'If I was closer, I'd do it myself,' he cut in. 'I need you to catch him up. Get close to him. You've got his signal on your phone?'

'Yes.' Not that she should *use* the phone when she was driving but if this was an emergency, maybe the Police Federation wouldn't throw her into jail if she had an accident.

'Get after him. Fast, Lucy. I don't want you hanging around, OK?'

'OK.'

He hung up.

Lucy took the next exit and looped back on to the M25 to head back the way she'd come. She quickly called her mum and told her she'd be late, but that she couldn't say how late. Luckily she had a fairly chilled mother who didn't freak out and just said, *I'll see you when I see you, love, and if you're really late, let yourself in as usual.* And that was it.

Lucy booted her car until she was doing just over eighty miles per hour. She kept her eyes peeled for cameras – the M25 was notorious – and tried to keep her speed up but it was difficult. Rush hour was at its peak and the lanes jam-packed with commuters heading home. She fought her way south, occasionally glancing at her phone, Blain's signal, and after a little while realised she was, miracle of miracles, catching him up. Slowly but surely she was narrowing the distance between them which meant he had to be keeping to the speed limit or below.

Darkness had fallen. Lucy followed Blain and when they switched south-east along the M20 towards Faversham, Lucy saw she wasn't far behind Blain, perhaps five miles between them.

She'd just passed a sign to Ramsgate and another to Canterbury when Dan called again. 'I know where he's going.' His voice was clipped. He gave her the postcode which she punched straight into her TomTom. Not recommended to do while driving, but what the hell.

'Drive straight there,' he told her. 'It's a safe house. There'll probably be a blue VW Golf in the driveway. There's a woman and child staying there. I do not want Blain anywhere near them, OK? Take them out of the house immediately and drive them away. Do not let them stop to pack. You've got to be *fast*, Lucy. I'm ringing the police but I want you there first, OK? Call me the second you know you're all safe.'

Holy crap, she thought. This is serious.

'Can't you ring them?' she asked. 'Tell them to get out?'

'I don't have a number. There's no landline, just a public phone box down the road.'

'Who are they?' she asked.

'My wife and daughter.'

Lucy was so surprised she fell speechless.

'Jenny and Aimee. Tell Jenny *Brimstone* if she hesitates.'

He didn't say any more. Simply rang off.

Brimstone. Lucy's adrenaline soared. She pressed down on the accelerator. Speeding tickets be damned. Dan's family was in danger. She had to beat the cops there. Protect his wife and daughter. But *why*? What was Blain going to do? And why didn't Dan have his wife's mobile number? Were they separated or something?

A car suddenly pulled out in front of her without indicating, forcing her to brake heavily and causing the car behind to blast its horn. She broke out into a sweat. She mustn't speculate or try and guess what was going on, she had to concentrate on driving. No point in getting herself killed as she charged to the rescue.

She was doing ninety-five miles an hour when she drove beneath a gantry studded with speed cameras but she didn't ease her foot off the accelerator. All she could hear was Dan's voice, *I want you there first, OK?*

When she spotted Blain's car ahead, her pulse pounded but she didn't slow. She was fifteen minutes from her destination according to her satnav. Would it be enough time to get Jenny and Aimee out of the safe house before him? She had to hope so. Blain was driving steadily in the middle lane, doing just over seventy she guessed. She rocketed past him with her head turned slightly to the right and praying he wouldn't recognise her or her car. If he did, then she would simply have to race him to the safe house.

Heart thundering she glanced in her rear-view mirror, waiting for him to pull out and give chase but no headlights loomed behind her. Nobody drove close, wanting to overtake. She was the fastest car on the motorway and, please God, there weren't any motorway cops around.

Lucy sped through Canterbury, trying to make progress without endangering anyone. She wished Dan was driving; he was trained for high-speed pursuits. She dropped her speed further. The last thing she needed was to have an accident or, God forbid, hit a pedestrian.

At last she was free of traffic and charging along a country lane. Before each corner she dipped her headlights to see if any headlights were coming the other way and floored the accelerator when it looked clear. Soon she passed a farm then crossed a river and as her satnav intoned, *you have reached your destination*, she spotted a cottage on the right and yes! A VW Golf parked on the gravel to one side. The sign read *Sparrow Cottage*.

Lucy jammed her foot on the brakes. Left the car in the road, partly across the driveway, to stop anyone from blocking her exit. As she ran to the front door security lights snapped on, briefly blinding her and making her stumble. Blinking fast, she was raising her hand to knock on the door when a fearsome barking sounded on the other side. Christ, she thought. Dan never mentioned a dog. Let alone one that sounded HUGE.

The dog suddenly fell silent.

Lucy rapped briskly on the door. She called, 'I'm Lucy Davies, a police officer. I'm a friend of Dan's and –'

The door was flung open. A slender woman in jeans, with sheets of ice-blond hair, stood facing her. She was barefoot. A rottweiler stood at her side. It looked at her silently.

'I know who you are,' the woman said.

'Jenny Forrester?'

'Yes. What is it? Why are you here?'

'We've got to go. It's an emergency. Dan's on his way but I was closer.' Lucy's mind flashed over what she could say and decided on the fastest route. 'He said to say *Brimstone.*'

What little colour that had been there drained from Jenny's face. She said, 'We're not safe here any more?'

'No. You've got to leave immediately.'

'Christ.' She spun round and pelted into the cottage, feet flying. Lucy followed fast.

'Aimee, honey,' Jenny swept into a small sitting room with a blazing log fire. 'I'm really sorry but we've got to go. Daddy just rang. It's another emergency, OK? He's sent Lucy to help us. She's a policewoman.'

The girl was a miniature of her mother. Straight blond hair, heart shaped face, bright blue eyes. She stared at Lucy, round-eyed.

'Hi,' said Lucy. She smiled. Aimee didn't smile back. 'Your Daddy's on his way, but we have to go now and meet him. He's in a big rush, so we don't have time to pack.'

'Daddy?' the girl's face lit up.

'Yup.'

'I need to get Neddy because Neddy has to come too, he goes everywhere with me –'

'I'll get him, darling,' Jenny said. She sent an urgent look to Lucy. 'You go with Lucy now and I'll be out in a second.'

'Is Poppy coming too?' the girl asked.

'Of course,' Jenny said. 'Now *go*.'

Jenny raced out of the room.

Lucy's heart was beating fast – *we've no time to waste!* – but she kept her expression calm as she held her hand out to Aimee. 'Better do as your mum says. She'll bring Neddy in a moment.'

'OK.' Aimee put her hand in Lucy's then turned to the dog saying, 'Come on, Poppy.'

Achingly slowly, they walked outside. Aimee asked Lucy to put the dog on the back seat of her car, where the girl then joined it. It was one hell of a squeeze but at least they were in. Lucy helped Aimee to buckle up.

Where was Jenny?

As she shut the rear door, Lucy heard a car engine. Her pulse spiked as she saw headlights approaching.

Lucy raced into the house and yelled, 'Someone's coming!'

'On my way!' Jenny shouted.

Lucy glanced over her shoulder to see the headlights sweeping over the rear of her car.

She couldn't wait any longer.

'We've got to go!' Lucy shouted. 'Hurry!'

As Lucy turned she heard Jenny racing down the stairs but she didn't wait. She pelted back to her car. Leaped inside and started the engine. Opened the passenger door in readiness.

A car pulled up behind her. Switched off its headlights. The security lights continued to blaze. Lucy's stomach hollowed as a man climbed out. Blain.

Jenny raced across the drive for Lucy's car.

Blain stood still for a moment, as though he was assimilating what he was seeing, and then he moved quickly to block her.

Jenny tried to get past him but he moved from side to side. He had his hands held high and he was talking fast, but Lucy couldn't hear what he said. Jenny was shaking her head at him and looking distressed.

Lucy began to get out of the car but paused when she saw another car arrive behind Blain's. Was it Dan? She put a foot inside the car and levered herself quickly up.

Her hopes crashed.

It was a Ford Mondeo.

The same Ford Mondeo she'd seen outside Irene's house last week. Horrified, she watched two people climb out and into the security lights. A good-looking couple in their thirties, the man with a broad face and cleft chin, the woman small and lithe. They weren't wearing tailored clothes tonight, but dark trousers and fleeces, black soft-soled shoes.

Every synapse in her body screamed *Run.*

Ivan and Yelena Barbolin.

The FSB agents were here.

CHAPTER THIRTY-SEVEN

When Jenny saw another car arrive and a couple climb out, saw the man was holding a handgun low against his side, she screamed at Lucy. 'Get Aimee out of here!'

The policewoman didn't hesitate. She ducked back into the car and slammed her door shut but to Jenny's horror there was a flurry of activity inside the vehicle – she couldn't see what was happening – and then Poppy exploded into view.

Everything went crazy.

The Rottweiler went straight for the man who'd said he was Nicholas Blain. Leaped through the air to land on his back, sending him sprawling to the ground. The air was filled with roars and growls from deep within the dog's throat.

Jenny made a move to run for Lucy's car but it was already moving, accelerating away. She'd never catch it up. Instead she began to back away. Sod *Brimstone* and Dan's instructions. She was going to return to the cottage and call the police. She spun and tore for the house. Flew through the door, slammed it behind her. Locked it. Hauled her phone out of her back pocket. Dialled 999.

Blain's screams followed her. *Help! Get it off me!*

She told the dispatcher she was under attack. That the men had guns. The police told her to go somewhere safe. She left the line open. Shoved on a pair of trainers. Ran to the back door, flung it open and raced across the orchard. She paused when she came to the little bridge that crossed the stream.

'Poppy!' she shouted. 'Come!'

She tore over the bridge and into the field. Her vision hadn't yet adjusted to the darkness and she stumbled over an anthill, nearly falling to her knees. She staggered forward, gathering her momentum. When she heard something behind her she turned, fear jagging, but the form that loomed brought a sob to her throat. A choking sound of relief.

Poppy.

'Here, girl.' She patted the dog briefly. 'Well done.'

Her vision was better now, and she could see the outlines of trees and hedges, the gap where a gate stood. She headed for it, jogging fast, her breath hot in her throat, her heart pounding. She'd keep running until she found a road, a house, a service station. Bright lights and people. Safety.

She chanced a glance over her shoulder. Outlined on the bridge was a man's form, headed her way. He held a torch. He was following her footsteps, made obvious in the damp grass.

She fumbled her pay-as-you-go phone from her back pocket.

'I'm in the field behind the house,' she told the dispatcher. 'A man is chasing me. He's got a gun.'

'Stay on the phone.'

She put it back into her pocket. Kept running. Poppy loped easily at her side.

As she neared the gate, a pair of headlights came into view. A car slowed then pulled over. Jenny saw a woman's outline emerge. Jenny veered away, ran flat out for the other end of the field, towards the trees.

Thank God Aimee was with Lucy. And that the girl had instinctively liked the policewoman and gone with her unquestioningly. Please keep Aimee safe. And where was Dan? What had Lucy said? *Dan's on his way but I was closer.*

Who were these people? Was it to do with Dan's job? Did they want to kidnap her to ransom her in some way? Aimee would be a more potent bargaining chip but if she was safe . . .

And what about Blain? He was English, he'd been watching her outside the house in Wales. Poppy had remembered him, could sense Aimee and Jenny's terror, which was why she'd attacked him. What did he want?

She stumbled again. She was tiring rapidly but she pressed on. If she could reach the trees, maybe she could hide, keep as still and quiet as a mouse until dawn and then creep to safety. *You fool*, she told herself. They're trained professionals and they'll track you until they've cornered you in your foxhole. Her safest bet was to get to a village, a pub, anywhere with *people*.

She reached the trees and paused. No vehicles. No music. Just the faint sound of a passenger jet overhead. Had she outrun them? She quickly walked through the trees, winding her way around thickets of shrubs and fallen branches. Poppy moved quietly alongside.

A tinny voice reached her. She snatched up the phone. The dispatcher said, 'A team is at the cottage. Where are you?'

Jenny gave them directions. 'They're behind me. A man and a woman. They're armed. I have to keep going. I don't want them to catch up with me. Please, hurry.'

She put the phone back into her pocket. Paused when she reached a dirt track that cut through the wood. She tried to take an aerial view, and visualise what lay at each end. She was pretty sure a village lay to the west, so she turned that way, launching into a run now she had a clearer path.

Finally she broke from the trees onto a road. A huge oak stood opposite. There was a road traffic sign indicating a sharp bend in the road and another saying NETTLETON WELCOMES CAREFUL DRIVERS.

Her spirits leaped. She knew where she was. Nettleton's pub was barely a quarter of a mile away. Saturday night, it should be busy. Noisy with people enjoying an evening out, *lots* of people. She accelerated down the road but slowed when she saw a pair of headlights shining ahead. The next second, a car appeared around the corner, just two hundred yards away. And accelerated straight for her.

Jenny pelted for the trees on the other side of the road. The engine gunned after her.

She ran as fast as she could.

She heard the sound of wheels sliding on damp tarmac as the driver braked hard. Heard a door slamming. The engine continued to run. She didn't turn and look back. She concentrated on running.

Nothing but the sound of her breath in her throat, her feet pounding, twigs and branches snapping beneath her feet.

Then came the sound of someone behind her. A man, breathing hard. He was moving faster than her. Much faster.

Please God, help me.

She grabbed her phone. She was half-sobbing as she spoke. 'He's right behind me. Help . . .'

She put every effort into running as fast as she could. She saw a wide, sturdy tree trunk and ahead. Came to a lurching stop. Grabbed Poppy. 'Get him,' she hissed. She pointed at the figure hurtling towards them.

The dog looked at her then back at the man.

'Poppy. *Get him.*'

She gave the dog a shove.

The Rottweiler launched herself at their pursuer. Jenny ran for the tree. Dived behind it.

She heard the man shout. Then came Poppy's throaty, snarling roar. The man shouted again. Fired his gun. Fired it again.

Poppy gave a single scream of pain.

Silence.

Oh God Oh God Oh God. He's shot Poppy.

Jenny put the phone to her ear. 'Help,' she bleated. She didn't waste time looking for the dog. She began running again but she'd barely gone twenty yards when she felt the man's hand close on her shirt collar. He dragged her to a halt.

She turned and tried to hit him but he warded her off easily. He was much bigger than her. She felt like a mouse swatting a bear. He trapped her hands in his. She lashed out with her feet but she was wearing sports shoes and they had little effect. She was shouting and yelling but he stood resolutely holding her.

The woman arrived. She said something in a foreign language to the man. It sounded East European, maybe Russian. The man nodded. The woman came close and leaned forward and that was when Jenny saw the syringe. Jenny reared wildly backwards, panic-stricken, yelling, 'They've got a syringe. Oh God, they're going to inject me, please someone *help* . . .'

And the needle went into her thigh and she was screaming *No!* but a cloud formed at the back of her head and she tried to fight it but it thickened, crept over her skull and her knees weakened, her mouth slackened and the last she remembered was the man leaning forward and letting her torso fall over his shoulder.

CHAPTER THIRTY-EIGHT

Dan pulled on to the verge and leaped out of his car. Ran to the ambulance. A man sat inside. His face was white. He was covered in blood. He was staring into the distance with a blank expression, obviously in shock. A medic was bandaging his hands, which looked as though they'd been through a mincing machine.

'Who are you?' Dan asked the blood-drenched man.

The man licked his lips. 'Nicholas Blain.'

Dan turned to the medic. 'Do not, under any circumstances, let this man go. I'm a policeman, OK? I want to talk to him.' He didn't care that he'd lied. It took too long to tell the truth.

Dan ran to the cottage.

'Sir!' A policeman stopped him.

'I'm Dan Forrester. The woman who was here, she's my wife. Where is she?'

He didn't ask about Aimee because Lucy had rung him fifteen minutes ago to tell him she had Aimee safely with her in a service station on the M20. He'd asked her to wait there until he told them what to do next.

'A team's been dispatched,' the policeman told him. 'To the outskirts of Nettleton. We're following your wife's phone signal.'

'TFU?' Dan asked. Tactical Firearms Unit.

'Yes.'

'Good. Show me where.'

The policeman didn't demur, which meant Bernard had obviously put things into motion since Dan called him earlier. The cop pulled out his phone. Brought up Google maps. Dan had a quick look, memorised the route. Neddy was lying on the driveway next to a big leather wallet, both no doubt dropped in the panic. The wallet contained their passports, all their paperwork, and Dan bet that's what had delayed Jenny. Picking up both Neddy and the wallet, Dan raced to Jenny's car. Ducked down to see a small plastic device attached to the chassis. A tracker, which Dan assumed Blain had attached. Had the Russians then followed Blain here? No time to think. He had to get to Jenny.

Four police cars were parked on the lane on Nettleton's limits. He felt a moment of relief that they'd taken his call seriously. He had a quick word with the officer operating the in-car comms before setting off into the wood. It didn't take long before he saw the team, fanned out and searching the area. He called out his name, holding his hands high, not wanting to get shot. One of the cops came over. Dan showed him his driver's licence as ID.

'Where's Jenny?' Dan asked.

'We found her phone by the tree.' He gestured at a female PC standing just ahead, next to an oak tree. 'But no sign of your wife. She kept the line open. We heard everything . . . she said they had a syringe . . .'

Dan's could hear every word the policeman said but he felt as though he was a very long way away, at the end of a long dark tunnel. Jenny had been kidnapped by the FSB. Despite his best efforts, he hadn't been able to prevent it. A dark dread rose inside him. An ice-cold feeling that crept through every vein and into his heart.

'We found something,' the policeman said.

Dan's mouth turned dry. 'What?' he asked, but the policeman didn't respond. Just led the way through the trees.

Next to a spreading rhododendron the policeman stopped and squatted down, pushing branches aside. Dan stepped close and for a moment he couldn't see anything, and then he saw a still, dark shape on the ground.

'Poppy.'

At the sound of his voice, the dog whimpered. It was a pathetic sound, filled with pain and desperation.

'We've called the vet,' the policeman told him. 'We believe your wife set the dog on her attackers, who shot it.'

'Oh, Pops.' He knelt down and stroked her head. The dog closed her eyes and made a groaning sound. He wanted to cry. He wanted to throw up, to scream. Anger, fear and rage thundered inside him but he took each emotion carefully and put it in a small black box deep inside his core. He would let them out later. When he'd found Jenny. Brought her home safely. Made the people who'd taken her pay.

Ice-calm, he rose to his feet.

The policeman said, 'We've put an APB on the hire car. It shouldn't be long until we find it.'

The FSB wouldn't let it be so easy. Dan bet they had a backup plan should they be forced to ditch the car, or another team in place that could pick them up fast.

Despite the fact his intellect knew Jenny wasn't in the wood any more, that she'd been kidnapped, Dan couldn't help scouring the area. It was only after the vet arrived that Dan felt it was OK to leave. 'Save the dog,' he told the vet. 'Whatever it takes.'

Dan wasn't allowed to speak to Blain until he'd been treated by the surgeon so he drove to the service station where Lucy and Aimee were waiting. He wasn't sure what to tell Aimee. He didn't want to frighten her, but wanted to avoid lying if he could. Giving her false assurances when her world might never be the same would simply instil false hope. He'd have to bite the bullet and give an accurate appraisal of the situation, but not right now. He didn't want to break this in public. He wanted to give her time to absorb what he said, ask questions, cry if she wanted, and be hugged as much as needed.

'Daddyyy!' Aimee lurched across the restaurant. She'd been lying fast asleep across Lucy's lap, wrapped in a new-looking pink blanket decorated with elephants, thumb in her mouth and obviously exhausted. Lucy, on the other hand, had been as alert as a meerkat and had spotted him the instant he stepped into view.

Now, his daughter hugged him, her legs wrapped around his waist, her arms around his neck. She was still half asleep and rested her head against the pad of his chest. He closed his eyes and breathed in the scent of toast and cheese clinging to her hair. Even though he'd locked his emotions away, inside his chest the sun flared, blue surf crested, children ran along the sand. He held her close, swearing silently he'd bring her mother back, that he was prepared to do anything, no matter how crazy. Things that might get him into trouble. Get him hurt. Beyond that, he knew nothing. He just had to get his family back together.

'Has Lucy been looking after you?' he asked, more to see what state of mind Aimee was in than check up on the policewoman.

His daughter yawned. 'She wouldn't let me have any chocolate.'

'Did she give a reason?'

Aimee wriggled. She didn't answer.

'Aimee?' he prompted gently.

She sighed exaggeratedly against his neck. 'I'd already had some ice cream.'

'What sort of ice cream?'

Another sigh. 'Chocolate.'

He leaned back to peer into her face. 'I'd say that was a good reason, wouldn't you?'

'I s'pose so.' Her words were reluctant but not because she was traumatised; it was her normal response to a situation where she wasn't allowed to have her own way.

He carried her to Lucy's table, his chin on top of her head. He said, 'I'm here with you now, munchkin. Everything's going to be OK.'

The fact that she wasn't showing any signs of bewilderment or anxiety meant Lucy had done an exemplary job in removing Aimee when she had and then explaining things so as not to panic her. He checked his daughter carefully. No overt signs of shock that he could ascertain, but it didn't mean that she wasn't feeling confused and overwhelmed by what had happened. Thank God she hadn't seen her mother kidnapped, or Poppy shot. Lucy told him that as far as she could tell, Aimee had seen a car arrive but had been chatting to the dog on the back seat and hadn't taken much notice until Poppy suddenly scrambled into the front, and bolted out of the open passenger door.

It was, Lucy told him, just after Poppy attacked Blain that Jenny had screamed at Lucy to get Aimee out of there.

'Where is Mummy?' Aimee wanted to know.

'The last we heard, she was with Poppy. Poppy got hurt and the vet's taken her to hospital.'

Aimee's eyes widened. 'How did she get hurt?'

'She was shot.'

He felt more than saw Lucy's blink of surprise at his honesty.

'Who shot her?' Aimee asked.

'A bad man.'

Long silence.

'Why?'

'Poppy was defending Mummy.'

Aimee's expression cleared. 'The man Poppy knocked over shot her?'

Dan decided to keep things simple. 'Yes.'

'That's why Mummy shouted for us to go away.'

'Yes.'

'When can I visit Poppy?'

Dan was glad her attention was more on the dog than her mother at the moment. It made his life easier. They talked about the vet for a while and when Aimee's eyes began to droop he tucked the blanket around her and cuddled her until she was asleep. Then he gently moved Aimee to nestle at his side. Lucy bought two coffees, a toasted panini and two chocolate brownies.

He wolfed down his panini, sitting close enough to Lucy so they could talk quietly.

'I don't understand,' Lucy said, obviously baffled. 'They've *kidnapped* Jenny?'

'It looks like it. An APB's out on their car and for good measure my old employer is activating all ports to look out for them.' He glanced at his daughter. 'I'll take Aimee to her grandparents tonight. I want to see Adrian Calder. I spoke to him earlier. He's already on his way south. Apparently he's got his mother-in-law with him.'

'Irene Cavendish.'

'That's the one.' He started on his brownie, speaking between mouthfuls. 'I know you've already told me on the phone, but I need you to tell me again exactly what happened.'

It didn't take long. From Lucy's arrival at the cottage to the second she'd raced off with Aimee had barely taken three minutes, but Dan went through the details meticulously, not wanting to miss anything.

When he'd finished the debriefing it was approaching midnight. Lucy was fiddling with a thread that had come loose on her jacket. She said, 'It's my fault. I shouldn't have let Jenny go upstairs . . . I should have grabbed her and forced her out. I'm sorry.'

'You can't blame yourself. She went to get our passports. Family documents. And once Jenny's on a mission, God help you if you intervene.'

'Even so . . .' Lucy bit her lip, looking mortified.

'Don't,' he told her, but he knew she'd beat herself up over it. She would rerun the event over and over, replaying how she thought she *should* have acted until she knew that next time it would happen the way she wanted. She was like him in that respect. A perfectionist.

They talked some more. Sharing information, going over everything they knew. This time, however, Dan told Lucy about his Russian sojourn. Although he could see she tried to keep her expression professionally neutral, emotions flitted across her face: horror, dismay, excitement. As he spoke, he wondered where Milena was, and whether Ekaterina had had her blood transfusion.

He finished by saying, 'The FSB are looking for a man called Zama Kasofsky.'

'Zama?' Lucy was electrified. 'That's the same name Calder mentioned. And I swear Irene recognised the name even though she denied it.'

The nape of Dan's neck tingled.

'Who is he?' Lucy asked but all Dan could do was shake his head. 'Hopefully I'll find out when I ask Calder tonight.'

'Let me know.' Lucy's phone buzzed. She answered it, mouthing, *my boss*. 'Hi Mac . . . yes, yes. Oh, that's fantastic.' She listened briefly before covering the mouthpiece and hissing to Dan: 'They've found the Mondeo.'

It was as though a thunderbolt had charged through him.

'Where?'

She listened for a moment longer. 'He says they were really lucky to have found it . . . It's only thanks to a PC noticing a farm gate was open when it was normally shut –'

'*Where?*'

'In a field just off the B2050 near Ramsgate . . .' She listened a bit more then added, 'Manston, to be precise.'

Dan could practically feel the blood drain from his head.

'What is it?' Lucy's face filled with alarm.

'Manston Airport,' he said. He was already reaching for his phone. *What if they're flying Jenny out from there?*

CHAPTER THIRTY-NINE

Jenny regained consciousness to find herself on a stretcher and being carried across what looked like a small waiting room. The man carrying the front of her stretcher was big with a badly fitting white tunic that bunched beneath his armpits. Jenny tried to say something but her throat wouldn't work. Her vision was blurred but she could make out a desk on the other side of the room, manned by two official-looking men. Behind them stood an open door. As the stretcher approached, Jenny tried to speak, to shout for help, but she couldn't move her lips. She couldn't move her hands, her feet or her arms. Aside from her eyes, which she could blink and move slowly from side to side, she was paralysed.

Terror flooded her. Her heartbeat picked up and her breathing changed, becoming shallow and panicky. Why couldn't she move? What had they given her? Would it damage the baby? Would she miscarry?

Help! she shouted soundlessly.

One of the men greeted her stretcher bearers. He wore a blue uniform with white piping. 'Hi there. How's it going?'

'We are OK, thank you.' A female voice spoke behind her. Then she said something in Russian. Slowly, the stretcher was put on the floor. A woman walked forwards. Although she'd changed out of her black trousers and fleece and wore a smart tweed suit with a silk scarf at her throat, Jenny recognised her. It was the same woman who'd stuck a syringe in her earlier. She gave the man what looked like a passport. He glanced at it, then down at Jenny.

'Anna Saburov,' he said. It was a statement.

Nooooo! Jenny howled silently. Desperately she tried to hold his eyes, pleading with him, but he looked straight back at the passport.

'We weren't expecting you so soon,' the man said. He frowned.

'But the aircraft,' the woman said sharply, 'it is here?'

'Yes. They're ready for you.' He looked back at Jenny. Gave a grimace. 'She broke her back?'

'Horseback-riding.'

'Terrible.'

'Yes,' the woman agreed. 'Terrible. Now, everything is in order? She may go?'

'Yes, she may go.'

The man didn't look at Jenny again.

Another man appeared at the corner of her vision. He wore a smart pair of trousers and checked jacket. He had a cleft chin. The man who'd shot Poppy. He greeted two men who came through the door, bringing with them a blast of icy air from outside. They wore ill-fitting grey suits and white shirts, bland ties. They looked like office drones. They all shook hands. Spoke in Russian. They didn't look at her.

'Bye, bye,' said the woman to Jenny. She was smiling. The man who'd shot Poppy didn't say a word.

The drones carried her outside. Sleet was falling. She could smell jet fuel and hear the whine of an engine. A man in an orange vest directed them towards a private jet. The howl of terror and panic inside her remained, unrelenting. Tears streamed down her face. As they approached she saw a pilot and co-pilot through the jet's windscreen. The pilot glanced at her then away.

A door in the side of the aircraft opened. Two men in reflective jackets brought a pair of steps over. Jenny tried to make eye contact with them but they weren't looking. They weren't interested. They were just doing their job.

Help me!

She was carried inside the aircraft where the stretcher was secured on the floor. The drones took their seats. Buckled up. The door closed, and then the jet's engines started. Another woman appeared. She was carrying a bottle of vodka and three glasses. She poured the drinks. They laughed, looked at Jenny, and drank.

The aircraft began to move. Jenny could feel the bumps of the ground travelling through the fuselage. She was crying, screaming inside.

Please, stop!

She felt the aircraft swing round, engines shrieking, and as it completed its turn it thrust forward, accelerating fast. Seconds later it lifted into the sky.

CHAPTER FORTY

By the time Dan had dropped Aimee off at her grandparents in Bath, it was gone three a.m. His eyes were gritty and his mouth tasted sour. He knew he should stop and sleep for a spell, but he couldn't. Not with Jenny God alone knew where and Adrian Calder and his mother-in-law at the hospital in Margate, the closest hospital providing full A & E to where Blain had been attacked. He must be one heck of a family friend considering they were still there.

He had to speak to Calder.

He needed to track down Zama Kasofsky and *get his wife back*.

So he jumped in his car and headed east, back along the M4, taking the cut-across through Bracknell for the M25 and M3. Being the middle of the night it was quiet, but there were always a few trucks in the slow lane, FedEX, Tesco, Maersk Line. As he drove, he thought of the phone calls he'd made. Trying to form a plan.

He'd spoken to Bernard earlier. Classical music had been playing, Debussy or something similarly soothing. 'I've informed the Foreign Secretary,' Bernard told him. 'He's going to kick up a stink, try and find out what's going on. Meantime, I'd like you to liaise with Oswald Lyons. Ozzie's running the show now. He'll keep me informed. Good luck, Dan. If there's anything else we can do . . .'

Dan had met Ozzie on the Russian desk at Thames House North last week. Tall, round-faced and muscular, he was in his late thirties, quick-minded and meticulous. For his sins he was also, he admitted ruefully, an amateur wrestler. Dan thought he could do far worse than have him on his side.

When he'd rung Ozzie, he'd learned that a Russian-owned private jet, a Falcon 900, had taken off from Manston Airport just after ten p.m. The passenger list included a woman who'd been on a stretcher, barely conscious due to a recent spine injury. Her passport gave the name Anna Saburov. The man who had checked her passport had been questioned. He'd agreed that Anna Saburov looked like Jenny, but as far as he was concerned Anna's passport had been genuine and he had no idea the woman was there against her will.

'Sorry,' said Ozzie. 'Wish we could have got the alert to Manston in time – thanks, darling, much needed.'

Dan imagined that his wife had brought him a brandy.

'Perfect. Where was I? Ah, tracking Jenny. The Foreign Secretary and FCO will be going through the official channels, screaming blue murder, OK? Meantime, I've alerted our Moscow desk. They're passing the word. The jet filed a flight plan to Moscow and we'll have someone there looking for it . . .'

But Dan knew that just because they'd filed a flight plan didn't mean they'd actually land in Moscow. It could be a diversion. The Falcon 900 flew at 590 mph at 36,000 feet. Eight miles per minute. Its range was around 4,500 miles. They could fly straight over Moscow and keep going to Irkutsk, in deepest Siberia. Or they could fly to Uzbekistan, Western China or Pakistan.

Six a.m. Dan parked in the hospital car park. All was quiet, nobody to be seen. Too early. A dozen or so cars were scattered between some skinny trees. He took his phone off the charger and pocketed it. Made sure he had his wallet and a handful of change. He was in desperate need of caffeine. He headed for the front entrance, eyes muddy, limbs sluggish. He knew he'd wake up once he was beneath electric lights and talking to Adrian Calder, but right now he felt as though he could sleep for a week. Stress and worry taking their toll; two of the most enervating things known to man.

He rang Calder to tell him he had arrived. It went straight to his voicemail. Dan simply said, 'I'm here.' And went to try and find a coffee machine.

Calder rang him back within the minute. He'd obviously been waiting for his call.

'Dan,' Calder said.

'Where are you?' Dan asked.

'How about we meet in the A & E waiting room? I'll be there in two minutes.'

Dan pushed through the doors into A & E. One nurse sat behind the reception desk, another stood at her shoulder. Both were looking at a computer screen. Five chairs were taken. A young man with a busted face. An elderly woman with a younger man that Dan took to be her son. A couple in their early thirties, smartly dressed, the man in a checked jacket, the woman a tweed suit.

Adrian Calder and Irene Cavendish came into view from a corridor to the right of reception. He recognised them from the photographs Lucy had sent him. Irene's skin was grey. She looked how Dan felt: exhausted.

Calder looked much older than fifty-five and he walked slowly, as though he had something broken inside. He saw Dan and raised a hand in greeting. As Dan nodded back, he saw the smart couple glance his way. As they took him in something shifted in them; something about the tension in their muscles.

A heightened awareness swept through him, banishing his exhaustion.

He stepped quickly across the room but the couple rose before him and moved towards Calder. Dan's alarm soared. He increased his pace. His adrenaline was pumping, his senses peaked, his thoughts moving with dizzying speed.

Was it the couple who'd kidnapped Jenny?

According to Ozzie the couple who'd dropped Jenny at the private flights desk hadn't boarded with her. Were this man and woman the FSB agents? He had no way of knowing. MI5 didn't have a photograph of them, but Lucy had said they'd been in their early thirties, good-looking, smartly dressed –

'RUN!' he yelled at Calder. He sprinted for the couple who promptly broke into a run straight for Calder. The man was reaching into his jacket as he ran. He was going for a gun.

Calder hesitated for a second as though he couldn't comprehend what he was seeing, and then he turned and fled.

He only managed half a dozen steps before the man had pulled out his gun and was taking aim.

Irene rushed between the man and Calder. She was shouting something at the man but Dan couldn't understand; she was shouting in Russian. The man with the gun shouted something back. And then he lifted his gun and shot her.

Irene toppled to the ground like a felled tree.

Someone screamed.

Dan was racing around the rows of chairs. He was too far away but the man had been taken by surprise. He hadn't expected Irene to try and protect Calder. Dan hoped he'd be off-balance enough to miss his next shot.

The man's gun spoke, spitting twice, and Dan heard another scream as he tore towards him.

Adrian Calder slowed but he didn't stop. He kept going.

The man took aim again. This time, he wouldn't miss. He'd take care to hit Calder where the damage would be fatal.

Dan was just yards away, preparing to rugby tackle the man when the woman grasped his arm and pulled. Dan spun to face her. He struck her under the chin with the heel of his hand. Her body was lifted into the air by the blow and she landed on to the floor with her neck twisted.

Another two spits from the silencer.

Calder had fallen, the back of his skull blown away.

Dan drove the man hard on to the floor, jamming his forearm against his windpipe, aiming to crush it, but he'd hit him a fraction too high and caught the soft skin beneath his jaw.

The men wrestled violently. Both were gasping. Dan could smell the man's breath; onions and cigarettes. He saw the gun, the man's wrist pivoting towards him. He grabbed the barrel and held it away. With his other hand he made short, hard punches to the man's throat and solar plexus. Then he tilted his body to the side and tried to plunge his knee into the man's testicles, but the man twisted aside, so Dan punched his elbow into his diaphragm instead. He heard the breath rush from the man's throat. Dan drove home his advantage and seized his wrist with both hands and broke it. The crack was like a piece of kindling being snapped.

Dan was about to grab the gun when someone kicked him in his side. Hard enough to break a rib. A security guard, who yanked the gun away from Dan at the same time as Adrian's attacker slammed a roundhouse into his face. Dan fell back against a chair that scooted sideways. Plastic, no arms, polypropylene. He grabbed it with one hand and swung with all his might.

The man rolled and Dan smashed the chair on to the floor, missing him. He scrambled to his feet but the man was lighter and more agile. He was upright and running, fleeing for the door.

Dan pelted after him.

Behind him, the security guard shouted, 'Stop!'

Dan increased his pace.

The man was fast but he was injured. Broken wrist, maybe a couple of busted ribs. It took the edge off his speed. As they approached the cluster of cars near the hospital entrance, the man's hand went into his jacket pocket and Dan knew he was after his car keys. He put on a burst of speed and launched himself at the man's knees, shoulder first, punching him hard.

The man flew to the ground.

Dan swarmed over him. Grabbed his ears and slammed his forehead and face into the tarmac. Once, twice. Three times.

The man lay still.

Straddling his torso, Dan rolled him over. He kept his fist high, ready to punch him if he moved.

The man's face was a mess. Broken nose, cheekbone shattered, a swelling on his forehead already blooming. He was out cold.

To one side, a man said, 'Stop.' It was the security guard. He was gasping, his skin greasy-pale.

'You've called the police?' Dan asked.

'Yes.'

Dan rose. 'Good. You can go now.'

When he hesitated, Dan took a purposeful step forward, bunching his bloody fists at his side. His demeanour shrieked, *You really want to mess with me?*

The guard took a step back.

'Go and help everyone inside,' Dan snapped, 'and direct the police to me when they arrive, or . . .' He looked pointedly at the Russian's prostrate figure.

The guard glanced at the shattered face, the broken wrist. He swallowed.

'Your choice,' added Dan.

The guard backed away.

When he was sure the guard had gone, Dan swiftly bent back to the Russian. He rummaged through the man's pockets, withdrew his car key. Pressed the unlocking button. The parking lights of a Ford sedan lit up. Dan raced to his own car. Yanked out a spare lead he kept for Poppy in the glovebox, along with a tow rope. Ran back to the man and tied his hands behind his back. Then he dragged him to the Ford sedan. Popped the boot.

He paused to gather his strength. He was panting and sweating, his heart pounding. He looked down at the man's mashed face. Heard his messy breathing.

He took a deep breath. *This man knows where Jenny has gone. He can tell me where she is.*

Dan put his elbows under the man's armpits and hauled him upright, exhaling sharply as he did so, transferring more energy to the movement and managing to get the man's torso to hang over the lip of the boot. He then took his legs and lifted them, twisting the body round, going to the shoulders and shifting them sideways. A trickle of sweat worked its way down Dan's face. More sweat gathered along his spine.

He tumbled the man into the boot, careful of the angle of his head. He didn't want to break his neck. Not yet, anyway.

Dan closed the boot. Walked around the car and climbed into the driver's seat. Started the car. Drove away.

CHAPTER FORTY-ONE

Sunday 8 February

Lucy awoke in bed beneath a duvet cover decorated with fire engines, police cars and ambulances. She gave a snort of laughter. Mum having a joke. She hadn't seen the cover since she was a kid and had pronounced it babyish. She could still remember her delight with it though, when she was six and had just decided to become a policewoman. She'd been at school when the police had come to give a talk, and the moment she'd sat in the police car and seen the radio, heard it crackle – a burglary had just been reported down the road – she knew that's what she wanted to be. At the weekend her mother had made police epaulets for her out of silver foil and bought her a toy police helmet from Wodworths.

Lucy stretched and rolled over to see what the time was. Ten o'clock. Not bad, for her. She'd had just over four hours' kip, which was surprising, because when she'd first fallen into bed she'd spent what felt like hours in the dark rerunning Jenny's rescue and trying to work out how to do it successfully the next time. She knew she'd done the best thing for Aimee, but leaving the girl's mother behind? If it happened again she wouldn't let

Jenny go upstairs. She'd take her by the wrist and *force* her out-side with her daughter, barefoot or not.

Thank God Dan hadn't taken it out on her. She wasn't sure if she could have coped with that. But he was a professional, he wouldn't see the point in going over something that had already happened, no matter how bad and when there were more impor-tant things to be thinking about. Like getting his wife back.

After Dan had left with Aimee, Lucy had returned to the scene and allowed herself to be directed to Canterbury Police Station where she was debriefed by the SIO. She'd made a statement and signed it. Taken a copy and emailed it to Mac. She'd been about to leave when the news came through about Calder's killing. Apparently she'd gone very pale and the SIO nearly hadn't let her join him but she'd rallied fast. She'd no intention of being left behind.

She'd seen Adrian Calder's body. Taken in the overturned chair in reception, the blood smeared all over the floor. From the description of the couple who'd attacked Calder, she guessed they were the FSB agents she'd seen on Irene's doorstep. The couple who'd kidnapped Dan's wife. One FSB agent was miss-ing, the other had been removed from the A & E waiting room. An overweight security guard described Dan to a T, and when Lucy intimated that Dan was with the Security Service, the man breathed out, obviously relieved. More questions from the SIO, until her head started to ache.

Finally, she was allowed to go. She wasn't permitted to see Irene, who was apparently alive but in a coma, and hanging on by a thread. More frustratingly, she couldn't see Blain either, who was under sedation and being treated for shock. She'd been torn between sleeping in her car – waiting until she could question Blain – and going to her mother's, but it wasn't long before the thought of a hot shower, a comfortable bed and all the home comforts won out.

Checking her phone, she saw she had a missed call from Mac. Climbing out of bed, she dragged on a dressing gown and padded downstairs and kissed her mum good morning, made a mug of tea, and rang him back.

'Where are you?' he said.

'At the kitchen table with a mug of tea. Why, where are you?' From the *ssshushing* on the line, it sounded as though he was in the car.

'You're OK?' he asked.

'A bit tired, but yes, I'm fine.'

There was a loud rumble and the distant sound of a horn. He was definitely in the car.

'Anything new?' she asked.

'Actually, yes.'

Something in his tone made her sit straighter. 'What is it?'

'Elizabeth Stanton,' he said.

The way he said her name, she knew. 'No way,' she said in disbelief.

'She was found first thing this morning. Shot dead.'

Her brain flickered green and blue in confusion. Why had Elizabeth been murdered? Why hadn't the killer tried to make it look like an accident, like they had Aleksandr? With Elizabeth so distraught over her husband's death, wouldn't it have been relatively easy to stage her death as a suicide? Drown her in the lake maybe? Or perhaps it didn't matter any more. Perhaps the killers didn't care. They were now, after all, in the open.

'I'm on my way south. I want to talk to the SIO down there, talk to Blain, get hold of Dan Forrester and find out *what the hell is going on.*'

A mass of interference made Lucy say, 'You're breaking up . . .'

'I want you there too,' he told her.

'What?'

'Margate Hospital.'

'What time?' she asked.

'Give me three hours.'

'OK,' she told him. 'I'll see you there.'

Lucy hung up. Her mind was spitting yellow, which she knew meant it had found a connection that her conscious mind hadn't registered yet. It had fired yellow when she'd been thinking about the killer staging an accident. Staging a *suicide.*

'Sorry, Mum,' she said.

Her mother sat opposite with her hair awry, glasses perched on her nose, reading the newspaper. 'Don't worry, love. It was nice to see you anyway.'

Lucy peered at her mum's paper. No mention of the killings on the front page but only because it had happened after the papers had gone to press. The media were going to go berserk. Would they connect Aleksandr and Elizabeth's murders to the mess at the hospital? The police wouldn't help them, and Lucy wondered how long it would take before a journalist began to connect the dots.

Lucy called the Queen Elizabeth The Queen Mother Hospital – a ridiculous mouthful but it had been the woman's title, after all – to find that Blain had apparently been moved to a short stay ward and that visiting hours were unrestricted. He was due to be discharged as soon as the on-duty doctor had given him a final check, probably later this morning. Galvanised, Lucy shoved her tea aside and pelted upstairs. Showered, dressed, pelted back down. She mustn't let him leave before Mac had seen him.

'Sorry, Mum,' she said again. They hugged on the doorstep.

Before Lucy turned the ignition, she checked her phone to see if Blain's car was on the move or not. According to Google, it was still parked outside Sparrow Cottage, which meant that Blain was hopefully still in hospital. As she drove, she thought about the list of the dead. Polina and her children, now Adrian Calder. Aleksandr and Elizabeth Stanton. Jenny Forrester kidnapped. What did it mean?

It was raining when she arrived. Great torrents of water pouring straight down from the sky, but it didn't seem to be deterring the media. Photographers stood beneath a cloud of umbrellas, camera snouts poised over the police barriers for any sign of action. Behind them stood white vans with satellite dishes, journalists talking, soundmen lingering. Some entrepreneurial soul had set up a mobile coffee shop and was doing a brisk business. Bored cameramen filmed the car park, the damp trees, the rain cascading down the hospital windows. Then they spotted Lucy. As she showed her ID to one of the cops and was waved through, a buzz rose and a wave of flashing and clicking ensued, snapping her every move.

Fame at last, she thought wryly.

She parked as close to the hospital entrance as she could. Incredibly, as she climbed outside, the rain increased. She broke into a run. Even though she used an umbrella, her shoes and trousers were drenched by the time she made it to the entrance.

Blain was sitting up in bed when she arrived, reading a newspaper.

'Hi,' she said. She hung her brolly on the end of his bed, dusted raindrops from her trousers.

'Hi.' He put the paper down. His hands were heavily bandaged, and he had more bandages on his upper arms and another on his shoulder, but his face held some colour and his eyes were clear.

'How are you?' she asked.

He looked at her hands then peered past her. He frowned.

Lucy glanced around to see what he was looking at but couldn't see anything. 'What's wrong?'

'I was wondering where the grapes were.'

'I don't come bearing gifts,' she said stonily. She didn't trust him an inch and wanted him to know it.

'How about a coffee then?' He tilted his chin at the bedside table. 'There's some change in there. Would you mind? And please, grab one for yourself.'

Lucy fetched him a coffee from the machine down the corridor. She didn't take his money. And even though she would have killed for a coffee, she didn't have one. She didn't want to make it seem like a social occasion. Pocketbook in hand, she took up position near the foot of his bed. She purposely didn't look at his medical chart although she was sorely tempted. Leave the man some dignity, at least until she'd questioned him.

'Last night,' she said.

He looked at her for a long time, expressionless. 'What do you want to know?'

'What were you doing at the cottage?'

'How about if I tell you what I told the police,' he suggested smoothly. 'And we take it from there?'

'OK,' she said.

'I'm a PI. Private investigator. Ex-Special Forces. My name is Nicholas Baker. My address . . .' As he continued to speak, he sipped his coffee carefully, his cup balanced between his bandaged hands. 'I was hired by Adrian Calder two years ago, to check on Jenny Forrester, maybe three or four times a year. To take a photograph or two, and write a brief report on her movements, her well-being. I wasn't given a reason why.'

He took another swallow of coffee. 'When he was arrested, Calder instructed me to increase the surveillance on Mrs Forrester and if she ever appeared to be in any danger, I was to call the police and defend her if necessary.'

'What did you make of that?'

'I've had far stranger assignments, believe me.'

'So you never knew why Calder wanted you to watch Jenny?'

He shook his head. 'I assumed he'd had an affair with her in the past and wanted to know how she was doing, but when he asked me to put a tracker on her car to monitor her movements, I knew things had shifted into another dimension.'

Lucy mulled things over briefly. 'So the photograph I saw you showing Justin Tripp wasn't of Dan Forrester as much as his wife.'

'Correct.' He put his head on one side. 'It wasn't all about Jenny Forrester, though. Mr Calder asked me to do other things for him. Like collect the occasional envelope on his behalf, and deliver it to his lawyer. He instructed me to drive Irene Cavendish to and from the police station so she could visit him. She doesn't have a driving licence. Adrian and Irene came and visited me in hospital last night. They were going to stay with Elizabeth Stanton afterwards . . .'

But then the FSB agents had turned up and shot Adrian dead and put Irene in a coma. Lucy wondered if Blain – she couldn't think of him as Nicholas Baker yet – knew if Elizabeth was dead, and decided probably not. He wasn't a policeman after all. No matter that he was ex-Special Forces, trained to perform unconventional and sometimes dangerous missions; today he was just a PI. A private investigator who knew nothing about Zama Kasofsky.

She stood quietly, drawing everything she knew together. The FSB agents had set Adrian Calder up, to make him look as though he'd murdered his family. Had they meant to kill Calder at the same time too, and made it look like suicide? But why had they killed the children? She recalled the warmth remaining in young Felix's body when she'd found the boy. His look of surprise.

'Who were the couple who attacked Irene?' Blain asked.

'They followed you to the cottage,' Lucy responded. She wasn't going to share any information with him that hadn't been released into the general domain. 'If it hadn't been for you leading them to her, Jenny would still be safe.'

'You can't say that for sure.' His eyes held a hint of challenge. 'They might have followed *you*.'

'They wouldn't have known which pool car I was going to use.' She refused to take any blame for his fuck-up. 'One last thing before I go, the SIO in this case is coming to interview you in a couple of hours. Please do not leave the hospital until you have seen him. DI Faris MacDonald.'

'Sure,' he responded. He surveyed her calmly, as serene as he'd been when she'd first seen him sitting in the station's reception. 'Now, when I get out of here, would you like to join me for that drink? I need something to look forward to.'

'No.'

'At least say you'll think about it.'

'No.'

'God, you're a hard woman.'

Lucy went to check on Irene but she was still unconscious. Two people sat with her. She recognised them from Dan's description: the two cousins, Robin and Finch. Their heads were together and they were talking softly. As Lucy approached, she did a double-take. Both were bruised, with scratches and scrapes on their cheeks and hands. Robin's wrist was bandaged, his arm strapped against his chest.

Lucy introduced herself.

'What happened to you?' she asked. They looked as though they'd been in a bike accident, or fallen out of a moving car.

'You wouldn't believe it,' Finch replied. Her skin was pale and she looked shivery and ill.

'All we were doing was walking down the street,' said Robin.

Lucy lifted her eyebrows.

'In Margate, this morning,' Finch took up the story. 'We were looking for a café to have breakfast. It was pretty early, around eight o'clock. A car came out of nowhere. It mounted the pavement and –'

'*Jissus*,' Robin said, shaking his head. 'I really thought our number was up. Honest to God I thought it was going to hit us. I pushed Finch out of the way and jumped after her . . .'

'It missed us by a whisker,' said Finch. She reached across and touched her brother's shoulder. 'Thank God.'

'Did you report it?' Lucy asked.

'*Ja.*' Robin nodded. 'The cops thought it was someone coming home from a party, pissed to the eyeballs. We didn't see the driver, or get a number plate or anything much. Just that it was a dark blue sedan.'

Although it sounded like a freak near-miss, Lucy's antennae were quivering. With Aleksandr and Elizabeth murdered, and Adrian and his family too, had this been an attempt on the cousins' lives? She warned them to take good care then went and got herself a coffee. She sipped it overlooking the car park, the rows of white media vans with their enormous satellite dishes perched on their roofs, waiting for Mac, waiting for Irene to wake up.

CHAPTER FORTY-TWO

'What the hell is going on?' Ozzie demanded. 'Five witnesses saw you break a woman's neck. Adrian Calder murdered in A & E. You fight the killer, chase him outside, and neither of you are seen again. And intimidating that security guard into backing off . . . well, luckily for you, we managed to beat the police to the CCTV tape that also shows you tying the Russian up and putting him in the boot of a hire car. What the fuck do you think you're doing?'

'Trying to find my wife.'

'And you think this is the way to do it?' Ozzie's voice rose.

'I need to know who the guy is. What makes him tick. Whether he's turned on by money and if not, what I can use.'

'No, Dan. Absolutely, not. We cannot have you doing this alone on some kind of –'

'Find out for me.'

Dan hung up. Ozzie rang back straight away. Dan switched off the volume and pocketed his phone. Looked at the two men Max Blake had talked about in the past and who Dan had managed, via a flurry of coded texts and emails, to track down. Ibro and Mirza.

'No carrot yet,' he told them. 'Just the stick.'

Ibro shrugged. 'It may not matter. It depends on the man and how fast we can get to know him.'

'It's my guess he'll be too afraid of his own people to talk.'

Ibro grinned. 'In that case, I will make him more afraid of me.'

Ibro and Mirza had been comrades during the war in Bosnia, which was where they had met Max Blake. They had headed military interrogation teams from Algeria to Lebanon and Afghanistan and Max apparently used them not just as interrogators but as information sources and couriers. *Extremely skilled*, was how Max described them. *Reliable. Use them any time. They owe me a favour.*

Which Dan now owed Max.

Ibro and Mirza knew his wife had been kidnapped. That she'd been put on a private jet that had left from Manston. That Dan wanted her back.

'Can we use water?' Mirza's voice was rough and gravelly, as though he rarely spoke.

Something inside Dan shivered. Waterboarding was a hideous form of torture. One of the worst, and although his intellect told him he could well have authorised such a thing in the past, or been part of such a decision, right now he baulked.

'What else?'

The two men glanced at each other.

'If he is as frightened of his authorities as you say,' Mirza told him, 'it will take us much longer without water. Perhaps a week.'

A snake of nausea coiled in Dan's belly. He couldn't wait a week. He needed to know where Jenny was *now*. But could he justify such a thing? Sanction such immense suffering on another human being? He allowed himself a glimpse of Jenny the last time he'd seen her, her blazing smile as she told him she was pregnant, and he gritted his teeth. Said, 'Do it. Whatever it takes.'

Ibro put out his hand. Dan gave him the keys to the Russian's hire car. He followed the men from the empty building into the quarry. Huge jagged walls of rock rose all around. Discarded mining equipment, crushers, screeners and conveyors, stood like silent metallic ghosts. Ibro had used the place before, apparently, not just because it was concealed and unused, but it had only recently been abandoned. It still had running water and electricity, security systems and electric gates. It was, as Ibro had said, perfect for their needs. Dan stepped over a puddle shimmering with diesel. It started to rain.

He watched the two men as they went to the car. Opened the boot. Silently, they manhandled the Russian out. Dan waited for the man to turn his head and look at him, but he seemed dazed. Ibro gave Dan a nod. Dan approached. The man swore loudly in Russian when he saw him, but although his voice was fierce and filled with venom, his eyes swam with fear.

Dan pulled out his phone. Took the man's photograph. The Russian fought as they dragged him away but he was no match for the Bosnians who'd done this a thousand times before and overpowered him easily and with professional skill. Dan watched them vanish inside a concrete block next to the outbuilding. The rain increased. Dan moved to stand under the shelter of a corroded mining bucket. He forwarded the photograph to Emily at Six and then to Ozzie. The man might have a bruised and bloody messed-up face but he should still be recognisable. Rainwater began to drip steadily from the mining bucket into a puddle. The minutes ticked past.

When Ibro and Mirza returned, they were dusting their hands together and looking pleased. 'We might get lucky,' Ibro said. 'The quarry has scared him. But we need the carrot, Daniel. Then we will have something to work with.'

'Just keep asking where Jenny is.'

'OK.' Ibro gave a nod. 'We'll keep in touch.'

CHAPTER FORTY-THREE

Jenny lay in bed, shivering. The room felt stuffy and overly warm, but she couldn't stop trembling. Shock, she supposed. She touched her wedding band and sent a prayer to Dan.

Find me, my love. Bring me home.

Tears rose but she forced them down. Tears wouldn't help her now. Planning might. Strength of will. Determination.

A nurse came in with a fresh jug of water and a cup. Short and dumpy, she had a pretty round face and mouse-coloured hair pinned beneath a white cap.

'Hello,' said Jenny but the woman gave no indication she'd heard. She put both the jug and cup on the bedside table. 'Please . . .' said Jenny. She raised her right hand and jingled the handcuffs. 'Why am I a prisoner?'

The nurse walked outside without a backward glance.

Jenny put back her head and closed her eyes, battling the urge to scream and shout, to weep. They would only tranquillise her, as they had before. She'd tried to fight the two men as they disembarked from the private jet. She'd bitten one on his wrist and lashed her legs at the other, and she was half-off the stretcher when a woman appeared and stuck a needle in her thigh. When

Jenny awoke, she was here, in this hospital-style room, shackled to the bed and wearing nothing but an olive-green hospital robe. She had no idea how long she'd been unconscious. It could have been hours or days. She decided to be as compliant as she could; she didn't want any more drugs inside her. What if they damaged the baby? And what about the stress? How would that affect the poor little mite? She had to try and remain calm and protect him, keep him safe.

Jenny studied her handcuffs for the hundredth time. Chrome-plated steel with a welded chain and double lock, they fettered her to the side of her bed. She'd already checked to see if she could dismantle the bed but when she'd begun investigating one of the screws holding together an aluminium tube, a sturdy-looking nurse had arrived fast. She'd wagged her finger at Jenny, shaking her head. '*N'yet, n'yet,*' she said. No, no. She had pointed upwards, towards the corner of the ceiling, and Jenny's heart sank. A camera. She was being watched.

She rattled the handcuffs. Fidgeted. A stack of European magazines stood on her bedside table – *Le Figaro*, *Deutsch*, *Elle* – but she refused to look at them. She didn't want them to think she was relaxing, making herself comfortable. She looked around at the windowless green walls, the grey linoleum floor, and wished she could meditate. She would have liked to be sitting serenely instead of being a restless mess. Anxiety gnawed in her stomach like a trapped animal. Acid kept rising in her throat. A side effect from the tranquillisers? Or was it simply her body reacting to being in a state of never-ending fear?

She tried to concentrate on Dan. Dan, who would move heaven and earth for her. He would have put Aimee with her grandparents, and would be on his way to rescue her. His love was a gleaming sword. These people would fall before him by that sword. Where was he now? Was he nearby? How would he find her?

Her thoughts were interrupted by two nurses. She recognised both. The sturdy one carried a metal kidney dish containing a syringe and some cotton wool and tape, the other with the pretty round face held a rubber tube.

When the pretty nurse went to wrap the tube around Jenny's upper arm, Jenny snatched her arm aside. '*N'yet,*' Jenny snapped.

The dumpy nurse held up her syringe. Jenny saw it was empty. 'Blood,' said the nurse. 'OK?'

They wanted a blood sample. Jenny shook her head.

Both nurses walked outside. They returned with two male orderlies. Both were over six foot and as square and solid-looking as a pair of industrial boilers.

Jenny relented.

The nurses took her blood. They were surprisingly gentle, the older one making soothing clucking noises when Jenny flinched, but it didn't stop her feeling deeply frightened.

When they left, she sat alone in the bed with tears seeping down her cheeks.

Come and find me, my love.

CHAPTER FORTY-FOUR

Lucy returned to Irene's bedside to find the cousins had gone to get something to eat. She could hear the sounds of beeping. Muted voices. As she fetched a chair – planning to sit with Irene until Mac arrived – a male nurse, early twenties, appeared.

'You're family, I take it? We're not allowing anyone else to see her.'

She almost said yes, but at the last minute decided to be prudent. 'Actually, I'm with the police.' She showed him her warrant card and gave him ten brownie points when he studied it carefully. 'But I've met Irene before, OK? I'm not cold-calling. I just wanted to see how she's doing. Has she woken up yet?'

'She came round earlier, which is a good sign, but she's on powerful painkillers so she's only conscious for short periods.'

'Is she out of danger?'

'Pretty much, but we're going to keep her here until we're comfortable she's stabilised enough to be moved to another ward.'

'It's OK if I sit with her?'

He hesitated. 'I'm supposed to ring DI Boden when she awakes. He wants to be the first to talk to her.'

'I understand,' she said. 'But is it likely Irene will be up for a police interview in the next ten minutes?' she asked.

'No,' he admitted. 'Her injuries are pretty severe.'

'Look, I'll sit with her for a bit and if she does wake up, I'll call the DI straight away.'

'I'd rather you called me,' he said.

'I'll come and get you immediately,' she agreed. 'You first, then the DI.'

Somewhere, an alarm rang, muted but insistent. His head clicked round. The nurses were rising from their station, moving fast towards a curtained cubicle to the right. He hesitated until one of the nurses turned to wave him over.

He said, 'You know the score . . .'

While he sped away, Lucy settled next to Irene. Gone was the broad-shouldered handsome woman and in her place lay a fragile-looking elderly creature who looked as if she was on her last legs. Her eyes were closed, eyelids puffy and grey. Her hands, broad and square-tipped, lay slack on the pale blue blanket. A thin tube ran into a bruise on the inside of her arm. More tubes ran from her nose and up around her ears, down her chest. Machines hummed quietly and soft plastic bags dripped.

'Jeez, Irene,' she whispered. 'You've looked better, you know, but apparently you're on the mend. They're going to move you to another ward soon. Good news, eh?' She took a breath. 'Not such good news about Adrian though. The cameras show you stepping in front of him but they still got him. You were incredibly brave. I'm really sorry he's dead. He seemed like a nice man. And then there's Jenny Forrester, Dan's wife. She's been kidnapped . . .'

As she talked, she was reminded of another victim she'd visited in hospital last year. A girl in a coma who later told Lucy she'd heard every word she'd spoken. Apparently Lucy's conversations had helped her regain consciousness and although the news Lucy had imparted at the time had been shocking and awful, it had helped the victim come to terms with what had happened in a strangely holistic way.

Lucy spoke softly, half-closing her eyes, letting her mind drift over everything she knew. The list of the dead. Aleksandr and Elizabeth Stanton. Adrian and Polina Calder and their children Jessie, Felix, Sofia and little two-year-old Tasha.

Why had they killed the children? She recalled the bloody mess the bullet had made of Jessie's chest. The girl's look of terror. Her mind began to spit yellow again, wanting to tell her something, make a new connection. It was something to do with the children. Staging accidents. The word *suicide*. Three strands, each with similar colouring and interlocking shapes.

Lucy let her thoughts drift as she continued to murmur to Irene, her legs crossed in front of her, staring at the pale grey curtain, and she just about had a heart attack when she felt a hand touch hers. She had to swallow her shout.

Irene's deep brown gaze was on Lucy, dazed and dulled with painkillers, but she was struggling to push past them. 'Where . . .'

'I'll get a nurse,' Lucy told her.

'*No.* Is she – where –'

She was fighting to sit up. Lucy's stomach rolled at the thought she might rip stitches trying.

'Nurse,' Lucy repeated. She sped along the ward until she found the male nurse in front of a computer at the nurse's station. 'She's awake,' she told him.

His face lit up. 'Great. Let's see how she's doing.'

Lucy waited on the other side of the curtain while he ran his checks. When he reappeared, he gave Lucy a nod. 'She's doing really well but I can't see us moving her for a while, though. I'll call the DI.'

Lucy slipped through the curtain. Put her hand on top of Irene's and said, 'You're doing really well, OK? As you no doubt heard.'

Tears coursed down Irene's face but she didn't contort her face, or try to hide her pain. 'Adrian,' she said in a thick, ragged whisper. 'He is dead?'

Lucy said gently, 'I'm sorry. I didn't know you could hear me.'

Her mouth started to convulse. 'And Elizabeth? They have killed her too?'

'I'm sorry,' Lucy said again.

Irene's head stirred on the pillow. 'I have to know.' Through the fog of drugs and injuries, something in her face glinted fiercely, hard and bright as steel. Lucy remembered what Adrian Calder had said about his wife: *She's a strong woman, like her mother.*

'But why did they kill Adrian?' Irene said. 'I do not understand.'

She gazed at nothing and for a moment Lucy thought she had drifted away, succumbing to the drugs, but then her hand tightened on Lucy's. She whispered, 'Why kill Elizabeth? She is not related. Aleks, yes. But his wife? I think they are cruel. I think they like the killing.'

Lucy stared at Irene. 'What do you mean, Elizabeth isn't related?'

'She does not share the same blood as Aleksandr. Adrian did not share the same blood as Polina but they kill him too. They have no mercy.' The steel flashed once again. 'When will they stop? When there is none of me left?'

Suddenly a firework detonated in Lucy's brain showering yellow and red. All the hairs rose on the back of her neck and along her arms. She scrabbled furiously through her handbag for her phone.

It was about the family blood!

Lucy's fingers flew over the keys, searching the BBC website until she found the report on the Bristol family annihilation story. She scanned the news reports, and then she found it. Apparently Oxana had married Philip Harris in 1984. Her maiden name was Stanton.

Lucy's heart was pounding. Her skull felt too small for her brain.

'Are you related to Oxana Harris?' she asked Irene breathlessly. 'She used to be Oxana Stanton before she was married.'

'Who?' The woman rasped. She looked genuinely puzzled.

Lucy heard Aleksandr's voice wind through her head. *I don't just have relatives in England but in Australia too.*

'What about Lewis Harris, Oxana's son?'

After a long moment, Irene said, 'No.' Her eyes began to go cloudy and her breathing dipped. She was beginning to slide back into sleep. Tears continued to trickle down her face.

Lucy ran outside. Called DI Penman.

'I need to know if Oxana Harris, née Stanton, was related to Aleksandr and Elizabeth Stanton.'

As they spoke, it soon became clear that although the victims shared the same surname, they didn't appear to be related, but Lucy wasn't easily put off. She continued asking questions, probing and pushing, trying to see if there was a link between the two families. Finally, she asked, 'Can you check and see if anyone, er, unusual or foreign, visited them before they died?'

'Like who?' The DI's tone was curious.

'A smartly dressed pair in their early thirties, posing as a Polish couple. Ivan and Yelena Barbolin. They're actually Russian.'

Long silence. She heard some rustling followed by tapping noises that she guessed was a keyboard. 'Visitors . . . hmmm. A South African relative dropped by just after the New Year. Finch Stanton. We interviewed her . . . she's doing a family tree for her father in Cape Town . . .'

For a moment, Lucy couldn't believe it. She'd found a connection. Her mouth opened and closed. She cleared her throat. 'Finch Stanton is related to Adrian Calder.'

'You're kidding.' The policeman sounded stunned.

'Yes, she's a cousin of some sort, but whether she's related directly or through marriage I couldn't tell you. But she is definitely related.' She took a breath. 'Nothing on a Mr and Mrs Barbolin? The Russians?'

When he said no, she explained who they were, and that they'd shot Adrian Calder in the hospital and also possibly killed Aleksandr and Elizabeth Stanton.

'You think they might have set up Oxana Harris's murder?' His tone was disbelieving. 'And her son Lewis's?'

'It's a possibility.'

'Jesus Christ. I'll get the SIO to call you as soon as I can.'

Lucy hung up. Her ears were ringing, her head buzzing.

Why were the FSB killing the Stanton family?

And what about the survivors? Lewis's wife had survived the drowning and Oxana's youngest son, Ben – who Oxana had apparently adopted – was still alive. So was Jenny Forrester. Did that mean they didn't *share the same blood*? A sense of urgency descended upon her. She had to warn the rest of the relatives. Get them to safety.

Before she called Mac, Lucy quickly checked Google to see that there were thousands of Stantons registered as living in the UK. The police would have to get in touch with the South African cousins and get a copy of their family tree in order to track the right ones down.

The cousins.

Her stomach clenched. The near-miss by that car now looked far less like a freak event. Had it been a failed attempt on their lives?

She raced back to Irene. She needed to warn Robin and Finch. She needed to know why the Stanton family had been targeted. But the Russian woman was comatose. She was out cold and didn't respond to Lucy's touch. Frustrated, battling the urge to scream, Lucy went outside. She paced the car park, making phone calls while she waited for Irene to awake.

CHAPTER FORTY-FIVE

Mac did his best to conduct his investigation from his car making phone call after phone call in between checking the satnav to make sure he hadn't missed a vital turning. By the time he parked his car and walked into the hospital, three police forces were conducting their own inquiries into the Stanton murders and every other police force had started looking at any recent deaths of Stantons with a questioning eye.

He ran the gauntlet of the media at the hospital car park entrance, camera lenses following his every move. They'd pore over his photograph and when they found out who he was, the brighter sparks would put two and two together and things would go ballistic. The sooner he found answers the sooner he could stick a cork in the media and prevent a nationwide hysteria.

His senses quickened as he approached the café, where he'd arranged to meet Lucy. He couldn't believe it. Here he was, in the middle of one of the biggest cases of his life, with fifteen people murdered, maybe more, and he was getting that feeling again, the one he always had when he knew he was going to see her.

He spotted her before she saw him. She was at the counter, buying a coffee. She wore tight jeans tucked into boots and a sweater coloured a sort of soft mulberry, which clung to all the right places and seemed to make her skin glow.

'Hey,' he said as he approached. She swung round, eyes alight, and he felt his heart lurch. God, she was gorgeous.

'Coffee?' she asked.

He didn't have time to stop. He was here to talk to the cousins, talk to Nicholas Blain or Baker or whoever he was, keep on top of the investigation, keep pushing it forward, taking on a thousand and one things that needed doing urgently, but he said, 'Great.'

'Another cappuccino, please,' she told the counter server before turning back to Mac. 'Anything else you'd like?'

You, he thought but instead he said, 'A toastie would be good. I'm famished.'

They ate standing up at another counter that overlooked a shop selling get well cards and trinkets. Lucy brought out her phone, sent a text. 'To the cousins,' she told him, 'to let them know where we are. Blain's being discharged. He knows he mustn't leave until he's seen you.'

Mac ate his toastie while she filled him in. Drank his coffee.

'So,' he said. 'You've found your hornet's nest.'

'Yup.' She gave him a grin.

He couldn't help it. He grinned back.

'I leave you alone for two seconds ...' He was shaking his head in mock despair, but he couldn't stop smiling inanely. And even better, nor could she.

'Lucy.' A man's voice.

Both of them looked around.

Nicholas Blain – aka Baker – was holding out a furled black umbrella to Lucy. 'You forgot this.'

'Thanks.' She reached out and took it from him.

'I have to say, it was one of the best debriefings I've had,' Blain told Mac with a smile. But he wasn't looking at Mac. He was looking at Lucy. 'I'd happily get savaged by an attack dog any time if it's Lucy who's sent to my hospital bedside.'

'Blain . . .' Lucy said warningly, but she was blushing.

Mac had never seen her blush before and felt such an intense rush of jealousy he would have liked to have planted his fist in the centre of Blain's smug, smiling face.

Lucy turned to include Mac. Her cheeks were still pink. 'You know each other, right? DI MacDonald. Nicholas Blain. I mean, Baker.'

When Blain put out a hand, Mac was tempted not to take it, but he couldn't refuse, not in his job.

'Call me Nick,' said Blain as they shook.

'DI MacDonald,' said Mac stonily.

Lucy stepped aside. 'I'll leave you guys to it, OK?'

Blain's eyes returned to Lucy. He said, 'I'll call you later.'

Lucy didn't respond. Just walked away.

For a few seconds Mac imagined Lucy with Blain. How Blain put his arms around her. Kissed her. How she kissed him back. And at the same time something fell loose from his soul.

When Blain looked back at Mac, the smile left his face. Mac realised his body language had shifted. He was like an animal growling at a competitor who was approaching his mate. *Back off or I'll tear your throat out.*

He looked Blain straight in the eye, held his gaze. Blain looked at the space where Lucy had been, then back at Mac. Amusement rose. The smile returned.

The two men held gazes.

It was the equivalent of a glove being thrown down.

May the best man win.

CHAPTER FORTY-SIX

Dan was on the Embankment waiting for Ozzie, walking back and forth alongside the RAF war memorial in an attempt to keep warm. The temperature had dropped to just below zero and snow was forecast. As he paced, a text came in from Emily at Six, attaching two files. Immediately he forgot the cold, the bleak grey of the Thames, the lowering cement-coloured sky. His whole being was concentrated on his phone.

The first file was labelled Ivan Golov. The photograph confirmed that it was the same man who was currently being worked on by Ibro and Mirza. The second was a file on Ivan's FSB partner, Yelena Mayask. Dan read both reports to see both agents had seemingly unimpeachable records with the FSB. Yelena was single and seeing another FSB agent. She had a four-year-old boy from a previous relationship, whose grandmother helped looked after him. Ivan was married, no children. He appeared to be faithful and wasn't a womaniser. He earned a fair wage. No gambling debts or prostitute bills or expenses fiddling that Six had found.

How to find the carrot that would persuade Ivan to tell Dan where Jenny was?

He felt more than saw Ozzie approach. Both of them wore thick padded jackets and hats and gloves. Ozzie's nose had reddened in the raw air and he clapped his hands, but whether he was simply trying to get his circulation going or cover a bout of nervousness, Dan couldn't tell.

'Nice weather for it,' Dan remarked.

'I thought you'd find it easier if we spoke in the open.'

Dan nodded in acknowledgement. The men surveyed one another.

'OK,' Ozzie said. 'Spill it.'

Dan described the scene at the cottage. Taking Aimee to her grandparents. Calder's shooting. Hitting the woman, Yelena Mayask. 'I did it to make her let go of my arm. She was stopping me from defending Calder.'

Ozzie pulled a face. 'I lied about your killing her. I was so pissed off with you . . . You broke some teeth and wrenched her neck, but she'll be OK.'

'I know. I saw her moving as I ran after Calder.'

'She's in the Margate Hospital, under guard,' Ozzie said. 'Not that we've advertised the fact, needless to say. She's not saying anything.' His gaze intensified on Dan. 'What about your man?'

'He escaped,' Dan said smoothly. 'I have no idea where he is.'

Ozzie looked at him. 'Bernard wants me to tell you that you must release him to us immediately.'

'If he hadn't escaped,' said Dan, 'and I could hand him over to you, what would you do with him?'

'Use him to negotiate the return of your wife.'

'With who?'

'The FSB,' Ozzie said.

Dan just looked at Ozzie. The officer looked away. Both of them were aware the FSB probably had no knowledge of the operation since, according to Ekaterina, the two FSB agents were rogue, working clandestinely for Edik Yesikov.

'Could he be useful to you?' Dan asked.

'Very much so. He's not just a grunt. He's fairly high up. He did his time in the field but he's been indoors for the past three years. He's with the BSEU. The Bureau for the Support to Export Utilities.'

Dan blinked. So, Ivan wasn't a foot soldier but an agent with a brain. Yesikov obviously didn't want to trust just anyone with this mission.

'Your man,' Ozzie said, 'is important enough for us to offer him half a million dollars and a new life.'

Dan was so startled something must have shown on his face because Ozzie nodded in concord. 'I know. I was surprised too. But apparently he's perfectly positioned to be able to tell us Russia's plans for its utilities future. Russia is already behind the anti-fracking movement in the UK and we suspect she's been undermining France's nuclear projects too. Our friend Ivan can give us the inside track so we can foil Russia's plans. Stay one step ahead.'

Ozzie brought his lower lip between his teeth for a moment. 'Trouble is he's got a wife. If the Russians get a whiff we have Ivan, they'll grab her and exert pressure. We have to get her first. But before we even approach her, we need Ivan.'

'I'll see whether I can track him down for you,' Dan said in an even tone.

Ozzie studied him. 'Don't fuck this up, Dan.'

Dan didn't respond. He was already walking away.

He had the carrot he needed.

Dan drove fast to the quarry. He'd left a message for Ibro when he joined the M25, but the Bosnian didn't call him back for over an hour.

'We have worked all day,' he told Dan. He sounded ebullient. 'He is terrified of the water. He went to pieces, you know? We didn't hurt him, just used water, but he's a mess.'

'He's coherent?'

'He needs to rest a little. But he's ready for you, Daniel. No problem.'

Dan arrived at the quarry at six minutes past four. He'd stopped en route for a packet of cigarettes and a lighter, and the smell of food prompted him to divert briefly for a hasty meal of steak and ale pie, mash and vegetables, and a Mars bar which he devoured while he walked back to his car. He didn't taste what he ate. His mind was too busy. He merely needed fuel. He might not get a break once he started interrogating Ivan Golov.

Ibro greeted him with a handshake and lots of nodding. 'He is absolutely ready for you. One hundred per cent. They don't train them like they used to, you know. Ten years ago it would have taken two days, but today it was barely six hours.'

He didn't want to go into the fact Ivan Golov had probably gone soft since he'd had an office job and he kept his expression perfectly dispassionate, forcing himself to suppress the revulsion that rose inside at the horror he'd instigated. He simply said, 'His clothes?'

Ibro showed him into the concrete building. It used to be a toilet and shower block and each cubicle was partitioned to the roof, which was also concrete. Light came from bare electric bulbs in the ceiling. Steel casement windows lined the far wall. Most were open to the elements, their glass having been broken. The air was cold and wet. Despite his down jacket Dan could feel a chill start to creep into his bones.

The Russian's clothes were neatly stacked next to one of the basins. 'Here.' Ibro passed Dan a small key, which Dan palmed. He put the clothes in the crook of his arm.

Dan found Ivan Golov at the far end of the shower block. He was naked and handcuffed to one of the iron windows. The room was freezing cold and slick and shining with water. It smelled of bleach. Ibro and Mirza had hosed not just the Russian but the walls, ceiling and floor. They had then put two plastic chairs against the wall, on either side of a small metal table.

When Dan stepped into view, Ivan cowered into a ball, eyes squeezed shut as he cringed to one side. He was panting, gasping with fear, his whole body trembling uncontrollably. Dan saw the man's wrist was swollen and red where he'd broken it in the hospital, but Ibro had eased the cuffs so they didn't cut off his circulation. When he said something in Russian – it sounded as though he was begging – Dan said, 'Good evening, Mr Golov.'

Ivan cracked open his eyes. 'P-please,' he stammered. 'No more.'

Dan waited.

'I beg you.' He began to sob. Tears streaked his face. His chest and stomach heaved in and out as he gasped. He had a strong body, fit and well muscled, but he was shuddering as though he was gripped in a fever. Dan could hear his teeth chattering.

'Help me,' he pleaded.

Dan knew he was taking a risk with such an athletic man but with Jenny's life at stake, he didn't see he had any other option. Hoping Ibro was right and that he'd broken Ivan, he stepped forward and unlocked the handcuffs. He was ready for the Russian to spring up and attack him, but Ivan collapsed to the floor, groaning and shuddering.

'*Oh, Gospodi, oh Bozhe!*' Dear God, oh, dear God.

Dan helped him up. Helped him get dressed. He would have fallen over if Dan hadn't bolstered him. He shook continually, mumbling beneath his breath. It sounded as though he was praying.

'Please,' said Dan. 'Sit down.'

Dan took one chair. Ivan took the other. He put a hand on his forearm, protecting his broken wrist. His teeth were still chattering and his eyes were jumpy, flitting between the door and Dan continually, no doubt in terror of Ibro and Mirza coming in again.

'Now,' said Dan. 'I want you to understand one thing. If you don't tell me where my wife is, you will remain here with the Bosnians indefinitely. They will ensure things will get worse. When you eventually die of your injuries, you will be buried in the quarry. Nobody will know what happened to you.'

'Yes, they will.' Ivan raised his chin, trying to find some bravado, save some face. His voice was raspy and rough, but his words were clear. 'My people have resources. They will find me.'

'If you're talking about the FSB, they don't even know you're here.'

'Of course they do.' But his tone wasn't firm enough and he seemed to realise it because he looked away.

'We've been in touch with Edik Yesikov. He denies knowing you or Yelena Mayask. Your mission was always deniable. You're on your own. So either you tell me where my wife is, or –'

'Yelena?' Ivan said. His mouth gaped. 'She is alive?'

He stared at Dan. He was astonished, Dan saw, but it was the light that began to glimmer at the back of the man's eyes that made Dan come alert. However, he didn't show he'd noticed anything. He continued speaking as though he hadn't been interrupted. '. . . Or I will kill you. Not with anything quick like a gun or a knife, but with water. Over the following days the Bosnians will work on you, non-stop, until your stomach ruptures and your lungs collapse.'

The trembling increased. 'No,' he said. His voice cracked. 'Please, not that . . .'

'Where is my wife?' Dan demanded.

Ivan planted a fist on the table but his trembling made the metal clatter. He jerked back and held the elbow above his damaged wrist, trying to hold Dan's gaze but his eyes kept sliding away.

Ten years ago Dan would have been tempted to grab him and punch him senseless, but he knew better now. He'd learned how to let silences work for him. He leaned back in his chair, scratched an imaginary itch on his throat and let the silence stretch. The air was now so cold ice had begun to form on the floor.

Eventually, almost imperceptibly, some tension left the Russian's shoulders. Dan breathed in a lungful of air, breathed it out in a gusting sigh. 'Ivan, you will leave me no choice.'

Ivan turned his torso away from Dan. Squeezed his eyes shut. 'I will tell you, if you send me home.'

Dan gave a bark of laughter. 'You really think Yesikov will give you a hero's welcome?'

Another silence descended, so dense that the only thing Dan could hear was the pulse in his ears and the soft flutter of cloth from the Russian's trembling.

'Then kill me,' Ivan said. His words were defiant but his body betrayed his terror by convulsing violently. He merely had to think of Ibro forcing the tube down his throat and his body reacted.

'I really don't want to have to do that,' Dan said gently. 'Look, I can see you're between a rock and a hard place. Damned if you tell me where my wife is. Damned if you don't.' He gave a long sigh as he brought out the packet of cigarettes and lighter he'd bought at the service station. Took off the cellophane and silver-paper membrane and shook out a cigarette. Offered it across the table. Ivan was shaking so much Dan had to help him light it.

'But what else can I do?' Dan continued. 'You're married. What would you do if we decided to kidnap Alisa? Put her under some pressure?'

The threat to Ivan's wife was unmistakable, and when the Russian didn't respond, didn't leap to protect her, Dan's instincts came alert once more. Ivan was dragging shakily on his cigarette, gaze fixed on the floor, his mind seemingly elsewhere.

Dan let silence fall again. He waited until Ivan had finished his cigarette before he rested his elbows on the table and leaned in towards him. 'Now, about Yelena Mayask . . .'

A tension came over Ivan. Dan tried to analyse it.

'Where . . . is she?' Ivan asked. It was a whisper, and although he'd only said three words, they gave him away.

Dan felt the beginnings of a wave of triumph swell in his belly but quickly quelled it. He didn't want his expression to change.

'She's somewhere safe,' Dan told him. 'She's OK.'

Dan had no doubt that if the Russian was fit and well and not terrified for his life, he would have retained a face like a board, but not today. The flash of relief was unmistakable.

'She hasn't told me where my wife is yet,' Dan went on. 'She said she wouldn't until she knew you were OK.'

Ivan's eyes widened. Dan knew he had to tread carefully and try not to let the man know he hadn't seen Yelena, and had no idea of her or her personality, her thoughts.

'How long have you worked together?' Dan asked.

Ivan's shoulders twisted. 'A few missions,' he mumbled. 'We work together well.'

'That's what she said. That you work together well. It's good when you find a reliable partner. Someone to depend upon.'

Ivan was still nodding. 'She is the best partner,' he agreed. 'And she is OK?'

Dan picked up the cigarette packet, put it down. 'It was her idea . . .' He looked away. 'I'm not sure . . .'

Ivan watched Dan, uncertain. 'She has an idea?'

'Yes.' Dan sighed. 'But I don't think my superiors will go for it.'

Ivan leaned forward. 'What is her idea?'

'I don't think you will like it.'

He was almost out of his chair. '*What?*'

Dan leaned back, frowning. 'Well, she said you could both be useful here, in England.'

Ivan stared at him.

'I mean,' Dan went on, 'you both know things that are of interest to us. But it would mean not returning to Russia. I don't suppose you've ever thought of living in, say, London. And what about your wife? We'd never be able to get her out, so you'd be here, all alone . . .'

Ivan's fingers were trembling so hard he couldn't take another cigarette from the packet.

'But,' Dan went on thoughtfully, 'there are lots of Russians living in London. You wouldn't feel out of place, you know. You can get cabbage pies, herring and sausage. *Pelmeni* and *Smetana*. We have Russian barbers, shops selling matryoshkas . . .'

Ivan had a cigarette in his mouth now, but his fingers were fumbling with the lighter. Whether from nerves, excitement or terror Dan couldn't tell. He hoped it was all three.

'I guess it would be easier if you had some money. Say if we gave you half a million in sterling. Enough to buy a little apartment, maybe start a little business, like a shop or café. We'd help you set up a new life. They wouldn't be able to find you, unless you wanted them to. And in return you give us everything you know about the Bureau for the Support to Export Utilities. And I mean *everything.*'

Ivan gripped the lighter in both hands and finally flicked on the flame. Sucked in smoke like a man starved. He said, 'This is Yelena's idea?'

'Yes.' Dan's lie came easily.

'Half a million sterling?'

'Yes.' At least that was the truth. Dan looked at the man straight. He said, 'Where is my wife?'

Although Ivan Golov didn't have any guarantee that anything Dan said was true, or any evidence Dan wouldn't send in Ibro and Mirza to torture him until he died, the Russian clutched on to the one thing that investigators had relied on for thousands of years: hope.

Dan only had to ask him a few questions. Jenny had been flown directly to a specialised private clinic on the outskirts of Moscow. Ivan knew the name of the place and where it was because he'd been told if for any reason he and Yelena couldn't get Jenny out on the jet, they were to get her there by any other means.

'Why?' Dan asked.

Ivan looked blank.

'*Why a clinic? Why does Edik Yesikov want my wife?*'

The Russian opened and closed his mouth. 'I don't know this.'

'OK.' Dan took a breath. 'Why did you kill Polina Calder and her children?' He switched the subject to try and see if Ivan was lying about Jenny or not.

Ivan looked surprised. 'We did not kill them.'

For the first time, Dan got a sensation of something very wrong. 'What do you mean? You killed Adrian Calder in the hospital –'

'Yes. We were told to eliminate him after we had your wife. But we did not kill his family. He did this, yes?'

Dan wrestled to keep his unease from showing. 'What about Aleksandr Stanton?'

'We eliminated his wife, on orders received yesterday.'

Dan's stomach tightened. 'You didn't kill Aleksandr Stanton?'

'He was killed by a horse, no?' The Russian frowned.

A short, snaking silence.

'No,' said Dan. 'He wasn't.'

The Russian seemed to make little of it and gave a shrug.

After a moment Dan asked more questions. Tried to work out through this dark and bloody mess what exactly was going on. Was Adrian Calder guilty after all? But what about Aleksandr Stanton? He studied Ivan carefully but couldn't be certain whether the Russian was lying, or if he was genuine and telling the truth.

'Half a million sterling?' Ivan said for the third time. 'Yes?'

Dan left Ivan Golov sitting on the chair being guarded by the Bosnians. Outside, it was dark and icy cold, no wind. His fingers tingled as he brought out his phone and rang Ozzie. Gave him directions to collect the Russian.

'Don't let him out of your sight,' Dan told him. 'In case he's lying about Jenny's whereabouts.'

'Don't worry,' Ozzie said cheerfully, 'we won't.'

'One thing you should know. He's holding a torch for Yelena Mayask.'

'Oh, poor boy. Because it's not reciprocated. She's in love with her FSB boyfriend. Does that mean Ivan's not screaming about his wife joining him over here?'

'Not a whimper.'

'That's rather good news. It'll save us a fortune.'

Dan went to Ibro and Mirza. 'Keep him here until he's collected. And thanks. It was a good job.'

'No problem.' Ibro and Mirza shook his hand. 'Thanks for the money.'

Dan was in his car when his phone rang. Lucy Davies said, 'Where are you?'

'On the M1 heading back to London.'

'Can I suggest you make a diversion to Margate? Irene Cavendish has woken up. She's just told me a very interesting story about your wife.'

CHAPTER FORTY-SEVEN

Jenny stood at the window. Before her stretched a vast sea of snow-covered grass and thistles dotted with clumps of frosted spruce trees and hawthorn. A copse stood to the left, icy branches reaching their bony fingers into a grey sky. On the right stood a low-slung barn and some stables. In between was nothing but snow. Snow as far as her eye could see. No point in running away. She'd only die of exposure.

They'd moved her from the clinic. Once again, they had injected her with some kind of anaesthetic and transported her unconscious. She had no idea what day it was, or what time, let alone where she was. Just that it seemed to be in the middle of nowhere.

There was no point in panicking. She was where she was, for whatever reason. She wondered what they wanted from Dan. Whether he was being compromised, what mission it was part of, and whether the FCO or MI5 were involved yet. She had to hope so. They would negotiate her release. Dan would come and get her. She had to hold on to these thoughts. Retain her sanity.

Despite her reasoning, her pulse was thudding and she felt short of breath. Her emotions were shimmering on the surface of her skin. Fear, horror, dread.

What had Dan told Aimee?

Immediately a wave of distress rose as dark and red as an open wound, and she pushed the thought away. She mustn't think of Aimee or she'd lose it, go insane. She would think about her later. She had to concentrate on the *now* and find a way to escape. But first she had to find out what she was doing here. Knowledge, as Dan always said, was power.

Slowly, she reached out and grasped the latch. Opened the window. The air was bitingly cold and fresh and she breathed in deeply, feeling her emotions steady. Leaving the window slightly ajar, she turned to survey the room. *Reconnoitre*, she told herself. *Gain information.*

Her eyes travelled over the heavy wooden floorboards. The wooden bed with a big headboard. Rough-woven rugs. More wooden furniture: chairs, bedside tables, wardrobe, two chests of drawers. An enormous flat-screen TV was bolted to the wall opposite the bed. Although a fire had been lit in the open fireplace, the radiators pumped out more heat. Cameras were positioned in the ceiling, covering what appeared to be the entire room. There were two doors. One to the left, the other straight ahead.

The first door led to a bathroom. A huge bath with clawed feet sat on one side. On the other was an open shower. The walls and floor were pale stone. She touched the floor to find it was warm. Underfloor heating. Fluffy towels and toiletries stood on a shelf next to the shower. Comb, hairbrush, hairdryer. Shower cap. More cameras.

She opened the other door. Looked up and down a corridor. More wooden floors. More radiators. To the right, a slab of light lay on the floor, indicating an open door. Jenny walked that way. Glanced at the pictures on the walls. Hunters with guns, dead wolves and bears. Sheep with huge horns.

She peered through the open door to find a sitting room with overstuffed sofas and armchairs, walls lined with stuffed animal heads: bear, foxes, martins and wolves, all snarling with their lips drawn back over frightening-looking teeth. There were stuffed birds too, duck and partridge, and a huge salmon hung above a massive open fireplace that glowed with burning coals.

Her spirits spiked when she spotted a phone on one of the tables. She rushed across, lifted the receiver but she heard nothing. No dialling tone, no buzz.

She dropped the phone back in its cradle when she heard footsteps. Light steps, quick and soft. Heart hopping, Jenny scooted behind the door. Listened to the footsteps pass. Quickly she ducked through the doorway and glanced down the corridor to see a petite woman in jeans and Ugg boots enter the room she'd just left.

Jenny crept along the corridor, in the opposite direction. A camera began to blink its tiny red eye and turned to follow her. She opened another door to find another bedroom, smaller than hers, but just as masculine. It appeared unused. She found a study lined with books and a games room with a full-sized snooker table, dartboard and cigar humidor. More bedrooms, all unused except one, which was covered in feminine detritus. Underwear, scarves and jewellery mingled with make-up on just about every surface. Did this belong to the woman she'd seen?

Jenny hurried to the room next door. For a moment she thought this was another unoccupied room but then she took in the vanity mirror on the table by the window, the hairbrush and creams. A sound, so tiny she thought she might have imagined it, made her spin round, her senses jolting.

A woman was propped up in bed. Slender fingers held a leather-bound book. A bandage covered half her face but Jenny could still see that she was beautiful. Wings of glossy raven hair flowed over her shoulders, framing an exquisite bone structure.

'You,' the woman said. It was like a rebuke.

Trembling, her veins prickling with anxiety, Jenny left the room.

She explored a huge kitchen, fridges filled with vodka and beer, fresh meat and vegetables. A pantry with more supplies. At the other end of the house were two more bedrooms. Both were in use, obviously by men. Men's shirts, underwear and shoes lay on chairs, on the floor. Lastly, she stepped outside. Cold air bit her throat and lungs. Not far away an engine rumbled. She tracked the sound down to find a large generator, which obviously powered everything in the lodge: heating, lights, refrigerator. Two massive polyurethane fuel bladder tanks sat to one side, which she guessed were airlifted in when reserves ran low. She crunched her way to inspect two top-of-the-range Land Cruisers. Both were covered in snow. Using her elbow, she pushed the snow away from the driver's windows. Both were locked. Neither had keys in the ignition.

'Come inside.' A man spoke. 'It is cold.'

Jenny looked at the seemingly never-ending steppe, felt the chill biting into her bones. Slowly, she sat down in the snow. The cold immediately start to soak into her jeans but she gave no indication. She didn't look at the man.

The man vanished inside. A few minutes later, the woman in jeans and Ugg boots appeared, except she wasn't wearing Uggs any more but snow boots and a padded jacket. 'Hello,' she said. 'I'm Milena.'

Jenny didn't say anything in return. Just looked at her. Milena was also beautiful, but in a completely different way from the dark-haired woman in the bed. She was tiny and blonde, like a doll, which made the bruises on her face all the more shocking. Her nose had been broken and her lips split. The scabs were deep purple and looked incredibly sore. Both her eyes were rimmed with blood. It looked as though she'd been punched repeatedly in the face.

When she asked Jenny to come inside, Jenny didn't respond.

'Come, you will freeze to death out here.'

Her English was surprisingly good, making Jenny wonder if she'd been to the UK. She wasn't going to ask though. She didn't want to make friends. Jenny shrugged. Looked away.

'You must be hungry and thirsty. Please, come inside and have some tea and jam. Hot soup. I made bread this morning. It's very good.'

Jenny shook her head.

'You must have something. You have come a long way.'

Silence.

'Please. It is not good for you out here.' The woman was getting increasingly anxious. 'It is minus twenty degrees.'

Jenny tried not to show her shock. She didn't think she'd ever experienced a temperature below minus two or three.

'You must come inside,' Milena pleaded.

Jenny shook her head again.

'I am here to help you. Tell me what you would like.'

Jenny just looked at her. *I would like to go home.*

Milena's hands fluttered agitatedly like trapped birds. 'I'm sorry.'

Jenny took a breath. Steadied herself. She said, 'I will stay here, in the snow. I will not eat or drink or bathe or do anything until you tell me why I am here.'

Milena looked at her a long time, her breath clouding the air like lace ribbons. Finally, she said, 'Ekaterina will tell you.'

CHAPTER FORTY-EIGHT

Irene could hear her niece and nephew talking in low tones. Her soul shivered as she realised it was time to tell them the family story, because although Timur had insisted his children would grow up knowing every word, Irene wasn't so sure. Their father might have been rabid about the truth, demonic and obsessed, but deep down he was a kind man and she believed he'd want to spare them from some of the more brutal facts. She would have to ask him. She'd sworn she'd never see him again, but today she wanted answers because if it had been Timur who had found out about her granddaughter and told the FSB, she would take a knife and stab him in the heart over and over.

Memories drifted through her mind like flakes of ancient ash: Timur five years old and shrieking in the bath; Timur with her and Anna helping him dress in his first suit on his ninth birthday, he had looked so *proud*. Timur standing there looking baffled as she hugged him goodbye the morning she'd run away, knowing something was wrong but not what it was. Timur ten years later turning up on her doorstep in Norfolk with a bunch of flowers and a bright smile.

'*Salka!*' he'd said. '*Surpriz!*'

She had stared at him like an idiot, mouth slack. She didn't know whether to scream, slap him, or burst into tears and draw him into a hug.

'Dmitry's parents told me where you were,' he added. His expression was filled with glee, and for a moment he was the boisterous, ebullient little brother she remembered putting a grass snake in their nanny's bed.

She still couldn't speak. She nodded. Her mouth had turned quite dry.

'I defected two months ago. They only released me last week. Lots of debriefing. Questions, questions. I'm a free man, now, though.' His eyes narrowed slightly. 'I didn't tell them about you, so you don't have to worry.'

Still she remained speechless.

'It's a nice place you have.' He ran his eyes over the stone-built farmhouse, the barns and caged areas where the chickens ranged in the open air. He looked at the stable cat lying in the yard, nursing her kittens next to the water trough, and then back at Irene. 'Aren't you going to invite me in?'

She didn't move. She stood there with her hands hanging at her sides and her mouth gaping.

'Who is it?' A boy's voice spoke behind her, breaking briefly mid-sentence and giving away the fact he was on the cusp of manhood.

Before she could move Timur's attention clicked to focus on the child. His eyes widened in shock.

She wanted to spin round and grab her son and slam the door shut in Timur's face but it was too late. Timur was looking at Aleksandr now standing at her side and he was staring and staring.

Aleksandr, her son, fourteen years old and tall and aquiline-featured, with bright blond hair and piercing blue eyes just like his father.

She said to her son, 'Inside. Now.'

Her voice was like ice.

'But I want to –'

'*Now.*'

Watchful, reluctant, Aleksandr backed inside the house but she knew he wouldn't go far. His curiosity had been lit. He'd eavesdrop if he could. Some would say he was nosy, but Irene saw it more as an intelligent inquisitiveness, because her son liked nothing more than knowing exactly what was going on at any time. It was a way of being in control, she supposed. Aleksandr had never liked surprises. Just like his father.

Irene stepped forward and into the farmyard. Closed the door behind her. She was trembling inside but she held her head high.

Timur was still staring at the space where Aleks had stood, as though the door was still open. 'How can you stand seeing him every day?' he asked. His voice was almost a whisper. 'I mean he's so like Lazar, doesn't it drive you crazy?'

Suddenly the air felt solid with fear. For a piercing second she saw herself and Timur, at seventeen and ten, her trying to hide her bruises and tears. *No, I'm fine, fine, don't ask again or I'll take away your train.* The look of horror from Timur who loved his train more than anything and her feeling of guilt at threatening him, but she didn't want him to know what was going on. She'd wanted to protect him.

'Lazar?' Her voice was thin and high. 'What do you mean?'

A trickle of pity inched into her brother's eyes. 'We all knew what was going on, OK? We couldn't very well miss it. He was noisy, yes? He didn't care if we heard. He *liked* that we heard. And you cried all the time.'

'Don't you dare say a word,' she hissed.

Timur's mouth opened and closed. 'He doesn't know?'

'And nor does Arthur. They think he's Dmitry's son.'

'*What?*' Timur's jaw dropped. 'But he doesn't even *look* like Dmitry!'

Irene bit her lips to stop their tremble. 'I told them his looks came from another branch of the family.'

'Jesus Christ.' He closed his eyes briefly, the flowers hanging upside down and forgotten by his thigh. 'You can't do that, Irina. You've got to tell him. He should know where his genes come from.'

The mere thought made her feel faint and her legs went boneless and she dropped on to the step. Put her head in her hands. Shame and hatred rose up her throat, hot and corrosive.

'Irene . . .' She heard Arthur's voice as though from a great distance. 'Are you all right?'

Her husband stalked into view. Arthur Cavendish, tall and broad with a ruddy face, brown curly hair thinning on top and kind brown eyes that weren't kind right now but guarded and hard and fixed upon Timur.

'Yes, yes.' She made a herculean effort to rise but when Timur offered to help, she rebuffed him, waiting until Arthur was at her side and putting his arm around her. 'It was a shock, that's all.' She tried to smile but it was tremulous. She could see the anxiety in Arthur's face and quickly tried to allay it. She didn't want him thinking anything was wrong. 'This is my little brother, Timur. He has come to surprise us.'

Timur half-heartedly offered the flowers. Both men looked at Irene, waiting for a cue.

'And what a surprise!' She gave a slightly hysterical laugh as she took the flowers. 'I wish you had given us warning! We could have prepared for you, but as it is . . .' She tried to give a shrug but it was more of a shudder. Arthur was watching her, concerned, and she saw she had no choice but to invite Timur in, pretend that everything was all right. And pray he wouldn't let slip her secret.

'Would you have a cup of tea?' she asked Timur. 'Coffee? Water?'

'Tea,' he said. 'Thank you.'

In the kitchen she put the flowers in a vase and set them on the table. Put on the kettle. Her hands were steady but her breathing was shallow and panicky. Arthur fetched cake and biscuits while Timur propped his hips against the counter and told them of his journey from Russia, and his plans to migrate to South Africa. He was, apparently, flying out the following week. Arthur laid four plates on the table, saying, 'Shall I get Aleks? He'll go mad to meet you, Timur. He's so proud of his heritage.'

Timur's gaze fixed upon Irene. He raised his eyebrows.

She said, keeping her voice level, 'Dmitry was the son of a former prince. As you know.'

Timur continued to stare at her.

'Aleks's grandparents were a former prince and princess,' she added in the same smooth tone. 'As you also know.'

Timur said nothing. His expression turned dangerously flat.

Sensing the chilly undercurrent, Arthur watched them uneasily.

'Which makes me . . .' There was a flurry at the doorway as Aleks appeared, all teenage angles and energy. 'The grandson of royalty!' He sped to Timur and looked at him closely. 'You're my uncle?'

Irene wanted to pick up the vase of flowers and hurl it against the wall. He'd been eavesdropping all the time.

Timur grinned at Aleks. 'Hello nephew.'

'Wow.' Aleksandr looked at him, awestruck. 'You're the first of Mum's relations I've met.'

Somewhere inside Irene's mind a cog continued to turn. Fourteen years' worth of lies and subterfuge hung as delicately and fragile as spun glass. As long as Timur kept quiet all would be well. As long as he kept the secret, things would continue as normal.

'Timur can't stay for long,' she said. 'He's got to be somewhere this evening.' She gave him a hard look. 'Haven't you?'

'Have I?' Her brother grinned easily. He appeared to be enjoying her discomfiture.

Apparently unaware of the atmosphere, Aleks grabbed a chair and pulled it alongside Timur. 'So, what's Russia really like?' he asked, tucking into a large slice of cake, speaking between mouthfuls. 'Everyone I know is terrified of it. Mum's told us stories of famines and purges, it's really scary stuff, but the country's meant to be beautiful. Wild forests and steppes, the lakes clear enough to see to the bottom. I've got pictures upstairs, do you want to come and see?'

'No.' Her voice was sharp and she hurriedly softened it as she added, 'You can bring them down if you like, though. We'd like to see them too.'

Aleks gave her an odd look but didn't demur. He crammed the remainder of the cake into his mouth and sped upstairs, returning with a variety of books and magazine cuttings. He spread them across the table and Timur looked through them, talking to Aleksandr about everything from his work (he was an industrial engineer), what the hunting was like in Russia (lots of deer, wolves and bear), to the political situation in Russia (since it was 1962, and at the height of the cold war, things were tense).

'You knew my father?' Aleks asked. 'My grandparents?'

Timur looked at Irene. 'Yes,' he said. 'I knew them.'

Her heart was beating as fast as a pigeon's fleeing from a hawk. So far, her brother hadn't lied. Would he lie for her? For her family?

'What was Dad like?' Aleks craned his neck to meet Timur's eye. 'I mean Mum's told me, but I'd love to know more.'

'What has she told you?'

Aleks scrambled for a photograph. It showed Dmitry's parents, Prince Vladimir Mikhail Kasofsky and his wife, Princess Sofia Varvarova, dancing with friends in the family palace in Lazarevo. The men wore tailored army uniforms and medals, the women ball gowns and jewels adorned their throats and hair.

'These two are my grandparents.' He pointed them out before bringing out another photograph. 'And this is my father.' It showed Prince Dmitry as a little boy at a picnic party on the Lazarevo estate. 'When their palace was burned down, they ran away to Moscow. My father grew up in poverty. It was hard for them, but they managed. He eventually became a teacher. Which is when he met Mum.' His expression was bright as he repeated what she'd told him. 'He was very intelligent.' Aleks looked proud. 'And strong. Not just physically,' he added quickly, 'but mentally. You had to be mentally strong to endure what he did. He went to a gulag, did you know?'

Timur nodded.

'He was a very brave man,' Aleks said. He was looking at Timur, waiting for him to agree, perhaps to add or make an embellishment of some sort, but her brother remained quite still, his button-black eyes crawling over Irene's face.

Irene said, 'Yes, he was brave. Now, Aleks. I would like to talk to my brother alone for a moment. Perhaps you could tidy up?' Which was an instruction to take his Russia paraphernalia back upstairs.

'But, Mum,' he protested. 'I've hardly shown him anything. I've got loads more –'

'Do as your mother says.' Arthur's voice was brusque.

Aleks blinked. It wasn't often his stepfather spoke harshly to him. For the first time, he seemed to become aware that something wasn't right and he looked at each of them, eyes sharp and trying to determine what was going on.

'Now,' Arthur added in the same tone.

For an instant Irene thought Aleks wouldn't go, but then he relented. The second he'd gone, Arthur said, 'So it's all true then.' He was looking between Timur and Irene. 'That Dmitry was a prince.'

'Yes,' said Timur at the same time as Irene said, 'Of course.'

'How amazing.' Arthur gave Irene a twisted smile. 'It's not that I didn't believe you, love, but it just seemed so incredible. And terrible, too, what happened to the family.'

Timur stared at Irene for a second. Then he nodded and turned his gaze to Arthur. 'It had to happen,' he said. 'The revolution. The people were nothing but slaves, dominated by just one hundred families who held all the wealth of the country.'

'One hundred?' Arthur repeated, shocked. 'Is that all?'

Timur nodded. 'The people hated the nobles with every inch of their fibre. They thought them selfish and greedy. The nobles on the other hand hated the people, thinking them stupid, rude and disgustingly filthy. Which a lot of them were, but with both sides thinking in terms of "us" and "them", they were never going to understand each other. Civil war was almost guaranteed.'

'You're saying no one was blameless?' Arthur looked surprised, and as the men started a discussion on the Bolshevik coup Irene moved around the kitchen slowly, feeling dizzy and off-balance with relief. *Timur was going to keep her secret.*

Half an hour passed congenially between Timur and Arthur, and then Timur looked at Irene and said, 'It's time for me to go.'

She nodded. Relief made her legs feel as though they might collapse at any second. She led the way along the corridor and outside, where she saw Aleksandr was playing with the kittens, but she was concentrating so hard on getting Timur away that she didn't take in what her son was actually doing for a few seconds.

He was watching a kitten flailing, struggling to swim in the water trough. He studied it without expression as it choked and floundered, half-drowned and wailing in distress, and when it suddenly vanished beneath the surface of the water, peered at it with a frown.

Timur exploded across the farmyard.

'YOU LITTLE SHIT!' he roared.

'But I only wanted to see if it could swim!' Aleksandr cried.

Timur plucked the kitten from the water trough and deposited it next to the mother cat and then he spun round and grabbed the boy by the head and forced him to bend over. Ducked his head deep into the trough. Water slopped wildly all around as Aleks struggled but Timur held him fast. 'How do you like it, you little fuck!' he screamed. Arthur pushed past Irene, running low and fast across the yard but as he came near, Timur released the boy who fell to his knees, spluttering and coughing and dripping wet.

'You're just like your fucking father!' Timur was screaming and pointing at Aleks, shaking from head to toe as though he was being buffeted by a storm. 'And I'm not talking about Dmitry, who was a decent man, I'm talking about Lazar fucking Yesikov who is a rapist and murderer! You've got a mass murderer's DNA stamped all over you, his genes crawling through every vein!'

Timur stood over Aleksandr, shouting so loudly the veins stood out on his neck. His face was puce. 'You think you're so fucking high and mighty, descended from royalty! Ha! What a laugh! Your real father's nothing but a psychopathic peasant who sucked his way into our father's favour where he'd slice open a pregnant woman's belly for the fun of it and leave the foetus for the dogs to eat!'

Arthur tried to get between Timur and Aleks but Timur kept sidestepping him, stabbing his finger violently at Alesksandr.

'And do you know who your grandfather is?' he yelled. 'Your mother's father? I bet she lied about that too!'

'No!' Irene found her feet. Began to stumble for her son. 'Please, Timur. Don't . . .'

'General Kazimir!' Timur roared. He was looking at Aleks, triumph lacing his voice. 'Ever heard of him? The Butcher of Ukraine? He's one of the most notorious mass murderers the world has ever seen. He helped imprison and execute tens of millions of ordinary people. That's your heritage. You're not a fucking prince. You're a nasty, cruel little freak.'

The last scatter of hope gusted out of Irene.

'And your children will be nothing but vicious little freaks too,' Timur said. He glanced round at his sister. He was trembling all over but his voice suddenly dropped, became calm.

He said, quite clearly, his voice carrying to each corner of the farmyard, 'If I were you, I'd get him sterilised.'

Without another word, Timur walked to his car, climbed in and drove away. He didn't back.

CHAPTER FORTY-NINE

Dan sat quietly, listening to Irene's story with a rising sense of frustration. Why had Lucy insisted he come? The policewoman was sitting next to him, while Irene's nephew and niece sat opposite. Apparently they'd heard the story before, but from their father's point of view.

'It sounds a bit different this way round,' Finch admitted. 'I feel really sorry for Irene. Dad behaved pretty appallingly from the sound of it.'

'I don't understand,' Dan said, trying to keep his impatience from view. He wanted to be organising a rescue mission for his wife, not sitting in a hospital listening to stories. 'What has all this got to do with Jenny?'

'My son, Aleksandr,' she said gently. 'He is your wife's father.'

Dan stared for a second.

'Your wife,' Irene said, 'is the granddaughter of Lazar Yesikov. Her great-grandfather is General Kazimir.'

Dan ignored the race of goosebumps that scurried across his skin. 'But her parents are Adam and Mary Shelby. They live in Bath.'

Irene's head moved heavily on the pillow, up and down. 'Yes. But they are not her birth parents. They are Aleksandr and Elizabeth.'

Dan's brain felt as though it was being squeezed in a vice. 'If you and Aleksandr were estranged – you said you hadn't seen or spoken to him for over fifty years – how do you know about this?'

Irene looked pleased at the question. 'The only time I saw my son after I left the farm, was at his wedding. Aleks hated me for lying to him all those years. He said that to him I was dead. However, despite his loathing of me, Arthur managed to persuade him that I should attend his wedding. This is when I met Elizabeth.' A smile unfurled as gentle as petals in the woman's eyes. 'We immediately felt a bond. We both loved Aleks. We both saw his stubbornness, and also his kindness. He could be a very generous and kind man.'

Dan's mind flashed to the drowning kitten and something must have shown on his face because Irene's expression hardened. 'So, he was cruel to a cat. This doesn't make him a monster.'

A twisting silence ensued.

'I suppose not,' Dan said. He didn't want to alienate her.

Irene nodded cursorily in acknowledgement of his concession. She said, 'Elizabeth and I, we secretly kept in touch. We became great friends. We'd meet in London from time to time. I'd show her Russian art, she took me to smart places for lunch. She was very upset that Aleks refused to have children, and when she fell pregnant, we truly believed he would be won round because of his love for her. But no. He went crazy. He demanded she kill the child. My son! Killing his baby!' Fire rose in her eyes. 'I hated him for this, what he did to his beautiful wife.'

Dan remained perfectly still. Every person who'd been shuffling in their seat or walking along the ward seemed to be holding their breath. You could have heard a pin drop.

'Elizabeth calls me, crying. She is hysterical. She doesn't want to lose her husband but she doesn't want to lose her child, either. Together, we make a plan. Aleks drives her to the clinic, where I lie in wait, hiding. Together, we see the doctor and explain Elizabeth no longer wants the abortion. She wants to have the child adopted. The clinic, they give us details of adoption agencies.'

She shifted restlessly. 'When Aleks collects Elizabeth, she doesn't tell him she has not had the abortion. He informs her he has had a vasectomy. They will never have another child. He is kind to her, but she is cold to him. She says she cannot stay with him at the moment. She needs time alone to recover from this dreadful thing. Elizabeth comes to me. I help her through her pregnancy, and I am with her when my granddaughter is born . . .'

Her voice became unsteady. Tears welled in her eyes. 'Ah. She is the most beautiful thing. So precious. So sweet. It is almost unbearable that we have to let her go . . .'

Her eyes were on Dan's, huge and pleading. 'But we had to. You understand?'

Unable to imagine what the women had gone through, he gave a nod. Irene exhaled.

'The adoption agency, they find the perfect parents for my granddaughter. Elizabeth registers what is called an "absolute veto" with the agency. This means that she cannot be contacted under any circumstances by her child in the future. Elizabeth is reunited with Aleks. The years pass. Our secret is safe.'

Irene's gaze turned distant. She plucked at her blanket. She had started shaking, a tiny unceasing tremor that jittered through her fingers and hands. She said, 'But then, I think I have made a mistake. When Polina has little Tasha, she looks so like my first granddaughter when she is born, I tell her all about her cousin. I feel someone should know about her.'

Her fingers pleated the blanket into narrow folds. 'I am always worried about my secret granddaughter, that she knows nothing of her heritage, her true parents, her medical history. What if she falls ill? What if she needs a kidney?'

Irene made a sound halfway between a sob and a laugh. 'I am always worrying! But Polina, she tells Adrian my worries. He is a kind man. He pays for the private investigator to check on my granddaughter from time to time. Nicholas Blain, he is very good. He gives us pictures, tells us about her life. I begin to sleep well.' She turned her head away. 'But then the killings start. When Aleksandr is murdered, Elizabeth and I, we are very frightened. Elizabeth is desperate to see her daughter ... We want to try and protect her in case the killers come after her also. We agree we should contact her and tell her the story. We do not know if Zama knows or not that she is adopted ...'

Dan felt as though he'd touched an electric pylon. His whole body stiffened, his skin flickering. 'Zama?' he repeated.

'This is what we call your wife. Zama. It is from the Russian word "*zamaskirovanni*", meaning hidden or disguised. Camouflaged.'

All at once, things began to tumble into place.

Zama Kasofsky.

Jenny was known in Russia by Dmitry's surname, Kasofsky.

Irene had told her daughter Polina about Zama. Polina had then shared the news of this new-found cousin with her journalist friend, Jane Sykes. Jane Sykes was then overheard talking about Zama in Moscow, saying that if it was true, it was one of the best stories she'd ever get. Pulitzer Prize-winning.

Somewhere along the way, Zama had become a boy. Had Polina or Jane Sykes tried to protect Jenny? Maybe it had been Adrian Calder, who would also know how important the story was.

Dan thought of the killings. The FSB exterminating anyone who knew about Zama. Exterminating anyone with the same genes. Why? Were they seen as potential rivals?

'Your Jenny is special to Russia,' Irene told him. 'Unique. With both Kazimir's and Yesikov's blood in her, she is like royalty except she is of the people.'

Dan mind snapped to Lazar Yesikov, the old man in Russia, the way he'd treated him. Yesikov hadn't wanted Dan to know he was married to his granddaughter in case Dan spirited her away. Yesikov had been checking him out. Checking Jenny out. Yesikov had released Dan from jail because he'd wanted Dan to lead him to his granddaughter, who had vanished.

Dan ran through his conversation with Lazar Yesikov. The talk about the Russian people responding to a strong leader. What would happen when Vladimir Putin was no longer around. Dan replayed Yesikov's words in his mind.

We will need another strong man to take his place. A man who loves Russia in his heart, and who they can trust and depend upon to look after them.

His heart stopped at his next thought: did Yesikov know Jenny was pregnant?

Irene was saying something but he couldn't hear her. The air had turned violent, pounding his skull, reverberating with what sounded like a million swarms of hornets.

If Kazimir was still alive, they'd probably walk through fire to follow him.

Dan felt shivery. He felt sick.

Lazar Yesikov wanted to take their son and, alongside Edik Yesikov, groom him to become Russia's next revered leader and secure his and President Putin's future in the Kremlin until they died.

CHAPTER FIFTY

Ekaterina finally stopped speaking. Her expression filled with pity.

Jenny longed for the woman's contempt to return. She'd much rather face her scorn than her sympathy.

She turned away. She was shaking so hard she struggled to catch her breath. Her world had turned inside out and upside down. The solid ground of everything she knew had vanished, become stretched and distorted. Her legs felt as though they didn't belong to her. She felt disconnected, unreal, and she was here in Russia, and nothing was the way it should be. She covered her face with her trembling hands and closed her eyes, wishing she was a child again and that she could make it all go away. That she'd had a bad dream and when she opened her eyes again, she'd be at home with the sounds of the sheep on the moors and Dan mowing the lawn, Aimee playing with Poppy in the kitchen.

Vaguely she became aware of a *whap-whapping* sound increasing outside, but she didn't wonder what it might be. She was too traumatised, too scared to make any sense of anything.

'Jenny!' The urgency in Ekaterina's voice cut through her upheaval like a blade. 'We have a visitor. He will want to see you, straight away.'

She was pointing urgently at the window. Finally Jenny realised the *whap-whap* sound came from rotor blades. Swallowing hard, she walked unsteadily across the room to watch a military helicopter land on the other side of the Land Cruisers. Great clouds of snow rose, obscuring the machine.

'Who is it?' she said. She couldn't get any energy into her voice. It felt as though she was struggling at the bottom of a river. Slow and weary, drained with shock.

Ekaterina shook her head but her almond eye, the one not covered by the bandage, had darkened in fear. She said, 'Milena. Take her to wait for him.'

Milena put out her hand and like a child, Jenny let her lead her out of Ekaterina's bedroom and along the corridor, into the sitting room with its sofas and armchairs, and walls lined with dead, snarling bears, foxes and wolves.

'Come.' Milena pulled her to stand in front of the fireplace but although the fire raged, Jenny couldn't feel its heat through the chill in her soul, her heart.

The woman left her briefly and returned with a shot glass of vodka filled to the brim. 'Drink this. It will help. The baby won't mind. Not just for this time.'

Obediently, Jenny drank. She didn't like vodka but now she could appreciate the burning sensation trailing down her throat and into her lungs. She felt her nerves steady.

'You will wait for him here,' said Milena.

Jenny begged the question with her eyes.

Milena touched her shoulder. 'Your grandfather,' she said softly.

Lazar Yesikov.

Who had apparently made love repeatedly with General Kazimir's daughter, Irina, before she'd run away with another lover. Irina had married this lover in Europe where her bastard son, Aleksandr, was born. When Aleksandr grew up he married Elizabeth. They had a daughter who they put up for adoption, but Ekaterina didn't tell her why.

Was it really true? That she was half-Russian? She'd only been told this crazy story by two damaged, fearful women, who in turn admitted it was hearsay, gleaned from a journalist called Jane Sykes who the authorities had been spying upon.

Footsteps came down the corridor, along with a tapping sound. Ekaterina had told her Lazar Yesikov walked with a cane.

Jenny's heart was beating like a rabbit's. She felt a wave of nausea. Swallowed it. Fixed her gaze on the doorway. Lifted her chin.

The instant she saw him, she knew it was true.

It wasn't just his appearance. Yes, they looked alike with their height and pale skin, their blue eyes and sharply cut features, but it was as though the second their eyes met her genes woke up and said, *hi!* A vital sense of recognition.

'Hello, Jenny,' he said. His voice was dry and rasped with age. She didn't respond.

'I hope Ekaterina and Milena have been looking after you.'

Recalling both women's fear of the man, she gave a nod. Ekaterina might not like her, but she wouldn't want either woman to get into trouble. 'They have been very hospitable,' she said stiffly.

'Good.' He stepped forward until he was barely a yard from her. Studied her at length. She did the same. His shoulders were bent, his skin wrinkled and spotted with age, but his eyes were as bright and avaricious as a seagull's. He wore a beautifully cut suit and his tie looked as though it was made of fine silk. European brogues and an expensive-looking watch completed the ensemble. He wouldn't have looked out of place in the Burlington Arcade. She didn't see a wedding ring.

'Ekaterina has told you who I am.'

A man at the highest level of government. A man who has the ear of the President and everyone in Parliament. A man who wants to take my son and give him to his own son, Edik Yesikov, to bring up as his own.

'Edik!' he called. 'Show yourself.'

A man appeared in the doorway. Shorter than the old man, with dirty blond hair, he had the same piercing blue eyes and cruel mouth.

'Edik can't have children,' Lazar Yesikov said.

'No,' agreed Edik. His eyes fastened on Jenny's belly. 'But this child will be like mine. He shares my genes. I have already named him Kazimir, after his great-great-grandfather. He will lead Russia with me, in General Kazimir's name.' His accent was guttural, his eyes gleaming with a combination of ambition and greed.

'Enough.' The old man flicked a hand at Edik who, after a long look at Jenny, disappeared.

'So,' said Yesikov. 'You know who you are.'

A surge of fight rose. She'd be damned if she'd let him get away with kidnapping her so easily.

'Hardly,' she snorted. 'Since it's all based on unfounded rumour.'

He reached into his suit jacket and withdrew two sheets of paper. 'Your DNA was tested. It is beyond doubt that you are my granddaughter, and General Kazimir's great-granddaughter.'

Her ears roared. She desperately fought a wave of dizziness. She had to keep it together. She must not show him how scared she was.

She said, 'I don't believe you.'

He pushed the papers at her. She didn't look at them. 'Forgeries.' She put a derisive snap into her voice.

He looked at her for a long time. She tried not to fidget. Hold on to her dignity. Finally, he turned and left the room. Jenny's eyes skidded to the window and then to the doorway. She forced herself to move around the room. She felt if she didn't move she would implode, crumple into a shrieking ball of fear and panic. She had to keep her blood circulating to help her think. She paced between the window and the armchair at the far end of the room, concentrating on the sensation of her feet hitting the floor, her breathing. It didn't matter what Yesikov said, she realised. Her birth father could be George Clooney and it wouldn't change the fact she had to get out of here. She had to try and make a plan, a deal, some kind of strategy that would help her escape with her unborn son.

Dan! she shouted in her mind. *Where are you! Hurry!*

Gradually, she became aware that although her nerves were still trembling, her hands had steadied along with her heartbeat. The shock was being replaced by anger. Fury at being treated like a chattel to be shifted across continents without thought for her or Aimee, or Dan.

'Jenny.'

She turned to see Yesikov walk back into the room. He was holding out a heavy-looking phone with a thick rubber antenna. A satphone.

He said, 'Speak to them.'

She blinked.

'Your so-called parents.' His voice sneered.

She gripped the phone. 'Hello?'

'Jenny?' It was her father. His voice quavered. He sounded old. But above all, he sounded scared.

Jenny swallowed. She blinked. 'Hi, Dad.'

'Are you OK?' He suddenly sounded close to tears. 'Where are you? Please . . .'

Yesikov reached over and snatched the phone. He snapped, 'Tell her the *truth*. She wants to hear it from you. If you don't . . .'

He passed the phone back to Jenny. She took a deep breath. said, 'Dad, he's told me I'm adopted. Is it true?'

The silence was so dense that for a moment she thought they'd been cut off.

'Hello? Dad? Are you there?'

'Oh, my love. I'm so sorry.' Regret and sorrow flooded his voice.

And with that, she knew the truth. There was no point asking anything more. It could wait. She turned away and began walking briskly to the other side of the room and at the same time she said quickly, 'Dad, I'm in Russia. In a hunting lodge. In the middle of nowhere. Snow everywhere.'

Yesikov shouted something furious in Russian, but she didn't stop. Her words came thick and fast. 'A helicopter's outside, registration RA-seven-oh-nine . . .'

She dodged as he came at her.

'. . . six-five. Two Land Cruisers, one number plate with white letters on a black background . . .'

Yesikov raised his cane and brought it down on her arm but at the last second she twisted aside and it slammed against her shoulder, making her gasp. She forced her words out over the pain. 'Zero-two-four . . .'

A brutish-looking man with a shaven head came charging into the room. Yesikov yelled at him and the man launched himself at Jenny.

She was shouting now: '. . .five-oh-K, five-one RUS –'

The phone was snatched from her.

'Love you!' she yelled. She crouched with her back against a bookshelf, her heart pounding, her lungs heaving.

The shaven-headed man loomed over her. He said something to Yesikov who snapped something back. The man left the room, along with the phone.

'So,' said Yesikov. His eyes were glittering. 'You're not just a beautiful woman. You are smart too. Quick thinking.'

'Yeah, and you're an ugly old man with a bad case of halitosis.'

'There is no need to be uncivil.' His eyes turned cold.

'Oh, really?' She affected sarcasm. 'You shoot my dog and kidnap me, snatch me away from my family, and you expect me to be *civil*?'

'I thought we could get to know each other.' He stood stiffly erect, as though he was on a parade ground. 'I am your grand-father, after all.'

Fury rose as hard and sharp as steel. 'I would rather fuck a donkey –' she hissed, wanting to shock him and show that she wasn't going to cower '– than spend another second with you.'

A flash of narrow, disgusted blue eyes. 'I didn't think you would be crude.'

She stalked out of the door. The shaven-headed thug was out-side and she was surprised when he didn't stop her. She walked along the corridor to the boot room where she put on a pair of snow boots and jacket. She walked outside to the Land Cruisers. No keys in the ignition. Not that she'd get far if she drove away – the snow was too deep – but it would feel good. There was no road, no path, but the line of trees facing the lodge along with the slight indentation in the snow indicated that a track of some sort lay beneath.

She began to walk.

The snow had a hard crust but below it was soft and powdery, making it hard going. She stopped from time to time to rest, but other than that, she kept moving. She needed to get away from the madness behind her.

Soon, the lodge was a speck on the horizon and she was sweating. But she didn't stop. She kept walking. The cold air was quiet. She could hear a faint breeze rustling through the trees to her right but that was all. Nothing moved.

Jenny walked until the afternoon began to darken. She saw nothing but snow and trees and a frozen river. No villages or farms. No people. No power lines. Somewhere a buzzing sounded and she snatched her head around. For a moment she saw nothing, then two vehicles appeared on the horizon, bounding and skidding across the snow like balls on ice.

Snow machines.

They must have been stored in the barn.

She stopped and stared ahead into an endless icy vista. The handful of trees stretching black-fingered branches into a bruised sky.

One snow machine stopped twenty yards away, engine running. The other pulled up next to Jenny. The rider took off his helmet. Dirty blond hair, vivid blue eyes. He was her uncle but all she felt for him was hate.

'It will be dark soon,' he remarked.

Jenny turned her attention to the horizon. 'How far is it to the nearest habitation?'

'Put this on.' Edik was holding out another helmet.

Jenny pointed ahead. 'How far?'

'Three hundred and twenty kilometres.' He then pointed left. 'Two hundred and seventy. But it is just a farm.'

'What is ahead?'

'Another farm.'

'How far?' Jenny persisted.

'You might get there after five days' walking.' He laughed.

Jenny felt something inside her collapse.

Edik looked over his shoulder in the direction of the lodge. 'We must go back. My father is waiting.'

Jenny felt quite calm when she returned to the lodge. Her body was exhausted and this in turn helped quieten her mind. She was given a bowl of hot soup by Milena, and some warm bread, and when she'd finished eating Yesikov came into the kitchen.

He said, 'You will stay here until you are ready to give birth. Then you will be taken to the clinic. Milena and Ekaterina will look after you while you are here. They will not help you in any way to escape or I will have them tortured and their families killed. When you have given birth to my grandson, you will be allowed to return to your country and your family.'

Like she believed him. He wouldn't want her launching an appeal to get her son back to the UK, highlighting to the world his insane plan. He would want her silenced. How would he kill her? she wondered. When? After the baby was weaned, or before?

She raised her head and met his gaze.

'How do you know I won't harm the baby?' she said.

He looked upwards, to the ceiling. Pointed out the cameras. 'I won't let you.'

CHAPTER FIFTY-ONE

Dan got the call when he was on the M25 and heading to Heathrow to fly to Moscow, where he was going to meet two contacts from Six who would help him launch a rescue mission. This time, his passport and credit cards would be in the name of David Rickman.

'You spoke to her?' Dan felt a moment's disbelief.

'Yes.' Jenny's father, Adam, sounded shell-shocked as he recounted the phone call. As Dan had asked, Adam had recorded all incoming calls in case the kidnappers rang, but Dan hadn't really believed it would happen. It must have been his training kicking in – covering all the bases no matter how unlikely – that had prompted him.

'Is she OK?'

There was a pause that went on too long.

'Adam,' Dan snapped. 'Talk to me!'

'Sorry.' The man's voice had thickened, indicating he was fighting tears. 'She sounded . . . strong.' His voice was surprised, as though he'd only just realised this.

That's my girl.

He went on to tell Dan that Jenny was in the middle of nowhere. A hunting lodge. Snow everywhere.

Ice twisted around his heart.

They'd moved her.

Dan increased his speed. 'Play me the tape.'

The quality was abysmal but Dan managed to hear most words. He latched on to the fact that the number plate Jenny had described was military, but he didn't recognise the five-one code. If she'd said one-seven-seven after oh-K, he'd know the vehicle was registered in Moscow. But five-one? He hadn't a clue.

He got Adam to replay the tape four more times before he knew he'd gleaned as much as he could. He thanked Adam. Told him he'd keep him informed.

'If you see her . . .' Adam said.

'I'll send her your love,' Dan agreed. 'Now. Can I speak to Aimee?'

'You're not going to tell her?' Fear filled his voice. 'Take her away from us?'

'You're Aimee's grandparents and I can't see that changing any time soon,' Dan said. Which wasn't exactly true because knowing his wife, she'd have a lot to say about being lied to all her life. In a snapshot Dan thought of Jenny's lies which had driven them apart – she'd hidden the fact he used to work for MI5, telling him he used to work as a civil servant in the Immigration Department, even making up stories of his old office parties, and who his boss used to be. He could see how Jenny's parents had lied to protect their daughter, as Jenny had lied to try and protect him and Aimee. And what about Irene? The lies she'd told to protect Aleksandr and Zama?

Lies layered upon lies.

When would they stop?

'Daddy?'

Aimee sounded small and tired, anxious.

'Hi Possum. How's you?'

'When are you coming to get me?'

'I've just got to pick up Mummy first. She's overseas at the moment, but when I've got her we'll come and get you. Hopefully before the weekend.'

'The weekend?' She sounded horrified. 'But it's only Monday today!'

'Let's try and make it before the weekend, then. You're with Grandma and Grandpa and they're going to take care of you until we're back. OK?'

He tried to be as comforting and reassuring as he could when in truth the only thing that would comfort Aimee would be to have one of her parents there. He had to force himself to hang up and when he did, he was shaken by the wave of anger that swept through him. He would take Yesikov down for this. Make the old man pay.

He spent the remainder of the journey making calls. He needed to change his flights as well as set up new contacts. He was still on the phone when he walked into the airport but he quickly terminated the call when he saw Emily from Six approaching. Emily briefed him as they walked to the departures gate.

'The number plate she gave is for Murmansk Oblast.'

Dan's gut tightened. The Kola Peninsula was in the north-west part of Russia and north of the Arctic Circle. It was part of the larger Lapland region.

The middle of nowhere.

How would they find her?

'We've got you on a flight to Murmansk, leaving in half an hour. It's the ten-twenty flight but it's been delayed.' She filled him in on Simonov, the contact who would be meeting him.

'I need a currency exchange.' Cash was always best in Russia, and since he might need to grease a lot of palms, he'd need a lot of it.

'There's one on the way.' She gestured ahead of them.

'Anything on the helicopter Jenny saw?' he asked.

'It's leased to Edik Yesikov on an ad hoc basis. No flight plan available, sorry. And we have no idea where it is at the moment.' She passed him his e-ticket and passport, credit cards, and ran him through his new legend. 'Good luck.'

CHAPTER FIFTY-TWO

Ekaterina let Milena change her dressings. The pain on her face glowed red-hot and she felt the muscles in her chest tighten. She forced herself to breathe. Tried to focus on Milena to take her mind away from the agonising ruin of her face. Even though her friend tried not to show any emotion, each time she peeled back the bandages and saw the burned and bloody mess, witnessed the disfigurement Ekaterina would have to endure, tears rose in her eyes.

'It's OK,' Ekaterina told her, but still her friend wept.

Ekaterina willed herself to keep still and not to flinch. *How had it come to this?* Was God punishing them? For their greed? Their quest for adventure? Excitement? Their hunger to experience new things?

All of these, she realised because she and Milena had been desperate to *live*. Neither of them had wanted to remain in Irkutsk earning nothing but a pittance in the factory, getting married the day they turned eighteen to some drunken slob and spending the rest of their lives looking after him and their children.

So when a modelling scout turned up in town, they were first in line, and first on the train to Moscow. And yes, they'd lived the high life. They'd been cosseted and coveted, revelling in the luncheons and parties, rubbing shoulders with the elite.

But all that had ended and here they now were.

As Milena moved to inject her with morphine, Ekaterina stopped her. She said softly, 'I'd like some cold milk.'

For a moment she thought Milena might ignore her.

'*Pozhaluysta, kotenok.*' Please, kitten.

When Milena heard her childhood nickname she nodded, but her eyes were scared. Her bruises and scabs were already healing and soon she would be beautiful once more, but only if she obeyed. Milena didn't want her face branded. Ekaterina could read it in every move her friend made.

'When?' Milena managed.

'In half an hour.'

Cold milk was their code for them to meet inside the walk-in pantry set at the far end of the kitchen. The pantry was the only place that didn't have cameras or recording equipment.

By the time Milena finished bandaging her face it was throbbing and sending waves of pain through the centre of her skull and spine, into every cell. It hurt to breathe, and she couldn't help the whimpers that escaped. Once again Milena offered the morphine. This time Ekaterina accepted. The pain she was in was so debilitating she couldn't function without it. Yes, the opiate blurred her thinking and made her mind feel woolly, but the pain was so acute it prevented any rational thought. She would try and use the morphine sparingly, but she couldn't do without it altogether.

It didn't take long until she felt a wave of warmth pass through her body. A sensation of weightlessness followed. The pain eased. She could have wept with relief except her emotions were floating on a cloud of contentment. She had to force herself out of bed to meet Milena.

The pantry was crammed to the ceiling with supplies; dried and salted meats, pickles, a variety of *zakuski*, *kholodets* and hard cheeses, beans, oils and cured fish. They wouldn't be resupplied until the snow melted and the roads became clear once more. If they needed fresh fish or meat, there were plenty of salmon and partridge to be had. All three guards were competent hunters and had already provided plenty of venison. They seemed to think of their assignment as a bit of a holiday and she'd heard lots of laughter late at night, and the sound of empty vodka bottles being thrown out the following morning. She didn't know what Yesikov had told them, but the guards didn't seem to see her and Milena as a threat. With no phones or wireless, no Internet, no way to contact the outside world, they were all prisoners of their environment.

The only piece of equipment that could help should there be an emergency was a satellite phone, but it was kept in one of the locked gun cabinets and neither woman was allowed the key. With their generator and barns full of wood, guns and fishing equipment, they were meant to be entirely self-sufficient until the child was ready to be born, whereupon Jenny would be flown to the clinic.

What would happen to her afterwards was anyone's guess but Ekaterina didn't think she'd be allowed to mother her son for long. They wouldn't want any maternal imprinting on the boy.

She pulled the pantry door shut behind her and Milena. It was cold enough that her breath plumed as she spoke. 'We have to get her out of here.'

Milena shook her head. 'No.' She put one of her small hands on Ekaterina's shoulder. 'Look, I know you're –'

Ekaterina moved her hand away. 'We have to do it while the Yesikovs are here. Nobody will expect anything to happen, let alone suspect us. We're –'

'No way!' Milena looked appalled.

'Come on, Milena. You know it's our best chance. They think we're completely cowed. They'll never expect us to fight back, let alone tonight. It's our best chance, believe me.'

'I don't want this!' Milena protested. 'I'm not strong, like you. I'm not a soldier. I've fired a gun once, remember, and that was only because you insisted. This isn't my fight, Katen'ka.'

'Don't you love Russia?' Ekaterina demanded.

'Of course I do!' She looked incensed. 'But there are five of them, and not only are they men but they're *combat-trained*! They're a hundred times stronger!'

'I have no intention of fighting them.'

'Why do you want to help her?' Milena's voice was indignant but then her look turned sly. 'She's Daniel's wife. I've seen your looks of poison. We all know what that means.'

Ekaterina felt like shaking her friend. 'This isn't about Dan and me! This is bigger than all of us. With this child presented to the people as their next great leader, there will be no pause in Putin's regime. No crack in his heartless, brutal control. We will kowtow to Edik when he inherits power from Putin, and then we'll kowtow to his so-called son, Kazimir.' She took a shuddering breath. 'If the child grows up as they want him to, with a heartless and distorted view of the world, it will be catastrophic!'

'No.' Milena shook her head again. 'I won't do it.'

Ekaterina gaped. 'You really want your children to live through another Stalinist regime? You know that's how it will be with General Kazimir's offspring at the helm. You really want people executed for looking the wrong way, the rest sent to slave-labour camps? You think your grandchildren will thank you for a life filled with nothing but starvation, fear and exhaustion?'

Milena looked away.

'Things have changed already,' Ekaterina said. Her tone was fierce. 'Haven't you seen it? Felt it? Where has our optimism gone? We used to rub shoulders with activists, journalists and politicians, remember? We all thought of ourselves as the post-Putin generation. Some were tied to the Kremlin, others the opposition, but we all went to the same parties. No more! Don't you get it? Our generation now accuses everyone else of compromise and collaboration. We've fallen straight into a pit of pessimism and paranoia. We are Putin's puppets. He enslaved us from when we were young. Our generation *is Putin*. We can't let the next generation follow suit!'

'You can't say it's going to be the same.' Milena's chin jutted. 'Jenny's son might make a great leader.'

Ekaterina gave a snort. 'If Edik and Lazar are paranoid psychopaths, just imagine what their prodigy will be like. He'll be even more brutal than his grandfather. And if he isn't, he'll just be a puppet to their ruthless machinations.'

Milena clenched her fists. 'Don't you think you're jumping the gun? He isn't even born! He might not even live that long!'

Even through the morphine Ekaterina felt a moment's shock. 'You're not saying you'd kill him?'

'No!' Milena looked horrified. 'He could get a disease or have a weak heart or something. That's all I meant.'

Ekaterina eyed her friend squarely. 'I know you don't want to help Jenny. That you want her to have this baby and then we can return to Moscow, to our old lives.'

Milena's eyes flared suddenly, filling with hope, and Ekaterina knew Milena was picturing walking back into their beautiful apartment, opening her wardrobe and choosing which designer outfit to wear, which shoes would match, which jewels, before wrapping herself in fur and calling for their driver and getting him to drop her at one of their favourite bars, where she'd glide inside greeting old friends as though she'd never been away.

'You know it won't happen, Milena.' Her voice was soft. 'Once the baby's born, he'll dispose of us.'

'But Edik promised.' Milena twisted her hands together. 'He said he'd reward us.' Her expression turned pleading. 'He's promised things to us before and never reneged.'

Ekaterina let the silence stretch. She wasn't going to tell her that this was a totally different matter. Milena already knew this.

'I can't let him kill my family,' Milena begged. 'How can you let him kill yours?'

It was the perfect opening. She said, 'We warn them.'

Milena evaluated this. 'How?'

Ekaterina outlined her plan.

CHAPTER FIFTY-THREE

Dan watched Heathrow fall away as the Aeroflot Airbus A321 rose into the sky. With a stop in Moscow, he wouldn't get to Murmansk for another nine hours, arriving just before ten tomorrow morning. His contact would, apparently, collect him in his car outside the terminal. Dan hoped it wasn't another Lada with the performance of a rice pudding, but something faster and more agile.

He prayed Yesikov hadn't moved Jenny again. Russia was enormous with great expanses of wilderness that hid a plethora of lodges and fishing huts. Yesikov could move her around the country, from Siberia to Kamchatka if he wanted, making it impossible to find her.

He was still assimilating the fact that Jenny had been adopted. After he'd called Emily from the hospital, she had contacted the adoption agency and overridden the absolute veto that was in place. There was no doubt that Aleksandr and Elizabeth Stanton were Jenny's parents, and that their daughter appeared to be directly related to General Kazimir. He'd only truly believe it when he saw the DNA test results, which he supposed Yesikov had already done at the clinic.

And what about the rest of the descendants? When he'd spoken to Lucy just before he'd boarded, she'd told him about the filicide case near Bristol, where Oxana Harris, née Stanton, had supposedly poisoned her two daughters and grandson, and how her eldest son had allegedly killed his two young children before killing himself. Lucy seemed convinced these people had all been murdered, but Dan wasn't so sure. What if they'd learned the truth about their history and had decided to commit suicide in order to cut the line? After all, that's what Aleksandr had done, by sterilising himself, albeit a bit late in the day and after his wife fell pregnant.

In Frankfurt, he checked his emails to see Lucy and her police colleagues were currently embroiled in contacting as many people descended from General Kazimir as they could, which sounded a major task considering they also lived in Australia. Ominously, the one descendant they'd managed to track down in Queensland had already died, seemingly in a kayaking accident while on holiday two months ago. A coincidence? Or was it, as Lucy believed, part of a sinister conspiracy?

He owed Lucy, he realised. If she hadn't been so dogged in her investigations, Jenny would have been kidnapped without anyone knowing why. It had been the policewoman who had traced the clues from Adrian Calder to Aleksandr Stanton, and uncovered Lazar Yesikov's monstrous scheme.

Well done, Lucy.

Now all he had to do was get Jenny and their unborn child home.

CHAPTER FIFTY-FOUR

Monday 9 February

Milena lay quietly next to Edik. She'd been surprised when he'd demanded she join him after supper – she thought he wouldn't want her with her bruised face but he hadn't seemed to notice. He'd taken her roughly, fucking her on the edge of the bed before flipping her over and fucking her arse, slamming into her so hard she felt her skin tear.

When he came, he groaned and fell on top of her. She wriggled to the side and he mumbled something as she dislodged him. He was already half asleep. He'd drunk a bottle and a half of vodka earlier and by the time she'd squirmed and twisted out from beneath him, he was snoring like a traction engine.

Quickly, she washed and got dressed. Tiptoed down the corridor. Everyone had gone to bed two hours ago and no lights burned. Everything was still and silent. She was nearing the boot room, planning on putting on her down coat and snow boots, when she heard the creak of leather nearby.

'What are you doing?'

Slowly, she turned. It was one of the guards. He was sitting on a chair in the corridor, a Kalashnikov at his side. Now he rose.

Hell. She hadn't realised anyone would still be awake but obviously the old man had left a guard awake in case they tried anything.

'Hi,' she whispered.

She slipped close to see it was Nik. The youngest of the guards. A nice young man who was frightened of caves and spiders. He'd fallen skiing and broke his leg when he was eight. He hated pop music, preferred heavy rock. He could build a camp fire and skin a deer. He loved his Mama. He was allergic to nuts. He held a gun and her fate lay in his hands.

'I was hoping you'd be awake,' she told him. She caught her lower lip between her teeth, looking up at him through her eyelashes. Even though it was dark, she could see his eyes flare.

She gave him a soft smile, shy and uncertain. 'I've been thinking of you, you see.'

'You have?' His voice was hoarse.

'Yes,' she whispered. She held out her hand. 'Let's go into the kitchen. Get a drink.'

He lifted his weapon uncertainly. 'I shouldn't.'

She raised herself on tiptoes. 'Nik,' she whispered. 'Everyone's asleep. Nobody will know. Just one drink with me, that's all.'

She held out her hand again.

Slowly, as though he was sleepwalking, he put his hand in hers and let her lead him down the corridor. Her heart was beating fast, her skin tight. Could she do it? Could she be brave enough? Or should she simply slip back into bed with Edik and do nothing? Let the gods decide?

She closed the kitchen door behind them. Looked at Nik, his messy brown hair, the pleading and anticipation in his eyes. He was like a puppy-dog waiting for a titbit.

I can do this, she told herself. *I can be brave. Just this once.*

She said, 'I've got some Zyr in the pantry. Edik will never miss it.'

'I've never had Zyr,' Nik said wonderingly. 'I've heard it's really good.'

Milena slipped into the pantry and picked up the prepared flask. Thank God for Ekaterina, who had foreseen that this might happen. Back in the kitchen, she poured them both generous tumblers.

'*Za nashi zdorovie!*' she whispered. She gently touched her glass against his. To our health!

He drank greedily, his eyes on her as she pretended to sip. Then she put down her tumbler and stepped back, raised her hands and stripped off her sweater. She wore a tight woollen undershirt beneath that clung to her body and outlined her breasts. His eyes bulged. She topped up his glass. He downed the rest of his vodka in four swift swallows.

'Sit,' she purred. Pointed at a chair. 'You can watch me.'

As he moved towards the chair he stumbled, putting out a hand to steady himself against the big pine table. Milena's heartbeat increased. Ekaterina's sleeping pills were already having an effect.

'Don't normally get drunk,' he said. His words were beginning to slur.

'Zyr,' she said. 'It's very strong.'

He almost fell into the chair. 'Shit,' he said. 'I feel dizzy.'

And at that, he was out like a light.

CHAPTER FIFTY-FIVE

Ekaterina replaced the fuel cap and stripped off her ski gloves, which were now soaking wet, and exchanged them for another pair in her pocket. She barely felt the cold through the morphine and knew she had to keep pushing herself to make sure she didn't slow down. She had to be quick. Make a getaway before anyone noticed.

She stamped the snow from the back door and around the helicopter to muddle her footprints with the guards'. She didn't need a torch to see what she was doing the starlight was so bright. Then she walked to the barn, where Milena was waiting. Her friend had prepared both snow machines, making sure their oil and fuel were topped up, and filled the gas cans and strapped them into the gas racks. She'd also laid out three helmets and snowsuits. Milena helped Ekaterina into her suit and pulled the hood drawstring tight, careful of her bandages as she made sure the fur trim was in position.

Then Milena made to hand her a survival pack. Ekaterina looked at it, then back at her friend. Her heart squeezed.

'*Kotenck.*' Kitten. Her words were gentle. 'I'm not going to need it.'

Milena stared for a second. Her eyes were wide and panicky. She thrust it forward. Her hands were trembling.

Ekaterina said, 'You keep it for you and Jenny. OK?'

Milena bit down on both her lips, but she didn't cry. Hope rose inside Ekaterina. Milena hadn't just managed to drug Nik, but she was making a real effort to be strong. That was good. That was *vital*.

The silence went on forever but Ekaterina didn't want to break it. Knocking out Nik had been easy compared with what was going to come. Milena had to come to terms with the situation in her own time. Ekaterina felt as if the very air was holding its breath, crystalline and as brittle as shards of ice.

Finally Milena nodded, turning to strap the pack on the second snow machine. She said, 'The compass won't work.'

'No,' Ekaterina agreed, grateful for her pragmatic comment. It showed Milena was trying to keep her emotions under control and endeavouring to be level-headed and sensible about what they were doing. They both knew compasses were unreliable near the Poles, and that they would have to be guided by the stars.

Together, they pushed one snow machine out of the barn. The lodge was silent. It was an effort, but they managed to force the machine a reasonable distance from the lodge, where they hoped its engine wouldn't be heard.

Ekaterina climbed aboard. She turned her head to Milena. They stared at each other.

Milena closed her eyes briefly. Her face spasmed. 'I can't believe this is happening.'

'You will be happy. You will find a good man who will adore you and shower you with gifts and spoil you until the day you die.'

'I wish things were different . . . I wish . . .' Her voice broke.

Ekaterina brought up her hand and touched Milena's cheek. 'I know.'

She looked at the pain in Milena's eyes and at the same time, felt the first pulse of fear at what she was doing. And as she recognised her dread, she felt a silence seep into her soul, a cool river of peace that soothed and calmed, drowning out all anxiety and leaving her thoughts distilled and clear.

She was doing this for Russia, yes. Also to help Dan and his wife. But it had become more than that.

She didn't want Lazar Yesikov to win.

As she drove into the wilderness, the air as cold and sharp as needles in her lungs, she held his face in her mind, his look of shock and rage when he discovered his prize had vanished, swept from beneath his nose by two *insignificant* women and making him look fantastically stupid.

CHAPTER FIFTY-SIX

Monday 9 February

The sky was only just beginning to lighten when Dan's aeroplane landed. Sunrise wasn't for another half an hour, which was a lot later than Dan was used to. Throwing his overnight bag into the footwell, he climbed into the passenger seat of a Lada Niva, a rugged Russian-built four-wheel-drive that, although new, looked as though it had been built in the 1950s. There was plenty of squeaking and rattling coming from the back that could have been the LPG tank moving on its mounting bracket, but otherwise it seemed OK. He wouldn't choose it as a getaway car on the streets of Murmansk, but with its minimal weight, narrow tyres, low-ratio transfer gearbox and diff lock, it would be formidable off-road.

'Any luck with the hunting lodge?' he asked. 'Or the helicopter?'

His contact, a squat man with a coarse face and intelligent eyes, said, 'The aircraft, I have trouble with. But the lodge . . .' He reached into his side pocket and withdrew a sheet of paper. Dan scanned the list of four names, all in Russian.

'Edik Yesikov has been a guest at all of these,' said Simonov. 'He doesn't own a particular lodge in the area.'

'What about his father?'

'I cannot find anything about him staying in any hunting or fishing lodge. He is like a ghost, that man.'

Dan studied the list again. 'You think she could be at one of these?'

'I couldn't say.' Simonov shrugged. 'But it's a good place to start.'

'Where are they?'

Simonov reached across and opened his glovebox and withdrew his satnav. 'I have already programmed them in.'

Dan had a look. He felt a curse rise on his lips. Two lodges were within a hundred k's of each but the third and fourth were almost at opposite ends of the peninsula.

'We'll need a helicopter,' Dan said.

'Yes.' Simonov glanced at him. 'You have cash?'

Dan nodded.

'I know just the person. He will be pleased of the business.'

Simonov made a phone call. When he hung up, he said, 'No problem. We will leave in an hour.'

CHAPTER FIFTY-SEVEN

Jenny wriggled, trying to get comfortable. She was hidden in a crawl space above the kitchen and it was so dark, she couldn't even see her hand in front of her face. Milena had shown her where to go after Ekaterina had left. She'd given her a pillow and two duvets from the storeroom and Jenny had struggled to convey them quietly to an area where she wouldn't be seen at first glance should someone poke their head through the trap.

She shivered continuously, her teeth chattering. The floor of the crawl space was heavily lagged to keep the lodge's warmth from escaping through the roof, but the air above wasn't heated. The temperature had to be hovering around zero.

Would Ekaterina's plan work? It was a crazy idea, and Jenny hadn't been convinced until Ekaterina pushed the point that the guards would be lulled into complacency by having Yesikov there as well as his son, the pilot and the bodyguard.

'When they see the snow machine has gone,' Ekaterina told Jenny, 'and that you and I are no longer there, they will assume we have both run away. They will send the helicopter after us. They will follow my trail into the wilderness. This is when you and Milena take the second snow machine and head in the opposite direction. Simple!' She beamed.

'But what about the guards?'

'I bet you ten thousand roubles they will all be in the helicopter, desperate to catch us.' Her gaze turned thoughtful. 'All except for Lazar, and perhaps his bodyguard. We can slip them sedatives, if we need to. I have many sedatives.'

'And the satphones?' Jenny pressed. There were only two that they knew of, the one in the gun cabinet and the one Yesikov had brought with him, but it would only take one call and they would be ruined.

'Milena will deal with them.'

Jenny must have looked sceptical because Ekaterina added, 'Because she will awake everyone and tell them we've gone, they will think she is on their side. She has given me up once before. She told them where I was hiding in my brother's apartment . . .' Her voice faltered briefly and she looked away as though the memory was too much to bear but she regained her composure fast. 'They will expect her to betray me again.'

Her voice wasn't accusatory or unkind. She was simply stating facts. Jenny looked at Milena but the woman's eyes slid away. She was scared, Jenny could see, and Jenny smiled, wanting to encourage her, thank her for her help, but Milena pretended not to see.

At the time, Jenny had thought it worth giving Ekaterina's wild plan a go – she couldn't see herself escaping on her own – but now she was shivering in the crawl space she thought it was ridiculous and full of flaws. If Dan had been there he would have thought of something far more sensible she was sure, like flying them out in the helicopter, but he wasn't here and her only allies were two women who'd done nothing with their lives except look beautiful and amuse whatever men they were told to.

She wasn't going to give up her hiding space yet, though. She was going to see how Ekaterina's plan panned out first.

Jenny didn't think she'd sleep she was so cold, but she jerked awake when she heard a man's voice. It sounded as though he was cursing. A chair scraped back. He mumbled a bit, and then he left, probably to use the loo. Another man's voice. Sleepy and untroubled. Lights were switched on. Jenny could see narrow beams coming through the corners of the floor. She heard the kettle go on. Then came the sounds of breakfast being made. The men fetching bread and cold cuts. The whistle of the tea kettle. Another man came into the kitchen, yawning.

She listened to the lodge awake. She tensed when she heard Milena's voice but it sounded casual, as though it was a normal day. They'd agreed she'd leave it as long as she thought credible before she raised the alarm.

Time crawled past.

Jenny lay and talked quietly to her son in her mind. Put her hand on her belly and soothed and loved him, told him everything would be OK. She thought of her grandmother, Irina, and what Ekaterina had told her earlier – retracting her previous story – that Yesikov hadn't made love to Irina but raped her continually until she'd run away with the love of her life, Dmitry, to make a new life in England. She wondered what Irina looked like, whether she had fair hair or not. If they'd recognise one another as her genes had recognised Lazar Yesikov.

To her surprise she found herself napping. She was dreaming of Wales, walking Poppy with Dan and Aimee across the moors, when she was jolted awake by a man's bellow. Then another. She recognised Yekisov's dry voice, yelling, enraged. Doors banged. Men shouted. Milena's voice joined in, high and panicky.

Footsteps ran back and forth. More shouting. Curses. Milena had obviously raised the alarm. Then Jenny heard Lazar Yesikov speaking. His tone was hard and brusque. He was giving orders. The guards responded fast. *Da, ser!* was repeated several times. Yes, sir!

Her stomach hollowed when she heard metallic clicks and whirrs of guns being loaded and primed. The men's voices were low, concentrated. Rustles of clothing and bullet belts being buckled up. Some final orders from Yesikov. And then she heard the low hum of the helicopter's engine starting up. She realised it had to be daylight. They wouldn't have been able to follow Ekaterina's snow machine's tracks in the dark.

The rotor blade started with a slow *whap*, gradually increasing as the whistle of the turbines wound into a high hum. Soon, the turbines were hissing and the blades a continual blur of sound.

She couldn't hear any more voices. Just the helicopter. She crossed her fingers. Counted down the seconds. It was less than two minutes later when the engine note changed, became fevered. The machine was lifting into the air. She wondered how many men were on board. She hoped all of them.

The engine note changed again and she held her breath but then it settled and the helicopter thundered away. Jenny exhaled. Closed her eyes. Pictured Ekaterina with her ruined face riding the snow machine north, straight to nowhere.

Go, Ekaterina. Go as fast as you can.

CHAPTER FIFTY-EIGHT

Ekaterina's snow machine had run out of fuel long ago. She'd used both of the spare fuel cans and managed to put over a hundred and fifty miles between her and the lodge. It would take the helicopter roughly an hour and a half to catch her up. That's if the helicopter made it. She'd shovelled handfuls of snow into its fuel tank earlier, and she had to hope it would interfere with the engines at some point, preferably when it was miles from the lodge.

She'd hidden the snow machine as best she could in a dense wood of tall spruces. If the helicopter was still flying, she hoped it would force the pilot to land in order to send the men in to check it. More time to help Milena and Jenny to escape.

She'd spent the journey thinking about Dan. All six-foot bliss of him. His hands, strong and broad, which touched her as delicately as silk. The feel of his heartbeat against her cheek. The depth of his voice. The way he said her name.

Kat.

Had he ever cared for her? She was never sure. She'd been an asset, an informant, and although he assured her his superiors didn't know of her existence, he was to all intents and purposes her handler. She gave him gossip and titbits from the privileged inner circle of politicians and the military, and in return he made endless love to her in his hotel room. He brought her up-to-the-minute clothes from London and read to her from books by up-and-coming novelists that he thought she'd enjoy. They had restaurants they always went to, and favourite bars. Dan loved to eat Beef Khartcho at CDL, she liked to drink Huertas in Bar Strelka.

She'd read Anna Akhmatova's poetry to him, a woman she admired for writing *The Requiem*, which the poet had worked and reworked in secret, because it showed the terrible suffering of the common people in the USSR during Joseph Stalin's time as well as exposing the truth behind the cult of his person. But it was Anna Akhmatova's love poems she'd shared with Dan.

To us, separation is just entertainment
The woes are dull without us.

He'd spoken Russian then. He told her she was the most beautiful woman he'd met. The most exciting, the most exotic. That she was stunning, glamorous, exquisite, and that he treasured every moment she gave him.

But he never said he loved her.

One day, she took him to St Clement's Church. It was spring and the row of trees flanking the massive building were budding vivid green. For the first time, she told him the truth. That Edik had asked her to befriend him. Ordered her to make the Englishman fall in love with her so she could drip misinformation into his ear.

Dan had looked at her a long time. Then he'd cupped her face tenderly with his hands. He said gently, 'I know.'

Which meant Dan had been feeding misinformation to Edik right back, which had amused Ekaterina enormously. Dan had warned her she was playing a dangerous game between the two men, their two countries, but she hardly cared. She was in love. And when Dan vanished one day, seemingly off the planet, Edik told her he'd heard that Dan didn't think she was of use to him any more, that he'd dumped her and wouldn't be returning to Russia again. She hadn't believed him until he'd taken her to a party and asked the British Ambassador how Dan was.

'We haven't seen him for a while,' Edik said. 'Is he OK?'

'He resigned from the Russia desk,' the Ambassador said. 'He wanted something more challenging.'

It was as though her heart had been ripped out of her. Her body emptied of blood. Her emotions blistered. She knew she had to hide her feelings but the shock of his abandonment – and without a word to her – was so immense, she swayed.

Edik twisted her aside. He was blinking rapidly. 'Shit. Don't tell me you *cared* for him?'

She saw his face begin to darken and knew her survival depended on the next few seconds. She pulled her arm free. Made an expansive, derisive gesture. 'Of course *I cared*!' she exclaimed. 'Who else is going to bring me my Fortnum and Mason hampers? My favourite perfume? My French lingerie?'

'Use the Internet.'

She pouted. 'It's not the same. He was my lapdog. I liked petting him.'

Edik laughed. 'I shall find you another, my sweet.'

Her love, her passion for Dan soured into loathing. She was so embittered, so angry, she couldn't even grieve for him, and the memory of him slipped into the hollows of her soul like poison.

Until last week, when she discovered that Dan had never abandoned her. When Fyodor rang Bernard Gilpin with the code words to alert him to the fact Dan was in danger, she'd told her brother to ask him why Dan had turned his back on her. Why Dan had broken her heart.

He didn't do it intentionally, the Director of the Security Service told Fyodor, going on to say that Dan had suffered a breakdown over the death of his son and had not only lost his mind with grief, but also his memory. Dan had no recollection of who he used to be, apparently. And no memory of her.

Her hate for him had vanished like a trail of vapour snatched by a breeze.

She remembered their standing in the cold of the street outside St Clement's Church. The way he looked at her, his eyebrows drawn in. His expression confused. The voice in her head told her that he couldn't see her like he used to, that he didn't know her, and tongues of pain licked her soul as she stood there, looking at him looking back.

When she asked him what happened, gazing into his ocean-grey, conflicted eyes, she knew a memory of her was in there somewhere. She'd wanted to beg and plead for him to remember her, but instinct told her she'd only alienate him. It had taken a monumental effort not to weep. Instead, her tears seeped hot and raw inside her heart as she'd turned aside, and talked business. Talked about Edik and his father's plans.

Did Daniel love her?

She'd never know, but she loved him. She'd never stopped loving him.

She stumbled, nearly falling to her knees. She was exhausted, her body beginning to fail, but she didn't rest. She kept going, spurred by her picture of Yesikov's infuriated expression, his disbelief that she'd outwitted him.

I will beat him.

I will win.

She'd had two doses of morphine and had another three to go, but she knew she wasn't going to last that long. Although she couldn't feel the frostbite where her hood had slipped, or the flayed raw skin where her bandage had fallen, every step had become an effort.

Where were Milena and Jenny? Had they left the lodge yet?

The weak winter sun began to rise. A grey, grainy light slipped over the endless snowy vista. Somewhere a crow cawed and she stopped to listen, trying to pinpoint its direction. She couldn't see anything but then a black shape flapped from the branches of a tree, wheeling over several dark shapes that seemed to be growing out of the ground. At first, she thought she was imagining things. She raised her goggles. Blinked her right eye several times. Her vision was blurred but the shapes remained the same.

She tried to tell herself that it was nothing more than her imagination borne out of desperation to live, but as her sight cleared she saw she'd been right. A collection of barns and buildings stood on the other side of the trees. A thin trail of smoke rose between two hawthorns.

She almost couldn't believe it.

She'd found a village.

CHAPTER FIFTY-NINE

'Where's the satphone?' Lazar Yesikov demanded. 'I put it on the kitchen table earlier. It's no longer there.'

His bodyguard, a thickset man with a dense red beard, stared at Milena with a dead expression, making her insides shiver.

She licked her lips. 'Perhaps one of the men took it.'

Yesikov's eyes bored into her, as sharp and cold as ice picks, until she felt he could read every thought she'd ever had.

'You wouldn't be trying to pull a fast one, would you little Milena?' he said softly. 'You know what will happen if you do.'

She swallowed. 'I think I saw it in the entrance hall.'

'Fetch it.'

On trembling legs, Milena walked along the corridor. She hated Ekaterina for putting her in this position. Why was her friend so intent on saving the Englishwoman and her child? They would be in their fifties when the boy became a man and walked into the Kremlin. They'd be *old*. Though fifty, her grandmother insisted, wasn't old any more. Fifty was the new thirty. Ha! Her grandmother looked like an old shoe she was so wrinkled, but Milena knew this was only because she'd lived most of her life outdoors. Not like her and Ekaterina, who kept their skin fresh and youthful with spa treatments and vitamins, never venturing into the harshness of the Russian sun or snow without protection.

She slipped into her bedroom and to the en-suite bathroom where she'd hidden the satphone. She had been going to disable it, maybe by immersing it in water, but she hadn't dared yet. The second she did, it would end the pretence she was on Yesikov's side and he'd order his bodyguard to kill her.

She held the phone in her hand. It was just her, Yesikov and his bodyguard in the lodge. Edik and the other guards had gone in the helicopter. Did she dare disable it? She began to shake. She wasn't cut out for this. She couldn't help replaying the way her stomach turned every time she changed Ekaterina's bandages. The bloody socket where her eye used to be, the skin on that side of the face bunched and corrugated where the brand had burned. The gaping hole in the side of her mouth.

Milena brought the phone to Yesikov. He immediately made a call.

'Nik. Where are you?'

He was talking to one of the guards in the helicopter.

'You've found the snow machine? Very good.' His lips pulled back over aged yellow teeth in a humourless smile but then it vanished. 'In a wood? They'll be on foot, get after them! No, don't land unless you have to. You should see their tracks leading out of the wood . . . Yes . . . Yes, you'll have them soon. Yes, be ultra-careful with the cargo . . . No, I want Ekaterina alive. I have something special planned for her.' He listened for a few seconds before he said, 'I expect to hear you have them soon.'

He put the phone on the kitchen table. His face was triumphant. 'We have them!' he exclaimed. 'Thanks to you, my precious Milena –' he blew her a kiss '– for alerting us when you did. You will die a wealthy old woman dressed in velvet and gold.'

Milena could have wept. The helicopter hadn't failed. The snow Ekaterina shovelled into its fuel tank earlier should have stopped it working by now but it was still flying.

'I am surprised at Ekaterina,' he mused. 'I thought she'd seen sense. You certainly did, didn't you, Milena? You don't like pain, and you certainly don't like not being beautiful.'

She managed a nod.

'Which shows how making an example of someone can work.' He stroked his chin thoughtfully. 'I think this time, I will cut off each of Ekaterina's fingers, cauterise them, then let her recover and understand how hard it is to live without them. Then I shall cut off her toes. Then one hand, then the other. Then her legs. Her arms. She will be a lump of meat in a wheelchair. I will keep her as a reminder to everyone not to cross me.'

A wave of nausea rolled over Milena. *How had it come to this?*

When the satellite phone rang, she jumped.

Yesikov answered. 'Yes?'

He remained silent for a few moments, and then he hung up.

He turned and faced Milena. His face was like stone.

'They can see only one set of footprints.'

Long silence while he surveyed Milena.

He said, 'Where is she?'

CHAPTER SIXTY

Ekaterina stumbled towards the village. It was further away than she'd thought, and she blamed exhaustion as well as her one-sightedness for her misjudgement.

A noise behind her in the distance. Something she couldn't identify. She staggered round, half-expecting to see Yesikov's guards charging through the snow for her, but there was nothing there. Only the gleam of snow beneath the faint dawn sun.

She went back to trudging through the snow. One foot, then the other. Plod-plod-plod. But the base of her neck was tingling as if a bony finger was toying with the fine hairs there. She glanced over her shoulder and pushed back her hood to listen.

The sound came again. The faintest buzz of a helicopter.

Ekaterina broke into a shambling run but she was so tired she lost control of her legs and went sprawling face down. She forced herself upright. Concentrated on putting one foot ahead of the other as fast as she could. She didn't look around again. She needed every ounce of mental energy focused on *walking*.

She had to get to the village.

The engine sound gradually approached, but slowly. They were following her tracks. They didn't want to lose them.

Ekaterina's head was down. All she could hear was the crunch of the snow and the brush of her snowsuit. Her breathing. She was sweating heavily. She felt sick. She kept going.

She didn't stop walking until one of the guards grabbed her arm, and even then she shook him off and kept going. He had to pin both her arms behind her back and haul her bodily into the air.

'Come on, Ekaterina,' he said. 'The game's up.'

Her mind hummed.

It was Nik. The youngest of the guards. He had a sweet face and soft, Spaniel eyes.

'Shoot me,' she told him.

'I can't.' He shook his head. 'We've been ordered to bring you back.'

'You know what he will do to me.'

He went rigid, staring at her.

She brought her hand up to her face. 'He will do something worse than this. Much worse.'

Nik's eyes shut for a second.

The humming became a strimmer reverberating in her skull. She thought if she moved, took another breath, she would splinter into a thousand icicles. Her mind flailed, trying to find something to say to persuade him.

'Tell him I fought. I tried to stab you. You did it in self-defence . . . Shoot me in the head. The back. Anywhere . . . you can show him the evidence . . .'

Nik shook his head. He wouldn't meet her eye. 'Sorry.'

'Please.' She hadn't wanted to beg, but she couldn't help it. She fell to her knees. 'Nik, don't let him turn you into something you're not. You're a good man. Yesikov is ... driven by something else.'

Edik's voice suddenly shouted behind them.

'*Davai, blyat, dvigaisya!*' Oi! Get a fucking move on!

Nik's face closed. He stepped forward and in two swift movements lifted her up and carried her into the helicopter. He could have been carrying a pillow of goose down for all the effort it seemed to take him. As he strapped her in, she said softly, 'It's OK, Nik. I understand. I forgive you,' but he pretended not to hear.

She closed her eyes as the helicopter took off, not opening them until she felt a slight bump. An air pocket? Or was it something else?

She looked out of the window to see they were flying above the wood of spruce trees where she'd hidden the snow machine. They were flying low, five hundred feet, and she could make out each individual branch.

They were still over the wood when the helicopter's engine note changed. Her heart soared but she didn't move, give anything away. *Please, make it happen. Please.*

At the same time a klaxon sounded in the front. The pilot said, 'What the hell ...'

Ekaterina closed her eyes. It was happening. Thank God, it was happening at last.

Seconds later, the engine note changed again. It sounded as if it was winding down.

'Fuck's sake,' said Edik. His voice was frightened.

The pilot was frantically working the controls. The rotor was still chop-chopping, the klaxon blaring, but the engines were silent.

'What's going on?' Edik shouted.

The pilot didn't answer. The other men also remained quiet but they were gripping the armrests hard, their knuckles white, their faces rigid with terror. She saw the pilot's left arm jerk down and at the same time his right hand slammed forward the control column. The helicopter's nose bucked violently.

Nik let out a panicking yell. The men started shout.

'Land this thing!'

'Get us down!'

Ekaterina looked down at the spruces below, their sharp branches jutting through the snow. She couldn't see anywhere safe they could land. Not unless the pilot managed to work the aircraft free of the wood, which wasn't possible. They were falling out of the sky, heading straight down.

All she could hear was wind against the fuselage, and the slow *whap-whap* of the rotor.

'Shit!' yelled Edik.

'Mayday Mayday Mayday,' the pilot spoke into the radio. 'RA70965 declaring an emergency.' He rattled off the coordinates but Ekaterina was no longer listening as the machine plummeted towards the trees at a terrifying rate.

As they careened downwards out of the sky, she felt as though her brain was shutting down. Nothing seemed real. Nik was weeping silently, tears streaming down his face. The others were screaming.

She had no concept of time, whether seconds were passing, or minutes. She tried to think of Milena but her mind was blank. Outside, the solid mass of dense foliage and wood was approaching fast.

She hoped it would be quick.

She closed her eyes. Out of nowhere a vision of Daniel filled her mind. He was lying next to her in bed. His grey eyes were calm, his expression kind and loving. He was brushing back a tendril of hair from her face and tucking it behind her ear.

Don't be afraid, he whispered.

She heard metal tearing, a noise louder than she'd heard before. She felt the underbelly of the aircraft begin to break up. The helicopter tumbled, rolling over and over. Objects flew at her; headsets, branches, a pistol, fragments of metal.

A smell of burning filled her senses and at the same time there was a dull *whump!* Flames burst inside the cockpit and then came a pause as though the world was holding its breath – and the aircraft was abruptly engulfed in a fireball.

Daniel tenderly pressed a kiss against her forehead.

Don't be afraid.

CHAPTER SIXTY-ONE

When the trapdoor lifted, flooding the crawl space with light, Jenny hunkered as low as she could and closed her eyes in case they gleamed, and gave her away.

'I know you're there,' called Yesikov. Then he barked something in Russian.

A man replied. She heard rustling sounds, then the man said, 'Come.'

She cracked open an eye to see a pistol aimed straight at her. She'd never had a gun pointed at her before and her insides felt as though they were going to melt.

'Come,' he said again.

She didn't have a choice.

She raised both hands. He lowered the pistol a fraction. Jerked his chin at the trapdoor. Pushing aside the duvet, she wriggled across the floor. Worked her way down the ladder. The warmth of the kitchen felt incredible.

'So.' Yesikov surveyed her. 'You seem none the worse for wear from your little adventure.'

She didn't respond.

'Milena,' he commanded. 'Bring us tea and cake. By the fire in the library. My granddaughter is cold.'

Without taking his eyes off her, he gestured ahead, to the corridor. Jenny tried to catch Milena's eye but the woman kept her head averted. *Traitor*, she thought, but then she saw the woman was trembling. Head to toe, she was shaking and her skin was the colour of dusty chalk. She looked so close to fainting Jenny felt a stab of shame. How could she blame her? Yesikov was controlling and terrifying and having to look at his handiwork on Ekaterina's face every day must have had a devastating effect.

In the library, she took the chair with its back to the window so it would make her expression harder to read. Yesikov sat opposite. She tried not to appear glad to sit in a soft chair, or revel in the heat radiating around her. She kept her chin high, her gaze level.

'It was Ekaterina's idea, wasn't it,' he said.

Jenny decided to remain silent.

'They're flying her back,' he said. 'They found her just outside a village. She must have been bitterly disappointed she didn't make it. She really thought she'd beat me. Ha!' He gave a dry laugh. 'As if that would happen.' He looked enormously pleased.

Jenny tried to work out what would happen next. Ekaterina would be tortured, maybe killed on her return. And what about Milena? She suddenly felt terribly protective of the petite Russian and hoped Yesikov would spare her.

'After this little attempt, I'm going to bring in more men,' he told her. 'I'm going to install video cameras in every room, and have someone watch the feed every minute of every day. You will not be allowed more than a hundred yards from the house . . .'

As he dictated the prison he was going to build for her, Milena came in with a tray piled high with cakes and chunks of bread and cheese. She set it down on the table between Yesikov and

Jenny and then stepped to the fire and picked up a metal poker. Jenny was fully expecting her to stoke the fire but instead, in one graceful movement, she spun on her heel and with her arms quite straight, swung it at the old man's head.

There was a sharp cracking sound, like a giant egg being broken. Milena gave a shriek and dropped the poker. Her hands went to her face.

Yesikov looked stunned.

He said, 'What . . .?'

Milena started to make a keening sound. She looked as though she was about to vomit.

Yesikov's eyes turned glassy and rolled up into his head. He slumped to one side. Saliva drooled from the side of his mouth and down his chin.

Stunned, Jenny stared at Yesikov's unconscious form.

Milena started rocking. The keening continued. She sounded like a wounded animal. The noise pulled Jenny to her feet. She was trembling and felt sick but she forced the sensations aside. They had no time to spare. She said, 'We have to get out of here.'

Milena looked at her blankly.

'The helicopter's on its way back,' Jenny added. She gave Milena a little shake. 'We've got to go.'

No response.

Yesikov made a moaning sound. Jenny's senses switched to high alert. She said, 'Milena. We have to tie him up. Where can I find some tape or rope? Milena!' She snapped her fingers in front of her face. 'Listen to me!'

Nothing.

'Milena!' Jenny patted the woman's cheeks sharply. 'I need some rope!'

At last, Milena came to. She stared at Yesikov. 'He's not d-dead?'

'No! Which is why we need to tie him up!'

'The u-utility r-room,' she said. The woman was shaking so hard she could barely speak. 'I will f-fetch it.'

'Wait!' Jenny said, 'Where's the guard?'

'H-he's in Katen'ka's room. I g-gave him a sedative, then a big shot of m-morphine.'

Unsteadily, she walked into the corridor. Jenny stood over Yesikov, watching him. She didn't know what she'd do if he regained consciousness and tried to get up. Did she have the courage to use the poker like Milena had?

When Milena returned she was still ashen but she seemed to be functioning OK. She'd brought a roll of duct tape. Perfect.

Together they secured Yesikov to his chair. Being elderly and muscle-weakened, he would find it impossible to free himself. He'd have to wait until his bodyguard recovered. Milena stood over him.

'I wanted to kill him,' she said. She turned an anguished gaze to Jenny. 'For what he did to Katen'ka. To me. Why couldn't I?' Tears filled her eyes. 'Why am I so weak?'

'You're not weak,' Jenny told her. 'You're a decent person.'

'No, I'm not.' The tears fell faster. 'I betrayed Katen'ka. I betrayed you . . .'

Jenny gripped her shoulder. 'You did well, OK? Now, we've got to go before the guards return. Have you tied up his bodyguard?'

'No. He won't move for hours. No problem.'

'Let's do it anyway.'

Once they'd secured the bodyguard, Jenny said, 'OK. Where's the satphone? Maybe we can ring for help . . .'

Milena brightened. She hastened outside. Jenny followed her into the kitchen, where the satphone lay on the table. Milena picked it up. She looked at Jenny. 'I need to know . . .' A look of anguish crossed her face. 'About Ekaterina.'

Jenny didn't move. She didn't say anything.

Milena studied the phone for a second, then pressed some buttons. 'I will call the other satphone,' she told Jenny. 'Which the guards took on the helicopter. Edik answered last time . . .'

She stood still, listening.

Impatience crawled through Jenny and she had to quash the urge to stride up and down the kitchen. 'Are you through?' she asked.

'It just rings and rings.'

Jenny looked at her.

Milena looked back.

Neither wanted to say the words, but they were both thinking the same thing.

Had the helicopter crashed?

Long, gnawing silence.

Suddenly, Milena gave a shake, like a dog coming out of a river. 'We may never know.' She turned brisk. 'If it is gone, then it is gone. Katen'ka would not want us sitting around worrying. She would want us to go.' Milena started walking for the door. 'I will get ready.'

Jenny picked up the satphone. She didn't know Dan's mobile number so she decided to ring the only number she knew by heart. She tried dialling double-zero for an international code but the call failed. She ran after Milena. 'What should I dial if I'm calling overseas? England?'

Milena paused in the doorway to her room. 'The prefix is eight. Wait for a dialling tone then dial ten and then the number you want.'

'Thanks.'

With trembling fingers, Jenny dialled. Several clicks came on the line, which she hoped meant she was being connected. Was it really this easy? Another loud click and she heard a phone ringing. Was it really England? What time was it? The UK was an hour behind Russia here, which would make it mid-morning. They could be in having their elevenses; percolated coffee and biscuits. Or they could be playing with Aimee in the conservatory. They *had* to be in . . .

She held her breath as the phone was picked up.

'Hello?'

One word from her father and the lid she'd kept on her emotions flew sky-high.

'Dad,' she said on a sob.

CHAPTER SIXTY-TWO

The second Dan rang Jenny and got the lodge's coordinates from Milena, he ordered the helicopter pilot to fly straight there and pick up Jenny and Milena's snow-machine tracks. The women hadn't wanted to stay in the lodge. They were too frightened of the guards returning, so he'd told them to head west, towards the Finnish border. Should Yesikov's guards follow them, he'd tackle the problem when the time came. In the meantime, he was willing the chopper to fly faster, *faster*.

Finally, in the distance, he saw a dot in the expanse of snow. He craned his neck and blinked, praying he wasn't imagining it. Soon, it became clear. A snow machine with two riders. Dan told the helicopter pilot to swing side-on to the snow machine so Jenny could read its registration number, and see that it was a different machine from the one Yesikov had used.

The second the pilot turned, he saw the snow machine's passenger bang the driver on the shoulder. The machine stopped and both riders clambered off. His heart clenched when he saw the taller rider pull off their helmet and balaclava and shake their blond hair free.

Jenny.

His wife.

His love.

Unsure of the ground, the pilot didn't set the machine down but hovered so Dan could leap out. He ran to Jenny. Scooped her into his arms and held her tightly. She smelled of woodsmoke and snow. She was crying.

'Sorry, my love,' he said. He cupped her face in his hands and kissed her lips. 'But we have to go.'

'I know.' Her eyes held his. Relief mingled with joy. She turned to Milena. 'Milena, this is Dan –'

'Yes,' said Milena. 'I know.'

Dan nodded.

Jenny looked between them. He could see curiosity flaring in her eyes but they didn't have time.

'We've got to get out of here.' He looked at Milena. 'You're OK to come with us, all the way?'

She blinked.

'To England,' he added. He didn't want there to be any confusion.

'London?' Disbelief rose in her expression along with something else he didn't recognise for a moment. Hope.

'If you want,' he said.

'London is good.' Her voice was definite.

They scrambled on board. Buckled up. Dan wanted to return to the lodge and Yesikov, to hit him or kill him he didn't know, but he knew it would be indulgent and foolish. His priority was to get them all to safety.

He got the pilot to fly them across the border and on to Ivalo, a small town nestled on the banks of the Ivalo River in Finland. Jenny couldn't stop looking at him. He couldn't stop looking at her. She'd lost weight but she was as beautiful as the first time he'd seen her.

'How is he?' He glanced at her belly and raised his eyebrows.

'As far as I can tell, he's fine.' She smiled.

They landed at the airport twelve miles south of Ivalo. From there they caught a flight to Helsinki, and thence to Heathrow, where Emily was waiting for them, planeside.

'We'd like to see you in the office first thing tomorrow,' she told Dan.

He nodded.

'Welcome home,' she said to Jenny, handing over her passport.

Jenny nodded. 'Thanks.'

Emily turned to Milena. 'Please, if you would come with me.'

Milena sent Dan a look of panic.

'Don't worry,' he told her. 'You'll be fine. Emily will look after you, won't you, Emily?'

'Of course.' She looked insulted that he'd asked.

Using a pen of Emily's and one of her cards, Dan scribbled his mobile number down on the reverse and gave it to Milena. 'I'll bring you a phone tomorrow but in the meantime I'll keep in touch through Emily, OK?'

She gave him a tremulous smile but the fear didn't lessen. He guessed she wouldn't feel secure until she had her residence card in her hand. He watched her walking away, her figure small and uncertain next to Emily's confident stride.

'How do you know her?' Jenny was also watching Milena.

Dan took a deep breath. 'Her friend, Ekaterina, used to be an asset of mine.'

Jenny gave him a searching look. Then she turned to look after Milena. She said quietly, 'They're both incredibly brave women.'

Dan didn't say anything. He took Jenny's hand in his and together they walked to passport control.

CHAPTER SIXTY-THREE

Tuesday 10 February

Lucy parked her car beneath a leafless tree and climbed out into a biting easterly peppered with sleet. Wrapping her scarf around her neck and half her face, she jogged for the hospital. This time, nobody was there to take her photograph. There were no hordes of journalists, no TV vans. Instead the killings were plastered over the front pages of every newspaper, double-page spreads of the victims' stories inside, great swathes of photographs, writers' comments, special reports. It was a media feeding frenzy, which the general public was lapping up.

She pushed open the door. Inside, it felt stiflingly warm and she quickly shrugged off her coat as she strode down the corridor.

While Mac had driven back to Stockton late last night, Lucy had stayed at her mother's. It had been Mac's idea that she should stay south for a couple of days' recuperation and she hadn't demurred. She felt she deserved a bit of a break.

As far as the police knew, the slaughter of the Stantons had stopped now the FSB agents were off the grid; one having been turned by the British Security Service, the other sent back to Russia in a diplomatic flurry of counter accusations. Not that there were many Stanton descendants left alive after the killings, which appeared to have spread to Australia as well. On the surface, every death looked like an accident, but nobody was taking this at face value any more. Apart from Timur and the two cousins, there were just two more that they knew about, and both were in England: the neo-Stalinist UKIP candidate in Sunderland and Jenny Forrester in Wales. The FSB had done a good job of wiping out most of the competition for Jenny's unborn son, which was no doubt Lazar Yesikov's intention. He had wanted his DNA to be passed on and lead Russia one day, but thanks to her and Dan, and the two Russian women as well as Jenny, his plan had been foiled.

Yesss! Lucy mentally punched her fist in the air as she turned into the hospital car park. *Result!*

Irene had been moved out of intensive care and was now in a long ward lined with windows showing a view of the car park. She was sitting up in bed with a newspaper, half-talking to her nephew and niece who, apparently, were due to leave for South Africa at the end of the week.

'It's been one hell of an adventure.' Robin was shaking his head. 'I can't believe it.'

'I can't believe we survived,' Finch remarked drily. 'Considering.'

Although Robin's wrist was still bandaged, his arm was no longer strapped against his chest. Their bruises had faded and the scratches healed. They could have a big story to sell to the media but so far they hadn't said a word. Lucy wondered how long the tale would remain out of the public view and guessed for as long as they wanted it to.

'How are you, Irene?' Lucy asked.

The woman had colour in her cheeks and a glint in her eye. 'I look forward to seeing Zama,' she said. 'Robin, he tells me she is pregnant. With a boy!'

Irene had lost her daughter and her grandchildren, lost her son Aleksandr firstly through estrangement, and then through murder, but she wasn't defeated. She had taken the one positive thing out of the mess and held it up to the light. Her granddaughter and great-grandson. Irina Kazimir was indefatigable.

'We're going to visit Dan and Jenny before we go,' Finch said. 'Now we know they're relatives of ours.'

'Wouldn't it be great if they visited us back home?' Robin asked. 'We could take them around some wineries.'

Lucy was half-listening to them talking about which bedroom they'd allocate for Dan and Jenny, which beaches they'd take Aimee and their baby son to, her eyes drifting over Irene's newspaper. More stories about sex abuse. More violence in Syria. A grandmother who escaped death when her light aircraft crashed. A UKIP candidate killed in a hit-and-run.

A magenta contrail streaked through her mind.

She reached across and picked up the paper.

UKIP CANDIDATE KNOCKED DOWN AND KILLED IN SUNDERLAND.

Gregory Stanton, 45, who was originally from Newcastle, was struck by a car late on Saturday. He was on his way home from meeting friends at a pub when he was knocked down at a pedestrian crossing. The driver of a Ford transit van is being sought after the hit-and-run.

The magenta contrail spread into a cloud that began to crackle into white lightning.

Another accident.

Another Stanton dead.

Her breathing tightened. Was it another murder? If so, why were the family still being killed if the FSB agents weren't around any more? Did Robin and Finch know about this? What about Irene? Why hadn't they mentioned it? Or had they just not read the article? As her thoughts raced the lightning increased, crackling and firing at a tremendous rate.

Numbers tumbled in her mind, agitated, urgent.

Times and dates.

It was all to do with *timing*.

Ivan and Yelena Barbolin, the FSB agents, had arrived in the UK on Thursday the twenty-ninth of January, the day before Adrian Calder's family were massacred. However, Oxana Harris's eldest son Lewis killed his two young children and himself by driving his car into a quarry and drowning *the week before*. The police had thought there might have been another FSB team in the UK, but what if they were wrong?

And what about Ivan Barbolin? According to Dan he'd been adamant he and Yelena hadn't killed the Calder family or Aleksandr Stanton. He had admitted to killing Elizabeth, however, and Adrian Calder.

Why?

She stared at the newspaper article, her mind fizzing as it scrambled to rearrange the information she had.

Irene's words tumbled past the lightning.

Timur's voice.

You're not a fucking prince. You're a nasty, cruel little freak. And your children will be nothing but vicious little freaks too.

If I were you, I'd have him sterilised.

Someone was still killing the Stantons.

'Are you all right?' It was Finch, looking at her warily.

'Fine, thanks.' Lucy felt dizzy. She had to ring Dan, she realised. Warn him. Then she'd ring Mac. She rose to her feet. Walked outside. She dialled as she headed for her car. She didn't feel the sleet pecking her cheeks or the cold teeth of the wind snatching her hair. Didn't register the diesel engine behind her. To her frustration, Dan didn't pick up. She began to leave a message.

'Dan, it's Lucy. I don't know if you know, but Gregory Stanton's been killed. I think it's still going on. I have my suspicions as to who it is, OK? But no hard evidence yet. I just wanted to warn you and Jenny to be careful of –'

She never got the next words out because something hit her very hard on the back of her head.

'Sorry,' said Robin and he hit her again.

CHAPTER SIXTY-FOUR

They had made love earlier, long and slow and lazily, as though they had all the time in the world, and now they were dozing together, luxuriating in the fact they didn't have to get up for anything and that Aimee was occupied playing nurse to Poppy downstairs. Jenny was blinking a little, yawning and thinking of nothing but how good Dan felt, how delicious he looked with rumpled hair and sleepy eyes, when the landline rang.

'No,' she mumbled. She didn't want to leave the cocoon of their embrace.

'I'll get it.'

She watched him lean over her for the phone, his chest broad and his muscles well defined. 'Nice,' she murmured, but he didn't respond. He was saying, 'Hello,' into the phone as he sank back on to the pillows, and 'Yes . . . Oh . . . I see. I'm not sure . . . Can you wait while I ask Jenny?' He covered the mouthpiece with a hand. 'It's the South African cousins,' he whispered. 'They want to come over today.'

Jenny felt a moment's dismay. 'But I thought they were coming on Thursday.'

'Their flight's changed.'

She started to shake her head. She was already having trouble getting her head around the fact she was adopted and the thought of being introduced to these cousins made her feel vulnerable and strangely frightened. She'd been an only child all her life with no cousins that she knew of, and she couldn't imagine what these two people around the same age, who shared the same blood, the same genes as her, might be like. She felt she needed more time before she met them. It was only now she could see how dissimilar she was to her mother, and how different she was from her father who had been so proud of his Scottish ancestry, trying to instil in her a sense of pride in her Scottish heritage. A heritage which she now knew didn't exist. A heritage of dust and lies.

She'd seen her parents once since her return and had demanded to see her birth certificate along with the adoption paperwork, and the absolute veto. And there it all was, proof that her birth parents were Aleksandr and Elizabeth Stanton. She'd looked at the two people who'd raised her as their own and felt the anger and horror of betrayal. She'd turned cold and aloof and, although she knew she was hurting them, she hadn't been able to help herself.

All my life, you lied to me! she hissed. *You stole my identity!*

We did it to protect you, pleaded her father.

We didn't want to lose you, sobbed her mother.

Jenny had left without another word. She knew she'd return because she wanted to know her life story from the very beginning in order to find some sense of self. She loved them, but first she had to forgive them. Her emotions were all over the place, partly due to the trauma of her kidnap but also not knowing who she really was. She felt abandoned and confused, and the knowledge that both her birth parents had recently been murdered added the extra burden of despair and grief.

Thank God for Dan and Aimee, and the baby who, amazingly, seemed to be doing just fine despite the stress she had undergone. They were her anchors, her security and sanity. At Dan's suggestion, she had contacted Adoption Support and booked herself in for private counselling sessions. The first one was next week. She hoped it would sort out the tangled mess in her mind and heart.

'Jen?' Dan said gently. 'They're really keen. And South Africa's an awfully long way away. You don't want to regret not meeting them while they're here, do you? They may not be back for years, if ever.'

Her mouth twisted. Some days she wished Dan didn't know her quite so well because he was right. She probably would regret them leaving without her having at least laid eyes on them. 'All right,' she relented. 'But not for long, OK? Just for a cup of tea or something . . .'

Dan gave a nod and returned to the phone. 'Hello?' he said. 'Look, that's fine, but we've only got an hour or so spare this afternoon.' He raised his eyebrows at Jenny who nodded and held up four fingers. 'Can you make it around four o'clock?' He rattled off their postcode and some final directions. 'OK. We'll see you then.'

He passed her the phone and she returned it to the cradle. 'You stay there,' he said. 'How about I get us some tea, and we can drink it in bed.'

They finally got up just before midday, something they hadn't done since their earlier days, when they'd been gripped by an intense, almost crazy and insatiable lust. They even showered together, which they hadn't done since Aimee had arrived. *And which will continue, even when our son is born*, Jenny promised. She'd lost Dan once – she wasn't going to lose him again.

She knew there was more to the story of Ekaterina Datsik from the way Dan behaved whenever her name was mentioned. He would blink and become strangely distant and although he told her she could ask him any questions about his mission in Russia and he'd answer them honestly, Jenny decided to let sleeping dogs lie. If he'd slept with Ekaterina, or had feelings for her, it was a long time ago. Besides, even though he'd recruited the woman he hadn't apparently been able to remember her, but Jenny knew how powerful the core of a memory was, and part of her – the fiercely protective wife and mother – didn't want him to have been in love with her.

While Dan cooked bacon, Jenny made the batter for some pancakes. They ate in the kitchen, Dan scanning the Sunday papers while Jenny and Aimee tried to decide which cakes to bake for their South African guests.

'Chocolate brownies,' Aimee insisted.

'Not everyone likes chocolate,' Jenny chided.

'They DOOOO!'

They'd decided upon a traditional Victoria sponge with buttercream when Dan checked his phone. Another first – he hadn't looked at it since they'd woken. Now, he listened to his messages. It was only because she knew him so well that she was forewarned something was wrong. His expression didn't change, nor did he stiffen or shift on his chair, but a predatory stillness came over him.

She watched him pick up the newspaper and flick through it, frowning. Then he fetched his iPad and opened up the BBC news site. Obviously, whatever he was looking for hadn't been in the paper. Jenny waited patiently until finally, his eyes locked on hers. He pushed the iPad over to her. As she began to read, she heard him walk into the utility room. A soft *thunk* indicated he'd pulled out the skirting board and then came the sound of him handling a set of keys. They had a distinctive bell-like jingle thanks to the novelty key ring Aimee had given him for his birthday last year. Every hair on her body rose.

The keys to the gun safe.

CHAPTER SIXTY-FIVE

Lucy awoke to plastic cuffs binding her wrists and ankles. She had a thumping headache that reached from her neck over the back of her skull and into her brain, her eyes. A sick dirty ache that made her groan.

Blearily she raised her head and looked around to see she was in a van. The vehicle was humming along smoothly, which Lucy took to mean they were on a dual carriageway or motorway. Two benches lined the walls. Carpet on the floor. Bits of rope and boxes of equipment scattered about. Her feet were secured to a metal ring at an anchorage point near the right rear wheel arch. Her hands were locked to another anchor point. Finch sat on one of the benches, watching her.

Lucy had been under the complete power of another person – absolutely helpless against whatever they might do to her – once before and a rush of pure terror bolted through her, loosening her bowels.

'Please . . .' she managed.

Finch looked at Lucy with an expression that was almost chiding. 'It's your own fault,' she said.

Lucy didn't say anything. Her mouth had gone dry.

'If you hadn't put two and two together,' Finch went on, 'we wouldn't be here. We would have finished our job and been long gone.'

'Job?' Lucy rasped.

Finch looked irritated. 'Not a job, *job*. We're not employed or anything. We're doing it because we want to, we *need* to. We're doing it for mankind. To protect future generations.'

The van turned left, throwing Lucy to one side. She was forced to use her hip and knees to brace herself against the movement of the van to avoid straining or rupturing a joint.

Lucy said, 'The hit-and-run in Margate. It wasn't real. It was to make you look like victims. Divert attention away from you.'

She didn't think it mattered if she challenged Finch. The cousin didn't appear to care if Lucy knew she was a murderer. She guessed she wasn't going to be released. *Don't think about it,* she told herself. *Keep Finch talking. Find an advantage of some sort. Work it.*

'Give Pc Plod a Mars bar for deduction.' Finch's black marble eyes were flat. She leaned forward, her hands between her knees. 'You must understand. We didn't want Elizabeth or Adrian dead. Only those directly related.' She shook her head, seemingly with regret. 'But I guess the FSB wanted all witnesses who knew about Jenny and her heritage, silenced. Then they could bring their little Kazimir up unimpeded, no doubt making up some wild story about him being conceived in Russia by pure-blooded Russians.'

Lucy worked her mouth but no saliva came. 'You killed Adrian's family?'

'They might have got the same ideas again. Genetics and behaviour. They could turn against minorities. Look at Gregory Stanton.' Finch's expression tightened into a mask of hatred. 'The world is better off without him. Fascist bastard.'

'You set Adrian up,' Lucy said. 'You made us think he'd killed his own children.'

'It was Robin's idea. We'd stayed with them earlier so we knew the layout of the place. The codes on the gun cabinet. Adrian was far too trusting, really. But then he thought he had nothing to fear from us. We were relatives. A trusted part of the family.'

'Robin wore Adrian's clothes,' Lucy said as she worked through what had happened. 'So they'd be covered in gunshot residue.'

'It nearly didn't work. Adrian turned up earlier than we expected. Robin dumped the clothes in the bin and set fire to them to try and make Adrian look guilty. Then he fled through the woods . . .'

Lucy felt a fleeting satisfaction that she *had* followed the killer's footprints through the snow. 'Where you were waiting to pick him up on the lane.'

A gleam of triumph entered Finch's eyes. 'We got away with it. We ran rings around you.'

'How does it sit with you, being a child killer?' Lucy asked. 'You murdered Lewis Stanton's little boys. One was two years old, the other barely six months.' *How could you?* she wanted to scream, but kept quiet.

Finch pulled her lips back, baring her teeth in an empty and chilling smile. 'We faced up to it. Other families wouldn't. They were in denial. They decided to ignore the past, sweep it away as though it didn't exist. The Australians simply said it was all lies and told their kids that their grandfather died of cancer. We couldn't do that: lie to ourselves, the family. Robin and I are riddled with guilt even though we weren't there. We're ashamed too, for what our grandfather did. But we're alive. Why? The only reason we exist is to put things right.'

Lucy stared. 'You can't play God.'

'Robin and me, we sterilised ourselves.'

An icy shudder gripped Lucy's stomach.

'Aleksandr,' Lucy said. 'You needn't have killed him. He'd had a vasectomy.'

Finch sent her a withering look. 'They can be reversed.'

'What about your father?' Lucy tried to think what role Timur, Irene's brother, had in this. 'Surely he –'

'It was Dad's idea, ages ago. He nearly didn't have us, you know, but our mum . . . she really wanted kids and he . . . well, he caved in. But he made us aware right from the start who we were, and where we came from. And how it was our responsibility to cut the line. Stop it from ever happening again.'

Finch's gaze turned distant. 'There are just two descendants left who are able to breed.'

Jenny Forrester and her daughter, Aimee.

CHAPTER SIXTY-SIX

'I don't know who it might be,' Dan told Jenny. 'Lucy didn't say, and now she's not answering her phone.'

He had loaded a shotgun and propped it amongst the umbrellas in the stand near the front door. A box of cartridges went into the hall table drawer, some in his pockets. He'd primed two handguns that made Jenny's eyes widen – she'd never seen them before – tucking one in his waistband, the other down the side of the armchair in the sitting room. Knives were to hand in the kitchen, pepper spray in the bedrooms, and he was now placing screwdrivers and hammers at strategic points around the house.

'Lucy didn't say when they might come,' he added. 'It could be today or tomorrow. I want to prep first, then I'll ring her boss.'

His nerves hummed like electricity through a wire. Whoever it was, he would be ready for them.

'We've got to warn the cousins,' Jenny told him. 'We shouldn't let them come. They're in danger too.' She glanced at a large pair of scissors he'd put casually next to a china vase filled with silk roses: another potential weapon.

'What's their number?' Dan asked.

Jenny went and fetched her phone, passed it across. He dialled. Waited almost a full minute. 'They're not answering.' He tapped out a text asking the cousins to stay away, and to ring back when they got the message. He passed Jenny her phone. 'Keep trying. If we don't get hold of them before they arrive, I'll go out and put them off.'

Dan rang Lucy's boss, DI Faris MacDonald.

'What did she say, exactly?' the DI asked.

Dan repeated her message, word for word.

'And she's not answering her phone.' MacDonald was brisk, but Dan could hear his concern for Lucy in his voice. 'If you hear from her, call me immediately. In the meantime, I'd like you to stay where you are. I'll ring the Gwent Police and get a car sent over until we know what's going on.'

Dan then called Ozzie.

'What do you mean, it's still going on?'

Dan explained.

'What can we do?' Ozzie asked.

'Nothing. The police are on their way. I thought you should be made aware.'

'Keep me informed.'

Dan went and found Jenny. Her face was pale but she wasn't panicking. 'I think we should talk to Aimee,' she said. 'Join me?'

He followed her to the kitchen where Aimee was colouring in a fairy book on the kitchen table. He watched Jenny fetch the kettle and fill it, switch it on, creating a sense of normality. She said to Aimee, 'Do you remember what we said about what happened to me? Those people who took me away?'

Aimee looked up at her mother. 'The man who shot Poppy?'

They'd shared the bare bones of her experience with Aimee after they'd returned from Russia. They hadn't wanted to frighten her, but they hadn't wanted to lie either. When Aimee asked why anyone would do that, they said things like, *There are people in this world who do bad things. This happens for many reasons. Some people are mentally ill. Others are just different from us, some full of so much hate that they become violent.*

'Yes,' Jenny said. She sent him an enquiring look, to which he responded with a nod. 'Well, they might come back. And if they do, we will be much, *much* better prepared. But if anything happens, I want you simply to do as Daddy and I say. Without question.' She looked at her daughter. 'OK?'

Aimee's eyes went to Dan, round with apprehension. 'Will they shoot Poppy again?'

'I hope not.' Dan walked to her, bent down so he was at her eye level. 'But we don't want you worrying about Poppy. If Mummy and I tell you to run, you run into the village as fast as you can and get help. Go the secret way, round the back, to the Taylors'. See if they're in, and if not, try next door. OK?'

'OK,' she whispered.

He looked at her calmly, wanting to instil confidence, not panic. 'And I know it may be scary, but if we tell you to hide in a cupboard, or the attic, you do that too, OK?'

Aimee nodded solemnly but her eyes were frightened.

'We're pretty sure nothing's going to happen,' Dan said, 'but we're prepared, just in case. We're all together and we're going to take care of you.'

He opened his arms a little and she stepped into his embrace. He lifted her up. 'Love you munchkin.' He pressed a kiss against her head before putting her down. He nodded at Jenny, who said, 'Now, Aimee. I think you were right, after all. We need some chocolate brownies. Could you fetch the butter for me?'

He left them in the kitchen. Toured the house. Checked and double-checked everything was secure.

The time passed slowly.

Four o'clock came and went. The police still hadn't arrived but they were, apparently, on their way. Jenny tried to calm the dog, but Poppy knew something was up and insisted on tottering to the front door and lying there, growling softly.

Dan checked the perimeter of the house again. He returned and double-checked that all the windows and doors were locked. With the Glock pressed against the base of his spine, he stood in the kitchen and watched his wife and daughter make a batch of brownies.

CHAPTER SIXTY-SEVEN

The instant Dan Forrester said the words *and she's not answering her phone*, Mac experienced an elevator-drop in the pit of his stomach.

He'd continued the conversation quite calmly before hanging up and ringing the Gwent Police, but inside something was screaming, howling with a fear of loss so great he thought he might implode.

He wanted to leap into his car and drive south, scour the hospital, track Lucy down, *save her*, but he knew he'd help her more if he stayed at the station where she knew where he was, and at the centre of comms on the case.

In his mind's eye he could see Lucy lying naked in bed, her dark hair flowing over her shoulders, her dark eyes on his, her beautiful body lit a rosy pink by the bedside lamp.

She was all that he wanted. He could see that now.

He was pacing the office like a demented creature when Detective Chief Superintendent Beacroft walked in.

'I heard your little constable might be in a spot of bother,' he said.

Mac stopped in his tracks. 'I'm sorry?'

The DCS held his gaze. 'I think we need to have a chat, don't you?'

CHAPTER SIXTY-EIGHT

'You won't get away with this,' Lucy warned Robin.

They'd driven for just over four hours, mostly on motorways or dual carriageways, and the cousins had swapped drivers a while back. While Finch drove, Robin rummaged through one of the boxes. He brought out a Beretta and, as Lucy watched, he racked the slide to chamber a round.

She couldn't help it. She started to tremble. Her muscles were aching from being restrained. Her head continued to thump from where Robin had hit her.

'I don't see why not,' Robin said. 'Just because you know what we've done, doesn't mean we can't disappear. Who says we don't have passports in different names? And why should we return to South Africa when there are so many other interesting places to live?'

Lucy couldn't believe they wouldn't kill her. Right now, she was the only person who knew the truth and Robin looked at her, seeming to read her mind.

'And no, we won't kill you,' he told her admonishingly. 'We only want to eliminate those related. We don't want anyone else's blood on our hands. Just those who might be contaminated.'

Lucy was genuinely puzzled. 'If you let me live, you'll spend the rest of your lives always looking over your shoulder. Do you really want that?'

'It will be worth it.' Robin was earnest. 'We'll be heroes. Just you wait and see.'

'Robin,' called Finch. 'Shut her up, would you? We're nearly there.'

At that, Robin pulled out a roll of gaffer tape, tore off a strip and stuck it over Lucy's mouth. 'Sorry,' he whispered. 'I'll take it off when it's all over.'

Like she believed him. Murdering bastard.

The van slowed, then slowed some more. Finally, it stopped. The ignition was switched off. She heard Finch open her door and climb out of the van. Heard her footsteps come down the side to the rear of the van. Crunch-crunch. The rear doors opened. Finch stuck her head inside. Lucy caught a view of moorland and cold grey sky before Finch hopped inside. She pulled out a Glock from the same box Robin had withdrawn the Beretta from. Lucy watched her load then attach a silencer to the weapon.

Lucy's heart was pounding, her mouth as dry as sand. Through her fear, she felt a desperate hope that they really were going to let her live. She didn't want to die yet. She wanted to make love with Mac again, swim with dolphins, watch the sun rise over the Pyramids, tell her mum she loved her.

Would Mac join her swimming with dolphins? He was a strong swimmer, much stronger than her. She wished she could tell him what he meant to her. Faris MacDonald. Faris, Faris, Faris. He'd never know she died with his name on her lips.

Heart knocking, feeling sick with dread, she watched Finch raise her gun and push the barrel into her forehead.

'Hey!' Robin knocked his sister's arm aside. 'What are you doing?'

'She's right. We should kill her.'

'No!' Robin looked appalled. 'We made a promise, remember? Only those with Kazimir's genes. Nobody else, no matter who they are or how much trouble they give us.'

'Look, it doesn't matter, OK?' For the first time, Finch looked tired. She pressed the barrel against Lucy's forehead once more.

Lucy lay there, feet and hands bound to the floor, heart pounding, terror bright white and scorched with fire.

Faris, she thought. Mac. The man who makes my body and my soul sing. My last thought will be of you.

'Of course it matters!' Robin was incensed. 'If we kill her, we're no better than our grandfather! Don't you get it? We have to let her go!'

Robin's gaze suddenly clicked up, past Lucy and through the cab of the van. 'Shit,' he said. 'He's seen us. He's coming outside.'

Finch's arm lowered. She took a look. 'I'll go first. We'll deal with her later.'

Incredulous, Lucy watched them climb out of the van.

Was one them going to come back and shoot her?

Both doors slammed.

To her disbelief, they walked away.

CHAPTER SIXTY-NINE

'They're here,' Dan said.

Jenny's nerves instantly wound themselves into knots.

'I'll go out and warn them. Send them away.' He looked at his watch. 'The police should be here any minute.'

She went to the kitchen window. She wanted to see what they looked like, these cousins of hers. She was surprised they were driving a panel van. She'd expected a sedan of some sort, something they'd hired from the airport. Perhaps they'd borrowed it?

She watched Dan walk across the drive.

She didn't realise she was holding her breath and exhaled when a slim, dark woman slipped around the side of the van. With her small frame and neat, birdlike movements, her name suited her. Finch. Jenny turned her attention to Robin as he came into view. He had similar features, but his face was wider, more open. He was smiling at Dan, but the woman was deadpan.

As Dan approached, the woman reached around behind her, pulled out a gun and levelled it at Dan.

She fired.

Dan staggered back as though he'd been pushed by an invisible hand. He dropped right, twisting, reaching for the pistol in his waistband, but he never made it. He crumpled into a heap.

Jenny froze in shock.

She watched Robin spin to his sister. His jaw was hanging open. Then the blood rushed to his face and he started to shout. Finch didn't seem to take any notice. Pistol in both hands, she moved towards the house.

Jenny turned round, grabbed Aimee, and said, '*Run.*'

CHAPTER SEVENTY

Lucy heard the *phut* of the silencer, then Robin was shouting at his sister, asking her what the fuck she was doing, had she gone crazy, what was she DOING?! – and then everything went quiet.

She yelled behind the tape but it was muffled, pathetic. The sound wouldn't be heard outside the van, but she couldn't stop yelling. What else could she do? She bucked against her bonds. Yanked and pulled against the plastic cuffs. Yanked and pulled again.

She kicked and lashed and pushed her feet. Flung her body from side to side. She felt the van rocking, and hoped someone would see, maybe be alerted that something was wrong.

She pushed her face against the van's floor, trying to scrape the gaffer tape from her mouth, so she could yell properly but it was stuck firmly. She fought and screamed, chafing the skin at her wrists and ankles. The blood made the plastic cuffs slippery, but they were still too tight to escape.

She kept fighting. She wouldn't stop until she'd cut her wrists to the bone. Her friends were in danger. She wouldn't give up.

Never.

CHAPTER SEVENTY-ONE

Jenny watched Aimee race across the lawn and scoot round the stone wall, out of sight from the front of the house. She was doing what Dan said and taking the back route to their neighbours'. She'd be there in five minutes, maybe less. She was going like a rocket.

Jenny picked up the phone and dialled 999. Her voice was trembling but she made herself clear. She needed armed police and an ambulance.

She felt a terrifying sense of déjà vu.

It was happening all over again.

But this time she wasn't going to be kidnapped.

She was going to be killed.

And if she didn't stop them, they'd kill Aimee too.

Jenny ran to the hall. Grabbed the shotgun. Flicked the safety catch to *off.* She didn't know much about guns, but she was pretty certain she could aim this thing and pull the trigger. Could she kill her cousin?

Damn right I could.

With the shotgun in one hand she grabbed Poppy in the other and hauled the dog into the utility room. Even though Poppy was dreadfully weakened after various operations she would still defend Jenny, but there seemed no point in letting the dog get shot a second time. 'Stay,' she hissed and shut the door. Turned the key in the lock and dropped the key in her pocket.

When she heard the front door opening, she slipped to the kitchen door and stood with her back against the wall, gun levelled at her waist, her finger resting on the trigger. The second one of the cousins walked into her line of sight, she'd take aim and fire.

Silence.

She couldn't hear anything above the beating of her heart, her ragged breathing.

Was anyone inside? Or were they standing still, listening?

She stood with her back to the wall, unmoving, alert.

No sound reached her. Nothing.

Then came a man's voice. He sounded furious.

'What the fuck, Finch?'

'Shut up!' the woman hissed.

'Why did you kill him?' Robin demanded.

Light footsteps on the hall floor. Jenny tensed. Finch was creeping into the house.

'Dad told us not to kill anyone who wasn't related, remember?'

'Fucksake, he's ex-Security Services,' Finch whispered furiously. 'I had to eliminate him.'

Standing in readiness, sweating, her heart knocking, Jenny didn't let Robin's words sink in. She couldn't afford to. She had to concentrate.

She heard a soft metal click. A safety catch being released? A weapon being primed?

'I smell baking,' Robin murmured.

'Shhh.'

Those light footsteps again. They were coming her way.

A moment later, Finch's slim form came into the kitchen.

Jenny stepped forward. Levelled the gun between the woman's shoulder blades. Squeezed the trigger and at the same time something came at her fast and the gun barrel was knocked high.

BLAM!

Her shot went high. Pieces of ceiling plaster drifted down.

Desperately she tried to wrestle the gun away from Robin, take another shot, but he was much stronger and in two swift moves he'd turned the shotgun against her. It was now levelled at her stomach. Instinctively, she put her hands over her belly.

In the utility, Poppy went crazy, barking.

'I'm not related,' Jenny stated. She spoke very clearly. 'Lazar Yesikov did a DNA test. We did one on my return. It proves I'm not Aleksandr's daughter.'

'What?' Robin looked startled.

Lie like you've never lied before.

Jenny said, 'Elizabeth must have had a lover. There were rumours of her affection for the master of foxhounds. His name's Edward Kinsey.'

'She's lying.' Finch came into view. Her face was pinched.

'I've got the papers upstairs,' Jenny said. 'I'll show them to you.'

Robin was frowning. 'But Irene says Aleksandr –'

'Do you really think Elizabeth was going to tell Irene she was pregnant by another man?'

Doubt rose in his eyes. 'I guess not. Finch, I think we'd better check before –'

'For Chrissakes, she's *lying*.' Finch raised her pistol at Jenny. Her eyes were as black and dead as a shark's.

Jenny felt her knees weaken. 'No,' she said. 'Please.'

Robin stepped forward. Towards his sister.

'Wait,' he said.

Without taking her gaze from Jenny, Finch swung the pistol and shot her brother in the chest.

Robin looked down, where there was a growing dark blotch. He said, 'Sis?'

Slowly, he collapsed to his knees. The shotgun dangled at his side.

'None of us are meant to survive,' Finch told Jenny. 'I didn't tell him before, because I knew he'd kick up a fuss.'

'But I'm not related,' Jenny bleated, sticking to her lie.

'It doesn't matter any more.' Finch suddenly looked exhausted. 'Because once you're dead, and Aimee's dead, I'll be dead too. We'll all see one another on the other side and it will be –'

A sudden movement caught both women by surprise. Robin was bringing up the shotgun, Finch swinging her pistol round but she was too slow – Robin pulled the trigger.

BLAM!

Finch doubled over as though she'd been punched in the stomach. Her pistol clattered to the ground.

For two beats, two seconds, nobody moved.

Finch collapsed to the floor.

'No,' Robin bleated. He began to crawl to his sister. His face was white, his eyes glassy with horror. 'I didn't mean to . . . Finch, please. I just wanted to stop you. I don't want to die. Finch, I didn't mean to hurt you . . .'

He started to weep.

The sound of his sobs galvanised Jenny. She dived and grabbed Finch's pistol. Pulled the shotgun from Robin's hands. Yanked his pistol from his waistband.

'Help me,' he begged. 'Please.'

Jenny ran outside.

CHAPTER SEVENTY-TWO

Lucy heard a shotgun's dull *boom*. She'd managed to scrape part of the gaffer tape away from her mouth and was gasping, panting in the small space she'd made.

Another *boom*.

Her face was grazed and bleeding and she scraped frantically at the tape until finally, her mouth was free.

'HELP!' she yelled. 'I'M IN THE VAN!'

Her wrists and ankles were bruised and bloody, her face half-raw, but she kept screaming and jerking against the plastic ties.

Distantly, she heard sirens and wondered if she'd imagined them. They grew louder. Police and ambulance. She yanked at the ties some more but was forced to stop when she was nearly overcome by a wave of nausea that threatened to black her out.

Cool it for a moment. You want to be conscious when they get here, not comatose.

The siren volumes increased. She heard a car arrive with a squirt of gravel, then another.

Soaked in sweat, her wrists and ankles in searing agony, Lucy screamed for help.

A uniformed police officer flung back the van's doors. Looked in at her, shocked.

Lucy yelled, 'Police!' Followed by her collar number. 'Free me!'

He grabbed a knife from one of the boxes and slashed through the ties. She scrambled outside.

Snapshot images. A patrol car parked next to an ambulance. Dan Forrester lying motionless on the ground, his wife with bloody hands pressing on what Lucy assumed was a wound. A uniformed cop running to meet the ambulance. Another heading inside the house. A woman sprawled on the ground near the front door. A smear of blood trailed from beneath her body into the house. She'd obviously dragged herself outside.

The cop inside the house appeared briefly, yelling, 'Another down inside! And don't let the dog out! It's fucking huge!'

She ran to the woman and saw it was Finch. Still alive. She pelted inside the house to find Robin slumped on the kitchen floor. No heartbeat, no pulse. Dead. She could hear the cop upstairs, checking the rooms.

Back to Finch. The cousin lay face down, breathing heavily. Slowly, she brought up her knee and pushed herself forward a few inches.

'No,' Lucy gasped. 'Keep still. The ambulance is here.'

But Finch ignored her and, using her elbow, inched forward.

Lucy saw two medics bend over Dan and begin inserting drips. They worked fast, and in less than a minute he was loaded into the back of the ambulance. Jenny hovered anxiously, eyes flickering all around.

One of the medics ran to Finch. Gently turned her over. 'No,' she mumbled. 'Don't stop me.'

'You're not going anywhere, love,' he told her.

Lucy was about to head for the ambulance to ask Jenny where Aimee was, when Jenny exploded into a run. Raced to where the medic knelt next to Finch.

'Don't touch her!' she shouted.

'What?' The medic looked up, startled.

'She shot my husband! She was going to kill me! Don't help her!'

'I'm sorry,' the medic said, 'but I can't do that.'

Lucy never knew how Finch did it, but somehow she found the energy – through enormous will perhaps, like an Olympian digging deep for the finishing line – and she reared up with a knife in her hand, a wicked hunting knife with a curved blade and a blood gutter – and she drew back her arm to plunge it in Jenny's belly.

Lucy didn't know where her response came from. She had no clear thought. She simply opened her mouth and screamed, 'ROBIN!'

Hearing her brother's name surprised Finch. It was barely a second but her brief hesitation gave Lucy the opportunity to launch her foot at Finch's arm. Kick the hand holding the knife. But Finch didn't let go.

'*Drop it!*'

Lucy was grunting as she kicked, sounds of anger and fear. She had to disarm Finch. She lashed out again and this time the woman's hand dropped to the ground. Lucy immediately stamped on Finch's fingers. Heard something snap. Finch's grip loosened. Lucy kicked the knife away from her. Kicked it further away.

'Fuck,' said the medic.

'Too right,' said Lucy.

CHAPTER SEVENTY-THREE

THREE DAYS LATER

'Will this happen to us again?' Aimee asked. Lucy flicked a glance across to see that the little girl had turned in her seat and was studying Lucy with a serious expression.

'Er . . .' Lucy tried to think what Dan would say. He seemed to tell the truth to Aimee when he could, or something as close to it as possible, but to Lucy she could have been stepping through a minefield for all the experience she had with kids, and how to talk to them about really serious stuff.

'I suppose so,' Lucy said carefully. 'But it's pretty unlikely.'

Aimee fell silent, seeming to absorb this.

They were on their way to the hospital. Dan had been operated on twice now, and was finally in a recovery ward and able to receive visitors. After Finch had been restrained and Dan raced to St Mary's Hospital in Newport, Jenny and Lucy went to find Aimee. As instructed, the girl had run around the back of the village to the Taylors' who were enjoying a leisurely weekend, and were washing up after hosting a lengthy Sunday lunch for the family.

The Taylors had rung the police and kept Aimee with them until Jenny and Lucy arrived. Jenny was going to rush in to Aimee but Lucy stopped her, gesturing at her hands, her clothes. She was covered in blood.

'You are too,' Jenny pointed out.

Lucy simply pulled her cuffs over her wrists and while Jenny cleaned up, went and spoke to Aimee. Told her that although her Dad was on his way to hospital, her mum was OK, and that the dog was OK too. For a moment it looked as though Aimee didn't know how to react, whether to panic or not, cry or scream, and Lucy quietly repeated what she'd heard Dan say at the service station what felt like years ago.

I'm here with you now. Everything's going to be OK.

When Jenny came out of the bathroom it was to find Lucy standing in the Taylors' hallway with Aimee's arms around her, the little girl looking up at Lucy and asking what she could take to Daddy to help him get better.

Now, as Lucy turned into the hospital driveway, she wasn't sure what to say to Aimee. She supposed they'd have to tell Aimee her true lineage in order to avoid the potential shock of it later. Much better to tell her when she was too young to understand the implications so it became part of who she was until she was old enough to ask questions and come to terms with it in her own time, her own way.

'They were very bad people,' Aimee said eventually. Very quiet, reflective.

'Yes, they were,' Lucy agreed.

'And the one that shot Daddy, she's in prison now.'

'Yes, she is.'

Finch was in a secure mental institution where she was being evaluated before her trial. Apparently the psychiatrist Lucy spoke to said it was doubtful she would ever be released into the general population. She and Robin had killed over a dozen people – men, women and children – and Finch was apparently obsessed with killing Jenny and Aimee. That's all she ever talked about, and nobody was certain if she'd always been like that or whether the killings had snapped something inside her mind. They weren't sure what label to give her but with words like psychopathic, schizophrenic and psychotic being bandied about, she was unlikedly to go to prison; she would probably be incarcerated somewhere like Broadmoor, where Robert Torto – the 'son of God' killer – once resided along with Peter Sutcliffe, the Yorkshire Ripper. An appropriate residence for her, Lucy thought.

As they walked inside the hospital, Aimee took Lucy's hand. It felt tiny and warm, very soft. Lucy felt a surge of protectiveness and pride that the girl trusted her enough not only to hold hands, but to ask for her to look after her while her parents were at the hospital. Aimee's grandparents had been a bit taken aback they hadn't been at the top of their granddaughter's list, but Lucy suspected Aimee's preference was because she'd driven her to safety when her mother had been under attack at the cottage, and then handed her to her Dad. She'd proved herself to the girl. That was all.

'Do you have a boyfriend?' Aimee asked.

'Er . . . maybe.'

Lucy thought about the past few days, how she'd had to endure endless debriefs by not only the local police but the Security Services as well. She'd met a moon-faced, muscular man called Ozzie, who'd grilled her politely but ruthlessly over every detail of the previous twenty-four hours.

'You say Dan Forrester asked you to follow Nicholas Blain. You didn't think to call it in?'

'Dan was informing the police,' she replied. 'I was concentrating on driving.'

'How did you know he'd called the police?'

He'd drilled down every action she'd taken until she wanted to scream *I'm not the guilty one here!* but somehow she managed to keep her cool, probably thanks to Ozzie's boss sitting in the corner like some kind of benign Buddha, oozing calm. Afterwards, Bernard – no surname given – came to her and said, 'Don't take it personally. Ozzie has a job to do and sometimes he's a bit overzealous. Well done on some excellent work.' He'd shaken her hand and she'd looked at it later, a little amazed she'd been congratulated by the head of MI5.

Blain had been debriefed in the same building and they'd shared several coffees in the corridor in between interviews. He looked like she felt: exhausted.

'I'd ask you out,' he told her at one point, 'but –'

'I'll only say no.'

He gave her an appraising look. 'Eyes only for your DI?'

She looked down the corridor. She didn't want to give anything away.

'It's OK,' he said on a yawn. 'I'm a big boy. I'll survive.'

For some reason, this small exchange lifted something between them and when he asked her to join him for a sandwich at a local deli, she agreed. He told her about his family and she told him about hers. He confessed he'd been married once but it hadn't worked out. His ex-wife had hated service life.

'My ex,' Lucy admitted, 'wanted to change me.'

He raised his eyebrows. 'How?'

'He wanted me to be boring.'

Blain put his head on one side, encouraging her to add, 'He wanted me not to laugh when I wanted, or rant at the TV when I wanted. He wanted me to wear floral dresses, be pretty, be "nice".'

'Sounds like Isabelle,' he said sadly. 'She wanted a humdrum nine-to-five man with a briefcase and a suit and instead she got . . . well, me.'

It was as though Blain had switched from being a potential suitor to a sort of brother and when he began gently teasing her about Mac, he did it in such a way that she didn't take offence but laughed.

After more debriefs in the afternoon, they left the building together. It was chucking it down and they shared an umbrella across the car park – he'd promised a lift to her car – and they were buckling up, laughing over something Ozzie had said when she thought she spotted Mac inside a Vauxhall driving past, but it couldn't have been him because he was up in Stockton.

When she walked into the beat office the next day, she received a round of applause, which made her blush. Mac, on the other hand, seemed to take her success in his stride. 'Leave you alone for two minutes, and you solve an international conspiracy.' He rolled his eyes but she could tell he was pleased. 'Drinks for everyone later. On me.'

Not everyone got along with Lucy, or she them, but at that declaration even the most reticent person came and congratulated her. Amazing what a free drink could do for your popularity.

She was in the pub and halfway through her pint when her mobile rang.

'Nick,' she said. 'Hi.'

'Hi. Look, I've just picked up a job in Berwick and I'm on the A1 and I'm starving. Fancy a curry?'

She checked her watch. She was aware that Mac was watching her, but she ignored him.

'Give me an hour. I'm celebrating with the team.' She gave Nick directions to her local curry house, which was cheap and cheerful, with Formica tables and fluorescent strip lighting, but the food was great.

'Not the most romantic of restaurants,' Mac remarked when she hung up.

'No,' she agreed. She was damned if she was going to explain that Nick was, to her surprise and delight, turning into rather a good friend.

He looked as though he was going to say something else but changed his mind. 'See you in the morning.'

It took all her self-control to be casual, as though they'd never slept together, never cared. 'See you.'

CHAPTER SEVENTY-FOUR

Five weeks later, Dan went to see Milena. Despite the .38 slug of lead that had travelled in and out diagonally through his body, he didn't feel too bad. This, he supposed, was probably because he was out of hospital, the sun was shining, and he was on his way to London. He loved London. The bustle and energy of the place, people on the move, people on buses and trains, aeroplanes overhead and flying into Heathrow.

Hospital had been a trial. Time passed at a snail's pace and he'd hated pretty much every minute, except when Jenny and Aimee visited, but eventually all the tubes were removed and he began to heal.

Lucy also came and saw him. She told him Finch had been transferred to Rampton Hospital, a high-security psychiatric facility for women near Retford in the Nottinghamshire countryside. If Finch escaped, she'd have a journey of two hundred miles to undertake before she got to his family.

'She'd better not get out,' Dan said.

'No chance,' she assured him. 'The place is like a prison. I've seen it.'

'Good.'

Dan parked in a narrow street in the heart of Streatham. The south London suburb had suffered over the years, its high street being dubbed the 'worst street in Britain' during long decades of retail decline. Funding from central government had been promised but much of it didn't appear to have had any effect.

He didn't park on Milena's street, but on the street behind. It wasn't a long walk, maybe five minutes, but when he arrived on her doorstep he was sweating. The bullet might have missed everything vital when it tore through him, but it didn't stop him feeling infernally ill.

'Dan.' The front door was open and Milena stood there in Ugg boots and a baggy sweater. 'You look terrible.'

Whereas she looked as beautiful as he remembered. Her hair hung loosely around her shoulders in honey-coloured waves and her eyes were clear, her skin unblemished. Her nose appeared to have re-set perfectly. No sign that she'd been beaten up by Yesikov's thugs.

'Thanks.' He gave her a weak smile.

'Come inside. Sit down. I will make us tea.'

The tea came thick and strong and with the usual Russian spoonful of jam.

'Delicious,' he said.

Her flat was small, and although it sported cracks running up the walls and had areas of peeling plaster, Milena had put up posters to hide the worst of it. She'd furnished it with items he guessed she'd picked up from the markets – mismatched but colourful lamps, battered but rustic-looking oak furniture and bright Indian throws – turning it into a homely and welcoming space.

'Nice,' he remarked.

Milena pointed at a small console table. 'See this? It was painted blue and below that, a hideous red. I stripped it down, made it beautiful again. I bought it for ten pounds, I can sell it for thirty-five. A good profit, yes?'

'Yes.'

'This is the business I am going into,' she told him. 'Buying things people think are junk and making them into something desirable.'

'A good business,' he said.

She asked him about Jenny, and he asked her about her situation. She'd been debriefed at length by Six and was still in touch with Emily, helping identify people of interest as well as looking at a variety of unprocessed information and substantiating what she could. She was apparently going to get her residence card soon and when it ran out in five years, apply for a permanent residence card.

'You like it that much here?' He was surprised. He hadn't been sure how she'd take to not being next door to Harrods or Bond Street with its five-star shopping and luxury restaurants and bars. Streatham was a long way from her old life of designer labels and chauffeur-driven cars.

She smiled. A real smile that warmed her eyes into the colour of a tropical sea. 'It reminds me of Irkutsk, except for the rain. And I am free.'

He'd forgotten she and Ekaterina had come from a poor background where they'd scraped a living working for the Irkutsk Aviation Association on an assembly line, manufacturing aircraft.

He'd rather thought the first thing she might have done in the UK was find a wealthy man to support her, but he'd obviously got her wrong. It appeared she was enjoying her independence.

He let a silence fall while they finished their tea. Milena looked out of the window where a mechanical street sweeper droned. She said, 'What news from Russia?'

He decided to be direct. He said, 'The helicopter failed and crashed into a wood where the fuel tank exploded on impact. Everyone died, including Ekaterina.'

Milena sat quite still as he spoke. She continued gazing outside.

'There is a bounty on your head,' he added. 'Thirteen million roubles.'

She looked amused. 'Nearly a quarter of a million pounds. Not bad for a Siberian peasant. And what of Lazar Yesikov?'

'He sustained serious head injuries and not long afterwards, suffered several strokes. He is in a wheelchair. He can no longer speak. He cannot walk, or feed himself.'

She seemed to think about this for a moment.

'He is like a baby?'

'I guess so.'

She turned to face him. Her gaze was fierce. 'Good. He deserves to suffer the fate he had in store for Katen'ka.'

Long silence.

He said, 'Can I ask you a question?'

'Of course.'

'When did I know Ekaterina? Where did we meet?'

She looked at him openly. 'It was before you were married. At an Embassy party.'

'And . . .' He hesitated and at the same time, Milena rose and padded to a scrubbed cabinet in the corner. Returned with a leather-bound, slim volume of poetry.

'Katen'ka. She wanted you to have this.'

'You brought it with you?' He was amazed at her presence of mind when she'd been in such a desperate situation at the lodge.

'It was her last wish.'

He opened it. His handwriting jumped out at him. He'd written something for Ekaterina in Russian on the fly page and suddenly he had such a violent shudder in his mind he nearly fell. He wasn't standing in Milena's little flat anymore. He didn't know where he was, but instead of shaking himself and trying to move on, he let himself become absorbed in the vision his ruined memory had recovered.

He was lying in bed with Ekaterina. He was brushing back a tendril of hair from her face and tucking it behind her ear. She was smiling. Her almond eyes were filled with love.

Don't be afraid.

ACKNOWLEDGEMENTS

I owe a big thank you to everyone at Zaffre for their endless hard work and enthusiasm for the Dan Forrester series. To Joel Richardson for being the kind of editor every writer dreams of having. To Emily Burns and Georgia Mannering for their tireless media campaigning. To Nico Poiblanc and Graham Evans for representing me so well.

Always thanks to my wonderful agent Rowan Lawton for her continued good advice and support. Thanks also to Liane-Louise and Isha for being so efficient and on the ball.

Grateful thanks to Angelica Semmelbauer, my expert on all things Russian, for making sure I don't make too many embarrassing mistakes, and for helping with Russian translations. *Za tvoe zdorovie!* Many thanks too, to Ed Hicks, editor of *Flyer* magazine, for his expertise on aviation issues. Thanks to Elinor Evans for sharing her insights into social media as well as getting me launched in Toppings and Company Booksellers of Bath – we had a great party.

Always thanks to my eagle-eyed proofreader, Anthony Weale. You won't find any loose Canons in these pages.

Special thanks to Group Captain Steve Ayres, whose extensive knowledge of everything from flying fast jets to the inner workings of NATO and Russian and military matters, has been invaluable. You are a one-stop research centre and I'm incredibly lucky to have you on tap.

Last, but not least, thanks to all the reviewers, bloggers, readers, librarians and booksellers who liked *Spare Me the Truth* and helped spread the word – I hope you enjoy this one as much.

As usual, I must finish by saying this book is fiction, and any errors of fact will be mine.

Also in the Forrester and Davies series

SPARE ME THE TRUTH

THREE STRANGERS. COUNTLESS SECRETS. ONE DEADLY TRUTH.

THE SPY

In the grip of amnesia, Dan Forrester believes he's just an ordinary man. Until a stranger approaches him with a startling revelation – and an explosive request . . .

THE COP

Banished from the Met in disgrace, Lucy Davies's life is falling apart. But when a serial killer strikes in her new provincial posting, might it be her chance at redemption?

THE DAUGHTER

Stunned by her mother's sudden death, Grace Reavey's grief is interrupted by a staggering act of blackmail – one that challenges everything she knew about her mother.

'Read it!' Meg Gardiner
'A top notch thriller writer' Simon Kernick

Look out for more in the Forrester and Davies series – coming 2018 . . .

Want to read
NEW BOOKS
before anyone else?

Like getting
FREE BOOKS?

Enjoy sharing your
OPINIONS?

Discove

REA
FIRS

Read. Love. Share.

Get your first free book just by signing up at
readersfirst.co.uk

For Terms and Conditions see readersfirst.co.uk/pages/terms-of-service